Praise for *Nine Lives of Sadie Briar*

"From the first sentence, Melvin Litton's *Nine Lives of Sadie Briar* immerses us in a story steeped in history, place, and hard-won lives. A singer-songwriter as well as a writer, Litton has an ear for the music of powerful writing in the treasure of each sentence, but this is a story driven by the surprising, fierce, brave, and quirky nine lives of the captivating title character. Spanning decades and generations, this story gives us a window into the dangers, losses, terrors, and changes of the west from the late 19th century deep into the 20th century as revealed through the uncompromising spirit of Sadie Briar."

– Caryn Mirriam-Goldberg,
past Kansas Poet Laureate,
author of *The Magic Eye*

"This is a remarkable story of a strong woman and her journey of sacrifices, love, loss, and perseverance. Melvin Litton makes you feel the raw beauty of the land and the struggles of the people that inhabited it. You feel you are along on a journey that spans across the decades, and this poignant story lets you feel what Sadie felt, a fierce loyalty to the prairie and a wisdom that comes with her span of time there. Once you start this story, you are immersed in it fully and you understand just what it took to survive with grit and determination."

– Sue Shoemaker-Shea,
Echo Dell Farm,
Ionia, KS

"Melvin Litton's book inhabits a woman's consciousness in ways that few male authors since Tolstoy have been able to do. *Nine Lives of Sadie Briar* describes the life of a 99-year-old Kansas woman who was born in the period of Indian raids – she herself was somehow spared by an Indian whose gaze would haunt her. From her awakening, self-taught love of the classics (she reads Plutarch, but the sacrifice of vestal virgins raises her hackles) to her consistent "free-thinking" on matters related to religion, politics, and customs, Sadie is ahead of her classroom peers and her time. Nevertheless, the extraordinary amount of detail given to the gathering of eggs, the milking of cows, the tending of gardens, and the bearing, breastfeeding, and constant tending of children shows how these everyday tasks eclipse one's urges to take action against what one sees as injustices and stupidities of the world.

"I read this book not once, but twice to catch all these loving details in the winding complexity of a woman's loves and many, many losses. I was immersed in another's consciousness, and yet never unaware of the great mystery of our brief existence. As Sadie said, 'a shy country girl, I'd stood apart, somehow marked, singled out by that old Indian's stare, beginning to learn that our lives are riddled with deceptive spaces largely unknown even to ourselves…'"

– Barbara A Kerr, PhD, Distinguished Professor,
University of Kansas,
author of *Smart Girls, Gifted Women*
and *Psychology of Liberty*

NINE LIVES OF
Sadie Briar

MELVIN LITTON

GOTHUS

PRESS

GOTHUS
PRESS

Cover photo by Félix Thiollier
"Lady and her Horse" (1899) – public domain

ISBN (digital): 979-8-218-77329-8
ISBN (paperback): 979-8-218-77328-1

Contents

"The best-laid schemes o' Mice an' Men gang aft agley,
An' lea'e us nought but grief an' pain for promis'd joy!"

— Robert Burns

I. The Cedar

Footfalls crunch the icy snow as their shadows pass over tufts of grass, an old woman, hunched like a straw-stuffed doll, leans to the hulking man who lends fond support in their trudge up through the pasture.

She draws a sharp cold breath and rasps, "Bing! Get back here!"

The little Scotty cocks one ear in pause, the other lost in a badger brawl the past summer, then zips on, tough and determined, his grizzled fur bur-tangled from flushing quail and rabbit through weedy patches thereby. "Dern scamp, off on a scent, be gone a week," she grumbles, needs him home to guard against possums, raccoons, and coyotes. Faithful but senseless, she thinks, like Paul here, powerful firm right up through the neck, at the head he weakens. Bless him.

"Same as you, Bing hears, just doesn't always listen."

"Yes'um…" the giant nods.

She didn't expect else, though the cold air and shout did waken her senses, feels her bones edge her skin, all but defleshed long ago, should have died then, and should have worn a third flannel shirt and double wool scarf. Once stood a trim five foot two, now stooped back to earth, barely scraps four foot ten, gravity drawn, soon to dust. But not yet. At least she'd shod her hooves in buckle boots fastened warm as they trek on. Not much further now, she thinks, gingerly picking her way on a crooked cedar cane cut and smoothed by Paul a few years ago when she finally conceded the need of a third leg, and presently glad of it.

"This one right here," she says, pointing her cane to a pasture cedar about the same height as he, though of wider girth with neatly skirted boughs. "Spied it last spring," her voice brightens, "it'll make our Christmas tree." It had once taken a half-day hike to find a nicely formed tree; the greater number held in check by prairie fires before a century of tillage checked the fires while draft animals kept the saplings grazed to the nub. But as horses gave way to tractors, cedars reclaimed the land, spreading more each year, another dozen, their dull-green foliage scattered among the russet-speared sumac, laced the upper draw. Not the comeliest of evergreen but the most enduring.

"Cut near the ground there so we'll have a fair trunk to set in the bucket."

Paul kneels down with the bowsaw, cotton tufts poking through his frayed denim coat sleeve as he scuffs a wedge of snow with his broad bare hand. Seldom wears gloves, hands scarred, calloused, now bleeding from a knuckle nicked in setting the saw blade. He pays it no mind and with a few deft strokes topples the tree then rises in slow motion it seems, looming up over her and his deed.

"We'll bandage that hand before you do the milking" — a task she yielded to him once she turned 90, nearly ten years ago, her hands so cramped and arthritic she couldn't grip a teat to fill a tea cup. Missed it, the milking, shedding so many things, right to the final skin. "Might strip that lower limb to shape it better," she adds.

He quickly snaps it free and proudly hands it to her, knows the ritual.

"Fine, now let's head on up," she glances to the hilltop directly west.

"To the old Indian?" he suggests in ready smile.

"Yes, to the old Indian…"

To ease the climb they follow a cow path meandering upslope. Near the top she pauses, leans to her cane to catch her breath and notes the dry grasses tinseled by the westering sun now touching the horizon. They slowly tread on until they come to the mound of stones gathered thereby long ago to protect the grave. Stones thrown up by ancient seas vanished with lifeforms still evident beneath the dormant grasses like ghosts of the buffalo and Indian. These chalky ridges and outcroppings, so prevalent through the surrounding hills, gained the region its name, the Limestone Valley. The old cairn, largely sunken to the earth and blown free of snow except in the crevices, catches the late glow of sunlight as the wind dies in the evening calm.

She steps over and lays the cedar bough on the grave. Paul kneels by and pats it in place, respectful of the old Indian's grave from the day she caught him searching through the stones for a relic. Ten years old at the time, already six foot tall and 200 pounds, but hung his head in shame, still remembers her tongue lashing. The only harsh scolding she ever gave him.

"The Watcher… right Gram?" — still kneeling, eyes level to hers till he stands, looking on as she gazes east toward the hills beyond, then to their homestead nestled below, her shadow and his reaching to the dusky tree limbs that web the creek.

"Yes, Paul, he's the Watcher…" she purses her lips, never certain over the years whether he watched in blessing or in curse.

II. The Raid

They emerged at dusk with the last rays of fading light as if riding from the spirit world beyond the sunset. Skeletal, wind-borne, sheathed in muscle, tendon, and animal skins, silent, without sign or signal, only their passing forms and pounding hooves witnessed by prairie dogs and burrowing owls wary in their earthen dens. The dust settled and a rattle snake uncoiled from a warm rock in hunt beneath the broad pattern of stars.

Blood slowed like the breath as unwary flesh slept to wake and labor, all a dream from night to day till the heart ceased. Still they rode — from where meant nothing, to where pregnant in plunder and promise. And horror to those awaking as yet unknowing while the wind twisted the trees and clouds skimmed the dark sky graying in wait of dawn. A horned owl scanned the scene, senses keen to twig snap and heart pulse as the shadowy forms rode in flesh and time with hoof, lance, and hate — feathered and painted, hungry and lean, unsated like reptiles lurching for prey…and vengeance.

On each horse's haunch and shoulder white circles flexed with yellow arrows and other symbols as suited a warrior's vision or mood. But each face painted black for war, lithe limbs naked, sinewed taut and supple — sworn renegades, ribboned in the tattered apparel of slain whites, set to avenge tribe and buffalo brother. From hair-rope bridles scalp locks fluttered in grim testament as the wind whipped the warriors' long greased braids that bore the scent of sun and earth, of blood and meat, of bone, ash, and the sacred breath of all the sweet grasses and precious waters that nourish man and beast.

———————◆———————

Enchanted by the land and each new dawn, she entered the day as the stars faded to walk to the creek and draw a pail of water. Pretty, of dark hair and eyes, today she planned to wash her hair and her sister's, flaxen like their father's wheat, a whole acre birthed from virgin soil. And since there were no threshers as yet in the region, they'd need to scythe, bundle, and flail it over blankets, let the horses stomp it like in olden times, then sweep away the straw and chaff leaving nothing but the golden grain. "Like panning gold on the prairie," their father laughed the previous evening. She shared his excitement, and while a bit envious of her sister's golden hair she still loved to wash, comb, and braid it.

She basked in the morning air enlivened by birdsong and wished she could make music, dreamed of a piano. As her father often noted, she owned a poetic heart, loved to sing and read, and dreamed of sharing all she'd learned, tales of China and Paris. Perhaps one day she would teach and later have children. But first a handsome man must appear. Blushing at such thoughts, she knelt smiling at her 15-year-old visage reflecting in the water — all which vanished in a blink, from innocence to terror, seized and yanked into a saddle, eye to eye with a fierce black-masked warrior, utterly limp in his grip. At his rank scent she shrieked, knew she'd never see China or Paris nor dream again.

Her brief cry, though quickly checked, roused those in the dugout on the upslope east. Sod roofed with a rough-hewn door and a shuttered window, both soon cracked open in question. Her father had just pulled on his boots and joined his wife still in her nightgown peering out the door at the war party riding forth, their daughter held captive by a tall warrior on a pale horse, their yelping dog swiftly speared.

"My God," he gasped, "they…they've got Katy," his heart shrank as if life had already left him. His rifle and shotgun gone with the boys, Liam and Glen, age 12 and 10, off on a two-day hunt with their Uncle

Pat. His younger daughter Lily, and wee boy, Will, another towhead, both stared up, wild-eyed and fearful hearing their older sister plea beyond the door, "Papa, Papa…Papa…"

He reached for his cap-and-ball pistol kept holstered by the door.

"Clay, don't go out there."

"I got to, Lizzie," he brushed her aside. "That's our first born. Now bolt the door," his last words to her as he stepped out, pistol barrel gripped in his left hand, arms spread wide to show he meant no harm.

"Trade gun for girl," he offered walking forth, pointing to the pistol then to his daughter in hope they understood. He met his daughter's despairing eyes as her captor clinched her tight and motioned him forth.

"Gun shoot?" the warrior grunted in question.

"Yes," he nodded, "it shoots."

The other lowered his hand and said, "Give."

He paused and again pointed to his daughter.

"Gun first!" her captor demanded, and he slowly handed up the pistol.

The warrior grasped the handle and held it to his eyes, seemingly pleased, and said, "Good gun. Think it kill buffalo?"

"Expect so, at close range," he answered calmly. "It's an Army 44…"

No sooner said, the warrior cocked the pistol and fired point-blank at his chest. Heart-blood-pain filled his vision as his eyes rolled white in death-fall to earth.

Seeing her husband abruptly slain, Lizzie snapped in anguish, rushed out, heedless to all, her long reddish locks catching the sunlight and the eye of yet another warrior who wheeled his horse, swung a stone ax and dropped her by her husband. With a war-whoop he leapt down to claim her scalp.

This last act Lily did not witness, having bolted the door and boarded the shutters. Only 13, but sensible and firm-minded, she knelt in the darkness to her little brother, a lone sunbeam lighting their eyes as she said, "William, listen, you must hide in the wood box. No matter what, you must not move or say a word. Not a peep, promise?" At his quick nod she gave a brief hug. "Here," she raised the lid and bade him lay and covered him with kindling.

Warriors were already pounding and howling at the door. Others scrambled to the roof to stomp it in. She had only time to grab the meat knife before the door burst open in splinters of wood and sunlight. In the blind moment she slashed the first to enter, but the second wrenched the knife away and dragged her out, ripped off her nightshirt and flung her to the ground.

She shrank back, desperately clutching dirt and grass in vain effort to cover her flesh. Then she crouched and clawed her hands, set to fight, full of animal rage for the beastly eyes feasting on their yellow-haired prey. They crowded closer. She lashed out, kicking, snarling, her cries as warlike as theirs amid the grapple to hold her down.

Meanwhile the older sister, thrown over the saddle, bound and gagged, stared on, helpless, mute. The flaxen hair she'd envied trampled by a dozen moccasins like she'd imagined her father's wheat being threshed by horses, only this a horrid mockery.

Lily writhed and cried to the God she prayed to daily but gained no answer save their pitiless howls. Held splayed, blood-splattered, the stark murder of her mother and father seemed a small kindness to this horror too vast to name, like her fickle God, and she weakened, a fragile wild thing wishing all to end.

Little Will remained hidden but heard her scream and fight, his heart in sync with hers. Lily, his favorite sister and he her singular charge, she scrubbed his ears and cuffed them when needed, read him stories, tucked him in, lately teaching him his letters on the slate. As her cries grew more piteous he tried to deafen his ears but could not.

He dashed from the dugout yelling his sister's name in desperate fury…

***

Toward midmorning, sated by mutilation and plunder, after trampling the garden, corn patch, sorghum and wheat, slaughtering the milk cows and chickens, feathers torn from tick mattresses strewn over the grass, sticking to blood and flesh, the warriors rode southwest with their dark-haired captive spared for later use and pleasure.

Roughly thereon, a mile east of the brutal scene, a young woman dressed in gray homespun and white apron glimpsed a crow land in a tall oak overlooking the clearing. She gave it little notice, enjoying the day and her new cabin built of split timber, chinks filled with lime mud, and a pitched shake roof just finished and nailed the day before. Her husband's pride and hers as well, the first settlers in the region, they'd wintered in a dugout, now housed in a cabin as promised her for their first born, a baby girl. And to celebrate he'd taken their nephews on a two-day hunt in hope to kill a buffalo — "We'll feast on the tongue, jerk 'n salt the meat. And all be fat come winter," he'd laughed in prospect.

Now in their second year, three more would make good their claim. Often a trial doing without, no sugar since early spring, the last traded to friendly Pawnee for baby moccasins and a cur dog that soon vanished. But praise-be they had molasses, goat milk, and chickens. Her baby, freshly nursed, tucked in her cradle, slept inside as she leaned over a wooden tub scrubbing laundry on a washboard. She straightened briefly, catching the warm sun on her face, prone to freckle, but she shed her bonnet through morning chores, her auburn hair, not so red as her older sister's, kept tied up against the dust and heat. Each evening she let it down and brushed it out to please her husband.

Seeing a second crow land, she glanced up, curious of their sudden presence and intent perch. Perhaps flushed by the distant shot she'd heard earlier, likely her sister's husband Clay had happened on a deer. They all took meat as chance and land provided. The intervening hills and trees muted most sound, and again she sensed no alarm.

Chickens continued to scratch the dirt, the goats browsed thereby. Not a bleat in warning as three mounted warriors suddenly appeared, motionless, as if set there. She had engaged with Indians on several occasions in friendly barter, but these were stripped naked save for moccasins and loincloths, their faces painted black, rifles held crosswise their saddles. Meeting their stares, she laid her laundry aside and brushed back a strand of hair, felt her heart race but did not panic, of tough border stock, raised to fear no man or thing and stand your ground. In nod to the lead warrior, she rubbed her belly with her left hand while bringing the fingers of her right hand to her mouth in sign of eating. Then she extended her open hands in gesture of giving — the frontier custom of generosity and a calm demeanor her only hope.

The tall warrior slid from his pony and approached in lank stride, rifle held relaxed in his left hand, his shadow cast her way. At several paces he stopped and motioned with his right forefinger to their immediate surroundings, then pointed to her and lowered his hand to his groin, forefinger held erect, asking, "Where your man?" At his crude gesture she did not flinch, merely raised two fingers to her eyes and pointed far south beyond the trees then mimed aiming a rifle to indicate he'd gone hunting. Again she made the sign for eating and waved him toward the cabin. He considered a moment then raised a fist to his fellow warriors signing them to hold and wait.

He followed her inside, instantly curious of the shadowed interior. He ran his hand over the back of a chair, the edge of the table, flipped a page of the book left open by the oil lamp, the wick blackened, unlit. Beyond the table he stopped at a wicker basket filled with mewing kittens, striped yellow, brown, and gray, recently weaned, their mother out in hunt. He stood transfixed by the tiny animals strange to his eyes. Fearing he'd notice her baby daughter asleep in the far corner, the cradle veiled by a thin towel to fend off the flies, she quickly uncovered a pan of cornbread and molasses, fresh-baked that morning. She sliced and offered him a piece which he promptly chewed and swallowed. He took another and gulped it down, grunting in satisfaction as she neatly packed the rest in a towel, the corners fashioned in a bow in gift to him. But the gift hung suspended, not taken, as his attention shifted to the cry of the baby awakened in want of the knotted cloth dipped in molasses to soothe her teething. He lay his rifle aside, threw off the towel and lifted the baby in an abrupt motion that stilled her cry as he raised her to the crossbeams, answering her bright chirrups with a low chuckle.

Pleased with his find, the warrior tucked the baby in his arm, snatched up his rifle, grabbed the proffered gift and left the mother standing, her arm still extended, stunned, as if he'd ripped out her heart. Desperate, faint, she recalled his fascination of the kittens. In a blink she plucked the basket and rushed out to intercept him before he mounted up.

"No, no…!" she cried, running breathless, then steadied herself and said, "Here!" holding forth the basket of kittens, "Swap for baby!" Firmly stated, but tense, waiting his judgement, she would rather die then and there than be stripped of her child. They stood eye to eye, the warrior and the woman, both fierce and proud in their want.

Finally the warrior shoved the baby to her and took the basket. He led his pony to the nearest tree and one by one lifted the kittens from the basket and bashed their heads against the trunk. Finished, he tied them either side of his saddle, then cast a stern eye, mounted up and rode off.

For a time she could not move, stood clutching her baby, seeing it captive in the warrior's strong arms, his teeth seemingly set to devour. Silent, numb, she watched them enter the creek timber. Not until they reappeared on the upslope and rode beyond the far hills southwest did she collapse to her knees and cradle her baby in full weep.

III. The Red Skull

I was that child nearly taken, Sadie, named for my mother, Sarah. She always claimed there were nine kittens and she never scolded a cat thereafter, seeing as they saved her child. But our kin, the Callaways, were not sparred — Uncle Clay and Aunt Lizzie, my cousins Katy, Lily, and little Will — all lost that terrible day. Except the two boys, Liam and Glen, who became like big brothers to me. So I visit at times the times I was told, before my birth and knowing, puzzling the wonder of my deliverance and this creature I became, speaking mostly to myself to counter the dread of the ticking clock. Time is not a friend but a measure. And this hugely stunted man-child cannot answer my questions. Of immense strength and scant knowing, a foundling burdened to me nearly fifty years now, my grandson Paul — no, not the Saint, though he sees through a glass darkly and could write the hymn of innocence and script the scroll of sorrow…

"Well Paul," she says once they secure the tree in the bucket and take it in the house, "you best do the milking while I gather the eggs and get the soup on."

The sun fully set, night walls in dense and opaque like crepe hung from the sky, then a single star glitters and another and soon all burst forth. Eggs gathered, she gazes up through her frosted breath at the heavens in full wonder then heads inside, grateful of the warm stove. She soon stands stirring a can of oysters into the pan of milk, adds a daub of butter, a pinch of salt and pepper, then turns the flame to simmer — purchased the range when she turned 90 to ease her labor, along with a refrigerator and small gas heater to supplement their old cast-iron wood burner. The merest task a chore, weakening more each day it seems, she reaches for the crackers to set before the bowls and spoons already placed on the table.

She steps out to check on Paul and observes a wedge of geese pass beneath the moon. Like an arrow of time soon fallen to earth, she muses, stuck in the ground, star to dust where all lie waiting, ever waiting for that ghostly action that made us. The moon in waxing crescent this night, and there glows Orion the Hunter in rise over the creek. And here's my boy.

She leans to her cane in wait of Paul walking up from the barn with lantern and milk pail. As he sets the pail down, she hands him the pan of scum cream she skimmed off the morning milk and says, "Give this to the cats and ol' Bing…if he's come in."

"He just showed up, Gram. Got a gimp paw," he shifts the lantern to show the little dog limping behind, clearly in pain.

"Aw now, what's happened here?" she eases down on the stoop and takes him on her lap, fearing he may have stepped in a trap. "Paul, bring that lantern close so I can see." She gently examines the hurt paw and spies a thorn stuck in a tender spot between the toes. "Poor puppy, got you a blamed locust thorn like the Prince of Peace born long ago this very eve," calming him with her voice. "No, that will be tomorrow. And seems he had not one but a whole crown of thorns stuck to his head when he died."

"Bing gonna die?"

"Heavens no, he'll be alright," she plucks the thorn then mushes his rough fur and brow. Bing hops down, his old self, firm of foot, nub tail wagging as he bulls in among the cats crowding the cream pan. Old pals, Bing sleeps with the cats in the toolshed next to the chicken coop. She grips her cane and slowly stands, relieved to have him home. Frets for the little cuss, fearless, always dashing in. Recently stood off the neighbor's big Collie, a chicken killer, sent it tail-tucked down the road.

Recalling which, she goes inside and returns with some crusted oatmeal and bacon bits left from breakfast and sets it down for an added Christmas treat.

"Here you little fool…" knows he'll one day tangle with one too big. "Aw well," she sighs, "we best go in and have our soup before it gets cold."

Soup is about all she eats lately, that and creamed oatmeal help soothe her pained stomach. The warmth helps for a spell then the pain returns. No, not much appetite. But she enjoys the soup, the rich flavor, though spoons the oysters aside, never cared for their taste or texture. She nibbles a cracker between each sip while Paul crunches a whole package in his huge bowl. Reached his full height of six foot seven by age 16, now 48, still gaining in girth, tipped the scales at 360 in the Ionia feed store last week. A wonder he doesn't tilt the earth. And her old body shrunk to a skin sack, nearly emptied out.

She gazes to the tree set in the corner, not yet adorned but soon would be, now a trying task for her old bones, but a joy for Paul. A pagan ritual in truth, practiced long before Christ. Old as the oldest tale. Even Plains Indians cut a cedar in the spring and attached tiny moccasins for each child born over winter then placed it by a flooding river or stream to journey to the afterlife in proof the tribe still prospered. All drew hope from the birth of a child, and she reckons one ritual as good as the other.

———————————————

Many called them red devils and savages, which they certainly were at times. But there was another side of the coin as I learned some years later from my parents upon reaching the age of understanding. Not a week before the raid that claimed the Callaway branch of our family, an Indian child was killed near Skandia, a Swedish settlement 20 miles east. Among the immigrants were some young rowdies who thought it great sport taking potshots at Indian children playing around prairie dog mounds thereby. All in fun, just aiming close, so they later claimed. But one shot hit a little fellow who dragged his guts some distance before he fell. The other children raced to their camp with word of the deed which in a day sparked a general uprising. Warriors from Sioux,

Cheyenne, Arapahoe, and even the usually friendly Delaware and Pawnee joined in, pitting their fighting spirit and rage against the white invader threatening their hunting grounds and way of life. While the ensuing raids made headlines and history, the initial callous act, like hundreds of others, went largely ignored, excused or forgotten.

Years before white settlement, in the heyday of the fur trade, trappers from the Rockies traveled north and south of the Republican River to skirt the fierce Pawnee whose villages dotted the Republican all the way to the Missouri. And merchants in St. Joseph, losing out on the trade, conspired to send a wagonload of infected blankets and clothing among the Indians. No doubt handed out by charitable missionaries blind to the fatal part they played. In a short time the Pawnee went from thousands to hundreds, utterly decimated by smallpox, the remaining few mostly pacified. But they never again welcomed missionaries in their midst.

And later on, with hostilities ended and settlements established, I was only a girl of 5 or 6 riding with my father one day, passing the Stanwick place, there sat a human skull on a fence post staring out at the rutted road. As I stared back father flicked the reins and said, "Sorry you've seen that. Damn thing ought to be buried."

My curiosity aroused, he told me of the Indian who'd appeared at the Stanwick homestead a few years prior. No threat, destitute, clothes ragged, he and his pony both half-starved. Couldn't speak a word of English, near to collapse, they dipped him some water. Offered food, he shook his head in grimace at a terrible pain in his stomach. He simply stumbled on, leading his pony up to their east pasture where he slowly knelt to the ground and lay. They no more than turned around when two drifters, white men, rode in asking about their compadre, so claimed, an Indian they'd camped with the night before. When Mr. Stanwick pointed yonder to the pasture, they couldn't hide their glee at seeing the pony standing next to the fallen body. Said they'd best go check on him. Stanwick followed and they found the Indian dead. Likely poisoned by the drifters, one of whom grabbed up the reins and said, "Reckon this horse is our'n." They rode off and Stanwick returned to the house. Winter coming on, he left the Indian to the coyotes, crows, and vultures. The following spring, kicking through the bones,

Stanwick found the skull and stuck it on a post to mark his southeast boundary.

Another callous deed, though I never saw the skull again. Shortly thereafter it was stolen by pranksters and ended up in a tavern there in Oakvale where it was painted red and men and boys pitched pennies to the eye sockets in chance of a free drink. The boys won a soda, the men a beer or whiskey. This I learned from my adopted brothers, Liam and Glen. Each hit the socket many times and felt no pity. No one could blame them after what they witnessed that dreadful day.

My father, Patrick Briar, had taken the boys on a hunt about 12 miles south where the Ionia Hills edge into the Buffalo Valley. Rumor placed a large herd thereabout and with more settlers arriving, the boys feared the buffalo would be shoved west before they got a chance to shoot one. Plus, both families needed meat. So they'd pleaded with their father and mine to go.

Each boy rode one of their father's plow horses while my father followed in the wagon drawn by his paired mules. After a half-day ride, they topped a hill and spotted hundreds of buffalo grazing through the broad plain that stretched to the Solomon further south. Wasting no time, they trailed on down and hobbled the horses and mules by the creek. They quietly entered the timber, hunched in shadow till they reached a gully then crawled the final distance through the brush, their scent cloaked by the south wind.

Caught unaware, the buffalo continued to graze and the hunters dropped two at 30 yards, both prime fat cows. They praised their luck and spent the rest of the day skinning and butchering the kill. Though they heard a number of shots off towards the Solomon, they thought nothing of it, likely other hunters out doing the same. By evening, the meat wrapped in the respective hides, they washed off in the creek, built a fire and feasted on buffalo tongues. They planned to jerk most of the meat and salt the briskets once they returned, making a goodly store for both families. Early next morning, about the time of the Indian attack, they headed north, facing another half-day ride but in high spirits from their bountiful hunt.

Nearly noon they spotted the dugout in the distance and the boys whipped their mounts into a lumbering gallop, anxious to share the news. My father quickened the mules and followed on, soon wondering of the wide patch of white feathers, thinking there'd been a freak snowfall. Then a black-winged vulture rose up from a cow's dark carcass as the boys leapt down frantically shooing the scavengers away from their dear ones. In that instant father realized what had happened and feared he'd face the same over the near hill east. Neither boy wailed, simply stood in vacant stare as he pulled rein and looked on. All dead, mutilated, nothing could be done.

"Boys," he said, "I need to check on Sarah. You gonna come or stay?"

"We'll stay," Liam answered. "Gotta cover 'em somehow…" Not a stitch of clothing left on the bodies, all carried off with the blankets and ticking. "C'mon, Glen," he called to his brother and each walked over to fetch an armload of hay.

Father hied the mules and whipped them hard the whole mile to our place. Found mother hanging laundry on a rope strung from the cabin to a tree, me in the cradle set by. Their joyful greeting and her brief tale of my salvation ended the instant he told of the grim scene just witnessed. She rushed inside and filled a basket of provisions at hand and emptied her dome chest of blankets, there being no time or material to build coffins. The bodies, already rotting in the intense heat, would need wrapped for burial.

When my parents arrived, Liam and Glen had fully covered the bodies and were digging the first grave using a shovel and hoe not taken by the Indians. Father added his pick and spade to the effort and they labored on into the night. Each grave dug a full six foot, my father's height. Each body cushioned in hay, gently wrapped and laid to the good earth.

Finished, they all stood silent, no words, just the raw beat of grieving hearts. Mother roasted meat on an open fire, which they quietly ate then stretched out on the remaining blankets and slept beneath the stars.

Next morning, making ready to return to our cabin, Liam would not budge.

"I gotta find Katy," he told them, "Gotta try…" and would not be dissuaded. Nor would he let Glen tag along. Told him to mind their aunt and uncle or else, stated firmly, now the eldest and instinctive head of the family. Gripped his father's Spencer rifle and passed the shotgun to Glen. Mother bundled some leftover roasted meat and other scant provisions and tied them back of his saddle along with a blanket rolled in oilcloth. Father gave him what few shells he could spare, shook his hand and wished him luck.

Liam mounted up and reined southwest. The Indians had left a broad deep trail and he was determined to follow in search of his sister. As mother once reflected, "He was a true Callaway, Liam, had his father's fight and his mother's fierce pride. Heard her warn him one day, *'You got more fight in you than is wise, my son. This world whups us all in the end, no matter how we whup it back. A fine brain stirs in that hard head of yours. Always choose the better o'er the bad else the good stands no chance. Nor do we. And never forsake your family…'"*

IV. The Search

The boy carried his mother's soft voice within, urged on by his father's fight. Though dead none were gone, not so long as blood flowed and warmed his flesh. Felt his lost kin in his breath and bone. Belly up all night in wait of dawn, he'd barely slept. Midmorning found him riding wholly alone beneath the burning sun, his shadow cast to the raiders' trail, harder to track further south, the grass heavily grazed. Then the trail spilt in half, then split again, the warriors parting in twos and threes till by noon there was not a sign or trace. Nothing but buffalo trails webbing the hills in meandering patterns from grass to water. All swallowed up in the vast land with his sister somewhere in pain many times his own.

Still he rode in the vague direction he'd started, crossing over into the Limestone Valley through bands of buffalo, antelope, and deer that mostly ignored his presence and he theirs. In descent to the creek he flushed some turkey then paused to water his horse and fill his canteen, the water clear and tasty. On the upland prairie west he saw nothing but diminishing herds of buffalo through the barren expanse.

Again he reined southwest, angling down the long gradient toward the Solomon Valley. In late afternoon he spied the faint line of the river that grew more timbered to the west where it forked north and south.

Further on, a distinct reflection caught his eye. Curious, he nudged his horse and in a short while arrived at a circular pool about 30-foot across surrounded by a natural mound that extended in gentle rise to his approach then dropped off in a sheer limestone cliff where water trickled down from the overflow above — the pool apparently spring-fed from a mysterious depth.

He slowly circled in wonder of how it came to be, then dismounted, drawn by Indian relics, or offerings, strewn at random over time: a knife sheath, beads and eagle feathers, a pipe stem floating at the edge. He knelt and dipped his hand, found the water harsh and salty. He stood and continued around the perimeter. And there, caught on a rocky overflow, dangling half in the water, he found a blue ribbon like the one Katy wore to tie up her hair. He pulled the wet end through his thumb and forefinger to press it dry. He raised it to his nose then gently folded and placed it in his shirt pocket; certain it held her scent — the rosehip she loved to gather for perfume and tea.

These thoughts suddenly eclipsed by the sight of men and horses grouped by trees along river less than a quarter mile away. On the high mound, exposed against the sky, fearing they were Indians, he dropped to the ground. Chancing a further look, he peered through the grass and discerned a cook wagon and uniforms and realized they were army. Relieved, he stood and waved his arms in shout to them.

"Captain, sir…we got us a straggler comin' in!"

The trooper pointed toward the approaching rider as the Captain, a tall, sandy-haired man with a full red beard, set his coffee aside and walked forth.

"Just a boy on a plow horse, sir…shall I send him off?"

"No, let's see what he has to say."

The boy halted at 30 yards, uncertain of self and strangers.

"Are you lost, son?" the Captain called out.

"No sir, I'm from the White Rock up north a ways."

"Well here stands Captain John H. Taylor, 5th US Cavalry. Suppose you ride up and state your name and business."

The boy rode forth and said, "I'm Liam Callaway. Two days back…Indians killed my family…" He choked on the last and sat staring off, hollow-eyed, fatigued, like he'd been caught in a horror that would never end. The Captain read it well, having witnessed that look often during the recent war.

"Climb on down, son, and we'll talk. Private Long," he said, turning to a trooper standing by, "will tend your horse. Now come along, Liam," he led the boy to a canvas stool beside the cook wagon, fetched them each a cup coffee then sat opposite, waiting till the boy had taken a few sips.

"Care to tell me what happened?"

The sugar-laced coffee loosened the boy's tongue and he told all in a rush.

"Me 'n my brother Glen was on a hunt with Uncle Pat. Come home 'n found 'em…Ma, Pa, my sis Lily 'n little Will…all dead. Killed bad. But they, the Indians, carried off my big sister Katy. Found this back up by the spring," he pulled the blue ribbon from his pocket. "It was hers."

"Son, thousands of those ribbons are traded across the plains each year. That's an old spirit spring up there. Called *Waconda*. Indians have tossed trinkets to those waters for centuries to gain favor in love, war, and the hunt. All according to their beliefs. Your ribbon could have come from any of a dozen different tribes."

"No sir, it's hers. It holds her scent," his voice adamant, certain.

"That may be," the Captain conceded, mindful of the boy's claim. "You say it happened two days ago? And you followed their trail?"

"Yes sir, but it give out up along the Limestone. I come on in hunch. Found this," again he raised the ribbon in proof.

The Captain met the boy's hopeful gaze and said, "Son, you can't trail Indians in summer. Not on a plow horse. Their ponies are too swift. Our cavalry mounts can't even keep pace. My orders are to scout for their main camp along the Solomon on west. Then join up with Colonel Carr at Fort Wallace till we hunt down Tall Bull and his Dog Soldiers. And we will, I promise."

"But they was Indians what killed my kin…maybe the same ones?"

"Sorry, son, we ride out directly at dawn and can abide no stragglers."

"But I gotta…gotta find her!"

"I know, but she could be anywhere, even clear to Colorado. Over the past week they've raided all through the Solomon and the Saline. Same as last year," he noted, "when Major Forsyth pursued with a band of volunteers, the Solomon Avengers. You may have heard of them, they made a brave stand on the Arikaree, at Beecher's Island, named for the young Lieutenant killed there. He and 50 others stood off a thousand Cheyenne and Sioux warriors. Dug rifle pits behind their dead horses and survived a 9-day siege on rotten horse flesh, risked sniper fire to fill their canteens. Even managed to kill Roman Nose, a big chief. For all the good it did. A year later Tall Bull and his Dog Soldiers are still at large, same Indians, same region…rape, pillage, murder." He glared in disgust. "I can respect the Indian until he turns predator, then I make him my prey. This time, I vow, we will find their main camp and ride them to the ground. Then good American folks like your family can fill this land. Live in peace and prosper."

"But I can help. Got my Pa's Spencer repeater same as yours. He rode Union Cavalry 'n taught me to shoot. I killed a buffalo three days back."

The Captain looked fondly on the peach-faced boy, just over five feet tall, willful and determined. Had seen his like many times in the war, particularly among the Rebel lads, charging bravely one moment then shot to pieces.

"I don't doubt your sand, son. But my final word is no." Meeting the boy's fierce eyes, he softened his tone. "Though there is one thing that might help. Can you describe your sister for me?"

"Near tall as me, I now beat her by a tad. Has long dark hair, brown eyes, is well-formed 'n pretty. Her birth name is Katherine, we call her Katy."

"Here's the best I can do. If we find your sister, I'll send a dispatch rider direct to the White Rock, where I strongly urge that you return."

"No, I gotta find her."

"Very well," taking a different tack, hoping to divert the boy from danger, "you might search back along the Solomon. Indians sometimes circle back, in part to hide their trail. Sometimes they tire of a captive and free them, or she may have escaped. Lieutenant Lawson and G Troop are patrolling through there to protect other settlers. Saw him yesterday along Asher Creek. You might try and seek him out. He may have word of her."

Nearly nightfall, the sun almost set, the wind calm, the boy listened in gaze to the fire, then glanced up in question, "What about the Saline? She could be down there?"

"True, that's possible. But be warned, if you head south you face a two-day ride and scarce water until you reach either Wolf Creek or Spillman on east. I still advise you return to the White Rock and help your family." With that he stood and tossed his coffee dregs to the fire. "I bid you good evening, Liam, and wish you well. You're welcome to camp here tonight and draw rations if you like." With that he gave a firm nod and strode to his tent to write his daily report.

Beneath the great oaks and cottonwoods, the boy lay watching the moon cross the sky while limbs and leaves heaved to the sighing wind amid soldier snore and horse stomp. Finally he dozed off in the wee hours only to awaken to the cuss and shout of troopers saddling up. He found his horse and did the same, standing apart from their scramble back to order.

At dawn the Captain led the double column west along the North Branch of the Solomon trailed by the commissary and supply wagons, moving like mounted shades through the heavy fog that drifted out from the river over the plain. The boy followed through the first mile, listening for the creak of wagon wheels that grew steadily faint then silent as the fog lifted to the warming sun.

The column had vanished, just wagon ruts and hoofprints in the dewy grass.

Pressing the ribbon to his chest, he reined south, somehow called in that direction. He forded the north and south branches of the river, both running shallow in early June, then ascended a daunting sweep of prairie to view an endless sea of grass and hot wind rippling to the horizon and nary a tree, even the buffalo diminished till he saw not a one. A few antelope drew close, briefly curious then bounded away over a rise. Later a pack of wolves crossed his path, intent and watchful as they dipped down a gully to reappear, fur blending with the grasses.

Otherwise, he encountered only the sun and wind over the continuous rise and fall of land.

In that emptiness he saw his guilt emerge ethereal from the ground, saw them tossing off their blankets, their mutilated bodies given image if not life, saw features of each amidst the flickering shift of sun, wind, and grass. He could have saved them had he not gone in hunt — with his father and brother he could have stood off the Indians like those brave men at that island the year before. But if the savages held Katy, what then? There was no changing what had happened. No escaping the haunt of his butchered kin as they whirled in blur through the midday heat. He turned his face to the sun to burn away the horror. Staring up till he clinched his eyes from the painful yellow-white fire, their ghostly remnants still vivid within, blind, dizzied, fatigued, he hung his head to his chest, riding in and out of dream until he fell with a jolt and awakened.

He blinked his caked eyes away from the sun and in a flash saw Lily combing her blonde hair, smiling as she and her hair merged with the mane of golden horse rearing to paw the air. He blinked again to clear his eyes and saw his horse had found water oozing from a chalky crevice to form a meager pool among the rocks. He bellied over, lowered his head and sipped, wet and cool to his parched lips, and not brackish.

Now close to sunset he chose to camp, placed his rifle handy and began to gather buffalo chips thereby, soon had a goodly pile. Wanted a fire against the closing night, not only in dread of ghosts but he'd sighted wolves several more times in his fitful ride. His Aunt Sarah had packed him a dozen matches in a little corked bottle. With none to spare he stuffed dry grass for kindling, but alone and edgy he lost the first flame to the wind. He cupped the next one with greater care and the grass caught, eating up through the chips in blue flame, all but smokeless, that cast a modest glow through the near radius. He drank more water, filled his canteen, then sat and slowly chewed the buffalo meat, chary of his supply, sufficient for a day or two. While there was game about, he dared not waste any shells, carried only seven in his rifle and four extra and would need every last one should he meet with Indians.

With these thoughts the wind roused, threatening to douse the low blue flames. He jumped up and quickly added more chips, shielding the fire with a blanket till the flames rose and steadied. From the surrounding shadows the mutilated forms again took shape, whirling about the fire in the spiraling patterns of the wind, hands seeking, reaching forth, and he did not want them to come and cried *"No! No!"* in animal fear and instinct, flailing his arms like when he'd shooed the vultures. Then the wolves appeared, their yellow eyes glinting beyond the fire. He dashed at them in crazed feint, gnashed his teeth and growled, eyes narrowed, wolf-like, then dropped to his knees and tore at the sod, flinging it at them. They simply shifted in wait and stared on like judgement. Then he found his voice and cursed, "You damn devils!" grabbed his rifle and fired.

The loud report scattered the wolves as he fell forward and blacked out.

The wind quieted and the flames gently hummed through the night. And there he lay, face down, gripping the rifle, when he awakened. The sun full up, an empty plain, for a moment he did not know who or where he was. Suddenly it came to him and he stood in panic — his horse gone! Turning west, he saw it still hobbled, calmly cropping the grass 40 yards off. He ran over and said its name, "Samson," for the first time since losing his family. He touched the soft nose, the warm breath, and repeated, "Samson," then grasped the coarse mane and led him back. Soon had the horse saddled and bridled, his blanket and food sack tied in place, canteen filled, he mounted up, head clear, relieved to have slept. Again he pressed the ribbon to his chest and rode south.

No real change in the landscape from the previous day until about midmorning when they crossed a wide marsh flat where hundreds of ducks and geese browsed and fed. Several score took flight in their passing, slowly wheeled about and glided back to land among the reeds and shallow water. Reining thereby, the horse tossed its head and refused to drink, too brackish like at the spring and they traveled on. The sun bore down and his canteen steadily emptied. Every few miles he'd take a sip, dismount and trickle a portion into his cupped hand for the horse. Barely enough to wet their parched lips till by noon there was not a drop. Despite which he urged his horse on, grateful there were no visions to plague him, just the hot sun, wind, and thirst.

Vaguely at first, then more clearly through the vaporing heat, he discerned the faint declivity that marked Spillman Creek in its winding descent to the Saline. Even the horse perked its ears, scenting water. They quickened their pace, focused solely on thirst, when he abruptly drew rein and hopped down, having struck the trail of a dozen or so riders headed west. Several horses were iron shod, the rest Indian ponies. Maybe they carried Katy? But he checked his urge to follow straight on, still needed water.

Mounting up, he sighted yet another group of riders southeast along the tree line, coming on fast considering the heat. In the anxious moment he thought to escape toward the creek. Then he noted their dark uniforms and took heart.

The riders, initially strung out, now formed a loose double column as they slowed, relaxed, in sync with their mounts — Buffalo soldiers led by a young white officer who presently called a halt and gave his name, Lieutenant O'Neil, adding that they were a troop of the 10th Cavalry. He then drew breath and said, "Young man," his eyes intent, "we're hard on the heels of Indian marauders. They have two white captives. You come directly in their path. It's a wonder they didn't get you. Did you see them?"

"No, but I crossed their trail yonder," his dry raspy voice brightening at word of captives. "Indians took my sister three days back up north on the White Rock. Maybe they're the ones as have her."

"Sorry, this concerns a mother and a child taken on a raid this morning. Mrs. Alder and her little daughter Alice, and we —"

"But they took my sister Katy," the boy insisted. "She's got long dark hair, stands near tall as me…" He waited, staring hard, expectant.

The Lieutenant grimaced and looked away, spat to the ground and answered, "Yes, briefly, at a distance, we did see a young woman that matches that description. They may have released her to lighten their load."

"Where? When?"

"About midday, east along the Saline. But she ran and hid, frightened like a wild creature and would not answer our calls. We scattered out in search. But saw and heard nothing more, we could not delay."

"You left her? You left Katy?"

Facing the boy's accusation, torn between moral and military duty, he felt like he'd halved the proverbial baby. "Listen, I'm sorry for your sister, but she's no longer at their mercy. We have to press on for the two still held captive."

A stout colored trooper mounted beside the Lieutenant sensed the boy's frustration turning to anger and said, "Lieutenant, suh…if I may…speak to the boy?"

Relieved to share the burden, the Lieutenant granted permission.

"Certainly, Sergeant Asa, but keep it brief."

"Yes suh," he nodded then addressed the boy. "Like the Lieutenant says, we seen her a couple-three times. Then she's gone, spooked like a ghost through the timber. Our dark skin mayn't helped her fear o' men after such rough handlin'. Could be she'll answer to a voice she knows. It's but a short ways east once you hit the Saline. A mile or so, maybe. There's a giant ol' cottonwood all stripped o' bark like the thigh bone o' God…bleached white 'n scorched black…lightnin' struck, I guess. It's thereabouts we searched…" Already riding forth as the Lieutenant waved them on, the Sergeant leaned back and hollered, "Hope ya find her!"

Gripping that hope, he rode to the creek, watered his horse and filled his canteen.

It was nearing sundown when he finally reached the old cottonwood that stood like a splintered bone charred to the marrow. He lashed his horse thereby and called for her again and again. Each time he waited and heard nothing but silence and the accursed wind. He entered the timber and searched the thickets along the river. The final rays of sunlight knifed through the limbs and leaves casting stark shadows and cross-hatchings as if to taunt the eye, both seek and conceal. Then he glimpsed something white. On a low bank above the roiling current, he found her hanging from a grapevine she'd fashioned to her grim task. Her tattered underclothes still clung to her wounded flesh. Her long hair tangled. Her eyes and mouth full open in final plea.

He clinched her waist, grabbed his sheath knife and cut the vine, then shouldered her limp body up through the timber and heaved her over the saddle. From there he led the horse to higher ground distant from the river, well above flood stage. Nightfall, early stars beginning to appear, he unrolled the oilcloth and blanket and gently lifted her down and laid her there, staring to the sky she once loved to gaze upon. He gazed as well, to the gibbous moon and gathering stars. Then he did his best to close her eyes, folded her hands across her breasts and tucked the ribbon beneath and covered her with the oilcloth and blanket. Too numb for tears he simply knelt for a time.

Finally he stood, removed the saddle and bridle and hobbled his horse. Then he pulled his sheath knife, dropped to his hands and knees and began to dig. Working by moonlight for he feared a fire would wake and draw her soul...and theirs. Now dead, he preferred they slept. Fleeing such thoughts he stabbed and clawed through the sod earth to gravel and rock, tossing off debris with bloody hands to reach a depth exceeding his height, all the while sensing her shade crouched above while the wolves circled calling across the night. On and on he labored, frantic to give her peace. At last he climbed out, edged her over and eased her down.

By dawn he'd filled in the grave and covered it with rocks. He sat facing the pale sunrise. His meat gone, felt no hunger, nor will to hunt, only a deep urge to lie down and never rise again. He stirred himself and stood, saddled up and rode north.

V. Liam

Mother said Liam was gone a full seven days, and not a bite to eat the latter half. A lean growing boy when he left, when he rode up to the cabin that evening he was so trail-beat and starved they hardly recognized him. Leaning in his saddle, half-dead, silent, he stared a moment then fell to the ground. Father carried him in and mother spooned him broth till he slept then cleaned and bandaged his torn hands. He didn't wake till late next day and they wondered of his hands and the fact his bedroll was missing, but when they asked about Katy, he turned his head away and simply said she was gone. More, they did not ask Thereafter whenever he heard her name or any of his dead family mentioned, he ducked his head and walked outside and stood staring off in silence.

By the second day he was back on his feet. Mindless of his hurt hands, he sat and honed his knife, then stood ready for whatever task ahead, ever willing and helpful, no longer a boy, not yet a man. But no, never cheerful, wore that deep silence, earnest and sober — and that was the irony, for hard drink and drunkenness would claim him. Though that came later.

By age 14 Liam was nearly tall as father and gripped each labor without grudge or complaint. Tireless behind the plow, likewise swinging scythe or ax. And he'd work a whipsaw till Glen gave out then set both handles to his end and keep a steady push and pull right up to the dinner bell. When he'd promptly come in and wash up. Sit and eat, speak when spoken to, polite but solemn. Never once spoke of what he'd found.

We all loved him, perhaps even more for that dark sorrow he carried.

When I was a little girl of 4 or 5, just learning my letters and numbers on the slate, he'd take me on his lap in the evenings and help improve my hand, patient, never cross. Sometimes he'd read one of the Grimm's Tales, of which Goldilocks was my favorite. Finished, I'd beg him to read it again and he often did. Always generous and kind to me, but never playful, and rarely smiled.

Whereas Glen could be a prankster, liked to run and chase. Laugh and tickle. All great fun till I could not breathe then I'd cry out, "Stop it, Glen! No more!" Still mother said that early on, like Liam, he was slow to smile. But father could draw him out and make him laugh. Called him, "Cut-a-hay" for Callaway, as in "Cut-a-hay…did you hang up that harness 'n brush them mules? How about that horse stall, Cut-a-hay, is it mucked out?" Unlike Liam, Glen could be lax in his chores and needed prodding. Fortunately, father preferred to coax a boy rather than whip him.

Liam, on the other hand, never once needed spurred. Crops sown, stock tended, he'd grab the ax and saw and head into the trees. And there was good timber along our creek that fed into the White Rock — ash, oak, walnut, red and white elm, hackberry and cedar. Among those virgin stands some giants measured 4 to 5 feet in diameter. Father, an experienced woodsman, having grown up clearing land in Iowa, helped fell the larger ones. Then left the boys to delimb, section, and split. Liam did the greater share while Glen snagged every chance to help father with carpentry on the various improvements that needed made, all of which required lumber. The boys would haul raw timber to a water-powered mill on the White Rock and trade for sawn lengths suitable for corrals, corncrib and the like. And they'd usually pocket a dollar or so in change.

The mill was owned by Heinz Roiter, a dark stout German so dutchy he seldom spoke beyond stating price and payment, shrewd to the last penny, then with an abrupt "Goot day!" went back to working his saw and maintaining the millrace. Folks took to calling him "That gruff ol' Beaver" which made him rather proud, I think. At least that's what father said. One day Liam and Glen let me ride along, but I stayed in the wagon for fear of the mean-looking bulldog that stood guard by the door.

Old Heinz winked and said, "No vorry, is goot boy…he bite, no eat. Ha!"

Leaving there, Liam and Glen stopped by the tavern. That's when I learned of the Indian skull painted red — spied through the open door while I sat on the buckboard and watched them pitch pennies to the sockets. When they came out each gripped a ginger beer and Liam handed me my first ginger ale in a blob-top bottle that mother later used for a flower vase.

Meanwhile Heinz kept his saw buzzing unless broke down or a drought slowed the water, then he suffered like Job to live a day without gaining one nickel. In a few years when the railroad came, looking to increase efficiency and profit, he ordered in a steam-powered saw. "No vaste time!" he loudly asserted, "Bring saw to trees!" This worked well enough until the day the boiler blew up, leaving Heinz stone dead, his head bashed against a fresh-cut stump.

As father wryly observed, "His damnable greed finally got 'im…"

Of course, father also had ambitions. The summer of the Indian attack, after Liam's return, he and the boys added another span to the cabin, nearly doubling its size. Over the next few years, they built a barn and corncrib. And to secure the Callaway land claim they built a small hut and tack shed there as well. From the ruins of the sod house they erected a stock shelter with adjoining corral. Nor did they neglect the graves, fenced them off and set a crude headstone at each and chiseled in the names.

By 1874 the boys had a stake. As head of the family Liam was now a landowner, yet showed little interest beyond his constant labor and made no plans. That same year, when he turned 16, father surprised him with a fine saddle horse. Both now the same height, father looked him in the eye, handed him the reins and said, "He's yours…" That did bring a smile. Liam loved that horse. Whenever he finished his chores he'd saddle up "Captain," as he named the horse, and ride out. The land largely unfenced, untilled, they could range for miles and miles.

This happened mostly on Sundays. And our family, the Briars, seldom to never attended services. Father joked that we were "Summa-the-time Christians" — the only honest sect, the rest "Mostly busy-body hypocrites 'n pretenders that'll praise you on Sunday 'n damn you come Monday," so he vowed. However, we did own a Bible from which he and mother read on occasion, claiming there was good teaching to be had in those pages, but neither of them cared for preaching. With no further Indian raids after the one that hit our family, settlers flooded in, among whom were many highly devout Dunkards, Friends, and of course Baptists. Most Sundays we did observe our rest, and in fine weather, while Liam was off on his horse, father would take us on a wagon ride. One hot summer day passing the Dunkard church, the door left open to catch a breeze, I witnessed their crude howl of a hymn which affirmed they frowned on singing, nor did they allow dancing or instruments of any kind. That dampened my curiosity of church and I proudly remained a "Summa-the-time Christian" ever after.

Father, like Uncle Clay, had served in the war, though only the final year. A volunteer in the Army of the Border, he fought in the Battle of Westport then rode mounted patrol in and out of Missouri, skirmishing with Rebel bushwhackers.

"They'd take a pot-shot from the trees," he'd chuckle, reflecting on the war to humor the boys. "We'd answer their smoke with a few rounds. Then they'd scatter. And we were happy to let 'em go. Just farm boys same as us, born in a separate region, caught up in a so-called cause. Some say we fought to free the Negro slaves. Others claim it was to preserve the Union. Partly both, I suppose. Me, on reachin' 18, I joined up to escape the gull-dern farm!" he'd slap his knee and laugh. This irritated mother, a staunch Lincoln Republican and he a casual Democrat, nearly a Copperhead in her view. Or as he liked to josh, "You're right, Sarah, I'm a summa-the-time Unionist," which further confirmed her opinion.

Yet he truly did dread sinking a plow in the prairie sod. His chief aim in settling on the frontier was to raise cattle. After five years, making good on both claims, he and his nephews ran roughly 60 head of Shorthorn roans, all red and white speckled, bearing the BC brand, for

Briar-Callaway. And Glen shared father's reluctance to plow. While Liam finished each task as bidden, Glen set behind a mule and plow was liable to wander off midday and be found fishing in the nearby creek. There father's good humor ended and the boy more than once felt boot leather on his hindside.

In spite of which Glen eagerly awaited his 16th birthday, fully expecting a gift horse like Liam's. But it took him another year to earn father's trust. And that gift delayed was a lesson learned. Glen grew prompt in his habits, and once granted the horse he shucked any grudges, mounted up and whupped and spurred like he owned the world.

"A natural horseman," father declared, watching him rein about with fluid ease.

Now young men, the brothers began asserting their freedom, both good looking, with light-brown hair that reflected their mother's reddish tint, Liam taller and stronger, Glen more slight and agile. Come Saturday afternoon they'd ride off to one settlement or another, Long Branch, Holsted, or Oakvale nearby. Maybe step into a tavern but mostly frequented dances. While Dunkards and others scorned such doings, there were weekly barn dances with lively reels, fiddles and banjoes, and the Bohemians among us always had their festive polkas and beer. And Glen, nimble afoot, loved to dance, took to it as readily as riding a horse. But Liam shied from girls and favored his beer, nursing a mug off in a corner alone. If a girl approached, he'd politely excuse himself and walk away. Yet should a ruffian try to rile him, he was quick to answer. Good with his fists and gave better than he got, venting his rage in a fury. Many nights he came home black-eyed and bloodied, lip needing stitched, hand bandaged, a finger splinted.

When mother shared her worry, father answered, "Just wild oats, Sarah. He'll grow through it," more doubtful than jocular. Mother, having sensed her womb go barren after nearly losing me, looked on the boys as her sons — each of differing bent and will, and seeing them drift apart, her worry only deepened. Though Glen was involved in several scraps and always helped Liam home, he usually steered clear of fisticuffs and drinking and their silences grew ever more telling. Finally the brothers hardly spoke or joshed at all. Then Liam started riding off alone, directly to the taverns. Skipped the beer and took to whiskey, often returning home late in a stupor.

Early one morning father found him fallen by his horse, lying so still he feared he was dead. Father gathered him up and carried him in. When laying him down his voice awakened in an awful moan, more animal than human, the cry of a deeply wounded soul. Listening by the door it was the most frightening thing I'd ever heard. In a day or so we learned he'd been in the Oakvale tavern where he grabbed up the Indian skull and dared anyone to stop him as he slammed it to the floor and stomped it to pieces.

Not two weeks later the brothers had a terrible row down at the barn. Which I witnessed, playing with kittens in the hayloft, holding one up to a misty ray of sunlight cast through the chinks when I heard angry voices and edged over to look. Liam had Glen by throat before father rushed in and pulled him off. When asked what the trouble was, Liam turned away, leapt to his horse and rode out. Faced with the same question, Glen shrugged and said, "It was nothin', Uncle Pat…just nothin'."

"Listen, a man doesn't grip another man's throat over nothin'. Is it a girl?"

"Naw, no girl," Glen mumbled in glance to the ground. Then he looked to father and said, "That time…us gone on the hunt, Liam says it's our fault they're dead…"

Father slumped his shoulders and pressed no further. Shared and felt that blame. Both walked silent in return to the house. I lagged a moment then followed. There was barely a word spoken over supper. Everyone separate, somehow broken.

Early December, the wind blew cold that night, howling from the north. Dawn saw our first snowfall and Liam's horse standing riderless outside the door. Father snatched up the reins, stepped to the saddle and reined hard, following the trail back through the trees. Found Liam beyond the creek crossing, his head at a severe cant to a rock, still reeking of whiskey, the bottle spilt nearby. Too drunk to break his fall and so broke his neck. Father hitched the buckboard and drove to the sawmill for a load of cedar.

All that day he and Glen sawed and planned then hammered a coffin, echoing the pang in my heart. Finished, they carried it to the cabin. And Liam, washed clean by mother and myself, dressed in his Sunday best, was laid inside, his pale face lit by the flickering candle as the lid shadowed over and was nailed shut.

The next morning as crows cawed from a near tree we all loaded in the buckboard and drove to the Callaway graves. Father and Glen broke the frozen ground and buried him with his family. A gray sky, the ground white like a shroud, we stared at the dark mound of earth then gathered ourselves home. That was in December 1879, and I was a month shy of 10 years old. I loved my brother Liam, a dear and cherished soul. Seeing him gone, I shared in part the pain he'd known in losing his family.

VI. The Limestone

Such dark thoughts, she needs something cheery, drains the dishwater and turns to Paul toweling a soup bowl and says, "Here, I'll finish that. You fetch that old red box up those spiral stairs…I'm too weak. Bring it down and we'll decorate the tree."

"With bubble lights?" — his favorite.

"Why of course, that's the first thing."

"And the angel's hair?"

"Sure, but that comes last, after we hang the colored balls and tinsel."

"Can we string popcorn?"

"Not this year, Paul. That's quite a chore. Let's just eat the popcorn and enjoy the lights once we're done."

He nods and clomps up the narrow stairs and soon returns, setting the box on the table. An old fruit crate painted red. And she recalls the broad, jolly whimsy of her second husband, Paul's grandad, wielding the brush — "Aye now, a Christmas box should be red, eh?" What good times we had, she smiles unraveling the twisted cord connecting a score of bubble lights, all different colors and all working when she plugs them in. Except the dull blue one where Paul points in disappointment.

"Gram, that one is dead."

She wiggles the cord and taps the glass cylinder and in a blink it begins to glow, first with a few bubbles then a steady stream entrained in blue light.

"There, it's come alive," she says. "I think it was a little slow last year too. Now Paul, hold out your hands…" She loosely coils them with the lights then begins slowly lacing the tree. First she leans to the lower boughs then up through the middle and finally towards the top has Paul clip the last one — a bright yellow glow above which he sets a thin crystalline star shaped like a snowflake that catches the light and casts it to the room. They stand a moment admiring the bubbly array woven limb to limb from floor to ceiling, pleased with their work.

"Come Paul," she says, "let's step outside." Noting his puzzlement, she adds, "There's something special tonight. Come see…" Opening the door, she points to the moon now nearing its zenith.

"The moon?" he asks, his mouth open in wonder.

"Yes. And tonight, this very minute, three men are up there in orbit."

"Or…bit?"

"Yes," she answers, stepping back inside, closing the door against the cold air. "Round 'n around they go…" she smiles watching Paul in slow sway to her words.

"Won't that make them dizzy?" he asks.

"You would think so. But it seems not, protected as they are inside a capsule like these colored balls we hang on the tree. Weightless, just floating in space."

He listens, munching a gingerbread man with cinnamon eyes while raising his own to the star and ceiling, and she knows he imagines himself floating, and she sees it too, like a giant gingerbread man buoyant in the air.

"But we're lucky, Paul. Here on earth we have gravity to keep us grounded."

"I like the earth," he says, settling his eyes back to her.

"So do I, for all its woes…I will sorely hate to leave it."

"You goin' somewhere, Gram?"

"No, not for a while, but as I've told you, my long life will soon end then I will return to the earth. And you know my wishes. Yet think of this, by next summer they plan to land a man on the moon. Step right down and walk there."

"Why?"

"Now there's a question. Just to touch it, I suppose. Same as you like to touch the star on the tree. Am I right?"

He smiles, reaching there in wonder if not understanding, certainly taking joy in the notion as they commence hanging the colored balls…

Why land on the moon? Why indeed? Try talking sense to an idiot, it will sharpen your mind and hone your reason with patience and doubt until you know that most of our efforts are futile. The other day he asked, "Gram, why does my shadow go sometimes in front and sometimes in back?"

"Your shadow is cast by the sun and which way depends on the angle of the sun," I answered as I was taught and others blindly repeat.

"No, Gram," he said, "it grows from my feet and stays on the ground. The sun hangs up there all by itself…"

Such questions arise often in a day and make you sigh in vain of an answer not drawn from books, but fit to Paul's understanding. And that sharpens the mind, and humbles it too. Poor Paul, I call you an idiot only in mind and lame habit. Though so branded you are no more so than other men I've known. All idiots in our way. Here I have a septic and a toilet in place of a slop jar where I can sit and think. No longer need to trek mud and snow. And while I doubt the hygiene of passing waste in the house, it is a convenience till the whole waste of me is gone.

Now in my ninth decade, my nine lives like an old cat it seems, once supple, now brittle as a twig. From year to year each decade tried to kill me…and maybe did in part. What was once was gone, then the world changed, fashion, clothing, and transport, what we ate and loved and feared. Even the terrain altered from grass to plow then fields left fallow gone to clover and weeds, thickets, thorny locust and cedar trees, which are fine when few but a plague when many. Yes, every ten years saw a new world, a new me in a new skin, which can be frightful or amusing, depending…

⸱•⸱

Mother claimed that when the Indians raided in '69 there was barely a score of settlers through our region. The following year, with Tall Bull and his Dog Soldiers subdued, several hundred rolled in. Over the next decade, by the spring of 1880, the population had swollen to 15,000 and growing. Nearby Oakvale counted over 400 souls. But our family had lost one more. Glen, having buried his brother, could no longer bear to look on a land that had swallowed his family. Young, restless, itched to ride west.

Father understood his urge and offered to buy him out.

"It's only fair, the Callaway half is yours."

"No, Uncle Pat," he answered. "You built all this 'n held us together. You 'n Aunt Sarah gave me a home. I'll not split it up in leaving."

"Well then, know you'll always have a home should you wish to return…"

With that they shook hands and Glen agreed to help through the spring planting. Father sold a dozen yearling steers to give him a small stake and traveling money. While the heyday of cattle drives was drawing to a close, open range ranching was booming in southeastern Colorado along the Purgatoire, and Glen wanted to taste the adventure and freedom. Plus, he yearned to see the snow-capped mountains, Pike's Peak and others rising like great white thunderheads in the distant blue. And he sure looked fine and handsome that warm spring morning all mounted up, dressed in a gray wool traveling suit, new gold watch in his vest gifted by mother, his carpet bag packed with wrangling clothes strapped back of his saddle. Reins in hand, he tipped his hat, wheeled his sleek sorrel horse about and rode. Aimed to catch the train at Smithville 30 miles west, where he and the horse would board and ride the rails on to Denver. All arranged by telegraph and scheduled to arrive the very next evening. Amazing.

After watching him go, mother returned to the house and cried like she'd lost a second son. But I felt the ache of joyous envy, wishing to see the mountains, a pull as strong as any desire to touch the moon. In my free time at school I loved drawing mountains on my slate, chalking in the jagged snow peaks. While I'd been learning from age 5 at Liam's knee, with more pioneer families moving in, I and their kids had been attending school for the past four years. The first was a crude sod structure and only offered a three-month session. Then the township built a wood frame school with a tower bell and increased the session to nearly six months. Blessed with a quick mind I did rather well in all subjects, but geography was my favorite. I gazed on the wall map, tracing the Continental Divide from the Rockies west to the Pacific then east to the Atlantic shore. I knew all the states and their capitols, and Colorado was the latest, admitted in 1876, marking our nation's 100-year birth as well as Custer's defeat. Still, hordes of miners rushed to the Black Hills. And recently gold had been discovered in Colorado at a place called French Gulch. My fancy envisioned Glen, his pockets filled with gold, returning to take us on a train to Denver to see Pike's Peak.

Shortly after Glen left the railroad arrived in Oakvale, a division of the Missouri Pacific, and overnight a thousand or more people poured in. Heralded as a gala event, a red-letter day, over 150 wagon teams jammed the main street. People crowded shoulder to shoulder along the tracks that extended southeast, straining to cheer the last rail laid to link with the broad turntable front of the roundhouse. The arched stone doorways gaped in wait of the locomotive parked 100 yards beyond, hissing steam from the boiler, smoke stack, piston, and drive wheel like a great iron beast of immense energy and will about to surge forth and flood our little valley with the rush and clamor of the wider world.

With the hammer ding of the last spike driven the coronet band struck up "Glory Hallelujah" and commenced marching back and forth through town while citizens feted the railroad workers and themselves. The band carried on with "Yankee Doddle" and other lively marches amid cheers and hurrahs for nearly an hour. Then gunshots and fireworks erupted filling the air with smoke, curses, rearing horses and howling dogs.

Never one for crowds, father shook his head in wry disgust, "A wonder someone isn't killed," then added, "Feel like the danged Indians must've felt seeing us come in."

But mother, flush with excitement, her recent sadness at seeing Glen leave all but vanished, frowned in question, "Don't you find it thrilling?"

"Oh, I suppose it is," he winked, "for one who enjoys a jostle now 'n then."

"You mind your tongue, Patrick Briar."

"Yes'um, Miss Sarah," he grinned, "I'll mind my tongue. But lookin' on this mighty throng, I've a mind to move us a mite further west...on over to the Limestone. There's a fine stretch of grassland 'n creek valley I've been eyein'."

"Hmmm…" she slowly nodded, none too surprised as he'd been hinting of such. "Perhaps so, if you promise me a nice frame house with plaster walls that I can paper pretty, and a hand-pump in the kitchen, I may be of a mind to join you…"

————•❖•————

That hand pump was a treasure more precious than gold, giving her water right next to the stove, handy for cooking, a wet sink for dishes, and she could fill a wash basin or tub in a blink. The house, while wood-framed with plaster walls, was not as large as our old cabin, merely four small rooms built on a square stone foundation, the roof pitched from all four sides to a Franklin rod and wind vane set dead center. No porch, just three flat stones placed in step to the door. Father promised in another year to add an upstairs and a wrap-around porch south and east. First he had to improve the barn, corral, and corncrib, rightly vowing that crops and cattle would pay for the house.

Yet all this waited as we did not make the move till the following autumn.

Beyond the aggravation of people crowding in, the Briar-Callaway lands sat at cattycorner, like diagonal squares on a checker board, cut by a sharp bend in the creek that created a choke point in driving cattle from pasture to pasture, dangerous to cross during thunderstorms and impossible at flood stage. So once corn harvest ended father finalized sale of our land and thinned the herd to 40 head of choice stock, then he and mother and I herded them 13 miles southwest to our new place on the Limestone.

Mother drove the mule team and buckboard loaded with household goods, chickens and cats caged in the carriage hitched behind. We had quite a menagerie: cattle, boar hog and five sows, the work horses, Samson and Thor, and our trusty frontier mongrel, Shep, who helped drive the cattle. And I as well, riding my own pony, an Indian paint named Patches, felt like a real pioneer heading west toward open range and adventure.

When we arrived father gave mother a hand up in his saddle and we all rode to the high hill west that overlooked the house and creek valley. Father pointed to the sweep of land running a full mile north and south by a half mile east, a quarter section of pasture on west. Nearly 500 acres all of a piece. Three tilled fields etched the creek bottom, one close by of 40 acres and two further down of 20 acres each. And east beyond the creek lay a rolling swath of fine prairie that father planned to leave for hay. No longer used a scythe, owned a horse-drawn sickle mower and hay rake, and with Glen gone he'd soon add a corn-binder and McCormick reaper. Reining his horse around, he pointed to a wooden windmill and water tank in the west pasture, then directly downslope to a spring oozing water through a marshy draw that broadened out before a grassy berm rising like a half-formed dam.

"Right there, Sarah," he declared, "gonna dam that whole draw. Buy me a buck shovel then hitch that drag pan to ol' Sampson 'n scoop the earth a spoonful at a time. By golly," he chuckled, "I can move a mountain. But heck, I only need a pond."

He'd bought the land from a woman widowed the past winter about the same time we buried Liam — her husband killed by a mule kick to the head. A hazard common to farmers daily hitching a mule or horse for one task or another, as father observed, "Any animal worked too hard is liable to hold a grudge 'n bite or kick when you least expect it." The woman with her 12-year-old son, two young daughters, and helpful neighbors had held on through the spring and summer, but after months of burden, when offered a fair price, she gladly took it and moved herself and kids back to her family in Springfield, Illinois. Thereby father basically swapped 320 acres above the White Rock for 500 acres along the Limestone and still had cash in hand.

That evening, mother, after showing the cats their new home and unloading a few essentials, already falling in love with the place, especially the hand pump in the kitchen, teased father about the deal, "Just how did you manage to swing this one, Patrick?"

"Just gave her what she wanted," he answered with sly grin.

"Hmmm…don't suppose that included your famous charm?"

"Oh now, I may've hinted as how an attractive widow stood a better chance of landing a new husband back east than stranded out here. But charm I save for you."

"Uh huh, as I recall you once charmed a certain Jefferson girl."

"So I did. But then you caught my eye 'n she lost out, poor thing."

"Ha! She was a flossy flirt."

"Well, lady or not, do hear that she makes a tidy living back up in Des Moines."

"Runs a sporting house, no doubt."

"Now Sarah, among the cultivated it's called a gentlemen's parlor…"

So they carried on, tit for tat, both showing a bit of gray and a few wrinkles, but when they laughed their love shone young as ever. And I was the little pitcher with big ears, perhaps catching more than they expected. Intended or not it furthered my learning. Now 10 years old, hardly a girl but far from a woman. And I was back in school, this one built of limestone and it stood only a mile northeast along the wagon road.

Any trepidation I had vanished the moment I entered the door and met my teacher. Fraulein Claussen, the lovely daughter of German emigrants, only 19, slightly built and graceful in black dress and white collar, her blonde hair neatly piled in ringlets to crown her sparkling blue eyes. Each morning she greeted us, "*Gaten morgan*, children…" and each day bid us home with "*Auf wiedersehen…*" her German not at all grating like Heinz the Beaver, but sweetly toned and dainty like herself. Her first name was Madalene, but we only addressed her as Miss Claussen. Adored by girls and boys alike, captivating in voice and movement, her delicate hand raising chalk to the black board, we hung on her every word and gesture.

Yet one day a rather loutish boy of 14 used a barnyard slur to express his disdain for the lesson. Miss Claussen slapped her ruler to her desk, marched to the wash stand by the door, picked up the bar of soap and said, "You come wash your mouth this instant, young man, or I will tell your father!" No idle threat, he walked over and washed his mouth out and thereafter governed his tongue. Which was her goal, to have us speak well, to read and write and respect our language…and each other. Except for her morning greeting and in seeing us off, she always spoke English. Strict but fair, kind and relentless, she put the grammar in grammar school. Stripped us of *ain't* and double negatives, made us attend noun, verb tense, adverb and adjective. Fostered correct spelling and pronunciation and daily introduced new words to expand our vocabulary. And I, a frontier girl with green eyes and dark curly hair that would not stay combed, strove to be like her, mimicking her polished manner and speech, soon thought myself quite the young lady.

Now looking on my tattered flesh, to think that I was ever young and dreamy seems a foolish fairy tale. And like my flesh given way to time and gravity, my language and grammar have backslid considerably. Brief and fleeting like youth, language obeys an inner will and need…and wonder. What word or group of words can rightly describe this life and thought? Yet wonder is ceaseless and strong, especially in youth. And we were all young, mother, father, and the land as well, new to our use and knowing…

VII. Visitors

Over winter father enlarged the barn, adding a forge shed off the west side. He'd always done his own smithing and horseshoeing. Glen gone, I often joined him at the forge to work the bellows, watching the iron glow red-hot, ready to hammer. And before dipping the metal to cool he'd let me spit and it was fun to see it sizzle white and vanish. Something we also did inside on the potbelly stove, which mother frowned on.

Hearing the hiss, she'd holler, "Don't be teaching her your dirty habits!"

"Now, Sarah," he'd caution, "just a little spit to check the heat. Swear I've never once let her spit tobacco." Though he did on occasion let me puff his cigar, but only a puff. Still she'd sniff the tell-tale odor and again father and I would suffer our scolding. Although this was seldom, mostly our lives were harmonious and busy.

Come spring mother expanded the orchard which stood beyond the garden and root cellar just north of the house, all nicely set to catch the morning sun. The ground drained east toward the creek that horseshoed north buffering cold winter winds. West, a gentle upslope funneled the late afternoon sun to further warm and ripen the fruit. To the many apple and peach trees already established she added a dozen cherry and apricot. With mulberry and gooseberry growing wild along the creek and sand plums in pasture draws, she had dozens of canning jars shelved in the cellar waiting to fill with fruits, vegetables, jams, and pickles. Last year's surplus onions and potatoes hung in gunny sacks alongside smoked hams and bacon.

The cellar, entered by a slant door leading down stone steps to a vaulted cave, measured about 12 foot deep by 7 foot high, laid up of limestone plastered smooth over the ceiling and walls to the flagstone floor. The whole domed structure covered by a mound of native sod provided a cool dry space for food storage as well as shelter from the violent winds and twisters prone to the prairie.

But predators were habitual. While mother penned and cooped her chickens each night, many a dawn saw another hen missing, carried off by a beast of field or air. Our dog Shep did his best to keep them at bay, in weekly battle with coyote, fox, possum, or raccoon. But the great horned owl proved a frightful nemesis that sent him cowering under the wagon as it shrieked down to snatch its prey. Despite which, mother's brood hens kept hatching chicks and their number held steady and grew.

A quarter mile lane led north from our house to the wagon road running east and west. The year before our arrival when the township built the school they also spanned the creek with a trestle bridge of railroad timbers and stout oak planks that held strong for 50 years until replaced by one of arched stone by the WPA in the 1930s. Most mornings I crossed the bridge at sunrise, arriving early to build the fire and wait for Miss Claussen. Faithful to her task she made each child feel special, even the loutish boy who jeered and called me "Teacher's pet!" But I didn't mind and do think I was her favorite. We both loved books, and quick and attentive, I read well above my grade level.

That winter she entrusted me with a new book only recently published that she had just finished, Lew Wallace's epic tale of *Ben Hur*. A magnificent story and I had to share reading time with mother and father. Many evenings we read passages aloud, reciting the hero's tragic fall into slavery, his rise to freedom, the chariot race, his vengeance against Messala, and the eventual redemption and salvation of his mother and sister. "That's quite a tale," father noted, "more of courage 'n quest than belief, 'cept there towards the end, them granted cure from

Jesus to me just serves to pin the tail on the donkey for the faithful…" Of all such miracles my parents held the more skeptical view expressed by Ingersoll in his *American Bible*, which I also began to sample, quietly questioning Miss Claussen's beliefs, for she was a devout Lutheran. Still, I idolized her and returning the book that spring, tearfully thanked her, for I hated to see school ending.

"*Auf wiedersehen*, Sadie, I'll see you in the fall…"

Closing the door on her fond farewell, turning west towards home, I'd never felt my isolation so keenly. Another six months before I'd hear her sweet voice or interact with other children.

Now distanced 9 miles from Oakvale and further from Mankato, the county seat, I suddenly felt marooned. Though Otego did lay only a couple miles north, a dismal little dust patch to my mind, of constant wind and a few stunted trees, nothing compared to the welcome shade of Oakvale nestled along the White Rock. But it did have a general store, grocery, and post office, so we headed there most Saturdays for essential trading. Father would coax me in the wagon with his little ditty: "*To Otego, Otego, to Otego we go…my wife 'n my daughter to Otego we go…*" and so on. He had a dozen versions and I'd soon hop up smiling at his side and help slap the reins, eager to reach the bleak little town.

There was always a candy or soda treat, and among the 50 to 60 folks some kids to see. Father invariably fetched his *Kansas City Evening Star*, a week late but timely enough to track the cattle market. And every now and then there was a letter from Glen with tidbits on his cowboy life along the Purgatoire, or "Picket-wire" as he called it.

Otego suited father fine, adjacent to the railroad with stock pens and loading dock. He could drive his cattle with ease and market them in Denver, St. Joe, or Kansas City. Our west pasture joined a prairie plateau that stretched 30 miles north and south from the White Rock to the Solomon, the whole as yet sparsely fenced. Many travelers used it as throughway and small bands of Indians often migrated between their tribal lands in the Dakotas and Oklahoma. Occasionally they'd stop by a farm to beg or barter food, more a nuisance or curiosity by that time than a threat.

School ended the last day of March and moping down the hill after saying goodbye to Miss Claussen, my heart gladdened seeing the first signs of spring, trees fleecing out here and there through the creek, upper branches tinted green. Other colors glimpsed in saunter up the lane as I stooped to pull a wild onion, its rosy petals speckled above the grass to tempt a cow and taint its milk. In rounding the house, I saw we had visitors.

Mother had just stepped out to quiet Shep and stood staring at three mounted Indians — an old man and woman of steel-gray hair and a younger woman, apparently their daughter, holding a small boy who peered through the cleft of a sooty blanket that wrapped her shoulders — all of them ragged and gaunt as their horses now shedding their winter coats. In the gnawing silence they reminded me of lepers, like Judah's mother and sister, condemned to darkness and squalor, shunned and delivered from some vile keeper to our mercy. Finally the solemn old man placed a hand to his slack belly and raised it to his mouth in sign to eat. Then from his pouch he drew forth a tiny pair of moccasins and uttered, "Swap…food," in two guttural huffs.

Mother answered with a slight nod, went inside and shortly emerged with two loaves of bread wrapped in a knotted towel. She raised her hand in sign to wait and rushed to the cellar and added a smoked ham stuffed in a gunny. All the while the old Indian turned his gaze to me, set deep in wrinkled flesh his dark fathomless eyes never seemed to blink. Not until she handed up the food did he shift his eyes to her, trading the moccasins with an approving grunt. Then they reined about and slowly rode up into the pasture and headed north.

She watched them ride beyond the hill, her breathing shallow and tense till she turned to me, startled, as if awakened, and simply said, "They were hungry."

Father had been sowing a field south beyond the creek and hadn't witnessed the encounter. Nor had I mentioned it, for mother bade me not to. That evening after supper, lying in bed, listening to the house settle, I heard her tell him that Indians had stopped by and she'd given them food.

"Well," he said, "better they ask than steal."

"Yes," she answered quietly, "and I think it was him." When father asked who, she answered, "The one that swapped the kittens for Sadie…"

Suddenly I was again transfixed by that solemn stare, felt it deepen, so vivid I laid awake a long while in silent thought and wonder.

But other wonders and labor soon filled my days.

At sunrise, taking advantage of cooler air, father would ride Sampson to the west pasture, hitch him to the buck shovel and continue panning out the earth, adding to the dam, working till noon then rest him for the day, switching to Thor or the mules for other tasks. I of course helped mother with daily chores, milking the cows, hoeing the garden, gathering eggs, mending clothes and sewing new ones. And I looked forward to days in the hayfield, the heat and sun, the mowed grass raked and ready to load. Mother and I both wore bonnets and long sleeves to protect our skin. She drove the team and wagon while father and I pitched hay into the bed. I liked handling the pitchfork and tossing the hay, the steady rhythm, the sweat and prickly stems, something of a tomboy, I prided in my blistered hands. Father taught me how to rig the hayfork and pulley to lift the hay into the barn then roll it down the center trolley and stomp it in place. Hot and dusty work, and feeling faint, I'd splash my face with jug water and catch the breeze then turn again to create a trove of winter fodder and bedding. The haymow filled, we stacked the final cuttings like large loaves of weedy bread just beyond the corral, convenient to feed our sheltered stock.

In the long evenings after a hard day and supper put away, we often enjoyed ice cream, for we had ice cut from the creek over winter, kept stored and layered with straw in a makeshift cave east of the cellar. Beneath the starry sky we took turns cranking till it would turn no more, then relished the cool creamy sweetness sliding down our throats.

On the 4th of July we traveled to Oakvale to catch the festive parade of wagons, horses, and the coronet band, folks waving and shouting all along the way, only to be trapped by a droning hours-long patriotic speech that at least included news of the near assassination of President Garfield two days prior. After a prayer for the president to fully recover, the speaker railed on, roundly denouncing alcohol while praising the state's new law limiting sale of the same. To which Father quipped, "Fat chance they'll have enforcin' that…" as he grinned to various listeners sipping brew. At last the speaker yielded to the inevitable fireworks and gunshots that greeted the night.

That morning I'd been anxious to leave my isolation and visit town, but once there I yearned to return to the sullen wind and solitude of the empty prairie. Arriving home I was fast asleep, carried in without waking as if the trip to town had been a fitful dream. Next day it seemed I'd never gone. Awkward and skinny, reaching my full height of five foot two that summer, a shy country girl, I'd stood apart, somehow marked, singled out by that old Indian's stare, beginning to learn that our lives are riddled with deceptive spaces largely unknown even to ourselves.

By summer's end father had finished the pond dam, overlaid with prairie sod to check erosion, the spillway riprapped in stone, awaiting only rain. In mid-September, after a morning cloudburst, we waded in the shallow water, feeling the mud squish our toes. Father cast an eye to the parting clouds and said, "Doubt it'll fill till spring."

The sky cleared like a big blue bowl, no rain in the offing. What did flood the valley was word of President Garfield's death from the gunshot wound, not wholly unexpected as he'd taken a turn for the worse a month earlier, they'd even called in Mr. Edison to work his magic and help find the bullet. No use, the wound terribly infected, he died on Monday, September 19th. Word went out over wire that night then neighbor to neighbor and we knew of happenings by Tuesday evening.

Rather somber over supper till father shook his head and said, "Sarah, that makes two Presidents shot dead in less'n 20 years. Now Lincoln, while a right sad case, I can understand, Booth a dern Confederate. But heck, this Guiteau fellow, they say he's a 'Stalwart' Republican 'n shot Garfield for bein' a mere 'Half-breed' Republican. Both Republicans, Sarah, it makes no sense."

"No, it doesn't. But they say he was disgruntled over not getting a job."

"Well he's got one now. Be bustin' rocks right up till they hang 'im."

"That's an awfully callous thing to say, Patrick...and our poor President dead."

"Callous? I didn't pull the trigger. And I'm rightly sad for Garfield, his wife 'n family. As a half-baked Republican he might've made a fair summa-the-time Democrat," he winked my way then ducked as she flung her towel.

This gave me more thoughts to ponder. All soon forgotten as another year rolled by, our tasks and rhythms much the same. April rains filled the pond. And father, done with spring planting by May, hired three Mankato carpenters who camped like a harvest crew over the next two months, adding a full upstairs, a washroom off the kitchen, and a screened-in porch facing south and east. To avoid the mess we lived mostly in the barn, but once they'd finished mother was delighted. In our spare time through summer I helped her paper the new plaster walls. From my new room up the spiral stairs I could seldom overhear their late-night chats, but I didn't mind, busy hatching thoughts and dreams of my own.

By autumn I and other kids again sat in thrall of learning from Miss Claussen. Spring of 1883 would complete my 8th grade and I was eager to attend the new high school in Oakvale — a large wood-frame building with a 52-foot-tall belfry, the pride of the town, though some chafed at paying $200 for the big brass bell. As Miss Claussen affirmed, urging my parents to send me, their staff and curriculum was superior to any in the region, and she prepped me daily on math, grammar, spelling, and geography. So I resented being pulled out of school in mid-October to help with the corn harvest, every hand needed. Again mother drove the team and wagon while father and I shucked ears of corn into the bed, a sorely tiresome labor compared to pitching hay, especially to my distracted young mind eager to return to school and learning. But we finished in timely fashion and there followed a week of storms thundering over the valley like an endless chain of corn wagons rolling over the bridge, filling our pond to well over half, not yet to the spillway but enough to prove it good and firm to hold water.

And I was thrilled to be back in school amid the heady anticipation of Halloween. Learning of the Salem Witch Trials in the 1600s, we thought of the little town 10 miles north by the same name, wondering if they harbored any such women and the stern cruel men that hunted them. When I shared this with father, he lightly scoffed, "Our Salem's just a dry-gulch town, Sadie, more haunted by lack of water than any witches…" Miss Claussen also assured us that those old superstitions had long faded away. Yet knowing that our Puritan forefathers had once drowned women so accused, I imagined myself strapped to a dunking stool and submerged forever in the cold dark water of our pond. What a horrid fate.

Still I aimed to be a witch on the coming day and borrowed mother's gray work dress and the cellar broom used to sweep spider webs and sundry bugs dropped dead from coffee grounds and tobacco tea set by. And father donated a black vest so torn and ragged, given scissors and stitching it made a perfectly ugly pointed hat. Among the girls were several other witches, a Goldilocks, and a Red-Riding Hood. The boys were mostly scarecrows, Indians, or sheeted ghosts. We played blind-man's bluff, bobbed for apples, and many parents brought pies and cakes. Towards sunset lamps were lit and to the hushed gathering Miss Claussen read *The Legend of Sleepy Hollow*.

Father had driven the carriage, and riding home that night between him and mother, the moon hanging over the valley, approaching the bridge, he pointed to a shadow cast by an oak bough arching to the wind in eerie rise and fall. "There he is!" he cried out, "the Headless Horseman! Damn ye, Phantom, let us pass!" He hied the horses and I clutched his arm though I knew he was only kidding as the wheels rumbled over the rough wood planking and shook my heart. Good frightful fun and I slept calm that night.

Soon the sun rose on the dreamy days of Indian summer turning leaves orange, yellow, brown and red, and the crisp nights frosted the silvery grass. Again I joined father in the cornfield for a day, only this time in pleasure, helping stack the bundled shocks all leaned center like teepees. Finished I crawled inside and breathed the sweet scent, nestled warm and dry from the cold wind and sleety rain. Thanksgiving came and went with a firm nod to our Maker for his bounty, or as father vouched in glance to the ceiling, "Grateful, you bet, just don't expect penance…"

On into December, nearing the shortest day of the year, darkness coming on as I walked up the lane and entered the house to find the lamp lit, the stove fire burning, but no one about. I looked to the barn expecting to see the lanterned shadows of mother and father at chore or milking. But saw nothing, only darkness. Stepping further outside I noticed a fire flickering on the hill west, and silhouetted against the sky a horse and two figures, one knelt and one standing.

Then I heard father's urgent voice, "Sadie! Bring your mother's tea kettle and a cup!" The tea was steeping on the stove, ready for supper. I gripped the handle with a hot pad, fetched a cup then gingerly picked my way up the hill so as not to trip or spill, curious of what was happening and why I was called.

Stretched on the ground by the firelight, his head propped on a rock, I recognized the old Indian who'd come for food. His hair nearly white, he lay like a fallen tree, his leather tunic and leggings soiled deep brown and wrinkled like his flesh blending to the earth. A coarse blanket drooped from his shoulders like peeling bark.

"We fear he's dying," father said quietly as mother raised a cup of tea to his lips. He sipped briefly then closed his eyes, apparently eased. Suddenly he awoke and from his tunic handed her a stuffed toy made of kitten fur with oval turquoise buttons stitched for eyes. As she accepted the gift I knelt by and he extended his arm in gaze to me, his deep old eyes dark and fluid as a river. His great hand, rough and gnarled, gently gripped mine before it slowly slackened and fell away. And his eyes lost their solemn depth, no current there, merely staring blank, reflecting the fire while his last breath faintly fogged the air then gone.

I accompanied mother back to the house while father led the horse to the corral. With pick and shovel he returned to the hill, a light snow beginning to fall. Waiting supper for father, mother carefully wrapped the kitten doll in a towel to place with other keepsakes in her bedroom chest. Returning, she told me that along about sunset they heard Shep bark and saw a man on a horse there on the hill, utterly still, just staring down. They watched him slowly dismount and walk to a small cedar thereby, break it over and build a fire. As it blazed he stood and spread his arms for a time then staggered and dropped to his knees.

"Can't say he fell," she said, "it was more like he folded to the ground." She paused as if thinking to herself. "I guess he chose his place to die."

We both sat silent for a time listening to the stove fire and the wind funnel up the chimney, pondering the old Indian and why he'd come. Then she clasped her hands and sighed, "Do wish Glen would write," having not heard from him in over two months, we pondered that as well. It was past nine when father finally stepped in and said, "I dug to a decent depth, Sarah. Tomorrow I'll pile on some stones…"

VIII. Changes

The stove fire snaps behind the isinglass, the wind moans beyond the door. She watches Paul hang the last colored orb, bright red, from the top left branch of the cedar. In an old shoe box her palsied hands sift the crumpled paper to reveal the gift kitten, its fur mangled by time yet the turquoise eyes still pristine blue.

"Here, Paul," she says. "Hang this on that upper right branch to balance things."

He takes it and pauses briefly — "This kitten come from the old Indian."

"That's right. And careful now, it's a lot like me, about to fall to pieces."

He cups it gently as if it lived and hangs it by a blue ribbon loop she stitched long ago. "There, that's good," she smiles, "before we do anymore let's have some popcorn and apples. And I'll turn on the radio, it's nearly 8:30 and they plan to broadcast their voices from the moon."

"All that way…we can hear?" He stares up at the ceiling through the unimaginable distance and says, "We can't even see them."

"You hear the train whistle as it passes on north, but can't see it. Same with coyotes crying off in the night. No, we can't see the men, but they use something like a telephone to send their voices. Only on radio waves that travel all the way from the moon in little more than a blink. Then from the radio to our ears."

"Oh, yeah…" Paul no more questions this than he questions snowflakes in the wind. One strikes the face, one strikes the ear, all that simple to Paul. His puzzlement ends with Gram's assuring words.

She turns up the radio in time to catch the voices with words from Genesis: *"In the beginning God made heaven and earth…and darkness was upon the deep"* — Paul listens enrapt, staring up through the ceiling to the far voice from the moon — *"And God said, Let there be light…and God divided the light from the darkness…called the light Day, and the darkness he called Night…And God called the firmament Heaven, the dry land Earth…and God saw that it was good…"*

Paul stares at the lighted tree, beholding a creation that also divided the darkness.

"They're just going to jabber for a while," she says, turning down the radio. "But that was a fine reading from Genesis."

Paul's puzzlement returns, trying the word, "Gen…gen-sis…like the Genie?" A character from his favorite tale, *Aladdin & His Wonderful Lamp*, a children's classic that he still thumbs through, pages torn and scrawled on, the binding taped and glued.

"No, but it's every bit as magical. The moon set there like a keyhole to the vast chamber of space where light shines through from the very beginning, even to Aladdin's lamp. And now down to us…right here, lighting our very own Christmas tree."

Paul gazes on the bubble lights of the star-tipped tree and swells with pride. To her eye he fills the room like a giant Genie. And if he could grant her one wish, what would it be? Nearly out of wishes but she holds one yet as she looks to the kitten and reflects on the old Indian's death. Only a dust of snow fell that night, next day she helped her father gather rocks and stack them on the grave. By Christmas Eve a deep snow blanketed the mound, surrounding hills and valley. The wind ceased and the sky cleared, a moonless night, the stars arrayed in vibrant glory, tinseling to the earth. So calm and peaceful, still pictured in her mind and she wonders of the old Indian sleeping there.

"Expect they're done jabbering by now," she says. "Let's see if they have some Christmas songs." She turns up the radio and catches Bing Crosby's "Silent Night…"

One chill morning, winter edging to spring, I recall the dim-eyed sun through a skein of clouds stretching east, the sky bluing to the west. As the day warmed a rider appeared along the upper pasture north and soon galloped down through the orchard to dismount by the front porch. My eyes widened and I gasped, for Glen had returned, tall, handsome, smiling in gray hat and suit, a pistol holstered at his waist.

"Sadie? Is this Sadie?" he laughed brightly. "Why you've growed near a lady!"

I leapt to his arms with a big hug, hardly lady-like, so choked with joy I could not speak. Mother rushed out the door and did the same, hugging him then stepping back to hug again. Both wiping tears as father hollered in run from the barn, "Glen! Glen Cut-a-hay! You young skunk!" Close up he gripped his hand in a hearty shake and said, "We feared you'd been ate by a bear!"

"Nope, just gone four years 'n ate up by homesickness. But here I am."

"Well you're a sight to see. Don't you think, Sarah?"

Mother nodded happily as I gushed, "Did you see Pike's Peak?"

"Flat did 'n climbed plumb to the top. From there I saw ever' mountain in the whole blame West!"

"Did you find gold?"

"Sure enough," he grinned. "About enough to crown a circus flea. My pard 'n I panned a couple weeks 'n decided to hit back to cowboyin' which paid 40 bucks a month. And you know what, Uncle Pat? I saved near every nickel. Got me a tidy sum here," he slapped his saddlebags, "like to throw in with you if you'll have me?"

"Say now, been hoping I'd hear that," father set his hands to hips and squinted in prospect, "been eyein' a quarter section just southwest yonder. Think the feller is about to pull up stakes. Hit with a dry spell last summer, planted a mite early 'n lost his whole corn crop to that hot south wind. Grew about knee high then burnt to the ground. With no winter feed, he sold me his cattle. His mortgage comin' due, bet he'll toss in his hand. Then we'll own this full section, one square mile. Join the Briar-Callaway up proper, yes sir, the BC Ranch. What d'ya say?"

"I say that's grand, Uncle Pat, just grand. If he'll deal, let's do it." This time they shook hands firm and business-like. Then Glen smiled to me and said, "Before I get sent to plowin', got something to show you, Sadie." He slowly drew his pistol and laid it on his left palm. "This here's a Remington .44 Frontier Army revolver. Some call it 'the Peacemaker' like its Colt cousin. Got a heavy 8-inch barrel, not a quick-draw, but mighty accurate 'n that 44 cartridge packs a wallop. So it works to keep a man friendly or wolf at bay. Now I ain't shot a single man or wolf, but scared a few off. Mostly just shot rattlesnakes 'n cactus. Had lots of time to practice out along the Picket-wire 'n got right handy. Yep, right handy…" he repeated, spinning it back to its holster. "Up in Denver last summer, drove a herd to market 'n caught the Ringlin' Brothers Circus. That was some amazing. A tale I'll tell later. But at a sideshow for trick-shooters, I joined in 'n won a few of these" — from his vest pocket he handed me a large gold coin. "Most got spent somewhere," he laughed, "but I saved this one for you, Sadie. It's a Double Eagle. Spend it on a pretty dress or a round trip to Denver 'n see Pike's Peak!"

Definitely gold, for it warmed my hand. But seeing Glen home warmed my heart and my urge to see the mountains faded like the clouds passing east. To celebrate father and Glen caught a chicken and wrung its neck, let it flop and bleed then dunked it in a bucket of scalding water I carried out. They soon had it plucked and gutted, the latter tossed to Shep. Mother and I carved up the pieces — legs, thighs, wings, wishbone, and giblets rolled in buttermilk and flour and fried in bacon grease, all piled on a platter then served with potatoes and gravy, green beans and bread, topped off with canned peaches, a favorite meal usually saved for Sunday, but this was a special occasion. Once fed, still in the thrall of reunion, sharing brief tales and laughter, mother showed off her hand pump and sink, washing the dishes while I dried. Suddenly she quieted and glanced to father.

"We should tell Glen about the grave."

Father gritted his whittled matchstick and rubbed his whiskered chin.

"Yes, Sarah, I suppose we should." He shifted his eye to Glen. "There's a fresh grave up there on that hill west. What happened is…here before Christmas an old Indian come by. We found him up there dying. Sarah recognized him. Said he's the one that swapped the kittens for Sadie. If you can't abide him, guess I can —"

"No need, Uncle Pat," Glen cut him short, glanced to the floor then to each of us. "Now I never talked of this…but one night, Liam drunk, he told what happened when he rode in search for Katy. Found her blue ribbon at that salt spring down by the Solomon. Two days later he found her body hung from a limb along the Saline. Said he buried her there with the ribbon. What they did to her is a thing you cannot forgive. But then, that Indian swappin' for Sadie is a thing you cannot forget. So no, let's not disturb the dead. Long as he don't rise up in haunt, leave 'im rest." A vague smile edged his lips. "Thing is, I got to know a couple Indian cowboys, the Sun-Walker brothers, Bill 'n Tom. Good hands 'n they could flat ride, taught me a few tricks. They was Cheyenne. As kids they survived that bloody day at Sand Creek. Saw most their kin killed in an ugly way, same as us. Now the dead are buried, let bygones be."

Listening, heartened by his tone and manner, I expressed my admiration, "Glen, that's very noble of you."

He leaned back and said, "Duchess," as he always did when he caught me acting high-toned, "I'm none noble a'tall. Just we're all stuck in this life 'n if you don't look forward, you're bound to fall back. Now here!" he slapped the table and grabbed me up by both hands, "Gonna teach you a cowboy jig!" In a blink he stomped the floor and commenced twirling me around for an evening of handclap and laughter. Father hunted up his mouth harp left untouched since Liam's death, a little rusty in reed and lip but both soon warming to the tune "Yellow Rose of Texas!"

⸻ ◆ ⸻

On a cash deal father and Glen acquired the quarter section and formalized their partnership — The BC Ranch, or as they proclaimed breaking out a bottle in celebration, "Before Christ 'n all Tarnation!" Mother hushed their heresy then joined in the laughter. The new land already had a small house and barn adequate to Glen's need, like he said, "After sleepin' four years on the hard ground, a tick mattress 'n roof overhead makes a palace…" And working with father each day he took most meals with us, which pleased mother and me.

Meanwhile my world and sense of things was rapidly shifting. Turning 14 that winter, I experienced a frightful change in self and flesh more disturbing than anything I'd known, sudden and unexpected, arising from within. My breasts swelled painfully, emitting a milky fluid. Then came the cramps and blood. "Expect it monthly," mother advised, showing me how to clean and care for myself. But my inner urge and dreams were more complicated. All the unmentioned, forbidden thoughts and passions hatched anew each night, fraught, implacable, and I could no more shoo them away than stop breathing. While my family was rarely puritanical and never preached damnation, others were and did, and steeped in that stew I felt judged by the hidden God, certain I would one day burn. Nightly twisting in torment and sweat till fear turned to feverish want to touch my flesh and I soon learned to enjoy my pleasure and regret it less. Outwardly modest, yet vowing to one day please my prince, someone kind and manly like Ben Hur, or my brother Glen. But heavens no, certainly not Glen, for him I would play cupid and conspire to match him with Miss Claussen. And he soon knew of our beautiful young school mistress, even glimpsed her a time or two driving the wagon to town for supplies. Hearts marked, I aimed the arrow.

On our last day of school, following a brief ceremony for myself and two other graduates, we filled the afternoon with the new game of baseball, pitched underhanded, and a series of footraces. Although shaping into a woman, I again outran the loutish boy. And I'd invited Glen to watch, anxious for him to meet Miss Claussen. Of course, she and the kids had all heard of my handsome cowboy brother and his adventures out west. For a grand finale he performed some riding stunts, leaping from ground to saddle with such ease it was amazing. Then he circled around, kicked free of the stirrups and sat riding backwards. He gave a wild whoop, flung his hat to the wind then switched front in the saddle, reined his horse about and raced for the hat, leaning down in the last instant he scooped it up and set it at a jaunty angle on his ginger hair.

Everyone clapped and cheered as he cantered over, tipped his hat to Miss Claussen, swung down and said, "Y'all stand back…" He took a silver dollar form his vest pocket, wrapped it in a red handkerchief and handed it to me. A trick we'd practiced, but only with a rock. And I could throw like a boy, overhand or sidearm, often skipping rocks on our pond. After making certain everyone was well distanced, Glen drew his pistol and shouted, "Pitch it high, Sadie!" At full arc, for an instant stilled, he aimed and fired, jolting it sideways through the air like a shot bird, promptly retrieved by a romp of boys. Glen unwrapped the coin and handed it to Miss Claussen, the Liberty face neatly kissed by the bullet. I saw her blush in smile to him and knew she was charmed. Already I pictured their wedding — she in white dress, him in dark suit, both showered with rose petals and shouldered forth in a jubilant shivaree.

From thereon through April into May, Glen squired her in the carriage to Saturday dances and Sunday socials. And though cautioned by father and careful of Glen, mother and I dreamed of a June wedding — hold it in the orchard and invite all the neighbors and her family, though conceding they'd likely prefer their own church and minister. Then one Sunday in late May, the carriage idle for a week, Glen unusually silent at supper, mother, with Decoration Day approaching, chanced to ask, "Perhaps Madalene would like to join us on a ride to the White Rock…to place some flowers on the graves?"

Glen shifted uncomfortably and said, "Doubt she'd be willin'."

"Why? Aren't you still seeing her?"

"No, Aunt Sarah, 'n likely nevermore. Seems she's steppin' up, now courted by that new young doctor over to Mankato."

Hearing this, my eyes teared and I lowered my head, utterly crushed.

Glen noted my distress and said, "Hey now, Sadie girl, don't cry over spilt milk. Heck, there's more heifers to lasso. Though admit I did like her some. Awful pretty, Madalene, but tight bound, I swear, corrected ever' this 'n that. Whether *saw* or *seen*, *was* or *were*, what the hay? Besides she can no more dance than a toad can fly!"

He and father slapped the table and had a good laugh, shucked his heartache and tossed it to the wind like he did his hat. While I sat appalled, him calling her a heifer and a toad in one breath, for she was still a princess to my eyes, graceful and perfect in every manner and thing.

Later that summer in Mankato we watched Glen ride in the July 4th parade, after which he reined by our carriage where we sat enjoying lemonade in the shaded breeze, casually observing various comings and goings. By and by he quietly directed our gaze to Miss Claussen strolling with her betrothed across the way. My heart sank seeing the pudgy little man, all slick and dandy, strutting like a toad in a fancy suit.

Glen leaned down and nudged my shoulder, "Duchess, you play your cards right, mind your Ps 'n Qs, you might catch you a feller like that."

"I shall not!" I snapped to his laughter, "No, no, never!"

But thereafter I readily practiced each dance step he showed me, more keen to heel and toe than to grammar, determined no toad would ever touch me. And I was confused, about to become a woman, still partly a child, soon off to high school, excited yet fearful. Glen would catch me downcast and say, "Head up, Sadie, 'n eyes straight. Good posture becomes a lady." Then he'd tease, "Yep, catch you a dream-feller someday."

Admit his grammar fell shy but his words held humor and made good sense.

Glen and father could both spin their meaning in a few words. Father always claimed that hiring men was like rolling dice, as liable to get sixes as snake eyes. Mid-summer, done with threshing, he'd hired two bindle-stiffs to help put up hay, Orlin and Greeley, the one quiet, the other sour-mouthed. That day I was helping mother with the garden and canning, but carried out the water jug wrapped in burlap and set it by. The men stood sweating in the hot sun, looking to the far field of mowed hay that waited the arduous task of loading to the barn.

Sour-Mouth puckered his lips, spat a stream of tobacco and said, "In a hunnert years won't matter one lick if we haul it out or leave it rot."

"No, don't suppose so," father allowed. "But it sure will come winter when the stock need fed. And if you want a noon meal 'n a dime to drink on come Saturday, best bend your back to it."

They didn't balk, perked right up and went to work, pitched hay four days straight without complaint. Took their meals with us and bunked at Glen's. After father paid their wages and waved them down the lane, he nodded to mother, "Not bad hands, Orlin 'n Greeley, once they got the gist of things…" In fact he and Glen offered them work come spring, once the ground had thawed, building fences. While disputes between fencers and anti-fencers continued to flare through parts of Texas and the southwest, in our region the day of open-range grazing was drawing to a close. Like others, father and Glen, though reluctant, bowed to the pressure of number and need.

Summer was also ending, as was my childhood, like a chapter gone in the reading and could not be reclaimed. Alternately thrilled and dismayed at the prospect of high school and leaving home, for I, like many country kids, would need to stay through the week with a family in town. Father and mother had driven to Oakvale in early August and arranged for me to stay with the family that owned the local livery, Howard and Martha Jensen. Their daughter, Darlene, two years older than me, was now a junior. I and another girl my age, Caroline Sawyer, would share an upstairs room and do the laundry and other chores to earn our keep, she in the kitchen with Mrs. Jensen while I chose to work in the livery and help tend the horses and mules and muck out the stalls.

Father stood by while Mr. Jensen, who seemed a nice man, walked me through my daily tasks. When finished he said, "Sadie, I've known your father since early settlement days. I assured him I'd keep an eye out. There's lots of men come 'n go here, includin' some foul types. More now as the railroad arrived. If anyone ever acts untoward, you let me know. Hear? I keep a bullwhip handy 'n I'll line 'em out."

Given his firm tone and that he and father were friends helped ease my qualms.

One thing I hadn't counted on, the Jensens were strict Methodists and attended church not only on Sundays but Wednesday evenings as well. Particularly Mrs. Jensen and her daughter, who expected me to join them. Actually more curious than concerned by this, having never attended formal services, and their church had an organ and piano and encouraged singing. As father joshed driving home, "Some of them hymns ain't half sad. So keep an open mind, Sadie, it'll further your education. Best to know the fish ya swim with. There's whalish good folk among the church-going, also some mean back-bitin' sharks!" — smoothing the way with laughter. And I'd have Patches for company. Planned to ride him to Oakvale Sunday afternoons, weather permitting, and return home each Friday after school. Classes set to begin the first Monday in September.

Seeking compass amid the whirl of change, I stood on the hill by the old Indian's grave that Sunday. Somehow felt centered there, comforted, like he had a hold on me, deep and enduring. And I wondered what would have happened had he not swapped me for the kittens. Had I lived I would have grown up an Indian and likely died in a raid or of starvation like so many young and old in the early 1880s. Was that the fate of his wife and daughter? And what of the little boy?

The previous evening after packing my personals and other belongings for the morrow's ride, alone with mother, I asked to see the kitten doll. She quietly opened the chest, took it out and handed it to me. Simply a stuffed toy, I thought. But no, the fur soon warmed my hands and the turquoise eyes grew faintly lucent, intimate and familiar. Uncertain of what I held or why its effect, I quickly handed it back and never saw it again for many years.

IX. The Circus

My first day walking out of school, adjusting my dainty new hat against the bright sunlight, directly west I saw a large colorful poster being pasted to the south side of the livery, visible through midtown and beyond. I hurried over, shoved along with many others curious to see as another section was rolled into place. A panoramic lithograph 6 foot high by 15 foot long depicting various scenes and astonishments of Miles Orton's Anglo-American Circus slated to hit Oakvale, show date Friday, September the 14th, less than ten days away. Four great shows, including The Royal German Menagerie, Le Gran Circo Zoologico, and The Mystic Circus of Japan!

Drawing closer I feasted on the fantastic images of exotic animals and costumes, bare-chested men in skintight leotards, and women also in tights, though bloused, their skirts cut at the knee, their neck and shoulders in naked décolletage. Amid gasps of shock and scandal there were more of delight and amazement admiring the pretty lady swinging forth, her knees hooked to the flying trapeze, her dazzling smile, arms, and cleavage reaching to the viewer. Thrilling to the eye and senses and I knew the words: menagerie, zoologico, and yes, décolletage. But what was *Bulalipus*, the rare beast from the Nile? Not in my dictionary, but already imagined like the acrobats and aerialists, jugglers, clowns, and bareback riders, and real live camels, lions, and giant elephants from Africa, India, and Ceylon! Then lower down, next to the monkeys, the Wild Boy of Borneo with tiger stripes and ravenous hunger! And I knew of Borneo, edging the South China Sea, next to Sumatra and slightly above Java. Breathtaking, all the strange names and wonders collected from around the world like a colossal hot-air balloon about to descend and spill a cornucopia of magic, splendor, and awe-inspiring feats!

Talk of the circus spread in contagion through the town and school, even teachers paused in mid-lesson, losing their train of thought to join us gazing out the window in joyous anticipation. Then they'd rap their knuckles and announce, "All eyes front!" yet more often in smile than in scowl. The very notion of the coming circus perfumed the air and colored our daily and nightly dreams.

Arriving home Friday, I galloped Patches up the lane anxious to surprise mother, father, and Glen with the news. But they already knew, word spreading like birds a-wing to the Limestone and all around. And they planned to attend, finish their morning chores and be in Oakvale by noon of the appointed day.

Likewise, I rose early that next Friday morning, school canceled for the big event. The train had arrived pre-dawn and I could hear the clank and rattle of sliding doors and dropped ramps, and the hustle and shout of men unloading wagons and animals. Excited by the occasional roar of a lion or elephant, I rushed through my livery chores then ran inside to tidy up, careful of my dress, blouse, and lady hat. Hurrying downstairs, I was met by Caroline, Darlene, and Mrs. Jensen, the latter waiting to chaperone "You three young ladies" as she addressed us "to witness proceedings at a proper distance." Of course, she and her daughter each wore white gloves and toted a parasol for protection from the sun, and, as she admonished, "From unwanted stares." Which trappings the kitchen maid and stable lass were relieved to forgo, the day already hot, high collars buttoned to our chins, we hardly desired further covering or encumbrance.

The broad swath of ground southwest of the depot, usually reserved for livestock shows and such, was raked clean and smoothed for the circus currently filling the same. Boxcars lined the track for a quarter mile or more, all nearly emptied out. Vast canvases lay spread over several acres tended by an army of men and women in various stage and motion readying poles, ropes, and pulleys to raise the big top. Others harnessed horses and hitched wagons, a few practiced stunts. Nearby a crew of stout men drove wooden stakes with huge mallets — one twice the size of others in the hands of a massive Negro, the first colored person I'd ever seen, except in newspaper illustrations, often cartoonish and exaggerated. But he was fully alive, strong, sweaty, and real. He set a fresh stake, tapped it straight, and with one mighty heave sank it deep. Then he swung his head like a big bull and grinned our way. Mrs. Jensen covered us with her parasol and hurried us on, something of a mother hen. Still we were entranced, taking in all the sights and sounds, foreign races, manners, and languages enlightening eye and ear.

Suddenly a steam calliope fired up and we turned startled, fascinated by the gold ornate carriage of carved cherubs and nymphs housing the boiler, whistles, keyboard and player. Amazingly sonorous, each steam-powered note enlivened the air nearly as loud as a rifle shot aimed to the horizon, only harmonious and musical. Nearby a discordant array of band members, including many Negros, donned their uniforms and warmed up, casually indifferent to our furtive glances. Trying not to stare, we often did so. Then in a hush of voice and air the great canvas billowed up and out of the earth, initially flimsy as if made of mist, but poles set and ropes tightened, it stood erect and sturdy like a dream castle come alive, ready to enter.

Mother, father, and Glen had seen it as well, only from a distance. Drawn by the magical sound of the calliope over the final few miles, in topping the long hill heading down to Oakvale they witnessed the far tent rise up "Like a three-masted ship filling the valley!" mother presently exclaimed, while father countered, "More like a great humped beast set to pounce!" We all laughed, caught up in the excitement, about to experience a pageant of novelty and wonder.

And I was happy to escape the scrutiny of Mrs. Jensen. Now escorted on Glen's arm, felt myself a veritable young lady strolling in greater range and freedom, and if I drew a stare or two, so be it. First thing I wanted to see was the Wild Boy of Borneo, or Tiger Boy, so pictured in front of a smaller tent pitched beside the large animal pavilion and the grand three-topped hippodrome. The sign read: *No*

Children Under 12 Allowed To View Such Ferocity! And young ladies such as myself must be accompanied by an adult male. I clutched Glen's arm and warily entered the shadowy interior, breathless at the sight of the wild boy, naked but for a fur loin cloth roped at his waist. He perched on his haunches at the center of a fenced enclosure, black and gold stripes artfully spiraling over his otherwise brown flesh. While his dark tangled hair and black-accented eyes lent a ferocious aspect, he looked vaguely familiar, like the feral twin of the handsome youth I'd seen earlier tending an elephant. Doubt vanished in the next instant as my eye drew his and he lunged straight at me and I jumped back. His attack stopped short by a chest harness chained to an iron ring skewered in the ground.

"Down, Zago, down!" his handler cracked a long whip, turned to me and warned, "Young Miss, stay clear of the wall and never reach your hand beyond. The same goes for everyone! You could lose a finger, hand, even an arm to his savage jaws. Indeed he is quick as a panther. Perhaps you've heard of the Wild Boy of Aveyron, lost as a child in the remote forests of southern France. Before his capture he ran with wolves and fed on carrion, rodents, anything he could scavenge. In time he was partly civilized, learned to dress himself, to sit and eat at a table, though only with his hands and mumbled but a few words. Yet regard! The Wild Boy of Borneo! After five long years, defying every kind and patient effort, he remains entirely wild and untamed, obedient only to the whip and harsh command. He cannot voice one human word and will not eat unless it's alive, fresh…and *bleeding!*"

No sooner said than he lifted a squawking chicken from a wire cage and tossed it to the wild boy who leapt like a cat and snatched it midair. In a swirl of dust and feathers he jerked off its head and raised it like a winged jug squirting blood to his open mouth. At this I did gasp, Glen too, everyone staring on, wholly convinced by this raw, ravenous act. Further heightened as he gripped each leg and ripped it open, plunging a hand into its entrails to claw forth the heart and liver then shove them in his mouth with a heinous yowl that chilled my spine.

The crowd stood silent in watch and wait. Not a breath.

Then Scully Harmon, a local n'er-do-well, often drunk, rudely scoffed, "Bah! He ain't no more vicious'n a chicken-killin' dog!" His guffaw immediately answered by the whip cracked near his ear.

"Bide your tongue, Rube," the handler swore, "I don't abide slander. One more word I'll have you marked. Now get out! There's good folk that's paid waiting to see the Wild Boy of Borneo!"

Silenced, if not shamed, Scully turned for the exit and the wild boy rose up and flung a fistful of entrails, striking the back of his head and the canvas beyond. Then everyone rushed out in shriek and holler as the wild boy tore and gnashed at the chicken, hurling feathers, guts, meat and bones through the air. Some ducked clear, others not so lucky. Once outside and safely distanced, we caught our breath and laughed, thrilled by the wild boy's performance, real or staged, he'd certainly proved wild enough.

Remembering which, I quickly checked my blouse for sign of blood or stain.

"Think you come through clean," Glen assured. "But by Golly, that boy can flat pluck a chicken lickety-split…'n eat it raw, whew! Think I'll have mine baked, fried or stewed." Sniffing the air, he turned and spied a brightly painted cart.

"Say, how about some roast peanuts?"

Waiting, I glimpsed the circus band, colorfully plumed, their instruments aglitter, marching through town followed by the show wagons and a select number of performers and animals. The Ringmaster stood on a platform in flared breeches and riding boots, red waistcoat and black top hat, his bullhorn raised to name the stirring events set to play that evening. While Glen and I had begged off going to the parade, mother enticed father by suggesting he could buy a cigar at Lloyd's Tobacco Shop.

"Just might do that," he relented as she hooked his arm, hurrying him on before he changed his mind. "And just might buy two, Sarah. Yep, have one for the drive home 'n promise I'll share."

"Hah!" she answered briskly, "that I will strive to endure and not do."

Glen shortly returned, handed me a bag of peanuts and asked, "Want to mosey on up 'n catch the last of the parade?"

"No, I'd rather see the animals before the flood of people."

"Well then, young Miss, right this way…" and we soon entered the huge tent housing the Royal German Menagerie & Le Gran Zoologico — a vast space sheltered from the sun through which a light breeze carried scents of straw and sawdust and scores of strange animals variously roped, chained, fenced, or caged.

"Holy cow, look at all these hay-eaters," Glen mumbled, astonished at their sheer size and number. "How in blazes do they feed 'em?" While I focused on a single muck that would fill a wheel barrow, aghast at all that cleaning, then gazed up to its author, a giant African elephant, and stood utterly riveted before the majestic creature, long-lived and knowing, seemingly old as the earth. As his eye looked to mine, I wondered what he thought of me. Then we moved on to the giraffe, its head stretched tall as our house, its elegant neck gently swaying like a sapling in the wind. It turned in a graceful pivot, long legs striding smooth and stately, barely skimming the ground, and fixed its eye far and away as if searching something lost. And I felt shrunken, like a mere rodent before such dignity. Yet pleased and grateful to witness, marveled at the very sight and presence of each. Again we paused, stock-still before the manly lion lazing in his cage, but head up, staring at us. He flexed a paw and rumbled low and throaty like a bull.

"Whoa now," Glen softly allowed, "would hate to meet him all by my lonesome."

So we continued on past ostriches, monkeys, zebras, a whole range of exotic shape, size, and color, each animal intimating further insight and astonishment. The wondrous spell soon shattered by the swarm of people coming in.

Back outside, mid-afternoon, the sun bearing down, Glen bought me a refreshment. One I'd never tried. Called a "snowball" — a fist of crushed ice held in a paper cone with grape syrup poured on top. "Careful now, Missy," warned the sweet-voiced colored lady handing it to me, "else that dark juice mess yo' white blouse somethin' awful. An' here, take this napkin 'n eat it 'fore it goes all drippy." I thanked her kindly and we sat thereby on a rough plank bench and enjoyed our treat. Finished, I wiped my mouth and hands and returned the napkin. She grinned and said, "Yessum, yo' blouse is still clean. But looky here," she held up a small hand mirror, "yo' lips is purple as mine." And she was right. I leaned closer, pursing my lips, and she chuckled, "Don' fret none, Missy, yos'll wear off." We laughed too, delighted by the icy treat and her good humor.

Ambling on in search of mother and father, Glen named me the Wild Girl of the Limestone for my dark lips and tongue. And I skipped to the notion of being a wild girl, fleet of foot, keen-eyed, lithesome and fierce. Then I suddenly felt awkward, weighted, common and tame next to the three performers practicing in the immediate foreground. A mustached man and two children all dressed in tights.

"That's Miles Orton himself," Glen observed, "the famous bareback rider."

"Are those his kids?"

"No, Sadie. Them's little people, all growed up. The midget marvels, Little Annie 'n Master Bernard…"

Given a second look I realized they were indeed a little man and woman, perhaps three feet tall, hard-muscled, lean and agile. Quick as a monkey the little man scampered up the large man from knee-thigh-hip to shoulder where he stood perfectly poised. Then Orton extended his hand to the little lady who in more delicate manner ascended as well, there taking the hand of the little man and in turn climbed to his shoulders. Wonderfully balanced, they held steady a moment, one atop the other, then in fluid sequence tumbled to the ground and stood arms spread to a scatter of applause, giving hint of their evening performance. For as pictured on many posters they meant to form their human pyramid while standing on a racing steed. Such a thing I could not imagine.

Yet seated that evening, third row up from the center ring, I watched the perilous feat unfold. Glen to my left, father and mother to my right, and hundreds more huddled in the immense canvas hippodrome. Dust haloed around the high gas-arc lamps that lit the general area while the limelight focused its bright circular beam on the entranceway open to the expectant darkness beyond. The band ceased, the crowd hushed, and the Ringmaster tipped his hat in a slight bow and announced, "Ladies and Gen-tle-men! Wel-come one and all!" Then raised his hand and turned to introduce the opening act, "Without further ado, the world-famous *tri-o-o-o…!*"

The crowd murmured as they entered to the lilting tune "Gary Owens" with Little Annie in front, then Master Bernard, then Miles Orton, all standing erect on the back of a magnificent dapple-gray with black mane and tail flowing to its smooth striding gait that lengthened to a full gallop. Impressive enough as they made a full circuit captive in the beam of light, their arms gracefully extended, then Master Bernard grasped Little Annie by the waist and with a hop she sprung to his shoulders, then Miles Orton knelt and deftly lifted the pair to his. As the crowd gaped Glen leaned to me and said, "That's one well-trained horse. If he shied a blink, they'd all fall 'n break their necks."

But the horse ran steady to the lively music and chorused *oohs* and *ahhs* until the Ringmaster abruptly silenced the band and cried, "Amazing, yes! Yet more amazing still, see them form the death-defying *Hu-man Py-ra-mid!*"

To a long drumroll we watched breathless as Master Bernard gingerly stepped to Miles Orton's head, then Little Annie likewise stepped to his. All the while the horse kept running as the brave trio, one atop the other, slowly arched their left leg back and balanced solely on their right. Everyone sat fixed to the moment, the whole arena silent but for the striding hooves and drumroll. And once they'd returned safely, so it seemed, to each respective shoulder, the crowd shared a marked sigh of relief. But they had not finished. Miles Orton held his palms out at either shoulder while Little Annie slid down and stepped to his left, Master Bernard to his right. Then Orton raised them like torches and they joined hands in arch overhead, holding the pose through another half-circuit before exciting to resounding cheers and applause — I, Glen, mother and father, nearly everyone rose to their feet in shout of amazement. By now I was dreaming of running away and joining the circus to enter the thrall and never leave the rich kaleidoscope of motion, color, and scene.

This instantly followed by more acts — aerialists, equestrians, jugglers, and acrobats answering to drumroll and trumpet call. I focused on center ring, on Princess Sonja, her beautiful blonde braided hair, her silken tights and glittery gold bloomers, reining astride three black stallions from the stables of the Czar, shifting, standing, leaping from one to the other, or dangling by her ankle from a rope looped to a muscled neck as they galloped at moments in line, at others abreast. In wide-eyed admiration I ached to do the same if given a chance and said so. Glen just shook his head, "Duchess, ya better stick to ridin' Patches. For them kind a' stunts you need to ride before you walk. Like the Cheyenne, start at age two 'n never leave off."

So he said, but I was not dissuaded, kept on dreaming, observing, taking it in.

Over the next hour acts continued to play in all three rings aside a swirl of stilt walkers, fire eaters, midgets and clowns staging a chain of mayhem and frolic, including a monkey tethered to a roguish clown who ranged in mischievous threat to performer and audience alike till the good clowns ganged up and sent him packing, though not before the monkey frightened several small children so badly their mothers had to carry them out to calm them. And there were many other characters trading antics, pantomime, and burlesque — a troupe of black-faced minstrels, a fat floozy clown, and a drunken tightrope walker who wobbled and fell, hooked a knee and swung aright only to stumble, slip, and wobble anew.

While the band played on and trapeze artists flew in summersault at daring heights, yet another bareback dancer entered center ring, Rosa Madeira of jet-black hair, silky blouse, red velvet jacket and skirt, bejeweled with gold earrings, bracelets and necklace, the bewitching Gypsy Ballerina! But who I admired above all, nearing the finale, was Senorita Alora, held in the limelight as she nimbly ascended a rope to spin and weave, performing the Spanish Web at the height of 30 feet or more. This I swore I could do given time and fearless will. Rig a rope in the barn and practice all next summer and run away with the circus when it next came to town. Gripped and determined, though I kept this to myself as I envied her dazzling descent to a groundswell of hurrahs!

For the grand finale they staged a dramatic reenactment of the fabled chariot race from the widely popular novel *Ben Hur*. Our hero, tall, blonde, and handsome, decked out in silver helmet and breastplate and flowing purple robe, rode a golden chariot. His opponent, Messala, was similarly accoutered, though his apparel was dark like his hair. Due to limited space each drove a single horse, respectively white and black. The rivals rolled into position and reined back their steeds. Trumpets blared, the Ringmaster fired a pistol and they were off, circling the arena in the narrow space between the audience and the center rings. The drivers reined hard through the dangerously tight curves, dusting the people seated close to the barreling wheels, whipping their horses and one another through the harrowing 10-lap race. Though partly protected by their helmets and armor, down the final stretch our hero sported a nasty welt on his bare shoulder but paid it no heed as he raced to the finish, winning by a neck.

Defeated and shamed, Messala exited to hisses and boos while Ben Hur took a victory lap, basking in a tumult of cheers and thunderous applause that continued ringing in our ears as we joined the mass of people streaming into the night to gradually trail off and disperse. Finally separate, looking back on the scene, standing numb and dazed by all the color, excitement, movement, and sound still rushing in blood, mind, and heart, indifferent to self and people, their passing voices and faces a blur until I heard Glen ask if I'd care to hear the after-show concert.

"Why yes," I answered absently, turning to see mother and father walking with scores of others towards the depot where the band was setting up to draw the crowd, safely distanced from the crews tearing down. Animals were led up ramps, loaded and secured. The large Menagerie-Zoologico tent shortly vanished, packed away for travel. As did the Wild Boy tent, the calliope, assorted confectionary carts and food wagons, all stowed in their respective boxcars with amazing alacrity and order. And soon the Big Top itself like a gigantic weary beast began its slow collapse to the ground. Crews busily labored by moonlight and lantern, coiling ropes, pulling stakes, rolling canvas, preparing to reset all at a distant town come dawn. What joy to travel on and on and see the many rivers, mountains, and cities, and the show would never end nor I ever age. Such were my thoughts as Glen and I joined mother and father listening to the band fill the night with a rousing "John Brown's Body" then the delightful "Suwannee River." And the air was sweet and balmy like my dream of ceaseless travel.

Pleasantly lulled, captive to that spell, the activity tapered down and the grounds emptied out. Then with the ever-favorite "Star-Spangled Banner" the music ended to brief applause, enthusiasm fading after the long day and growing fatigue.

As the band stood packing their instruments, the crowd trickling away, a drunken voice shouted, "C'mon now, play us one more!"

To which the band leader politely answered, "Thank you kindly, Citizen. But the show must end, for a new day waits and we must travel."

"Hell you will…" and shoving forth, bottle in hand, came Scully Harmon, drunker than before and with a second rowdy in tow. "Call that a show? That's damn thin gruel you serve. Why I seen the Ringlin' Brothers in Saint Loui —"

"Whoa now, fella," Glen stepped over and tried to calm him. "No call for such talk. These folks put on a whale of a show."

"Whale my arse!" Scully spat as several circus toughs loomed, the Wild Boy's handler standing foremost.

"Mister, I warned you earlier today, now you are marked," he growled as other circus men urged the crowd back, warning there would soon be trouble. "And Mister, when I put my foot down, I put it flat!"

"Flat, hell! I'll knock you flat ya damn clown —"

The handler ducked Scully's wild swing and laid a tent stake hard against his head, adding a second blow as he fell. Glen lunged to block the third, shouting, "Don't kill the fool, he's already out!" Then a second club blindsided Glen, knocking him face down in the dirt where he was instantly stomped and kicked amid the signal cry *"Hey Rube!"* as a score of circus men and townies clashed with fists and clubs, cursing, kicking, slugging in violent fray. Father threw several quick punches and fended off others while mother and I dragged Glen clear, even managed to grab his new hat, crumpled and dusty like himself moaning bruised, half conscious, bleeding from the head. Father broke free and helped us carry him to the platform by the depot then stood guard against the riot.

I cradled Glen's head while mother ripped a sleeve from her blouse to bind the wound, a nasty three-inch gash above his right ear. "Sadie, press your hand here," she said, "It'll help stanch the blood." Then she checked his swollen eye and lip and looked him over for other wounds or broken bones.

"Let me up…" he rasped, wanting back in the fight, but father held him down.

"You stay put, young man. You're hurt bad enough, leave it be."

Glen arched briefly against restraint then his eyes rolled back and he passed out. My heart pounded no longer in thrall but in panic and fear for Glen lying wounded amid the ongoing shove and shout, faces masked in tribal fury, snarling like beasts, no longer human, their rage frightful and deafening.

A loud pistol shot stilled the night as Mr. Thomas, the town marshal, and two deputies waded in to separate the combatants. Once parted the opponents continued glaring eye to eye, clubs, staves, and ax handles held ready to resume battle. Underfoot others lay wounded and groaning, one man cursing, "Ya broke my arm, ya bastard…" Among the dark mass of heads and shoulders I saw Mayor Morgan and Mr. Thomas standing toe to toe with Miles Orton and his lead men, their faces lit by a lantern on the ground between them. Their tempers lowered but simmering as they spoke.

"Damn this one-horse town…"

"Then take your rabble of thugs and get…"

"Circus folk are one family and we protect our own!"

"What? One fool opens his mouth and you leave a dozen wounded?"

"Insult leads to injury. I'll not have my people abused by a rube."

"Granted, our man was out of line, his remarks uncalled for. As mayor of Oakvale I apologize. You folks put on a great show. And perhaps he deserved his pummeling. But back here we have at least two broken arms and a half dozen bashed heads that may prove serious."

"A stitch in time saves nine, Mayor. You should've jailed your man sooner."

"Yes, could have, should have. I can abide tit for tat, fair play and a fair fight. But this time, in this fight, you overplayed your hand."

"As I said, we protect our own."

"By God, so shall we!" Mayor Morgan stoutly declared then thought better and lowered his tone. "But for sake of all…I'm prepared to call it even this very minute, if you and your people agree to load in peace and be on your way."

Though neither man offered a smile or handshake, Miles Orton gave a firm nod and said, "So agreed…" Then he hailed his men and in short order they finished loading. The last of the crew hopped aboard the trailing car to join others standing at the handrail with rifles and pistols to assure their safety.

Town folks stood tense as well and I was relieved to hear the distant chug of the engine and hiss of steam, the drive wheel churning to tug car-to-car till all jolted forth. At about 40 yards out a lone figure emerged from the onlookers, Mort Stanley, a sidekick to Scully, slightly unsteady as he stepped to the tracks. And before anyone discerned his intent he raised a shotgun and yelled, "This is for my pal, you sonsabitches…!" He let loose both barrels peppering those in the trailing car, not lethal at that range but no doubt stung. This promptly answered by flash and crack of gunfire, bullets riddling the air. And flesh. Mort spun dropping his shotgun to clutch his left shoulder. Mayor Morgan buckled to the ground. A young boy hobbled in frantic pain, streaming blood, his boot heel shot away.

More bullets whizzed by as father shouted, "Down! Down!" and spread his arms to shield us at the base of the platform. Yet another volley struck the depot, shattering glass and splintering wood amid the desperate shriek and cry and I heard a heavy thump land directly overhead. The shooting ceased, leaving an acrid drift of gunpowder, the reek of whiskey and pooling blood. Toward the tracks the Mayor lay flapping his arms in question, "Can't feel my legs, can't move, what happened…?"

Men rushed past, some for help, others shook their fists at the receding train.

Father slowly raised up and looked around then offered his hand and I too stood. The station master stumbled out the door, his face bleeding from shards of glass. Turning eye level to the platform, I met the dead stare of Finn Winchell, the town blacksmith, his shop next to the livery, a bullet hole in his right temple, the left side of his head splattered against the wall. His young children knelt clutching his coat sleeve, calling, "Daddy, Daddy…" His wife slouched over him in weep. His oldest son Seth ran pleading for a gun to fire at the train. While his daughter Shannon, the brightest girl in our class, who I was just getting to know, slowly sank to her knees beside her mother, her face contorted in anguish like her scream funneling with the train whistle into the far night, leaving only blank, dark silence.

X. Hwinums & Yahoos

"Gram? Gram…? Don't go, Gram, don't go away…"

Paul leans by gently nudging her shoulder, his voice urgent, "Gram?" Her eyes are open, but seeing no response, again he nudges her, "Gram, Gram…?

"Paul…" her lips move, her voice faint. "It's okay, Paul. Just dozed off awake, I guess. Lost in a memory."

"Thought you was gone, Gram," his concern close to tears. "Don't want you to go."

"I know, I know," she pats his hands still gripping her shoulder. "But my old body wears out…like your old work gloves. Maybe Santa will bring you a new pair…would you like that?"

"Sure," he answers softly in glance to the tree then back to her. "But no new Gram. Won't throw you away like work gloves."

"No, not throw away, but you must lay me down when I grow cold and no longer breathe or move. Will you do as I ask, carry me there and lay me down?"

Again he looks to the tree so as not to answer her.

"Will you?" she asks hopefully.

He avoids her watery old eyes and points to the blue bowl on the table.

"I left you some popcorn, Gram. Want some?"

"That was kind of you, Paul, but popcorn doesn't set well on my old stomach. Believe I'll just have a slice of apple." She takes one in her mouth and slowly munches it to mush, letting the tart juice soothe her gums and freshen her breath. He continues staring off, fidgeting with the tinsel, as if a thing not spoken of will not happen.

"I'm sorry to burden you, Paul. But it is my last wish, and you're the only one I can trust. When I am cold, gone from this flesh, will you do as I ask?"

Finally he looks to her and nods, "Yes'um. But I don't want you to go."

"We all have to go sometime, Paul. And my time is near."

"Why do we come if we gotta go?"

"That's a question been pondered from the beginning. Even the wisest give pause, puzzled by that. Though some pretend to know, no one does, not really. Just look at our tree here, Paul. We know where it grew…in our pasture. We know where we cut it and how…today with a saw. And we know it now stands there in the corner decked with pretty balls, star, and lights. But the whole of it, how and why it came to be, is a wonder of wonders…where one question begets a thousand more. Even Einstein, perhaps the smartest man who ever lived," she notes, her eyes alive and quizzical, "and who's hair was wild and white as mine. Even he, who could gauge the speed of light and track space and time, shook his head at the strange workings of things. Stumped by the comings and goings, and why. Because the sun, moon, and stars are all ornaments hung on a great tree beyond all knowing. And that tree grew from a tiny seed, Paul…so they claim. Like this apple seed here," she takes the seed from her mouth and rolls it between her thumb and finger. "Seeds I once loved to nibble…" she smiles in memory of their lavender flavor, "and now cannot, my teeth so poor. But we both know that if you plant this seed it will grow into a tree. Yet they say the first seed that grew the world and all beyond to the end of time was tiny like this seed to the size of the earth, only more so. Wonder of wonders, like you and me, Paul, and all that comes and goes."

"Like Genie in the lamp. Tiny like this," he pinches his finger, "but can grow big as this room. Big as the whole house even!" He stands amazed at the thought.

"Yes, Paul, and in a snap of his finger he can make a castle the size of a hill…or a mountain. Or swallow a whole sea and blow it plumb across the desert."

No longer troubled, Paul takes a string of tinsel and turns in wonder to the tree while she turns in wonder of events long ago.

***

"Still wanna join the circus, Duchess?" Glen sat gamely by the lamp, his swollen eye and bashed lip lending irony to his smile as mother clipped the hair near his wound, blood still oozing, she daubed it clear. He'd regained consciousness on the journey home, cursing his aching head and the jolting wagon.

I didn't answer, simply looked at my hands folded on my lap, still haunted by Shannon's scream and her father's dead stare. My dream of joining the circus had died that night, trampled by the fierce violence that flared like a match, fists and faces set to murder. Then, as father by chance had alluded, the humped beast pounced.

"Dang it, Aunt Sarah!" Glen cursed. "Done been clubbed, gonna scalp me too?"

"Hold still, else I will," she warned, stropping the razor.

"Clipped 'n sheared both?" he groused.

"Yes, I need to see where to stitch."

"*Aye-yie-yie!*" Glen grimaced under the scraping blade.

Father had stepped in from tending the horses and stood amused by their banter. As she daubed the wound and laid the razor aside, he reached for his whiskey bottle and said, "Here, Sarah, splash it with this. Good for a wound. And by gosh, if not legal to distill or brew, we can still buy 'n use."

Glen intercepted the bottle, "Thanks, Uncle Pat, could use me some right now…" He took a good long swig before mother snatched it away.

"That's enough," she scolded, tipping his head to douse the wound.

"Ow, that burns! Better give me another shot."

"No!" she handed it back to father and began threading the needle, preparing to close the wound. Glen gritted his teeth and gripped the edge of the table. Father leaned back in his chair, taking a nip, watching Glen wince stitch to stitch.

Daring not look, I sat numb next to the fluttering lamp.

By and by father read my mood and said, "Sadie, there's a hidden beast in man, in us all, that leaps forth when we least expect it. Once you see it you never want to see it again. But it's always there, waitin'…" He paused, looking past mother and Glen to the shadows cast by the flickering flame. "Funny thing, during the war, at times we'd call a truce, us 'n the Rebs, and make friendly for a spell, usually along about sunset, by some stream or road. We'd chat 'n trade tobacco for coffee or bacon for eggs. But for canned peaches you could about name your want…" He chuckled at the memory then sobered and leaned forth. "They were good fellas and we could've been friends in another time 'n place. But next day they went back to bushwhackin' whilst we rode hell-bent to hunt 'em down. A cruel game, war, politics, life…each got our own tribe 'n take offense at the drop of a hat, once the battle starts each fight on their own hook…farmers, ranchers, railroaders, townies 'n circus folk. Then there's religion, the most vicious beast of all, and why I'm only a summa-the-time Christian. All those blood feuds in Europe 'tween Protestants 'n Catholics who swear by the same God, the same prophet, same book, same words, yet quibble over ritual 'n meaning. Whether one favors wine 'n wafers, or coffee, cornbread 'n beans, or praises good work over prayer, all whittle down to the same faith in things hoped for, evidence unseen. And each will kill the other in proof."

He glanced out the window to the far night. "That old Indian on the hill, I bet he smoked cedar bark in nod to the Great Spirit. His returning you to your mother 'n me was a true act of mercy. But what his brethren did to Glen's family, the devil himself could do no worse. Good 'n evil spins heads 'n tails through all our doings. That's the beast in us, Sadie." Again he caught my eye. "And I'm sorry you had to see that poor man dead on the platform. I truly am…"

⸻ ❖ ⸻

For a time I attended Wednesday evening devotions with greater fervor, yet found no solace or redemption from the grim tragedy I'd witnessed — could not reconcile event and belief, it made no sense, so shallow and common, a silly quarrel that left a good man dead and his family without a father or husband. The smith shop closed a week then reopened under a new owner, gaining the family meager funds to cover the funeral. Shannon never returned to school. She and her mother took in laundry and sewing to make ends meet. The oldest son, Seth, hired out shucking corn through the fall harvest then apprenticed under the new blacksmith, a Swede named Jons Thornsen. On occasion I'd glimpse Shannon but she always turned away as if shunned, like a door had closed and she no longer had hope and it pained her to see those who did.

One day about a month later I chanced to see her hanging sheets in the afternoon sun. I approached thinking to share a book I'd just read. She wiped a strand of hair from her eyes and smiled faintly. When offered the book she shook her head and said, "Thank you, Sadie, but with all the work and the little ones, I simply haven't the time." Facing her I felt empty. She needed the fruit of salvation not the fallen leaves…or mere pages pressed from such. Like the many I offered my sad condolence, said I was so sorry for what had happened then left her stranded to her fate. I sank deeper into my studies and sought refuge from the present by exploring the past.

Others had suffered as well. Though he walked with a limp the boy shot in the heel eventually recovered, as did the two men with broken arms and those with head wounds like Glen. But Mayor Morgan would never walk again, shot through the spine and left paralyzed from the waist down. An intelligent, worthy man, he maintained a positive outlook and resumed his official duties but required nearly constant care from his wife and daughter, leaving two more women essentially marooned.

The night of the shooting Marshal Thomas and 30 other Oakvale men formed a posse. Next day, along with Sheriff Johnson and his deputies, they ran a special train from Mankato in pursuit. By noon they overtook the circus in Marysville, 80 miles east, where a score of circus men were detained and questioned. No doubt a dozen or more had fired on the depot, but as they had been provoked, only two were charged. One, a shady drifter self-named "Buckshot," received 10 years for murder in the second degree. The other, a powerful Negro they called "Big Muddy," drew 3 years for manslaughter. Hearing this, I wondered was he the one with the huge mallet who smiled at us that morning?

Many claimed that the two were just patsies taking the rap for the whole lot, which further befuddled my young mind.

As autumn lost its colors and leaves turned brown, my perplexity deepened. How could a dozen men fire repeatedly from the train, killing one man, crippling another for life, wounding several more, yet only two were charged and found guilty? The question lingered, haunting me like the bloody scene that replayed nightly in my dreams.

"Why all this melancholy 'n no spunk?" father observed one evening, watching me piddle through my Latin studies. "Where hides my green-eyed girl 'n her bright smile?" He grinned and tweaked his mustache, trying to draw me out.

So I told him and asked, "How come only two are guilty and not the whole bunch?"

"Oh yes," he squinted his eyes in thought, "the law is an odd thing. You see, Sadie, the aim for justice often falls short. Like the Gospel tries to teach us to love one another, the law tries to keep us from killin' one another till that hallowed day comes. You may not know this, hardly believe it myself," he furrowed his brow in wonder. "For a couple years followin' the war I read for the law, recitin' all the where-asses, whyfors, hereins, be-it-resolved 'n such. Up in Des Moines, understudy to an attorney-for-hire named E.G. Bayne, not a bad sort, had a nimble mind 'n easy conscience. Could argue his case either way, please his client, claim his fee 'n dance to whatever tune played. Me, I was not so flexible regardin' the law 'n its uses, or people 'n their concerns. As you know, I detest the throng. Much prefer horses 'n cattle…and of course, your mother."

"Are you lumping me with your cows?"

"Why heck, Sarah, you are my favorite, almost…" He ducked her playful swat and continued, "Point is, Sadie, the Gospel 'n the law work parallel in a way. Both imperfect, at times harsh 'n oft-times leave us confused. Beyond which we're left to dangle by our lonesome. And that, my dear daughter, is the sum of what I have to tell you. But here, this'll shed more light on things…" he stood and reached for a book on his cluttered shelf. "Been holdin' this back, but deem it time you peer into *Parallel Lives* by Plutarch, an old Greek who wrote in Roman times. Admired 'n read for centuries, compares the lives of famous Greeks 'n Romans, nigh on every page speaks of the good 'n evil that runs in the blood of all. Wise 'n vivid, his words will enlighten and entertain. Another good reason I'm a summa-the-time this 'n that, albeit full-time sweet on your mother" — he winked to her then handed me the heavy book. "Volume one, it'll make you ponder and for certain enliven your Latin, I guarantee."

I began reading then and there, and on through the winter into spring, every spare moment I turned another page, engrossed in the churning drama of thought and deed that played through the lives of men and women therein. Finished with volume one I went to volume two, through wars, battles, rivalries of politics and love, full of action, argument, and blood. From King to King, Caesar to Caesar, there was rarely a succession without murder, whether by sword, dagger, or poison. While I paused in thought of Lincoln and Garfield's recent assassinations, the ancients slew the families as well — wives, children, parents, brothers and sisters, if not executed, given choice of suicide. A practice so common it seemed casual, many calmly submitting to their fate, their veins opened by self or others as they reclined in warm baths to speed the bleeding, conversing with a loved one to the last breath. Strangely, reading of their stoic acceptance of death amid the violent cycle of things worked to relieve my melancholy.

Freed of gloom I grew pensive, less uncertain, though plenty puzzled. For while Plutarch had lived a full generation after the death of Christ and wrote extensively on persons then current and past, he never once mentioned Jesus of Nazareth, nor a single disciple. Yet Romans and Greeks both practiced religion, Plutarch himself a priest of Apollo, with rituals similar to later Christians, even sharing the same titles and names, Pope, Priest, Nun, Vestal Virgin — and any such who broke her vow, if found out, was buried alive. That young women were once smothered, literally, by men who shared the same urge and likely pleasured in them angered me. And I began to see that women had long been and still were closeted, cosseted, and in a sense chained.

As mother would remind father, "The war freed the men, not the women. By law and religion, we all remain chattel." Seeing him start to protest, she'd add, "I may have voice here in the kitchen, but not to vote." With that I grew somewhat proud and aloof, remembering what she once confided, "We must be brave or be fools."

More and more a free thinker, I did not express my thoughts freely except to my parents. In town and at school I guarded my views. Taking meals with the Jensens, I quietly bowed my head in prayer, and at church gladly sang along for I enjoyed singing. But asserted neither belief nor nonbelief, and beyond Wednesday evenings I skirted any further devotions. While Mrs. Jensen frowned on my lack of zeal, she never insisted and I think Mr. Jensen understood, for he too avoided church, like as not. But their daughter Darlene followed after her mother, vague of thought and prone to sloth, hated to dirty her hands and seldom did. And never let Caroline and I forget we were hired girls. Though seldom tyrannical or harsh, she looked down her nose, often smug and haughty, deigned not touch dirty dishes or laundry, and never set foot in the stables. However, she did make excellent pies, evident by her ample form. Caroline and I secretly joked that we were Cinderellas made to slave for the wicked sister. But we were not ill-treated, simply galled at times.

Caroline was a pleasant girl, easy-going and not at all studious or curious minded, but diligent at every task and loved to sew. Finished with chores, I delved into books while she stitched a new blouse or dress. Our evenings passed quietly, the clock ticking on till ten or so before we doused the lamp to sleep and rise to another day. Occasionally, prompted by something I'd just read, I did share a notion. She'd smile politely and listen, perhaps purse her lips in brief thought then wave it aside and resume her sewing.

One night reading *Gulliver's Travels* where the hero escapes from a race of savage humans to take refuge with a tribe of intelligent talking horses, I glanced up excitedly and said, "You know, I think Swift is right, horses are superior to people."

For once Caroline actually paused her stitching to answer. "Well, they don't cuss. And another thing, their manure sure smells better than ours." And immediately two girls had to cover their mouths to stifle their giggles else they'd wake the entire house.

A week or so later, arriving at school after morning chores, a smart-alecky boy smirked and said I smelled like horses. To which I sharply replied, "If you spent less time picking your nose and read your Swift, you'd know tis better to smell sweet as a horse than stink like a Yahoo!" Yes, in that instant I did speak my mind and the boy never taunted me again. Proud to have read Swift, loved his fantastic plots, his wit and satire, but tripped over his invented spellings, especially *Houyhnhum*, much preferred it spelled *Hwinum*, as it was pronounced. And did so in my written report, and persisted despite receiving a red mark. Again proudly assertive, choosing the practical over the persnickety, certain that Swift, a writer who sought to vex and challenge, would approve. However, I found it peculiar, his hero's disgust at sight of a Brobdingnagian woman's giant breast, a feature to which few men in my experience were adverse. Particularly as my maiden buds swelled to their fulsome form, drawing men's eyes, some furtive, others more direct, focusing like wolves eager to feed.

Young and innocent, shy of my breasts, the girl in me wished to conceal, somehow turn away and hide them, but could not. An embarrassment I dared not share even with Caroline, for hers were rather small and she felt envious and said so one morning as we dressed. I simply blushed and hurriedly buttoned my blouse.

At home I did confess my embarrassment to mother.

"Pshaw…" she waved off my concern, pinched my cheek and said, "You should be proud. You are becoming quite a lovely, well-endowed young woman." Her blessing worked like magic, her using the very word *proud* made me no longer ashamed of my breasts. I stood erect and moved more freely.

And of Hwinums and Yahoos I spoke freely. Father had always placed horses and mules before men, extolling their graceful strength, virtue, and good sense. And Glen heartily agreed, "Dang circus Yahoos near stove in my head. Least when a horse or mule kicks ya, they generally have cause beyond fool mayhem." While his wound had healed, the blow had impaired the hearing in his left ear. We'd each noticed how he favored his right in tilt to our voices. Before supper one night, father stood back of Glen and snapped his finger to the left side, getting no reaction, he did so on the right. When Glen glanced around, father asked, "Did you hear me snap by your left ear a moment ago?"

"No, Uncle Pat, just a dang ringin', aches like the devil out in the wind."

That night mother knitted him several tiny balls of yarn to tuck in his ears. And it did help, he and father worked in the wind a great deal that winter, busting out post rock in the west pasture. Knowing they needed to fence, father swore he'd only do it once. Wood posts, easily cut from the creek, would soon rot or burn in prairie fires common to the region, whereas rock posts, though laborious, were durable and readily at hand. Over autumn, before the ground froze, father had hitched Sampson to the buck shovel and cleared several areas where rock strata edged the hillside. By mid-winter, using an auger and bit to drill the holes and applying feathers and wedges, he and Glen had busted out roughly half the 500 needed to enclose our mile long pasture. Then in late February to father's surprise the two bindle-stiffs, Orlin and Greeley, showed up dead broke and sober, anxious to hire on, and they helped bust out the rest.

Through those many cold hard weeks father rarely cracked a book, and joked, "This fencin' is gonna leave me nigh illiterate as those two cusses. But reckon it's a small price to pay to keep our Hwinums safe from Yahoos."

During a late winter snowstorm Sampson died. Found him lying in his stall and father said, "Might have spared him that last tug on the buck shovel, but he loved to dig in 'n pull." He and Glen wrapped a log chain to his hindquarters then hitched the mules and skidded him over the snow on south of the cedar gully. Not long thereafter the old Indian's pony died as well. Again they dragged him out to lie beside Sampson.

Glen quietly gazed on and noted, "Seems those two mark the end of an era."

By spring coyotes and other scavengers had picked the carcasses clean while ants and beetles burrowed through the marrow until the sun bleached the bones white and the summer grass sprouted green amid the remains of our faithful Hwinums.

XI. Mystery Woman

"*Salubrious…healthful…mild Mediterranean clime*" — we laughed at the captions from railroad brochures and local boosters phrased to entice immigrants and folks from back east to settle on the plains, painting an illusion of plentiful water through a fertile expanse begging to be plowed and harvested. But they found a climate and terrain more extreme than Biblical lands, less forgiving and hardly temperate, where dearth as often occurred every two or three years as the proverbial seven. Winter went from a mere frost to a killing blizzard in a day. Dust storms blew through most of March. And you could bet on 40 days of drought nearly every summer, especially in July and August. And there were veritable plagues of locust, the worst in the summer of '74, which still haunted mother's dreams. Though my memories were sketchy, only 5 at the time, I recalled the creatures burned in great heaps like foreskins of the infidel in the Old Testament. And glancing to the sky, seeing hordes of the demons darkening the sun, I screamed. Mother scooped me up and rushed us inside and I remember nothing more.

Then came the Great Blizzard of '86, which hit January 1st and howled three days straight, soon followed by a second Norther. Scores of people froze to death and cattle perished by tens of thousands wandering lost in drifts further west and into Colorado. Fortunately, father and Glen had finished fencing our pasture, and while we lost a few head to the bitter cold, most survived huddled in the creek bottom, delivered wagonloads of hay by father and Glen who returned to the house half-frozen and hunched by the stove rubbing their numb hands and feet. We all felt grateful, safely cocooned from the cold wind, feeding chunks of wood to the fire. Out of long habit father always laid up an abundant supply of wood, as he said, "You never know when you'll break an arm or leg. It takes weeks to starve, but you can freeze inside an hour."

That winter entire families, having run out of fuel, were found frozen to death in their houses. And throughout the west, cattle losses were so massive that they soon called it "The Great Die Up." For a time beef prices rose as did railroad rates which ate up half the profits. Yet grain prices fell so low that many farmers, rather than ship for nothing, burned their corn for fuel or simply let it rot in the field.

Even still people flooded onto the plains. Father would shake his head at all the comings and goings, "I swear one farmer goes bust, two more jump in. Trouble always starts when the few become the many. Then the many want what only a few can have 'n hope to hold. Fool tinhorns 'n speculators don't know anthill sticker-patch from sweet creek bottom. Grab a handful of dirt and expect to reap gold the next. Can't go on, I swear. A house of cards will soon collapse. Like here last winter, Chrissake," he said in gaze to the creek, "we're just lucky we had the fencin' done 'n hay to feed. And damn lucky we own our land 'n owe no debt."

Though luck hadn't purchased our land, as father well knew, it was hard work and blood. Over half our family that homesteaded in '68 and '69 lay buried above the White Rock. Each year we made that pilgrimage and stood in homage to the price they'd paid, knowing the slightest shift in time and chance that fatal day would have seen us buried there too. And what of the old Indian, his band by now all but wiped out by disease and starvation. Yes, we were lucky, and grateful, as father observed standing by the graves that spring, "There but for fortune. The three sisters, the old Moirai, spin 'n weave to the last stitch. Drought, dearth 'n debt. Then the Pale Horseman stomps all to dust."

Or horsewoman…my thought, recently seeing less and less of Glen, in fact upon returning home from the graves he immediately rode off, didn't stay for supper. When I asked why, mother smiled archly and said, "Seems he has a new lady friend."

"Oh…" I blinked, instantly surprised and curious, but before I could question more, father cautioned, "Don't you two be gossipin' on Glen." I held my tongue, waiting till he went to chore then rushed to mother and asked, "Who?"

When she told me I was at once astonished, proud, and intrigued.

Holly Hazelin, the mystery woman, had been a subject of rumor for several years. Ever since she'd abruptly abandoned her studies at the University in Lawrence where she had thrived for a time but it had ended badly. Some whispered of an abortion. For certain it had ended and she returned home to assist her widowed father run their ranch.

The Hazelin Ranch tipped our land on the lower quarter Glen had purchase and extended southwest for two square miles. Mostly grassland with little more tillage than Briar-Callaway, they mainly grew oats and alfalfa along the creek valley that edged their stately house, huge barn, and wood panel corrals. Her father, Jude Hazelin, contracted with the U.S. Army, supplying quality horses and mules. More than help her father, many claimed that since his decline she pretty much ran things, a sharp-tongued boss that none dare rebuke else they were gone. Yet few sassed her — fair-minded, she won their respect, rolled up her sleeves, joined in every task, whether birthing, training, grooming, feeding, even mucked out the stalls. Not only that, she dressed like a man in shirt, pants, and boots, mostly kept to herself, but donned a jacket and black ribbon tie when she went to town, strictly business, no jewelry, lace or ruffles. Let her long hair flow, never put it up or wore a hat. Women were appalled, nearly to a one, excepting mother, though an honest few did allow she was quite pretty, perhaps beautiful. To which men's sidelong glances aptly attested.

So yes, hearing that Glen had ridden off to Holly Hazelin, the mystery woman I'd never met, my lodestar of wonder burst with curiosity. But Glen slyly ducked my every question and made himself scarce.

Finally I chanced to spy them one day riding up through the west pasture. Knew it was her by her long hair flowing in the wind like the mane and tail of her sorrel mare, and almost the same color. At my tentative wave they reined in and waited my approach.

Glen cracked a smile and said, "Holly, this here's my sister-cousin, Sadie Briar. What d'ya think?"

"Oh, I think she'll do." They both smiled like they knew something I didn't.

Then he nodded, "Sadie, this here's Holly, who you've been so curious of."

My throat went dry, I felt accused. Face to face she was even prettier than I'd imagined. Her hair fell in lush folds nearly to her waist. She wore a denim shirt and jeans like Glen. Her waist cinched with a leather belt and a silver Spanish buckle. She sat erect, full-breasted and proud — her eyes so keen and direct I had to lower mine. Her knee-high boots, scuffed and soiled with manure, in the warm sun and grassy air she smelled sweet as a horse.

Braving a smile, I raised my eyes and said, "Pleased to meet you."

"Likewise," she answered, adding, "I hear you're a budding young scholar."

At that I blushed and stammered, "No, not really, but...I do like books. And I hope to attend university, like you —" then caught myself, fearing I'd said more than I should.

"Ah..." she raised a brow in further scrutiny as I again blushed.

"But that would be...next year," I hurriedly explained, thoughts overrunning my words, "I and two boys will be the first to graduate high school...in Oakvale. Then go to university in Manhattan...or Lawrence...perhaps."

"How nice," she smiled, "such a fine thing to strive and dream. I wish you luck, Sadie," then she reined about and headed upslope. And Glen did not tarry, tipped his hat and spurred to a gallop. Both soon riding abreast, they traded love taps and laughter, then she quirted her horse and he his and they were off, racing over the hill, at one with their mounts and one another.

Next trip to town I begged mother to purchase some tough denim cloth and once home I set to work sewing my own jeans on her prize new Singer treadle machine. She peered over my shoulder with a doubtful look and I promised to only wear them at home or while riding in the pasture. "Very well," she said, "but cut snug as they are, you better double-stitch else they will rip." I did so, even riveted the pockets, hip and seat.

At the very next haying, helping Glen work the hayfork and trolley in the barn, I wore my new denim jeans and no bonnet, my hair loose and tangled with straw.

"Why look at this," Glen teased, "wild girl of the Limestone. Better watch it, startin' to look 'n act like Holly."

"Well, what of it?" I said then straight away asked, "How did you two meet?"

"She just sort of appeared one day," he grinned.

"Come on, Glen, stop teasing."

"It's a fact. We was fencin' that south end last fall 'n up she rides. We get to talkin' about horses 'n such. Tradin' a few pointers. 'Course I boasted some on my ridin' which she dared me do. So I hops on my ol' Monty 'n show her some Cheyenne stunts 'n the like. Then heck, she showed me hers."

Just what he meant I dared not imagine.

"Are you two in love?"

"By golly, you're quick on the draw. Admit I do like her some. Quite a woman," with that he turned to work the rope and pulley.

"Are you going to marry her?"

"Whoa now," he squinted to me and grinned, "doubt she'd wear a halter to the altar. A mite high strung 'n likes to canter her own way. Which suits me fine."

"But you and her…are you…do you?"

His grin told me enough and nothing more as he answered, "Sadie, Sadie, you should know. A gentleman never tells 'n a cowboy never lies…"

XII. Hagan

Never lies…smiling, she rocks her chair, remembers Glen pitching hay in a shaft of sunlight that long ago day in the barn, now only a shadowy form in dusty nimbus but still moving, speaking through her mind. She repeats absently, "Never lies…"

"What's that you said, Gram?" Paul turns in question from hanging the tinsel.

"Nothing, just old memories talking…" again she smiles then glances to the clock and sees it's on past ten. "You know, Paul, there're folks coming home from Christmas Eve service about now. Others getting ready for midnight mass."

"I like it here," he mutters, diligently placing another silvery tinsel.

"Yes, and you have our tree looking awfully pretty." She purses her shriveled lips thoughtfully and asks, "You ever sorry I don't take you to church?"

"No, Gram. You took me once, remember?" So she had. He was only 7 or 8 and tall as her. They went to a little Baptist church west of Ionia, the preacher shouting fire and brimstone. "That angry man, remember? He said the Devil was gonna get us and I ran…" Paul had taken every word to heart, jumped up and dashed out, causing quite a stir, even silenced the preacher. She offered a quick apology and rushed after.

Had a terrible time calming the boy, even home safe inside the house still certain the Devil was out there. "That man was simply spinning a yarn," she assured him, "like on Halloween when we tell ghost stories or read about the Headless Horseman." Finally, Paul caught his breath and sniffled, "I…I like Aladdin and His Lamp best" — which they must have read a dozen times that evening then agreed, no more church.

Again she thanks her lucky stars that her parents were freethinkers and spared her the curse of religion. Yet she had turned around and visited the selfsame curse on Paul.

What a fool thing, she thinks, shaking her head at the memory and chuckles at the thought of them once dressed for church — Paul in a starched white shirt, overalls, bowtie and cufflinks, and her in a fussy dress, hat and veil.

------------------------------◆------------------------------

While I wore my denim pants boldly around the farm that summer, I also sewed three new dresses, fine and frilly with lace, bows, and ruffles. Set for my final year of high school. Like most girls anxious to be fashionable, attractive, I too wore hats and occasionally a veil to add mystery and allure at various town concerts and picnics. I enjoyed being a young lady, and while I admired Holly Hazelin for her daring dress and manner, I was more determined to follow her former path to university than shuck it all and remain on the Limestone. That year would be my stepping stone, eager to enter the world, learn and experience all that waited. Although money was tight, father vowed to pay my tuition and ticket to Manhattan if I earned board and room. This hardly seemed an obstacle as I'd done so the past three years in Oakvale with the Jensens. Simply a matter of finding a new situation and I was already promised a letter of introduction from a teacher native to the town. Doors opening, everything seemed possible, I merely had to dance my way through.

Meanwhile Caroline was no longer my roommate. The previous winter she'd finished her *trousseau*, the one French word she knew, and left school, judging her education sufficient to her needs. In late spring she'd wed a young farmer, Theodore Hunsfelt, who she called Teddy — already working his own acreage under his father's guidance. I'd see her on occasion when they came to town, looking rosy-cheeked and happy as they reined briefly by the livery to chat.

"I'm sewing a new dress," she'd recently beamed, "A maternity dress!"

So our lives diverged, hers centered on husband, home, and motherhood, mine as yet undecided, though certainly not marriage. Like other girls I'd cradled my rag doll as a child, but the stuffed kitten handed to me by the old Indian, and that gesture, for good or ill, gave me pause at thought of self, birth, and motherhood. And pausing, I thought of Shannon, daughter of the slain blacksmith, who by now had also wed, likely to escape the burden of raising her brothers and sisters. Sadly, I fear she'd only doubled her woes, her husband, Amos Gridley, a dour middle-aged man, owner of the local grocery-hardware, chintzy of money, kindness, and warmth. At least they had food. But Shannon showed little joy tending their young son while carrying another baby near term, only 17, her eyes downcast, stressed and sullen.

No, matrimony did not tempt me, like Holly Hazelin I tossed my head at the notion.

And while harboring the natural impulses and urges of youth, I was wary of the primrose path and remained outwardly modest and determined in my studies. Whereas Darlene Jensen, who'd also left school, courted regularly, caught in the swirl for there were considerable doings even in Oakvale, community theater, dances, concerts, church socials and the like. One fair day in early autumn she even stepped from her haughty cloud and extended an invitation. Asked me to join her and several other young men and women on a carriage ride 20 miles south to Cibola City.

"They're having a *love-ly* Chautauqua," she hinted slyly, "with poetry and music."

I politely declined, sighting my studies and chores.

"Well suit yourself, Sadie Briar," she huffed, adding, "There's more to life than your silly books, you know."

"Undoubtedly, but no thank you," I replied, didn't care for all the dust and jostle, not to mention some rude whiskey breath trying to worm his way under my dress on the long ride home. And don't think it didn't happen, often right in back of the buckboard years before the "sin wagon" as old prudes labeled the early cars, like as not once guilty themselves. I too was restless, full of question and want, but reined my lust by constant study and for a time remained chaste and innocent.

Not so Darlene Jensen, fancied herself quite worldly and winsome, utterly embraced her notoriety and danced for a season. Then one chill November morning, in a dreary fog and drizzle, her father loaded two large traveling trunks in the carriage. Her mother drove her to the depot and purchased a one-way ticket to Denver and saw her off. "To Madame Chevelle's Salon, a finishing school," she later vouched to one and all, "they stress style, etiquette, and grace…which shall improve her prospect of a fine marriage." Apparently it worked. In any case she never returned to Oakvale. Rumor claimed she'd gone to a home for wayward girls and unwed mothers. Fair or foul, watching her go that morning, I pitied her fate and parried all advances and offers of courtship.

My senior year, I'd forgo matters of the heart and focus on learning. My love of geography still held, extending to other countries, continents and oceans. And history gripped me, past events and those current with snippets of political battles brewing north, south, east, and west. Odd terms and phrases flitted to my ear: Free Silver, Bimetallism, Greenbacks, Goldbugs…curious and foreign as new words to a child. "The Crime of '73" and women's suffrage and temperance movements, issues vexing as locusts clouding the sky, all given voice by two rival weeklies, *The Oakvale Republican* and *The White Rock Gazette*, the latter of Democratic bent, each hurling invective and insult at the other, those on high, and the many stirring to rise. Yet they joined forces to condemn a third weekly, more pamphlet than newspaper, *The Thinker*, its editor, an avowed agnostic, championed the inherent goodness of man and brotherhood of all, rousing consternation among the devout. One editor fumed: *"Why, the Thinker hardly thinks, condemned by his very word and thought. Ignorant of his own belief. If there be goodness in man, it is surely there by Divine Grace. For there is no good but for God!"*

Reading which, father had a good laugh, "I give the Thinker credit, but you can't unconvince a believer. A waste of breath. They'll twist black to white, up to down till Hell freezes over 'n Devil take the hindmost. Wonder they haven't burned 'im out."

But the Thinker they merely scoffed at or belittled, aimed their full ire on a fourth newspaper that had recently landed in our midst, its sign hung in big black letters directly across from theirs, *The Prairie Advocate*, which published news and editorials in support of *The Farmer's Alliance & Industrial Union*, decrying the yoke of the wealthy few over the indebted many, claimed the game was rigged and challenged the old pabulum that solely by thrift and hard work a people could thrive. Worse than a nonbeliever, they branded its young editor a "Socialist! Anarchist! Rabble Rouser!" This the common view, folks suspicious of an outsider, yet many were beginning to question the iron grip of Eastern Banks, Industry, and Railroads. Just the day before, while I readied for my weekly ride to Oakvale, father had grumped, "Dern shippin' rates for cattle, might as well take a dime for the hoof 'n horns and give the meat away."

Monday afternoon, walking from school, I glimpsed the suspect young editor standing under his sign, casually nodding to people, taking in the day. Unlike his stodgy rivals, he looked more swordsman than penman, tall, lean, and as other girls attested, handsome dressed in dark pants, vest, and white shirt, sleeves rolled to the elbow, his brown Hamburg cocked to one side. He caught me looking his way, tipped his hat and smiled. I ducked my head and hurried on.

A few minutes later, changed to my works clothes, doing chores in the livery, Mr. Jensen nodded to the street and said, "See our latest newsman has his sign up. Been out there all afternoon, greets the gents, charms the ladies, makin' himself known. Corbett's his name, H.R. Corbett. Met him Saturday, stalls his horse here. What the 'H' stands for I don't yet know. Maybe '*give 'em hell*' cause he sure has 'em riled. Tell you one thing, if he writes half as good as he rides, he may prove out."

"Oh...?" I looked up in question.

"Yep, he's a goer, rides hard I swear...Saturday, Sunday 'n again today, up 'n saddled by sunrise 'n gone past noon. Come ridin' in a while ago, his horse lathered up, pulls off the saddle 'n I ask, 'Been ridin' a far piece?' He says, 'Yes 'n no, just out and around to meet folks and gather the news.' Strikes me as a right fine fellow for a bomb thrower...so some claim. But I think he may prove worth a read now 'n then. And say," Mr. Jensen pointed to the near stall, "that's his horse there, the tall black, still wet from his ride. Might give him an extra combin', Sadie, to cool 'im down..."

And I did so, gladly, curried him twice over as he snorted and quivered his slick coat under my hand, and I wondered at the strange mystery man who'd come to Oakvale. Now I knew his name, Corbett, H.R. Corbett.

Several days thereon, again working in the livery, sifting other thoughts entirely, in fact ciphering the shipping costs against the market price of beef in Chicago and Denver, I determined that father was right — the railroads were filching half the profit. *Why it was highway robbery!* Incensed, I stabbed my pitchfork and noticed a shadow suddenly cast my way through the large doors open to the street and afternoon sun. Alone, Mr. Jensen out on an errand, I faced a burly man staring in as men sometimes did. To avoid his leer I turned and continued pitching hay to the horses, careful not to bend over or show profile, glued to my task, hoping he'd soon grow bored and move on. But his shadow steadily loomed closer, larger, rising over the stall panels to the far wall.

His stench hit me before he gripped my shoulder and spun me around. A soiled derby topped his ugly head, brutish, unshaven, feral-eyed like a pig, flesh and clothes filthy, reeking of sweat and worse, I nearly retched, his whiskey breath full on mine.

"How 'bout it, girlie? Got a kiss fer ol' Jonesy?"

As he gripped my other shoulder I shot a knee to his groin, angry, fierce, instinctual, summoning the spirits of my cousins once raped, vowing "You shall not!"

Though he winced and reddened, he did not cease. Flung my pitchfork, twisted my hair and hissed, "Ya little barn whore, gonna spread ya out 'n do ya…"

My head wrenched back, eyes clinched in pain, I did not see but sensed another force. Heard the *thwack-thwack* of fist to flesh as my attacker abruptly released his grip and dropped me to the straw. All slowed, sound and motion elongated and enlarged as two shadowy forms grappled in a flurry of punches till one drove the other to his knees and added a mean kick that pitched him sprawled on his back.

Still shaken, dazed, I had no idea who was helping me stand.

"Are you alright?" he asked softly and repeated, "You alright?"

I simply nodded, gazing past the voice and person to see my attacker stagger to his feet and grasp the pitchfork, and I cried out, "No!" My scream answered by a cracking whip that wrapped the pitchfork and snatched it away — *Slick as a circus act*, I thought, looking on as the other man again felled my attacker with several quick blows. This time he yanked him up and pinned his arm. And I recognized him now, the other man, as he turned to me. The young editor, Mr. Corbett, even more handsome up close than at a distance, his hair mussed, having lost his hat in the struggle, his mustache as dark and broad as father's.

"What happened, Sadie?" Mr. Jensen asked, rolling up his whip.

I walked forth, breathing hard, so mad I could kill and spat, "This…this pig…he grabbed me and I…I kneed him!" Only this time I had the range and kicked like a Can-Can dancer catching him directly on the toe of my boot and didn't care if they saw the flash of my thigh. He gulped and buckled, puking whatever he had drank.

Mr. Corbett let him spit it out then jerked him upright and said, "Sorry for your trouble, Miss. I saw this wretch stumble off the train yesterday evening, fully soused, gripping a bottle, he probably passed out in the trees. Today I saw him pass by as Mr. Jensen headed out. My shop window angles right to the livery. Saw him check the street both ways, seeing all clear, he slipped inside. That's when I stepped out, rather briskly I might add. Glad I did. But he won't bother you anymore, Miss. He plans to catch the night train to Kansas City…right, Bub?"

"Hain't…hain't got a dime," he mumbled, snorting blood from his nose.

"Fancy that. I'll see your ticket. You just see you don't return."

And Mr. Jensen fisted his coiled whip and added, "You ever show your face round here again 'n touch one of our girls, I'll whip you all the way to Hell. By God, I will!"

Standing by, I picked up Mr. Corbett's hat, dusted it off and handed it to him. He set it to his head in nod to me then grabbed the culprit by the collar and shoved him into the sunlight. When the fool started to balk, he again pinned his arm and on they went. I reached for the shovel and prepared to scoop his vomited muck.

"Sadie, no need you doin' that. You go rest. I can finish up here."

"Thank you, Mr. Jensen. But…I want to be rid of him to the last spit!"

He chuckled and said, "Suit yourself, Sadie. Think I understand. Just know this won't be spoken of…at least not by me."

But others peering in had already seen and heard and many more witnessed the young editor of *The Prairie Advocate* march the villain to the depot. The whole town soon knew the story, which didn't hurt his reputation, or mine. He the champion of the farmer-debtor, now defender of young women, and I the intrepid damsel, general object of adore. And conjecture. I myself stumped in wonder, all quite unsettling really, for I had sighted afar and scorned all notions of romance and told myself it was curiosity I felt, and gratitude, him coming to my succor.

The very next day, Friday, after school and before returning home, I determined to fetch a copy of his paper. Somewhat daring for it was still considered unbecoming for a young woman to walk uptown alone. But I did not hesitate, boldly opened his door and entered. Then stood silent, frozen in his gaze as he turned from the slanted work bench where he'd been setting type. He doffed his hat then laid it aside.

"Beg your pardon, Miss," he said, "I often wear my hat while working, helps me focus. But I do recall my manners in the presence of a young lady."

Meeting his smile, I quickly asked, "May I buy a paper? It's…for my father," I added, promptly holding up a nickel.

"Save your nickel. As my sole customer today, you shall have one gratis."

"Thank you, Sir. That is very kind."

"Hagan…Hagan's my name. Hagan Corbett."

I glanced down hesitant to say his name and muttered, "Pleased to meet you."

"Likewise, I'm sure. And you are…?"

"Sadie…" I glanced up, "Sadie Briar."

"Very well, Miss Briar, take a copy of my humble words with compliments to your father." Then he raised a brow in sly appraisal. "And do you read?"

"Oh yes, I recently finished *Frankenstein* by Mary Shelley."

"Ah…a most prescient tale, it sounds the tocsin on monsters soon to hatch and those to come. Yet thought and written 70 years before our time. And she was only 19. What a fertile, far-seeing young mind. A remarkable woman, I'd love to have known her."

"I too," again glancing away to avoid his dark eyes searching mine and changed the subject, "I also read *The Thinker*."

"Yes," he answered amused, "our local agnostic, George Linwood, interesting fellow, quite earnest, like old Saul's Letters to the Philistines, albeit given a contrary slant. But that's his province. I never argue religion."

"That's what my father says…it's a waste of breath."

"Your father's a wise man."

Again meeting his eyes, I curtsied and had no idea why. Feeling foolish as he leaned back in grin and said, "Having seen you deliver a most wicked kick, I'm delighted to see you have your more gracious aspects…" I blushed red, grabbed a paper and was gone, relieved to be safely distanced. No, harbored no desire for romance. Yet in his presence I felt my body lighten, my breath quicken, and I began to realize that the heart has its own ambitions, once awakened, not easily denied.

Riding home I repeated his name…*Hagan, Hagan, Hagan.*

XIII. Blood

The mind's a sort of prism, she thinks, and memory passing through gets cast in separate colors on the inner skull, like Paul's Christmas lights, some red, blue, yellow, while others blink and darken to nothing. This one fades brown and brittle.

She gently lifts the old newspaper from the box, hands tremoring like they do late at night. Forgot she'd put it there, that first copy given her, a single page folded twice. The header missing, having crumbled through the years, the lower text remains.

She fidgets and casts her eyes about, "Paul, I can't seem to find my glasses."

He turns and sights them, "Here they are, Gram." He steps over and hands them to her. "Hid behind the red box they were."

"Thank you, Paul…and one more favor. Would you fetch that quilt off my bed? I'm feeling a chill, even here by the stove."

He quietly nods and goes to her bedroom while she slowly rises from the rocker and stands. Returning shortly, he drapes the quilt over the back rocker, quill lining facing up. She shuffles close, grips the armrests to steady herself then eases down, dropping the last few inches to the seat.

"There now, that's better," she sighs, wrapping her arms and shoulders. The old quilt has covered her bed since she was a girl, sewn by her mother, of variegated pattern and color, every stitch a memory like in her mind and on the tree. "Thank you, Paul. I just may sleep here in the chair tonight…help my old stomach keep the soup down."

"Can fix you some tea?" he offers. "Them red berries you like?"

"Oh yes, the sumac…that would be nice. I would like that."

While he fills the kettle and sets it on the stove to heat, she lightly tips her rocker, reaches for the paper and lays it on her lap. She adjusts her glasses, words coming clear like on that long ago night, read it so many times she knew it by heart. Hears his voice again so fresh and bold speaking through her mind till she barely needs read a word…

"These are perilous times for the farmer, debtor, and small merchant, for artisans, mechanics, and workers all across this land. The opportunities granted you following the War in opening the west and settling the plains rudely yanked away like cloth from under a table setting, spilling every promise to the ground. England, whose yoke we once threw off, returns, investing heavily in railroads, timber, mines, and lands throughout the west. While their cohorts on Wall Street and The Chicago Exchange tangle all in a web of debt, draining our lifeblood, choking our breath.

"I point to the Coinage Act of 1873 — nay, the Crime of '73! — passed by sleight of hand, even Grant had no idea what he signed. Snuck it through like a cat creeping in the night, or better yet, a snake wrapping all in a coil of debt! How? By demonetizing silver — the People's Money since 1792 — its value now halved as is the worth of your labor and toil, likewise your wheat, corn, and beef bring only a fraction of their former price. Yet your debts double. Interest, taxes, freight charges take their pound of flesh and leave you with crumbs to nibble. Thereby England, on the Gold Standard since 1844, and her Tory allies, the Vanderbilts, Harrimans, and Morgans, aim to beggar the world and you!

"Robbery and worse! A chorus of thieves runs the railways and rules the cities, bilking the farmer from field to market, paying a dime and selling for a dollar. These Goldbugs would have you sit a toadstool in hope to hatch a leprechaun then point to the rainbow's end where they sprinkle a glittery dust, a trifle. But the dust that burns your eyes blows from droughty fields and vain effort while they laugh and feast.

"Always and finally remember this: they've halved your worth and doubled your debt to bend to their will. The Captains of Finance claim that gold is the sole rational means to resolve transaction and pay what's owed. They descend into endless detail of ratio and percentage, graphed and footnoted to obscure their ends, to tire and tame you into submission. The Devil not only has a subtle tongue, but works a subtle math.

"So skip the detail, this dust they throw in your eyes, and know that since the Crime of '73 you have been robbed of half your worth, your pockets picked of your rightful fruit and labor. Looking on, the powers that be, both Republican and Democrat, shake their heads and wring their hands at what can be done. Don't let them wash their hands of you. Remember, they are your servants, are they not? Then urge them, nay, demand that they change their platforms, write legislation and pass laws that serve your interest and not the Gilded few. And if they will not heed your just anger then we should form a third party, a People's Party, come together and act.

"First, repeal the Crime of '73 and restore silver! Give it parity! Overnight prices of wheat, corn, and beef will increase. No longer shackled to gold, debts will be more easily paid. Sure, the wealth hogs will howl at the layer of fat cut from their carcass, but the many will cheer! Next, we should nationalize railroads so they serve and are paid for by all. Finally, and perhaps most importantly, we should give women the vote. Many of you fought in the recent war to preserve the Union and thereby freed the slaves. And now that they have say, how can we deny the same to our mothers, wives, and daughters? It's high time we give them equal voice and the right to vote!

"I am but one, and admittedly I have much to learn. But I have traveled this great land from coast to coast, seen its mountains, rivers, and cities, and met many people of different views. I write from what I have gleaned. Of all the people I've come to know there are none more diligent and deserving than the good folks of the beautiful White Rock Valley of north-central Kansas, here in the nation's heartland. And here I choose to stake my claim and raise my voice on your behalf in fight for greater justice and equity to improve the lot of all. Respectfully, H.R. Corbett..."

"Hagan R..." quietly sounded his name as I read and reread his proclamation late into the night. No, didn't know what the 'R' stood for as yet, didn't know many things, but by dawn I had memorized the entire page and rushed downstairs to share it. Anxious for Glen to see it too, I held off till the noon-day meal. Shortly after eating and clearing the dishes away, I handed father the paper and said, "This is the new one, *The Prairie Advocate*. Like you, he says that railroads are nothing but thieves and robbers."

"Hmmm…" he took it in hand and glanced down while Glen piped up, "Hang the railroads! That's my two cents 'n ain't read a blame word. Ought to do like the James boys 'n rob 'em right back. 'Cept out here there's sad little timber to hide in!"

Father swiftly seconded the notion, "Yep, ought to 'n dern tempted. But what the hay, guess I'll read this instead…" he laid the paper to the table, leaned to his elbows and focused line to line, gave an occasional nod. Finally he straightened up and laced his hands behind his head, mulling his thoughts as he spoke, "Got to give this Corbett fellow credit. He does seem to know a thing or two." Then he squinted an eye to me and asked, "Don't suppose you've met him?"

"Only briefly…to buy the paper."

"Oh…?"

"But he wouldn't take a nickel. Just gave me one free."

"You don't say," father noted in widening smile.

Then Glen cut in, "Bet he's short 'n pudgy, ain't he?"

"No he isn't! He's taller than you and —" Fearing I'd betrayed myself, I checked my tone and feigned indifference. "Some might say he's rather nice looking."

Glen popped his knuckles and grinned, "Actually I hear he's right handsome 'n handy with his fists."

"How do you know?" I stood astonished, mouth slacked in surprise.

"Holly, she told me all last night."

"Last night…?" My turn to insinuate.

"Uh, evening…yesterday evening," he corrected sheepishly, hurrying his words, "had us a little social. Like Uncle Pat she hates crowds, takes her buckboard to Mankato for supplies most Fridays. Some women in the general store were a'gabbin', one calls her over 'n asks, 'You hear 'bout your neighbor north? That Briar girl? Why, yesterday she was attacked by a drifter in the Oakvale livery. Lucky that new editor happened by and gave the bum a lickin'. They say he's a mite radical, but handsome 'n gallant all the same. And you know most girls would've wilted, attacked like that. But that Briar girl, they say she just scooped up that bum's vomit 'n tossed it out. Rid of him to the last spit, they heard her say…'

"To the last spit," Glen affirmed while father beamed, "Mighty proud of you, Sadie, mighty proud…" And my eyes did tear hearing that and remembering the terror of being seized. But again I did not weep or wilt, wiped my eyes and held steady, basking in their good humor and warm praise.

Until Glen teased, "So? Don't suppose you like this Corbett fella some?"

"No!" my answer came too abrupt and emphatic, like I'd been found out, exposed. But it was not 'liking' I felt, it was something else, something more. And it frightened me nearly as much as being seized.

"That's enough from you two," mother stepped in and gave me a hug. "You did fine, Sadie, just fine. And we're all very proud."

"Yes 'n damn grateful too," father said. "Like to meet this Corbett 'n thank him myself. Till then, though he advocates for silver, to spur his cause 'n gain us a paper he might could use this" — he slapped a 5-dollar gold piece to the table.

Glen rose from his chair and rustled a coin from his vest pocket, eyed it a moment and said, "Was savin' this back for my watch chain, but so goes the aim of mice 'n men," then slapped it down beside father's. "Best double up 'n make it a Double Eagle, 'cause we're twice grateful. But mind you, Sadie…" he lowered his eyes to mine, "when you meet with this fella, you mind he behaves a gentleman."

Hesitant, uncertain, yet grateful for their concern and assurance, I quietly gripped the coins and clasped them to my breast. At this point it seemed they knew my feelings better than I myself.

It was midweek before I again ventured to his shop. Though I'd seen him once passing the livery, doubt he even noticed me working in the shadowed interior. And standing at his door, hesitant, clutching the coins from father and Glen, I summoned my courage, took a deep breath and entered. Startled by the bell I stood head up and wild-eyed like a frightened deer as he turned on the tall stool in front of his type cases.

"Why, Miss Sadie Briar," he smiled, "what a pleasant surprise."

"Mr. Corbett," I nodded, greeting him in turn, gripping the coins in wonder of how to present them as he removed his hat and stood. In laying his type stick to the counter, the bent ring finger of his right hand caught my eye.

"Did you break that in the fight?" I asked.

"No, not recently, long ago, now mended," he answered, nimbly flexing his hand. "In my earlier days, you see, to supplement my income, I fought a number of bareknuckle bouts. But at the sensible age of 28, other than a chance fisticuff, I only engage in gloved matches, a more gentlemanly sport. And do so but seldom."

To which I faintly smiled, not knowing what to say.

"So…" he tapped the counter, waiting, "what brings you to the den of the wicked wordsmith, as my rivals claim?"

"Oh, you are not wicked. Those are fine strong words you wrote. Father thinks so, my brother too. And they want…would like to buy a subscription" — offering the coins in my open palm, I asked, "Will this be enough?"

"That will do nicely," he said and gently took them from my hand. "Only hope my words are worthy of their generosity."

I blushed at his touch and quickly explained, "They would've paid themselves, but we live some distance…on the Limestone. Their next trip to town they hope to meet you. Mother as well…they all want to meet you."

"I would be honored," he said. "And really, you may call me Hagan, if you like." Reading my hesitance, he added pleasantly, "Forgive me, Miss Briar, if I sound forward. I come from many places and meet many people. Perhaps it is not proper for a school girl to address an unwed man by his first name."

"I will graduate next spring," I announced, asserting my maturity. "I and two young men will be the first to graduate high school in Oakvale."

"That is truly commendable, Miss Briar, my compliments."

"Then I may attend university…in Manhattan or Lawrence. But…in these uncertain times, as you say, money is tight."

"That it is, and will likely worsen. The market at its peak, prices set to fall, given drought and debt, at the slightest tremor encumbered farms will drop like ripe fruit into the hands of speculators waiting to snatch the spoils."

"Father and Glen own our land," I declared proudly. "And owe no debt."

"Good for them. I hope they maintain their status. But many are caught, trapped, close to busted. Folks further west are already pulling up stakes, heading back east by the thousands, hungry, desperate, so I have many issues to address and a mountain of type to set. And you, your studies. But wait…" he reached under the counter and handed me a book. "Here, you may enjoy this. It's by a Frenchman, Jules Verne. A fantastic tale of men who journey from the earth to the moon and back in a capsule shot from a cannon."

"Is such a thing possible?"

"Not just yet. But take electricity. A few decades ago, all theory and mystery, now it lights the night and sends the human voice over great distances. X-rays can read bones through the living flesh. And as surely as men worked and breathed underwater in diving bells to build the Brooklyn Bridge, they will one day walk on the moon. Once dreamed, all is possible. So dream, read, and do. Now good day, Miss Briar…" he abruptly raised his hat and tipped it to me.

I simply nodded and left, clutching the book, feeling a bit slighted as if dismissed, yet pleased I'd delivered the coins and expressed gratitude without inviting familiarity. Fooling no one but myself, I suppose, for his touch set my flesh tingling and my thoughts reeled. Nevertheless, when tempted to say his name, I did not. And for a time we remained Miss Briar and Mr. Corbett.

A week or so later father and Glen did ride into Oakvale to thank him, as I learned stopping by the Advocate before returning home. When I entered, he greeted me with a smile and said, "Miss Briar, I met your father and brother yesterday, Pat and Glen, both fine strong men, of a cut I admire. As thanks, they gave me this," he held up a bottle set nearby and proclaimed, "Old Kentucky! And a fine brew it is. Like Glen joked, 'It ain't ol' rotgut I've sipped in cowboy saloons, stuff worse'n coffin varnish, I swear…' We had a good laugh over that and as you can see, sampled a fair portion while we bantered and traded views. Mainly on anti-fencers out west and down into Texas still lamenting the loss of the open range, and we agreed they'll stand fierce a day then fold to the bitter fact of things. Like your father said, 'Admit, it's damned hard work, fencin'…but sure beats finding your cattle froze in a drift 50 miles yonder…' And I just might quote him on that in the future. Yes, I do believe so, Miss Briar…" In leaving, I smiled to him, proud he'd found them worthy men, and father's words worthy as well.

Later that evening, arriving home, father told me of their visit with Mr. Corbett.

"Yep, walked right in, each shook his hand 'n thanked him. He's got a firm grip, Mr. Corbett. For a young fellow he's sure set foot in lots of places. Thinks deep, and unlike some thinkers, seems to know the lay of things. What can 'n can't be. Yes sir," he added vaguely, "think he'll do."

"Do what?" I asked.

"Oh, just say I'm grateful, Sadie," casting me a kindly look, "grateful he's hereabout to keep an eye on things." Then he smiled and went to chore.

Other than that, week to week, on through autumn little changed except the color of the leaves and grasses. Some days warm, some brought a chill. While all three weeklies came out on Thursday, I waited till Friday to fetch my copy, and kept my visits brief and cordial. Though I looked forward to catching his smile and gladly shared mine. Then the day before Thanksgiving, as I tightened the cinch on Patches, preparing to ride home for the holiday, he walked into the livery and surprised me.

"Brought this issue out a day early, Miss Briar," he said, handing me a folded copy. "I wanted you to have one since I'm closing up early to board the train for Dallas this evening. I'll be gone a week, maybe two. Charles Macune, a leader in the Southern Alliance, is forming a Farmer's Exchange, cooperative effort to beat back these Country Stores that bleed the farmer nearly as badly as Company Stores bleed the miner. While they grow more cotton and less corn and wheat down south, our interests do overlap and I want to see what's brewing, so to speak."

"I imagine so…" I allowed faintly, baffled by the swirl of issues, admitting, "I know little of such things."

"No shame in that. There's always more to learn, for all of us. And I hope your father and others will forgive next week's lapsed copy, as I aim to follow with a double issue upon my return…relating events and any promise thereof."

"Yes…well…father always looks forward to reading."

"Good, that's good to hear, Miss Briar." He glanced to the near stall then back to me and said, "There's something more personal, a favor I'd like to ask…" again looking to the stall, "That black there…he's my horse. His name is Blood."

"Blood?" I answered, curious of the name and the pending request.

"Yes, of uncertain pedigree, but definitely has blood. Quite spirited for a gelding and tends to go wild if not ridden every few days. So, as a favor, I was hoping you might ride him once or twice in my absence. If you're willing?"

"Blood…" I whispered softly, walking to his stall as he raced his head to my hand and let me stroke his neck and mane. "Blood, "I repeated then answered, "Yes, it would be my pleasure…Hagan" — at last saying his name, I felt strengthened and relaxed.

"Pleased to hear that, Sadie," he smiled, "truly pleased. And I know you can handle him. I saw that dog attack your horse last week. You held steady, reined about and sent the dog packing. An admirable bit of horsemanship," he observed, eyeing Blood and me, "Seems you two are prior acquainted?"

"Yes…Blood and I have been friends for a while now."

"Good, now that you know his name…and mine. There's one thing, Sadie. Be forewarned, that incident, you and the dog, is included in the current issue. What we call in the news trade 'an item', a little story of local interest to entertain and draw the reader. So, like it or not, Sadie, you're in the news…"

With that he bid me "Good day" and went to board the train, leaving me stunned, exposed, elated. Tempted to read it then and there, instead I tucked it in my saddlebag and rode home, heart throbbing, anxious, uncertain, but thrilled to be an item penned by the hand of Hagan Corbett. All that evening I said nothing, hid it away through supper then rushed upstairs and lit my lamp. I sat a moment then slowly unfolded *The Prairie Advocate*. Beneath the large header, the first item in the upper left column read:

"Local Girl Wards Off Another Attack! Last Friday while calmly riding out of town on her weekly journey home, Miss Sadie Briar, an Oakvale High School senior, drew the vicious attack of a mangy cur that set her horse to bucking. But she took heart, held her seat like a bronc-buster, spun her mount and sent the cur yelping, tail between its legs. What a splendid display of horsemanship by a spirited young lady! And we should draw inspiration, indeed, all of us need to bring that same fierce fight to our politics to defend our freedoms and fruits thereof, remembering the vital words of Old Hickory, another fierce soul who for whatever his faults, sums it best, 'Equity for all, privilege for none!' And the same holds for Goldbug or mangy cur..."

⁓ ❦ ⁓

Returning to Oakvale by noon Sunday, I unsaddled Patches, stowed my bags in the corner, and immediately saddled Blood. Still in my riding skirt, I mounted up. No, not so bold as Holly Hazelin to wear my pants but this time I loosened my hair and let it flow long and free like Blood's mane and tail as we galloped north out of town. Now an item in more ways than one, riding Hagan's horse, and I didn't care who saw. I set my heels and leaned low, letting him run through a mile or more, releasing his spirit, sensing his reach and surge, matching his rhythm to mine, attune to breath and pulse.

Mindful of his wind, I reined back and eased him to a cantor and a short distance thereon we halted before the cabin where I was born. The roof sagged over the north wall staved in, the whole falling to ruins next to a fine frame house, empty as well, the screen door torn, hanging ajar. Evidence of yet another family that had pulled up stakes. A sign tacked to the porch read: For Sale, 320 acres, house and barn, for details see A.W. McCloud, Oakvale Land Office.

I reined away, feeling robbed, wronged, my memories sullied, and headed down across the dry creek bed, not a pool of water, only rocks and sunbaked mud crunching under shod hooves. Then we rode on over the hill southwest and descended to the site of the old Callaway place. Nothing left now except the graves fenced off against grazing cattle. I dismounted and lashed my reins to a post, opened the gate and stood gazing at the graves all level with the prairie, fresh headstones in place of the old. Father and Glen had traded several steers as payment-in-kind to an Oakvale stonecutter to carve each name and year of birth — the year of death all the same, 1869, except for Liam, ten years thereon. My kin, and having known only one, I focused on Liam's stone and grave. His bones and mine the same, yet his blood no longer stirred and I heard no voice beyond the wind rustling the leaves yet to fall, speaking of lost, uncertain things. Listening, cast in a spell of warm Indian summer, I felt that gone life flow from them to me then down Oak Creek to the White Rock and over the rolling hills to the Limestone. From that moment certain I'd live my life in that flow; that they underground like the old Indian on the hill had a hold, a claim that I neither could nor cared to shake.

A week passed, and midway through the next, choring after school, I noticed Blood's stall was empty and knew Hagan had returned. Out on business I supposed, hanging up my pitchfork, nearly finished when Hagan rode in.

He swung down with a big smile and said, "Sadie, you tended him well, thank you. He's never handled better." Then he asked, "You did run him, didn't you?"

"Yes, twice…" I answered shyly, surprised to see him, "once to the future and once to the past…" Spoken without thinking, relieved he did not ask my meaning as he simply gave a nod and allowed, "Well, that's quite a range. And I thank you again."

As I reached for the reins to lead Blood to his stall, Hagan intercepted my hand, "No, no," he said, "you've done quite enough. I better tend him a spell else he'll forsake me for you. For you are most adorable to horse and man…" He held my eyes and gently released my hand.

Before he dare say more I asked, "Your trip to Dallas? Did you learn much?"

"Yes, learned a great deal. The co-op is a grand idea. A mite too grand perhaps, like the man himself. I sense Macune harbors ambitions beyond the cause, has an eye on Washington and sees the Alliance as a stepping stone rather than a path to walk or row to hoe. But with or without him, given cash flow, the co-op may succeed. Much hinges on the fate of the Sub-treasury Plan now being hatched. A notion that…" Hagan fell silent as Blood turned his head to my hand and observed, "Seems you've already won him over."

"Oh, he just remembers our rides," I said, fondly rubbing his nose and forelock. "But you were saying...about Dallas?"

"Dallas, yes..." he gazed off briefly to gather his thoughts. "Broadly speaking, the Southern Alliance has strong organization and good leaders, particularly Leonidas Polk from Carolina, who edits *The Progressive Forum*. Overall, they have a better grip and more discipline than the Northern Alliance headed by Milton George, Jay Burrow and others I've met who have heart but less spine. So for the long pull, I expect that Kansas, Nebraska, and states out west will hitch their wagons to the Southern Alliance. The main weakness that I see, and like Achilles, self-inflicted, carried within, is what they call 'The Negro problem.'"

"The Coloreds? Why is that?" I asked. "Are they causing problems?"

"Only to whites, North and South, who hate to see them rise and aim to keep them down."

"But there was a war...emancipation? There are laws...can't something be done?"

"Very little, an issue that I fear will plague us far beyond our time."

And I knew he was right, recalling the circus shootout, people seldom mentioned the chief culprit, the white drifter "Buckshot," but never tired of cursing "Big Muddy," out of prison, having served his two years, who some would still lynch if given the chance.

"You see, Sadie, unlike money matters such as gold and silver, grain prices, interest and railroad rates, which can change and will, race and religion are set like rocks in most people. Like the Rockies, once risen, impossible to move. Sure, we can plant cities and settlements, carve new pathways for commerce and travel, even brave a few inroads of thought. But the Rockies remain. Down South the gains made under Grant were stripped away when Hayes withdrew Federal troops. Closed the door and made a devil's bargain. And when you dance with the devil, he names the tune. Again, freedmen are no longer so, and if not quite enslaved, theirs is a beggars' democracy. If they raise their voice, they are silenced...or worse. Most live in shanties, ill-fed and ragged clothes, scorned like lepers, or Untouchables in Hindustan. Yet we strive for a better world, and if we touch the underbelly of such, we've done some good, perhaps..."

His doubtful smile defined him as I was to learn. For all his energy, effort and ideals, he knew that old blood coursed strong like rivers, determining ends and means, and seldom abides our druthers. Much of what he told me there in the livery formed the gist of his next column, focused mainly on the Southern Alliance and the potential of a farmers' co-op, all given a positive slant. Of race and religion, however, he made no mention, only alluding to the Rockies, their majestic mute presence, indifferent to all yet offering resource, inspiration, and challenge for those who would struggle to ascend and touch the underbelly of creation. The darker aspect of things he summed in an aphorism set off in the lower right-hand column: *Of our knowledge so dearly gleaned, the bulk goes to utility, a mere speck to understanding by which all pivots and turns...*

XIV. Voice & Vote

Flesh cold, feet numb, she feels life ebbing drip by drip like the leaky faucet and asks herself why she still breathes as Paul, finished hanging the tinsel, hands her a cup of red-berry tea, nicely steeped. She takes it gingerly in both hands, savors a sip then sets it aside. Refreshed, she watches Paul fold his letter to Santa, a few words in jagged scrawl, then bending to the stove he adds a log and feeds the letter to the flames. He closes the door and gazes up the stovepipe where the letter rises through the chimney then off to the North Pole.

"Did you send your Christmas wish?" she asks.

"Yes'um," he answers, "Asked Santa to keep Gram here" — the same request for many years running. She nods vaguely and they sit quietly admiring the tree. Simply waiting, it seems, the last ornament yet to hang clutched warm beneath the quilt next to her heart, deeply personal and tragic. Is this my last task, she wonders, to remember?

Glistening snow ushered in the year 1888, gently blanketing droughty fields and pastures, briefly raising spirits. Like carolers' voices soon muted by the howling wind. As Hagan predicted, prices fell with the thermometer. Wheat at 50 cents a bushel only paid the farmer two bits after shipping then dropped to the lower teens, then to mere pennies. "Lends new meaning to Penny Dreadful, don't it?" became a common joke as debt mounted, threatening farm payments and prospects all around. With hard times the issues Hagan addressed gained traction, his subscriptions doubled, then tripled. Money tight, he accepted payment-in-kind, eggs, milk, firewood, a smoked ham or baked pie, and earned most of his cash doing job printing for bulletins, handbills, legal notices, or sales postings like the one I'd seen at our old home site. But the Advocate remained his prime focus and passion. He even hired a boy, Ian Winchell, youngest son of the slain blacksmith, to deliver papers and tack up notices around Oakvale. A bright boy, Ian was soon learning to set type.

By midwinter Alliance literature was flowing in from other parts of the state and nation. Various speakers passing through addressed civic groups, Grangers, and railroad workers, drawing disaffected Democrats and Republicans alike, shaking the platforms of both major parties, demanding new policy voiced and formed by the people. And Hagan threaded in and out of each gathering, interweaving ideas, framing the argument while here and there adding a humorous item or cryptic note.

We met intermittently at the livery or print shop, our exchanges polite, increasingly familiar, perhaps a warm smile or chance touch that set my flesh tremoring like a softly tapped bell. At my demurral he'd defer and pivot to other matters, often lending me a book — *Les Miserables* by Hugo or *The Narrative Life of Frederick Douglass* — speaking briefly of each, ever busy, active, putting out another issue or giving Ian another pointer on setting type. By and by rumors arose that while gathering the news he also gathered women. This voiced within my hearing by other girls no doubt jealous of his attention. I feigned indifference and said nothing, thought it likely and only natural that a vigorous attractive man would attract women. Whatever the case, he behaved a gentleman to me and kept his womanizing discreetly distanced in Red Cloud or Mankato.

And one day I met his fellow carouser, also rumored of, when they entered the livery like a gust of wind, each with an arm over the other's shoulder, obvious they'd been drinking. Hagan doffed his hat and said,

"Pardon the intrusion, Miss Briar…" oddly formal in the moment, "I do confess we've shared a pint."

"Awe, just a nip or two agin' the cold," the other growled amiably, a big burly man sporting a wool flat cap on his curly red hair, his broad mustache red as well.

"Hah, with one nip this lug empties a bottle!" Hagan laughed and said, "Sadie, meet my oldest and truest friend, Maximus Ross. Maxie, meet Miss Sadie Briar."

"Aye, Maxie, ah am," the other took over, fogging the air with his deep brogue and breath, "Come to Mankater in November, ah did. All the way from ol' Philadelph. This pug," he slapped Hagan's back, "sends a wire 'n says, 'Come, tis beautiful country!' Had me doubts, ah swear, till laid eyes on thee, me lass. Aye, tis beautiful indeed."

"Don't embarrass her, Maxie. This is a stable, but she is a lady."

"Ah said no other…"

"Don't let him worry you, Sadie. He may sound rough, especially given a cup, but deep down he's tender and poetic."

"Tender? Why ah've pulled ye outa many a' scrap, ah have!"

"Really, I don't mind," I smiled to steady things. Nor did I mind, more curious than offended, I asked, "Truly, what brings you all the way from Philadelphia to Kansas?"

"Twas a wild notion," he said, crinkling his lively blue eyes, "one o' many. Ah works railroad, see, some years now. 'N Hagan here, he did say, 'Come!' Ah has me con-nections, so works the switches 'n lands a job in Mankater. Section boss thar to Marysville 'n tend the spur t' here. Did so today. Lines the track, ah does," he raised a clenched fist, "aye, 'n lines the men. Takes a few knocks 'n all runs smooth. Aye," he repeated relaxing his hand, "had me doubts, ah did, till meetin' you, Miss Sadie…then, like that" — he snapped his finger — "all me doubts are gone. Now," he said, shifting to Hagan, "ah'll be havin' the full snort ya promised 'fore boardin' to Mankater…"

With that, still locked shoulder to shoulder, they gave a slight bow, wheeled about and exited in gibe and josh. While I stood wondering at what had blown in — friends in contrast, one gallant and dashing, the other, Maxie, bullish and rough. But charming, and I liked his big red-faced smile.

My thoughts stewed and stirred as winter shed its icy crust and warmed into spring, veering by the moment from the past to the present to the future, attempting to divine my place and path. Mother and father squeezed pennies into dimes, Glen as well, to help me toward university. I'd yet to share my misgivings, my change of plans. But what plans? Beyond Hagan, his mystery, all else paled, and I feared my heart's pull, helpless to resist, dancing a dance old and recurrent as spring.

Easter Sunday, I stood at the old Indian's grave, looking down on my home, the creek and farm, while scenes from my youth folded into the land like hands in prayer. But turning west to where the sun passed and set each day, all stretched before my arms too vast and distant to embrace. Unlike the past that dimmed, ever receding, what lay ahead remained untouched, unknown, and unnamed. The rock-post fence faded to the horizon. I looked to the grave in wonder of the kitten doll — was it a token of life taken and returned? What was expected of me? Were we all fragments of them to come and them now gone? Standing beneath the endless sky, I sensed no answers, only the barbed wire humming in the wind.

My thoughts settled on an essay assigned to the seniors soon to graduate, our general theme, "Pioneer Days," to be both written and given orally, and judged by the editors of the Oakvale weeklies. No need to slight the Thinker, over winter he'd packed up his press and moved on, "To undermine other souls!" many claimed, including Mrs. Jensen who bid him "Good riddance!" But father and I missed his quirky little page, as did Hagan. And my essay was inspired in part by Hagan's recent column on Frederick Douglass's speech at a Women's Suffrage convention in New York that spring where he'd urged women to lead the fight and advised men to "Give her fair play and hands off!"

Of course I did not win, gaining only one vote, Hagan's. First prize went to Calder Elwell for his moving account of an uncle shot and left for dead in an early Indian raid. Hearing shots, his brothers arrived within minutes and found him still breathing. They made a litter of the cabin door and carried him miles to the nearest town, only to watch him bleed to death later that night. One of many tragedies among early settlers and rightly favored by his listeners. I too could have touched their hearts with my family's story, told of Katy's abduction, of Lily and the others slaughtered, left for Liam and Glen to bury. Or told of the baby swapped by a savage for a basket of kittens, though hearing which many would have suspected Satan's hand at play. While it was generally known that Sarah Briar and her child had been spared in the raid, whether by chance or grace of God, none but my family knew the full truth of that encounter with the very Indian buried on our hill. That mystery and those deep wounds would remain our own.

Instead, I spoke to the moment, titled my essay, "Grant Women the Vote," which opened with a quote from Frederick Douglas, *"I would join with anybody to do right and with nobody to do wrong..."* Before that assembly of students, teachers, townsfolk, the judges and my family, my first words quivered forth, but drawing courage from mother, father, and Glen, their quiet smiles, and Hagan keenly attentive to each word, my voice soon steadied and strengthened:

"True, it was mostly men," I granted, "who went forth and traded gunfire with the hostiles, who sank the plow and broke the sod. But women, too, stood steadfast, loaded their rifles, bound their wounds, and cleaned and dressed the dead. They bucketed water, washed clothes in lye, calloused their hands planting seeds and tender shoots, constantly growing, gathering and preparing food…giving birth, often dying, seldom complaining, all while taxing their bodies without voice or vote. Though yes, this past year Kansas women did gain the right to vote in city elections, by which they helped re-elect Mayor Morgan. But this is neither full vote nor full voice. So I say, pioneering never ends and courage is needed each day. We fight today for suffrage, a word that discomforts many listening, as it did King George in 1776 and more recently the Southern Bourbons. The discomfort of guilt, knowing they have long denied others equal voice, for which women still struggle and pioneer.

"Finally, as a woman, I say this…" and I glanced briefly to Hagan in more subtle, personal appeal, "to whoever man I may one day wed, vow to love, honor, and obey, then join my body with his to make one flesh, I say yes…if he vows to cherish, hold, and forsake all others. But do unto others and grant to others what is granted you. If all men are created equal, and all are certainly born of women, how can she be less than thee?"

I left the question hanging and concluded with a brief poem:

Cannot she who rocks the cradle, knits and mends have say
like he who plows and plants, harvests grain and mows the hay?
Why must the voice that lullabies the babe asleep,
beg pardon, wait on, and ask to speak?
Women too have heart and mind and raise our heads in hope
that if not prayer, then reason, may one day affirm our vote!

While I didn't win the prize, I won the applause. Women initially, then given a nudge, the men joined in clapping their hands with franks smiles and scattered hurrahs. Stunned in the moment of exhilaration, my young heart beat certain that after 40 years of suffrage, the sacred Biblical number, women would surely achieve the vote, perhaps in time for the presidential election that fall? Little did I suspect it would take another 32 years before the 19th Amendment came to pass, finally allowing mother and I to vote in 1920. Yet many things were about to happen, my life soon to change.

Mr. Jensen, sitting in the front row with his wife, was the first to step forth and shake my hand, "You made a grand speech, Sadie. Don't think I'll let you muck stalls any longer, no…" Though I smiled and thanked him, hearing that made me a little sad, for I'd always enjoyed my time with the Hwinums. Even Mrs. Jensen had a kind word, along with others lining up to extend their regards to all three graduates. Our essays concluded, we were each presented our diploma.

Amid the confusion of voices and faces, mother appeared, clasped my hand and drew me aside, "I'm so proud of you, Sadie." Overjoyed, near to tears at her touch, I merely smiled and cast my eyes about in search of father and Glen. "They're over this way," she said, leading me through the milling crowd. I spied them along the wall near the door, father and Glen leaning in to share some quip with Hagan at which they reared back and laughed then quieted at my approach.

Glen was the first to speak, "Duchess, you really kicked up the dust. Better'n a bronc-bustin'. You sure got my vote!" This made me laugh as father beamed, "Mine too, Sadie, those were quality words, like you, nothing shoddy, no. Even Mr. Corbett, our wordsmith, says so."

"That's right, Miss Briar, sterling, first rate anywhere on any day. Once you've seen your family off, I'd like you to stop by the Advocate, if you would…and please, bring your essay…"

I simply nodded slightly puzzled by their combined look, as if they were privy to something I was yet to learn. After seeing my parents and Glen to their carriage, out of habit I paused by the entrance to the livery and peered in. Mr. Jensen saw and shooed me off with a laugh, "Now you git, you've got better things waitin'…" It seemed he knew something as well.

I went to my room to freshen up, gathered my essay and walked to the Advocate, flush with excitement, anticipation, like an aerialist about to leap and grasp a handhold. Hagan stood waiting on the boardwalk out front. He opened the door and bade me enter. He hung his hat on a hook and asked for my essay. He skimmed it briefly then tapped the pages and said, "This is good, very good. I should like to print it. And I think we could work it up and send it out as ready copy. Under your name, Sadie Briar. And likewise, your poem. I know other papers that would gladly print it…the Vincent brothers in Winfield for one. From which you will earn a modest fee."

"I…I only wrote what I thought and felt."

"Exactly, and that's the key to writing. The boy's essay was worthy, but typical. Yours was stellar. It struck the heart and ear of each listener. Even those who would disagree were roused. You have talent, Sadie, as I suspected. That kind of writing cannot be taught, only honed and crafted. I know you've had your eye on attending university, as you should, and I would not dissuade you. But I spoke with your parents and have their permission to offer you a job for the summer. It's not much money, but enough to help defray your future school expenses. Or, should you wish, you can stay on, write copy and learn the entire printing business. As your father said, 'That's up to Sadie. She's her mother's daughter and has her own mind.' So, no need to rush, think it over, you can have the job for the summer, or beyond. That's up to you."

"Well I…I should like to learn. And I think…I should like to stay."

In answer I felt I'd grasped my handhold as he took my hand in his and said, "Come, let me show you the ropes. There's much to learn but don't let it overwhelm you. This strange contraption is the Liberty printer, what we call 'the Jobber.' We use it for job-printing…handbills, flyers, bulletins and the like. Back here stands our trusty workhorse, a model 1880 Washington hand-press…the mainstay for small newspapers since the 1840s. And over here," still gripping my hand he showed me to the type bench where I'd often seen him at work, "is where we set the type for the galley, thence to the form. But first…" he noted, placing a rectangular device in my palm, "we use this, a printer's stick, on which we select type and compose each line, using the longest line to determine the width of the column, gradually adding to the whole. And all must be done in reverse, as I've been teaching Ian. These upper cases," he drew open the top drawer, "hold larger type for headers, capitals and such. And these lower ones contain various small letters and symbols. To be honest, setting type is tedious, and again, all must be done in reverse, every letter, word, and line. But a necessary drudgery to an exciting result. Always a thrill to see a story you've gathered, composed, completed, and printed out…ever mindful of the old verities, who, what, when, where, why, and how. For ours is the search for truth, near and far. And it all happens back here at the Washington press where we carefully place the galley in the form and lock it in with spacers and fillers we call 'furniture.' Then we take the brayer and roll on the ink, lay out a fresh page, crank the tray under the platen, then pull this lever and press it home. Each fresh sheet of print is like magic, a drama, a trace of life to delight the mind and eye. And I can teach you all…if you wish."

"Yes, Hagan…I do wish."

"Then there's something more. I think it's no secret I've been courting you. And I confess, I've wooed women, but never courted…till now. You are different, special, an intriguingly difficult young woman to know. Today I asked your father's permission to court you. He just grinned and said, 'Well, again, that's up to Sadie. But I should warn you, she was once nabbed by a wild Indian 'n he gave her back in a blink…' I swear, he nearly had me convinced, then you appeared and we all laughed."

"That was not a joke."

"You mean…he wasn't pulling my leg?"

"No, and that he told you means he trusts you."

"Then it happened. But how…when?" he grasped my hand in wonder and question.

"Will you promise to never make it a story or item in your paper?"

"Yes, you have my word, Sadie. It will never be printed nor spoken of by me."

"Then you surely know that Glen's family, the Callaways, was massacred while he and his brother Liam had gone hunting with my father. All part of Oakville lore. But that same morning, three warriors surprised my mother at our cabin. She signed to them and offered food. One entered the cabin and ate. Then grabbed me from my cradle and walked out. She ran after with a basket of kittens and demanded he swap. He coldly did so then bashed their heads against a tree, tied them to his saddle and rode off.

"Some years later, after Liam died and Glen left for Colorado, we moved to the Limestone. The Indians were peaceful by then and occasionally they'd pass through along the pasture ridge east of our place. One day, the spring I turned 12, an old Indian showed up at our door with his wife and daughter and her baby boy. They signed for food. Mother fed them. Later I learned that it was he who'd nearly taken me. Then the following winter, just before Christmas, the old Indian returned. This time alone. We found him dying on the hill. He stared in a strange way, reached forth and touched my hand. Father buried him there in the cold wind and snow."

Hagan gently clasped my hand and searched my eyes.

"Now the hand touched by a savage, touches mine," he said. "Your story, sadly profound, yet marvelous and beautiful, like yourself. And since you bare your heart, I shall tell you something that no one, no one knows…" He released my hand, turned and gripped the press lever as if to steady his thoughts, looking from the past to me.

"Like my horse," he began, "I'm of uncertain pedigree. What they commonly term, a bastard. Never knew my father. My mother never said who or which one, a handsome devil, no doubt. She was an actress, beautiful, wooed by every leading man, rose of the limelight. Angeline Corbett. I took her name as she'd taken hers. The Corbetts were actors since Elizabethan times, perhaps before. Like the circus, the theater is a world apart, a new stage, new city, week to week, season to season. A life of greater freedom, joy and pain.

"I learned to read watching rehearsals, turning page to page…or seated on her lap, helping her recite her lines. I memorized every part, schooled by Shakespeare, Dumas, Goethe, Dunlap, Aikens…from *Hamlet* to *Faust* and *Uncle Tom's Cabin*. And for each new production the theater manager would write up the show date, name of play and actors to appear and send me to the print shop. I stood by, often for hours, observing the type set, the pages printed, then rush out and hand playbills to passersby, more fascinated by the printing and the activity in the street than the play being advertised and staged.

"Soon I was working as a newsboy, hawking papers on street corners, scrapping with other boys for a choice spot. And still small, age six, I lost more battles than I won. But in whatever city we landed, I kept scrapping and growing and soon held my own. In Baltimore, Boston, New York, Cincinnati, Denver, San Francisco and a dozen towns in between, I worked as printer's devil, like Ian. Till by age 12, my eyes and hands quick and able, I was a full-fledged typographer, working at *The Public Record* in Philadelphia where my mother appeared in a production that lasted two seasons. When she moved on with a new role, I stayed. By 15, hungry and eager, I was writing copy, reporting on horseraces, baseball, prizefights, crime, tragic death and murder with all the blood and thunder of theater, only real-life drama from the street.

"My first big story came three years later, the Railroad Strike of 1877. It started in West Virginia when the B&O, Baltimore and Ohio Railroad, cut wages for the third time that year. Workers struck, demanding they cancel the last pay cut. The Governor called out the National Guard, and when they refused to fire on the strikers, he asked for Federal troops. From there the strike spread to nearly all major cities. The most violent was in Philadelphia. Only this time the state militia did the Governor's bidding with 20 strikers killed, shot and bayonetted, and many more wounded.

"That's where I met Maxie, a young railroad worker, hurling rocks, tending the injured. Then the strikers struck back, burning hundreds of locomotives and boxcars, the depot and scores of other buildings, and another 20 workers shot dead. I too was caught up in the moment and ever since, a spreading drama I aim to write and stage to aid the fight for workers' justice…a fight that extends to the farmer. There are winds astir all across the nation, regions of promise ripe for change, none more fertile than here in the White Rock Valley…" He laid his hands to the print tray and repeated, "Right here lies the seedbed where we can plant a new politics that roots to the pioneering spirit that finally serves…the people. Good folks like your father and mother, and Glen.

"And you may wonder," he added, turning to me, "of all the places and cities I've seen, what drew me to Oakvale?" To my quiet nod, he continued, "Several years ago a story went out over the wire that caught my eye, concerning a shootout between a circus crew and citizens of a small Kansas town. Perhaps you were there?"

"Yes, the man killed was Ian's father. He was only a bystander."

"So I've lately learned. A sad, senseless death which I'd largely forgotten until recently, watching the Alliance movement spread through the south, mid-west, and the plains states, then rumor and instinct called me here. To the very scene of that tragic event, to a rural county beyond influence of any large town or city, where settlers who'd faced off Indians and hazards of nature now suffer the crush of prices, shipping rates, and debt while both major parties turn a blind eye. Last summer, on route from Denver to Kansas City, I got off in Mankato and rode the spur to Oakvale. I stayed several days, taking in the land and people, and sensed a vibrant pulse. Still, after arriving last fall and opening the shop, I had my doubts. Till the day I met a certain young lady in the livery." Once more he took my hand in his. "And now, Miss Sadie Briar, I've said a great deal, and you, very little. Are you still willing to join me?"

In answer I rose on my toes and kissed him. Our lips parted briefly, our tongues touched then I slipped away, savoring the taste of his breath on mine.

"Lovely," he smiled, "most succinct and lovely."

Fearing a full embrace would arouse me to passion, I quickly asked, "Your mother? What…became of her?"

His smile faded as he glanced off and said, "She died…of a disease common to actresses. Old age…only 36…I was 16. She'd returned to Philadelphia, having missed her brush with fame, losing a choice role to a younger woman and fearing she could no longer appeal to an audience or man. Loathe to do burlesque or comedy, one night she drank laudanum. The whole bottle, and drifted off in a dream. And there I leave her."

As I leaned to him the entrance bell rang and Ian rushed in, and all stopped, as if caught in a camera flash. Hagan immediately brightened and waved him forth. "Ian, my boy, come…we have work to do. And good news, Miss Briar will be joining us…"

XV. Courtship

Still clutching the lone remaining ornament, she sits in her rocker by the stove, capsuled in her quilt of memories. Paul sits thereby engrossed in the play of bubble lights and tinsel. She reaches for her tea; finding it barely warm, she sets it down.

Paul shifts in notice and asks, "Want me to warm it, Gram?"

"Yes, that would be fine…"

While he pours the tea back in the kettle and puts it on the stove to heat, her thoughts return to the past. To Hagan…like the sun, he radiated, inspiring all around him. I, the moon, reflected his light, and like the men there in orbit I revolved about his center. How we did reach for a time, aspiring, then fell…as all must, I suppose. Yet I would not trade my journey for any. Nor for theirs, those three brave men soon to descend…safely, I hope, and taste their moment's glory. But I'll be gone.

The wind moans low beyond the window and door; she hears the cry of a coyote echoed by another faint soul. Gone, gone, a frail note to the swirl of silence. No ache or memories, only ashes, a drift of smoke. But what of Paul, she wonders? How will he fare? For the world is both kind and unkind.

By his surprised smile upon entry Ian knew our courtship had begun. Many times thereafter he caught us embraced as we circled and waltzed ever closer to our fiery want. Not a week later Maxie too walked in, interrupting an intimate moment.

"Aw, a kiss it tis, the lad 'n his lass…as ah did suspect."

"Hold on, Maxie, I was just explaining the p's and q's of typesetting. Reversed, they're easily confused, then paper becomes *qaper* and no one pays the *qrinter*."

"Wha…? Ah'm no blind, tis lip to lip I saw. A kiss! Properly placed it was 'n tis the season 'o the birds 'n the bees. Hear 'em hummin' 'n singin'. But hang me, been a long day o' labor 'n hungry, ah am. Care to join me for a meal 'n a pint over to the Hotel? Ah'm buyin'. The lass is welcome too. What say ye, Sadie? A pint o' beer'll redden the rose o' yer cheeks…"

Now early June, I'd been working with Hagan for over a month, still rooming with the Jensens, yet skipped many evening meals, working past 8 learning to set type, among other tasks. So I was happy for the break and eagerly joined them, walking arm in arm between the pair. Maxie, lively and fun, put me at ease as we settled at a table near the bar. We all had fried chicken, corn bread, and beer. Maxie soon on his second urged me to raise my mug to his.

"Aye, me lass, ya catchin' on. Drink up!"

I sipped my beer but found it bitter, set it down and asked, "So, you are Irish?"

"Half me is. Ya see, ah have me Mum's tongue, the Irish. But me Da was German. Aye, Ross…thar's Scotts o' that name, but *das Ross* in German means *horse*. Met comin' down off the boat, they did. Din't know a word the other spoke. Took one look, sparked 'n had me, hah! Nay, me sis come first then ah pops out. Me Da ah barely recall 'cept his face black from coal. Swallered in a Skullkill mine he were, when ah's a lad 'o three. Near Pottsville nor'east o' Philly. What few times ah saw 'im washed, it spooked me, his face pale white like a ghost. But died black-faced he did, buried full deep in a mine, him 'n a dozen others."

Charmed by his frank manner and crisp brogue, as the bitter beer loosened my tongue, I dared ask, "That cap of yours…" nodding to where it hung on the back of his chair, "is that a miner's cap?"

"Me paddy? Aye, worn by miners, rail workers 'n a good many others back east. Not so much out here. A paddy cap it tis, worn for centuries in the old Isles, decreed by law, it were. To set us apart from the high-born, like Hagan here," he laughed, "with his silver tongue 'n golden mind. Only Lords 'n such wore hats or went without. Common folk doffed the paddy, aimed to keep us down. But a man's a man 'n ah wears it now out o' pride. For me Mum, me Da, for all 'em o' dirt 'n mud, blood 'n bone."

Further emboldened, as I did with Hagan, I asked of his mother.

"Aw, she died o' ca'sump, coughin' blood…ah's 14, bless 'er. Been on me own since. Aw, hang it, me mug's gone dry…" He held it up to the barkeep, "Kind sir, fetch me a'nuther, will ya?" A full mug soon in hand, he took a swig and resumed.

"Aye, me 'n me sis, Polly. A'nuther boy 'n girl died enfants 'n after Da died, Mum opened a boardin' house, down by the tracks. Polly as runs it now."

"In Philadelphia?"

"Aye, Philly. Thar she lives with her man 'n four bonny kids. He's no bum, good hand he is…a railroader."

"Hagan says that's where you two met, in Philly, during the big railroad strike."

"Right we did" — he snapped a leg bone, sucked the marrow, wiped his lips and said, "Smack dab in the battle, it were. We teamed up 'n lugged a dozen bloodied fellas. Aye, 'n bashed a few heads ourselves. When they come shootin' we ducked for cover. Same again two years ago in Chicago, stood shoulder to shoulder in Haymarket…right a'fore the Big Riot, they called it. Fightin' for the 8-hour day 'n guess who throws the first punch? Hagan here steps up 'n slams a copper a hard right. Lays 'im low. Then three pugs jump Hagan. So ah wades in, ah did."

"Maxie flattened all three."

"Aye, then grabs up Hag 'n we scram. 'Cuz when the shootin' starts no fist can whup a bullet," he laughed. "Been in some scraps, Hag 'n me. Aye, he's got a golden mind, he does. But ah got a fist o' stone 'n know how to use it."

"And a true heart, my friend," Hagan raised his mug to Maxie.

"Aye," said Maxie as they slugged their beer, "true 'n loyal to me lads 'n lasses."

Then he winked to me and I felt blessed.

We left the amber swirl of overhead lamps and entered the warm June night. The fading sunset darkened to a blink of stars in the west as we crossed the street to the print shop where Hagan lit the lamp and poured Maxie a cup of whiskey.

"There, that should hold you a few minutes," he said then snatched up a page of writing and checked his watch. "Good, only 7:15, need to hit the express office and send this out. And you," pointing to Maxie, "see you mind your manners while I'm gone."

"Aw, plug it, Hag. Always a gentleman to a lady…on me oath," he tipped his cap and waved Hagan on. "Thar he goes, off with a'nuther chapter. Writes 'em 'n lives 'em. Always at it, he is. Aims to make his name or die tryin'. Ah've known none like 'im. 'N he's keen on you…'n you on him. Ah know, ah loves 'im too, like a brother. But ya should know, Sadie, 'n ah'll say this but once. Like the hero in those big books ya read, thar's many a chapter in Hagan's life. Many…"

To his kindly notice I smiled, thinking I understood, but no one truly understands another's meaning. "As long as I'm the main chapter," I calmly assured, "I'm happy to turn every page."

"Aye, ya're the main chapter…'n may it read to a happy end," he raised his cup and emptied it as Hagan returned. "Why here's the devil home he is. Fill me cup, Hagan, the sprites have nipped it dry 'n the lass pierced me heart."

Hagan uncorked the bottle and topped his cup — "What have you been blowing on about, you big lug?"

"Only a wee gust, a trifle whiff o' yer wicked ways. But what ah aim to say, ya ought to marry this girl a'fore she smarts up 'n finds one better."

"Got anyone in mind, Maxie?" Hagan grinned.

"Might…just might. But mind, she's a keeper. If ya don' wed her ah will. Thar!" he gulped his cup dry and slammed it down. "Ah said it 'n ah meant it too."

"Getting the horse a little before the cart, aren't we?"

"Cart? Hah! Ya be forgettin' ah'm the horse…das Ross! Remember? Tis for yer own good ah speak…'n hers. Time ya got hitched, Hag. 'N time ah catch the 8:05 back t' Mankater. G'night!"

He stood, slapped his gut and shoved out the door, banging the bell as he left.

Caught in the tentative moment, fraught with humor and meaning, the shop silent and still, we both smiled, somewhat embarrassed. Hagan took a deep breath and exhaled. "Oh Maxie, Maxie…" he groaned, "ever the enthusiast, no penny ante, all in or all out."

"I like him though. He reminds me of Glen, blunt and direct. Now I better go before Mrs. Jensen shuts me out."

"Wait…" he grasped my shoulders and we shared a lingering kiss, tender and warm then full and fervent till I pulled away and hurried off anxious of all the chapters to come.

That night my dreams grew ardent as well…folded in Hagan's arms, opening to him, lurching, moaning, soon passing to a moment even more passionate, deeper, spreading, forcing me down…Maxie, a centaur with reddish fur and hot breath, not devilish, but a bullish man-stallion plunging unto me. I awoke in a sweat, ashamed and confused. Why this? For Hagan held my heart utterly. Only a dream, a silly dream, I told myself. And the beer, I mustn't drink beer. Yet I was no longer so certain of chapters to come.

Over the next several weeks farmers were busy reaping, binding, and threshing their wheat. Not a bumper crop, but still an imperative, and despite meager prices, a generally joyous time. Hagan and I were busy, and others as well — Grangers, suffragettes, silver advocates, and temperance ladies, all coming together under one tent. The Alliance Movement, barely nascent six months before, steadily catching fire and gaining steam, holding their first big regional meeting, Saturday, July the 14th, to mark the end of harvest and echo the jubilant Fourth. Others across the state were doing the same, rallying hard-pressed farmers to nominate and elect sympathetic voices to the state legislature.

And Hagan gave me voice; my own column titled *The Last Spit*. As he suggested, "People stop me on the street and say, 'Hear the last-spit girl is working for you now.' See, you've already got your handle and caught their interest by your natural spunk. Like Eva Gay's *Mong the Girls* about factory workers in Minnesota, *The Last Spit* has the grit that folks will grab up and read. Just heed the old verities and how you use them."

While I had my doubts, at his urging, I sat down determined to write. Took my initial inspiration not from the verities but from recent dreams and qualms of what lay ahead: *"Like one who cannot see,"* I began in a rush of thought and words, *"speaking to one who cannot hear, we each glimpse only a part, a mere fraction, especially of the future. But see here, as surely as the magic of electricity now lights far-off rooms, streets, and cities, and the wire that sends telegrams will soon carry the human voice coast to coast, bringing all these wonders even to Oakvale, so will women gain full and equal vote and wear trousers the same as men. What's more, men will still notice and court them. Some may say, 'Sooner will pigs fly!' But I say one day we may all fly, even to the moon. That's the Last Spit for now from Sadie Briar..."*

It was fun and engaging, weaving the serious and the whimsical, aiming for a poignant conclusion. I wrote a new one each week. Approaching the big day of the Alliance gathering, Hagan warned me, "You're growing popular, Sadie. Beyond the slated speakers I have a hunch the crowd will want to hear from their own White Rock girl. So might have something ready, just in case..." Forewarned, I prepared, nervous, expectant, worried they'd call on me and anxious lest they wouldn't. Mustered my courage and practiced in quiet moments, rephrasing my words, imagining the crowd. Father, mother, and Glen would be there, plus hundreds more.

Nor did our kisses cease or weaken, adding to my roiling thoughts and emotions, but nightly grew more ardent and I relished the urge of him to me. Finally, on the eve of the coming event, Friday the 13th, lucky or unlucky, my ripe flesh could no longer resist. Our kisses deepened, my breath to his, our yearning long held in check spilled forth.

My lone plea, "You must respect me."

"I do..." he hushed me with a kiss, "respect, adore and desire you." His finger traced my cheeks, chin and lips, his soft whispering breath warmed my ear and neck, "Love you, your hair, your lively green eyes, your smooth creamy flesh..."

He slowly unbuttoned my blouse to cup my eager breasts, tenderly pressing my nipples till they ached then loosened my waistband and caressed my essence. His hands strengthened, firm, insistent, he swooped me up and bore me to his back room and bed, and there were no more words, only sweat and grapple as his flesh met mine and I grew weightless, willing, opening fully to the press of him. I gasped in pain, then wonder, helpless, drowning, clenched breathless, floating skin to skin, my dress, petticoat, thighs spread in pleasure and surge…and it was wonderful.

Later, wholly naked and disengaged, I lay trembling at his side, shocked at my passion. I pulled the sheet about my shoulders and sat up, uncertain of what to say or do. He stroked my hair and said, "Your curls frame your face and fall to your breasts…" He undraped my shoulder and I flinched at his touch. He smiled, "Don't be shy. Even the old theologian Calvin asked, 'Has the Lord clothed the flower with great beauty that greets our eyes…yet it is not permissible for our eyes to be pleased by that beauty?' No, don't be shy or ashamed. Calvin also said that intercourse between man and wife is a pure thing, good and holy."

"But…we're not married," I muttered. "And I'm a mess."

"You've lost your maidenhood is all. You'll clean up nicely."

Clothed in the sheet, I picked up my bloodstained cancan and said, "I'm going to burn this…" I took it into the shop and used the clean portion to wipe myself then tossed it in the stove like a crumpled flower. Lit a match and watched the stiff lacing take flame then crinkle to ash and swore I'd never wear such contrivance again. Now a woman, partly proud and partly frightened, I waited till the embers darkened then returned, still wrapped in the sheet as I sat at his bedside.

"I'm afraid it's too late to return to the Jensens."

"You can sleep here with me."

"But they will know."

"I imagine so."

Suddenly worried, I searched his eyes — "What if I'm pregnant?"

"Then we shall need to find you a husband."

Fearing ridicule, or rejection, I looked away. Faced the dark silence, the ticking clock, and my anxious heart. Then Hagan stirred and asked, "Your parents? Are they still coming tomorrow?"

"Yes, they and Glen. About midmorning, they thought."

"Good, there's nothing really planned," he suggested, "no festivities till early afternoon. Perhaps we've time for a prior event, one more private. First thing in the morning I'll check with Mayor Morgan, he's Justice of the Peace. You go to the Jensens and gather your clothes and such. Wear whichever pretty dress you choose. Then we'll meet your parents and Glen around 11 and they can stand in witness. And I'll be your husband, if you'll have me?"

I threw off the sheet and fell in his arms, laughing and crying, and we made lusty love till I lay curled at his side, listening to the warm wind, his slow breathing, clutched in fervent hope of our chapters to come.

XVI. Joy & Promise

Toward dawn I slept then awakened to birdsong. Hagan had already washed, shaved and dressed. "There's a pan of clean water, soap and towel," he nodded to the bureau then turned to the mirror and finished lacing his tie to his crisp white shirt. "You freshen up, Sadie," he said. "We've got a big day ahead. I'm off to find the mayor and set the stage."

A half hour later, the sun fully risen, a dog barked at a distant wagon rolling into town as I walked to the Jensens. I paused at the door, attempted a casual demeanor and entered, smiling brightly, "Hi, I've come for my things," I said as they both looked up, still seated in the kitchen, taking their breakfast.

"Why, Sadie…" Mrs. Jensen observed, narrowing her eyes, "we were worried."

Not wishing to explain, I simply answered, "There's no need for worry. I'm to be married this morning…Hagan and I."

"That's quite a surprise," she offered in a tight smile, "bless you, my dear."

"Thank you. Hagan thought that since my parents were coming to the Alliance gathering, a small civil ceremony at the mayor's house would spare them a second trip."

"How thoughtful," she added dryly.

"Darn thoughtful, I'd say," Mr. Jensen affirmed, standing to greet me, "and makes good sense, my best to you both. Darlene's wedding way out to Denver last year cost an arm 'n a leg. Half our savings. Mayor Morgan'll get you hitched for a two-dollar fee."

"Now Howard, don't you be going on."

"Right, a little late, ain't it."

"Why, it made her so happy, and me too."

"Sure, always happy spending money…"

I left them to squabble and hurried upstairs. Changed into my favorite summer dress, light blue with ruffled white collar and pleated front. Then coiffed and pinned my hair just so, topped by a broad-brimmed sun hat with a blue bow. All set I packed my things in one large bag and one small then crept down the stairs. Hearing and seeing no one, I made my escape.

By midmorning we met and told my family. Both surprised and delighted, mother teared in smile and gave me a hug while father and Glen heartily shook Hagan's hand.

"Hey now," father enthused, "the day's a'wasting, let's get 'er done…"

And straight away we headed to Mayor Morgan's house and rendezvoused in his front parlor where he sat smiling, blanket over his lap, tended by his wife and daughter, ready to perform the ceremony. He bade us step forth and in a few words prompted us through the required vows. We said our "I do's" and he pronounced us "Man and wife!" We happily kissed and headed outside.

There in the stark sunlight, wholly unexpected, over a score of townsfolk waited to greet us. Mr. and Mrs. Jensen stood foremost, and Martha actually wore a pleasant smile as both offered their blessings and best wishes. Likewise from others gathered thereby. Moving on, I spied Ian and his sister Shannon. Her sad smile brightened as I approached and she quietly offered a bouquet of white roses.

"Fresh cut this morning," she said. "When Ian told me what was happening, I had to come and wish you long life and happiness. If you press one in your Bible it will hold the scent of this day."

Thanking her, I held the soft petals to my nose. Before I could say more, a buoyant voice and presence intruded. Striding from the depot, Maxie called out:

"What's this? What the devil, Hag? Ya gone done it without me? Your best bud? Afraid ah'd stand 'n object, was ya?"

"Too late to back slide, Maxie. I had your say and urging, remember?"

"Aye, that ya did. Ah'm glad for ya both…" He loomed up and squeezed us in the mighty sweep of his arms. "Thar, that done, how 'bout a kiss from the bride, eh?"

I happily raised my lips to his and caught a whiff of cigar and whiskey. Then he stepped back and laughed, "Lordy me, ah'll carry the blessing o' those sweet lips to me dying breath!"

In the dizzy moment others cheered us as Maxie gushed, "Wha' a day! Wha' a blessed day! 'N praise be, luck 'o the Irish, ah brung two keggers shipped straight from the brew caves in Saint Louie! Aye, got con-nections, ah does. Two big keggers thar at the depot, still cool but soon heat in the sun. Ah needs a wagon to haul 'em 'n straw 'n ice to pack 'em in."

Father readily volunteered our wagon and Glen said, "I'll have it there in a jiffy."

Then Mr, Jensen chimed in, "After you fetch ice, swing by the livery and I'll pitch on some hay." That's when Mrs. Jensen reclaimed her stern voice and warned:

"There'll be no liquor at our Oakvale gatherings."

Before the Jensens renewed their squabble, Maxie stoutly clarified, "Nay mam, na rum nor whiskey. Tis righteous beer, liquid bread, the staff o' life! Aye, to bless their weddin' day 'n the hardy toil o' our farmers." Then he winked aside and slapped Glen's shoulder, "Come on, lad, les' load up 'fore the blasted sun boils the lot…"

<hr>

About a half mile west of Oakvale the White Rock looped north then south then flowed east under the bridge out of town. Stately oak and walnut trees lined the creek and through the low bottom tall cottonwoods stood nicely spaced, shedding their white fluff gently to the grass. The area, prone to flood following big rains, had by long use and general consent become the city park. Nearby, water flowed over the dam where the old beaver, Heinz Roiter, once milled lumber, since replaced by a Swede named Linsborg who milled wheat, oats, and corn. Back of the dam where water pooled, venturesome boys jumped from high limbs, splashed and swam. Centered in the open space facing west, a large platform anchored by posts set deep in the ground gave stage to various outdoor functions, square dances, songfests, and the like. Presently the city band was setting up to provide music for the festive occasion.

While I knew better, the bride in me embraced it all as part of my wedding day.

A special day indeed, folks were arriving from every quarter of the countryside for miles around — families in wagons, and many ahorse, trailing in to camp and picnic amid the grassy, shady environs. Like a new settlement coming alive in the very moment. On our way, father, mother, Hagan and I had stopped by the print shop to place my bouquet in a quart jar of water. From there we proceeded to the park and met Glen wheeling the wagon around directly north of the platform. He jumped down to stake the horses while Maxie walked up to father and said, "Got the kegs stowed in ice 'n straw. Hope ya don' mind we leave 'em thar a spell?"

"Don't mind at all, handy to wet my thirst. And appears the horses agree…" father grinned as they stomped and blew in want of their water bucket and nose bags, content to laze in the shade through the hot afternoon before the long pull home.

Then Maxie tagged Hagan's shoulder — "What say ya shuck that coat 'n tie? Some boys yonder gettin' up a game o' pasture ball. Play a few innings whilst folks trickle in."

"Tempted, but…I'm speaking here in a while. Need to focus my thoughts."

"Aw, focus-pocus. It'll limber ya up, do ya good. You pitch 'n ah catch. Sadie don' mind, does ya, girl?" He leaned to me and pointed to Hagan's hand, "Has a mean pitch from 'is broke ring finger. Aye, 'n see no ring," he winked. "But we'll fix that. Ah'll buy yer rings as a weddin' gift ah will. That watch 'n jew'ler man in Mankater's got rings, he does.

Anyhow, Hagan spins the ball in a wicked curve. Hellish hard to hit. C'mon, Hag, let's show the boys yer stuff."

"Maxie, you're one smooth talker, should make you speak in my stead." Hagan jauntily shed his coat and tie and delivered them to my care as Maxie slapped his back, "Atta boy, now let's go have some fun…" hustling him off, once more vowing to buy the rings, "Aims t' see ya wed proper, by gosh or by gar!"

Meanwhile father and Glen joined in cranking ice cream as mother and I helped women prep the food on makeshift tables, benches, and wagon beds. Now and then I glimpsed the game beyond the trees, hitting to the pasture further west. And I clearly heard Maxie's great beller, "Fire it, Hag! Fire a spitter…" as he crouched on his knees, his cap turned backwards, catching the hard fast ball with his bare hands.

They continued in shout and play and occasional crack of the bat while we draped patriotic crape from the platform and nearby bushes and trees, entertained by the Oakvale Glee Girls and the city band through a medley of popular songs that all but drowned out the distant game. Then in a pause between songs there rose a far gust of oaths, mild to strong: "Damn! What a wallop! Dad-gum ball is gone, gone, gone…"

As we shortly learned, Maxie hit one so far they lost the ball and called the game. The men came herding in, hungry, thirsty, laughing and arguing over who had the most runs, the farmers or the workers.

"Don't matter none, can't win if you don't finish the game!"

"Why, you fellas lost the ball?"

"Lost, heck? He hit it too blame far…" Back and forth they bantered, all in fun, soon hatching the tall tale of the ball hit plumb to the clouds.

* * *

People took their food to join with family and friends beneath the trees. Others spread blankets and sat on the ground, eating and chatting merrily for a time. A moderate breeze shooed the flies. Cottonwood seeds drifted here and there. Gradually a rippling hush quieted distant children at play. Even the birds aflutter limb to limb seemed to settle as all eyes turned to the center platform, now absent of glee girls and city band, where the first speaker stood straightening his jacket, making ready with notes in hand.

Professor Jerome Hayworth Constance of the State University in Manhattan had generously accepted the invitation. Accustomed to lecturing, his voice carried well as he diligently covered issues of the day, granting deference to both major parties while urging local merchants and farmers to keep faith and remain patient in face of challenging times and the current drought. He finished with the usual optimism, "Be assured, better days await us. Indeed, a limitless horizon with new seed varieties and machinery to improve production. While we've learned that planting trees does not bring rain, it does reduce erosion. And new methods of tillage will preserve precious moisture in your soil. Yes, God willing, through persistence and honest effort all citizens will prosper…"

People listened dutifully throughout and gave polite, modest applause.

Then Hagan took the stage like one who knew the stage, sleeves rolled up, collar unbuttoned from playing ball. Hatless, his hair catching the breeze, he cast his eyes to the crowd, wiped his sweaty forehead and with a flick of his finger announced, "It's hot, damnable hot!" to scattered laughter as he flicked it again and firmly declared, "Yet this is but a trickle to the sweat of our farmers and workers who earn their bread by the sweat of their brow. And they should be justly paid —"

"Hear, hear!" interrupted by fervent shouts as Maxie roared, "Give 'em hell, Hag!" He and Glen now buddied up, shoulder to shoulder, each a beer in hand.

"I agree with the good professor," Hagan continued. "We all stand in hope for a better day. But that promise has been broken time and again. How many centuries have they preached 'Love thy neighbor' only to deny their neighbor his daily bread, always to their profit. This is an old fight that began long ago…among English speakers with the Magna Carta when feudal lords revolted against divine rights, demanding equal voice to King John. Though he conceded, and it was so written, he reneged. This stuck in the craw, festering for two centuries, until 1361 when peasants led by Jack Straw revolted against a poll tax and rallied for the abolition of serfdom. To which young King Richard, cornered in the Tower of London, aptly agreed. Then next day he sent his henchmen to hunt the rebels and hang them. Scotched for a time, but in time this sowed the seeds of our own rebellion against King

George, bound by the self-evident truth proclaimed in our great Declaration in 1776 'that all men are created equal, endowed by their Creator with certain unalienable Rights, among these are Life, Liberty, and the pursuit of Happiness...' Would that not include a living wage for our workers and parity for our farmers?"

To sudden hurrahs Hagan repeated "Parity and a living wage!" then continued:

"In 1833, the tiny parish of Tolpuddle, England, six farm workers led by George Loveless, or luckless George as things played..." he quipped, drawing them in. "Yes, luckless but brave, for he began to organize his fellows to gain a living wage, to put food on their tables, feed and clothe their children. These were not shiftless hoe-bums and bindlestiffs, but good, honest, literate men with homes and families. Yet the Tolpuddle Martyrs, as they came to be known, were forthwith charged and convicted of treason. Shipped down under to serve as convict labor. Finally, after five years of protest against the rank injustice, their sentences were revoked. Pardoned, they returned to England. Having been ill-dealt, and hoping to improve their lives, most of them immigrated to Canada or the United States.

"Now here, in the land of the free, the very forces that framed the Tolpuddle Six resist our common efforts for simple justice, and seek to ensnare, twist, and squelch our rightful demands. Yet all we ask is a fair price for our grain, a fair wage for our labor. When we gather in number to peacefully petition, do they listen? No, they turn us away, urging patience. If we persist, they visit violence and force. Recall the Great Railroad Strike in the hot summer of 1877 when in city after city they used militias and thugs to put us down. Then did the same just two years ago at Hay Market Square in Chicago, where thousands of workers gathered, asking for '8 hours of labor, 8 hours of rest, and 8 hours of what we will...' And they were answered by billy clubs, bayonets, and bullets. Not until workers were killed did the protest turn violent. Then yes, a bomb was thrown and policemen died. And the culprits were tried and recently hanged.

"But name one Governor, one railroad magnate, one grand banker who has ever paid for the wrong they inflict. Not in our time, not in this land, not a single one. Yet these selfsame hoarders of wealth, who keep gold among the few, claim the rules are set. That the scales of justice must tip their way, else it lead to chaos and bedlam, blood in the streets…like the Paris Commune. To any just request or question, they rail, 'Anarchist! Ingrate! Socialist!'

"I say, Bunkum! We're not fools to be fooled. I know that most of you here are farmers. The fight for the 8-hour day is not your cause or concern. You toil sunrise to sunset, as you must to plant and harvest, to sustain your farms and families. And like the worker, you want to educate your children and see them prosper. For that you need and deserve fair prices, just shipping rates, ready loans and debt adjustment. A democratic people, we do not seek violence or anarchy, only a voice at the table when they slice the pie. We reach farm to farm, neighbor to neighbor, forming an Alliance, like workers do to form a union, steadily gaining strength and number all across this land. Already they yield, albeit grudgingly, the kings of finance, railroads, coal, and steel.

"As our ranks swell, the Goldbugs sweat and gather in their marble chambers to plot how to counter, dissemble, and deceive. They slice and deal, attempt to pit us one against the other and scatter our efforts like chaff. Then once more reap the greater spoil. But if we unite, stand strong, they will yield. I'm a printer, a newsman, I know paper. A single page you can easily tear" — Hagan pulled one from his hip pocket and did so — "Even ten or twenty pages a strong man can rip in half. But a thousand pages pressed into one book will blunt the blow of an ax!" Then he raised his fist and shouted:

"They will yield if we unite! Unite! Unite…!" answered by scores then hundreds pumping their fists, joining in the chant — "Unite! Unite! Unite…!" riling the air like a sudden storm, gradually subsiding to voices eager for Hagan to run for the legislature — "Go tell 'em that in Topeka!" — "Mister, you got my vote!" — "By heck, I second that!"

Hagan shook his head and raised his arms to calm them.

"I thank you, truly thank you," he said. "But no. I write the story, your story. That's my job. You need one of your own to represent you. One who's lived your story. Who knows and shares your burden. Who can speak plain words and stand for the truth. Look around you, find several you trust. Bring them forth and have them speak. Then choose one, be he Democrat or Republican, send him to legislate on your behalf…"

Amid the general mumble and stir groups formed in random caucus and in a short while two candidates emerged, by turns coaxed and tugged forth. Nearing the platform, one shook off his handlers and stepped up, a sturdy dark-bearded man in his mid-thirties.

"Welp…" he said, casting his keen blue eyes over the crowd, "my name's Jordan Miller. Like most you folks, I'm a farmer. Settled here 'n broke sod in '74. Each year I sow 'n harvest and I'm heckin' tired of no gain…" This sparked a chorus of "Amens!" to which he answered, "I hear ya, folks. And we all know that homestead land is long gone, been claimed for some years. The land we got right here is where we make our stand or lose. Lose like those poor folks that settled the dry counties on west. Some did fine for a spell, but lately they been burnt dry 'n blown out. Drought 'n debt and no money to be had. Many of us got kin among 'em. Had a cousin of mine come through a month ago headed for some point east, hoping for a job. 'Any work that pays 'n feeds my kids,' he said then repeated that sorry refrain, 'In God we trusted, in Kansas we busted…' Welp, we fed 'em 'n sent 'em on with a couple loaves of bread, some ham. A sad sight to see your kin knocked low. Like Job, it makes you doubt. Still I trust in God, the God that helps them as help themselves. Now I was schooled through 8th grade is all. But I can read 'n reason well enough to tell a lame lie from the hard truth. Y'all know me and I know our troubles are most the same. Can I fix them? No! But with your vote I sure aim to try and I promise to shoot straight…"

Ending his speech on that firm note, he stepped down to vigorous howls and applause. After which the second fellow was ushered up. Evan Wainley, a thin balding man, stood facing the deafening silence. He cleared his throat and muttered, "Good day…" then slumped his shoulders and nodded to his opponent, "Jordan Miller, I think you'll do…" And the crowd heartily agreed.

Then a far voice called out, "We want the Last-Spit Girl!" answered by another close by, "Let's hear from Sadie Briar!" Soon others were shouting, "Sadie Briar! Sadie Briar!" Hagan, who'd been standing aside, reached down and gave me a hand up. We traded smiles then I walked to center stage, so happy I felt no fear.

"Here's something you don't know," I promptly announced, "I woke this morning, Sadie Briar. By noon I was Sadie Briar-Corbett!" I beamed in joy, sharing my moment to a round of cheers, then had my say, "Yes, and as I am proud to be Mrs. H.R. Corbett, if given the vote, I would proudly vote for Jordan Miller…" Again they cheered as I quoted my poem, "Cannot she who rocks the cradle, knits and mends, have say…" then threaded back to women's suffrage, "Just last year, our Kansas legislators, for the first time ever, granted women the right to vote in school and city elections. And we are grateful. But state and national elections are still denied us. And here's the last spit," I concluded, "You hear it said that the bull outlasts the cow. That may be, but the bull whiles away the day while the cow gives milk, butter, cream —"

"Why heck!" a wiseacre exclaimed, "He gives the cream o' life!"

"I grant you that, good sir," I answered, locking eyes with my heckler, "The bull does give a dribble. A mere spit at the bottom of the pail, praise be, for which he gets one mighty vote. But the cow gives milk by the bucketful and it's high time she gets a full vote too!" I clenched my fist in mimic of Hagan and shouted, "And so shall we! So shall we! So shall we…!" Women stood in unanimous chorus while men roused as well. And even the rude voice hollered, "By Jesse, jes' might vote for that!"

Hagan drew me to his side and waved them forth.

"Come on in!" he called. "Join the Alliance! Sign and add your name. Women too! We'll lobby and petition to gain you the vote. Band together and they'll hear our voices in Topeka and all the way to Washington!"

Over half lined up, stringing back along the creek, orderly but animate, determined to add their names. Nearly an hour passed, the sun tipping the distant hills, before the last signature inked the page. The crowd thinned, many returning home to evening chores, others closing round in wait of further doings. Hagan thumbed through the pages of signatures and glanced to father.

"See you haven't signed, Mr. Briar. There's still space to add your name."

"Gave it some thought," father allowed and tapped the ash off the cigar Maxie had spared him. "Twice in my life I've signed 'n joined up. First with the Border Army to preserve the Union…set me to killing my fellow man which I did not savor 'n still doubt the worth of. Then I joined with my fair lady, Sarah, who I do savor each day and regret not one. To here I break even. Hate to see a third joining ruin my luck."

"But the Alliance, with cooperative grain storage, could help market your wheat and corn?"

"Could…but won't help my cattle. No co-op can store beef or keep coyotes off my calves. Besides, we crib our corn. Plus Glen 'n I just finished a granary. With tongue 'n groove floor and walls 'n a tight roof to keep our grain dry till the price improves, which it usually does come winter. Meanwhile Sarah's cats keep the rodents down. So, much as I'd like to oblige my daughter's husband…believe I'll remain a proud member of the Briar-Callaway clan."

"You're a hard sell, Patrick Briar."

"Well, you did win my daughter. Not bad for one day."

"That took far more than a day," Hagan laughed. "And judging by her father, the deal may not be fully sealed."

"Why now, think we can help you there. What say you, Sarah? Shall we stay the evening 'n help celebrate? Them ol' bossies won't mind a late milkin'."

"Oh, they'll kick 'n moan some," she smiled. "Like all us females, they must learn to endure…"

But mother was happy to lengthen her stay. Glen too, for there would soon be dancing, the city band being replaced by string players — two fiddlers, a banjo and guitar, and a big double bass to add bounce and rhythm. The food put away, a score of lanterns were soon lit and hung from surrounding tree limbs. A spry Bohemian, Johann Alba, again topped his beer, preparing to call the square dances interspersed with jigs and reels, starting off with "Soldier's Joy," popular from the Civil War.

Father grabbed mother by the arm and spun her away while Maxie and Glen ladled beer to all around. I sipped from Hagan's cup till we emptied it then he took me by hand and waist and we skipped across the grass beneath a canopy of stars, spinning in a blur of lanterns, and he danced as wonderfully as I had dreamed. Lithe and aswirl in his arms to the vibrant music and warm fragrant night till Glen, who'd taught me to dance, cut in and flung me high in wild stomp and laughter. Likewise, mother and father stepped lively arm in arm. Then Maxie demanded his turn, bulled in, waging his finger at Hagan,

"Recall, twas ah urged you wed! Now scram 'n leave me dance the bonny lass..." And dance he did, amazingly graceful and light on his feet for a big man, swinging me round and round with such power I feared he'd fling me into far orbit like the ball, gone, gone, gone...

XVII. Foment & Birth

"Paul, the coyotes are getting awful close. Why don't you grab that double barrel in the corner, step out and fire a salvo off over the creek, and one up to the hill. That should send them packing. Ol' Bing is no coward and would love to take on the whole lot. No need to tempt him…" Plus she knows that Paul loves to cock back the hammers and fire the shotgun. Certainly no toy, her father's twist steel 12 gauge, but looks like a toy in Paul's hands as he goes outside. He swiftly delivers two blasts and steps back in smiling. She feels comforted for Bing's sake, the night now quiet.

"Thank you, Paul. Any closer, Bing would've been up and at them. And those darned coyotes might've scared off Santa's reindeer. Can't have that, can we."

His grin widens as he stands the shotgun back in place. Paul knows Santa doesn't really come. He knows Santa sends the presents to Gram and Gram puts them under the tree. He knows that and other things. Paul walks over and pours Gram a fresh cup of hot tea then sits down, feeling mostly content…except he worries for Gram. She should be in bed now, him too.

Still she sits, eyes to the stove, sipping her red-berry tea, remembering. The tea settles her stomach some, the sumac mildly sweet and citrusy like warm spring air, yet her old bones remain rigid in ache and long for release. And she would trade her tea, she thinks, for a bottle of laudanum and like Hagan's mother float free and be gone, another memory. And she remembers when she fell in love. Yes, she loved him, and loves him still. They once shared such pleasure and promise.

The bouquet of white roses was still lovely when I touched them late that evening. Still lovely the next morning when I pressed a fallen petal in my Bible next to the line in the Song of Solomon, *"His hand is under my head, and his right hand doth embrace me…"* And I stood wreathed in memory of the whole lovely day that framed the hope of many things to come. Many fell by the way, and the few that came to pass were never so brilliant or wonderful as our first kiss, our first lovemaking, and our early fervent dreams.

Along with the hundreds of signatures gathered that day, Hagan's subscriptions doubled. With the coming election he decided to close shop in Oakvale and move us to Mankato, the county seat.

"Elections are like harvest time," he explained. "That's when the news business makes hay. And now that we're married, Sadie, we need more room."

Later that week Hagan made a down payment on a suitable building on the north edge of Mankato business district, convenient to the depot, telegraph and express office. A wide-framed structure with a storage attic, living quarters in the north half, business space south, it had previously housed a fine clothing and hattery store. Facing hard times and a dearth of customers, the owners had moved on to try prospects in Wichita. An awning shaded the front window and boardwalk that bordered the main street east. In the large lot in back there were several fruit trees, a garden, and clothesline that caught the afternoon sun. The wash porch extended to the cistern supplied by well water. With a hand pump in the kitchen, I rolled up my sleeves, happy as a princess in a palace, eager to make it my home.

Maxie, who had corralled his crew to load and freight our belongings and print equipment to Mankato, after seeing all unloaded and carried in and me ready to work, stepped back and laughed, "No-

no, Sadie girl, not jus' yet. Not gonna let ya dirty yer pretty hands 'n go t'scrubbin' til ah see a ring put proper on yer finger. Ye too, Hag, here it tis…" He took a tiny box from his pocket and presented the gift he'd promised. "Aye, 'n since ah missed the weddin', les hear 'em words 'n see it done proper…"

Maxie stood in wait as his crew looked on.

Hagan gently took my hand and said, "With this ring I do thee wed." After he placed it on my finger, I took his hand and did the same.

"Now kiss, kiss!" Maxie urged, his crew joining in. We kissed to their loud jest and holler while Maxie clapped his hands and shouted, "Thar, ya's wed proper! Man 'n wife! Bless ya both. Now ya can git to work. Ah'm off to have a pint with the boys."

And work we did, a heady wonderful time, harvesting news and printing campaign ads and brochures. Ian had moved with us, having finished 8th grade and well on his way to earning his printer's license. Showing keen interest in photography, Hagan helped him purchase a camera and supplies and they made a space at the far end of the print shop for a dark room and living quarters. He took his meals with us and helped with the laundry. Soon settled in, I immersed myself in the hustle bustle of printing chores, housework, and Hagan's various Alliance events.

Over the hectic months leading to the election the rally in Oakvale replayed many times, featuring a slew of popular speakers — Mary Lease, Annie Diggs, 'Sockless' Jerry, among others — a few famous for a day, footnoted and gone. There again it was Hagan's breath, his flint and steel that kindled the fire and fed the flame. While I spoke on several occasions, my enthusiasm faded like petals from the rose bouquet. Vaguely aware that I blossomed within and the life that grew took stronger hold than issues buffeting around me, people and voices receded like chatter in the wind.

"What's the matter, Sadie?" Hagan asked, puzzled by my lack of zeal, my growing reluctance to speak or even travel a short distance.

"Each morning…a sickness…" I answered faintly. "Perhaps it's…a baby."

Hagan broke into a smile, "I should have known, my beautiful Sadie, fertile as the prairie given rain and seed. You need to slow down and rest." Thankfully the sickness soon passed and my energy returned. By October my pregnancy began to show.

Meanwhile talk and activity centered on the coming election, and Jordan Miller looked to be a shoo-in. But the big story was the bomb in Coffeyville, allegedly planted by anarchists and accidently detonated awaiting shipment to Winfield, leaving two innocent women badly injured; soon rumored dead. So claimed in Governor Martin's proclamation out of Topeka several days later offering a $300 reward for capture of the culprits and another $300 for information leading to others involved. Hagan advised me to be on guard for unwelcome visitors — "I have a good idea what's afoot."

That was a Tuesday. On Thursday morning they appeared. I had just finished cleaning up after breakfast and was putting clothes to soak when I heard an annoying voice from the print shop and entered to discover Hagan facing two strangers. I knew it was not a friendly encounter as he stayed me with his hand and offered no introduction. Both wore suits and rounded bowler hats; the larger man, standing mutely rigid by the door, reminded me of the letch in the livery, only well-dressed and apparently sober. The other, slender and hatchet-faced with a ridiculous hair-patch beneath his nose, proceeded to speak in his grating nasal tone.

"We have tracked your activities, Mr. Corbett, you and Max Ross. Both known members of the Knights of Labor and suspected Videttes, very likely connected to if not responsible for the recent bombing. For certain you are agitators, and we are here to serve notice that your kind are not welcome in the free state of Kansas and firmly suggest you move on." Succinctly stating his case, he raised his chin in wait.

Hagan smiled evenly and answered, "I like it where I am. My feet are planted, my mind set. My affiliations are no secret. I'm a proud advocate for the Farmer's Alliance and the Industrial Union. As for Videttes and Knights, it sounds thrilling, but I am just a newsman. My pen is my sword. And until they scratch the First Amendment, I'll wield my pen as I will. In so doing I gather the humble voice of workers and farmers to make them heard. If the Governor and his men would listen to and serve the people instead of themselves, they'd have no need to hire the likes of you."

Hagan held his smile, poised and relaxed while hatchet face clenched his jaw and reddened in anger. Then the door banged open and Maxie strode in, gave the large man a hard shove and eyed the other.

"Feared ah's too late, but nay," he showed his teeth, "twas out on the section when ah got word ya had visitors. Pumped me hand cart like the devil, aye 'n see the deuces pair. Mr. Roberts 'n Mr. Gridley, am ah right?" Maxie, blunt and assertive, laced his hands and popped his knuckles, glaring from one to the other.

Hatchet face slacked his jaw and gaped, "How…how do you know our names?"

"Names is easy," Maxie growled. "Thar's rail 'n telegraph to towns large 'n small. Eyes 'n ears…got con-nections. Knows when ya come 'n when ya go. When 'n who ya meetin' with. Ah knows ya dealt with the Governor's boys not a fortnight back. Here to plant another bomb 'n point the finger are ye?"

"How dare you —"

"We don't dare a thing," Hagan challenged, "We know you met recently with Mr. Greer, editor of *The Winfield Courier* and confirmed ally of Governor Martin, both rabid opponents of the Vincent brothers and *The Nonconformist*, another paper that gives voice to the people. We also know you're chums with a certain itinerate printer in Topeka, a Mr. Henri, the willing courier it seems of the package that exploded in Coffeeville. Facts known by few and for the moment kept hidden by those few in charge. But in little less than a week there'll be an election. And given a new Governor, an honest investigation, the facts will come to light. Until then, take comfort knowing that the two victims, Mrs. Upham and her daughter, have regained consciousness, though lamed, they are expected to live. So when you're found out and cornered, you may not hang. But the noose will tighten, and before your handlers throw you to the dogs, you're the ones who should seek new borders and identities."

"Hear me as well," Maxie said, pointing both to the door, "ya ever show yer mugs in Mankater, me 'n the boys'll do ya worse. Now git!" he kicked the door wide and shoved them out. They headed directly to the depot while Hagan and Maxie shared a good laugh and my heart throbbed in panic.

"Who were they?" I asked, relieved to see them gone.

"Pinkerton men," Hagan said, "licensed goons eager to bloody their hands for pay. Threat is the one thing they understand and respect."

Although he admitted later that day to playing a hunch, he had most of the facts in hand. Governor Martin lost to Governor Humphrey and over the next several years an investigation revealed the conspirators. But to little avail or consequence. As Hagan observed, the law proved an intricate maze by which the few controlled and ensnared the many. And therefore should be called out and defied.

That was the Hagan I loved — direct, confident, handsome, fearless, a prince of a man. And Maxie his staunch loyal soldier, both knights in a cause. But with the election past, activities waned. Hagan made a brief trip to Topeka that winter, otherwise settled in and our affections grew along with the baby. On the Ides of March, heavily burdened, I planted potatoes by the light of the moon and felt my spirit rise, my flesh strengthen. Then in mid-April, a bright sunny day, mistaking early cramps for a minor backache, I chanced planting peas and squash. That's when my water burst and I shrieked more in surprise than pain. Hagan rushed out, catching me in mid-faint.

"Silly girl," he lightly scolded, "trying to work in your condition."

"Only planting a few seeds," I gasped in cramp, dizzy with excitement. "Think I'm having a baby."

"Hold on," he urged, hurrying me inside, "we need to get you to bed." Then he called for Ian to bring the doctor, "And be quick!" That was Dr. Sudlow, the very one who'd married Miss Claussen. Hagan helped me undress and eased me down. Seeing the baby starting to come, he calmly coaxed my effort. When the doctor and Madalene arrived, the head was fully out.

Dr. Sudlow laid his satchel aside, peered down as he rolled up his sleeves and said, "Hmmm, you've done well so far, young lady. The head is clear and no tear, appears to be a fine natural birth. Now give us another big push, if you please…"

While Madalene gripped my hand, I heaved and strained and felt myself pull in half, breathless and empty. Briefly submerged, dazed, I surfaced, opened my eyes and beheld a new life being dangled by its heels and given a sharp slap. Hearing its cry, I seemed to waken as well, reborn with my baby. Dr. Sudlow cradled its head and laid it down.

"There now," he said, "you've birthed a fine male specimen of good heft and length. He should grow tall as his father." Then he tied and cut the umbilical and wrapped the afterbirth in a towel.

"Mother Nature has done well today," he stated, turning to wash his hands in the porcelain bowl Hagan set by. "You need simply hold your baby and rest. He'll find the nipple by and by and begin to nurse. Mrs. Sudlow will stay and help clean and ease you. I have other patients to attend. So…" he finished drying his hands and looked to Hagan, "if I may collect my fee, Mr. Corbett, I will be off."

"Certainly, Dr. Sudlow, we appreciate your timely arrival. Let's get you paid."

Left alone, so exhausted I could barely raise my hand as Madalene quietly washed me and my baby, tender and careful of us both. Wishing to thank her, I smiled and said, "So kind of you to stay and help me, Miss Claussen. Oh, I'm sorry…" quickly correcting myself, "I should say Mrs. Sudlow."

"That's quite alright, Sadie, just call me Madalene. And it's my pleasure to stay," she added warmly, a hint of envy in voice and eye. "My husband, Dr. Sudlow is a most formal man. Punctual and precise as he must be in the medical profession with all there is to know and learn. And Willard, which is his first name, is a good man, I think…" she winced in question to the window, searching her thoughts. "Of all my students, Sadie, you had the most inquisitive mind. I thought it certain you would continue your studies and attend university."

In thro of my baby and numb to such notions, I simply said, "Yes, that was my plan. Then Hagan happened. And once the heart chooses, the flesh follows."

"I wouldn't know…" she answered, looking down and away. For a moment she reminded me of Shannon in her sadness. Then she perked up and asked, "What of your brother? How is he?"

"Glen? He does well. Ranches with my father and helps out on the Hazelin Ranch, training horses."

"That would be Holly Hazelin's place."

"You know Holly?"

"Yes, her father is a patient of Dr. Sudlow. Holly brings him in from time to time. A most interesting woman…" Again she looked away, then finished tidying up, lifted the stained towel and asked, "Shall I dispose of this for you?"

Focused on my baby, I merely nodded and she quietly left. Apparently Hagan saw her out, for he shortly entered with a bemused groan, "Good God…that doctor and his missus are an odd pair. Wonder if she calls him Dr. Sudlow in bed?"

"She is pretty, don't you think?"

"Pretty, yes, but prim. Prim and tightly corseted. Not lively and full of spunk like my Sadie." Then he lifted the sheet to see the baby, "Sure is a tiny little guy."

"Didn't you hear the doctor say he'll grow tall as you?"

"Well, he is a hungry little wolf."

By now he'd nuzzled to my breast and found the nipple and latched with such force, exciting warm spasms of delight to my very center.

"May I name him Daniel?"

"Of course you may. You're the mother, suffered the agon. It's your victory."

"Daniel was my mother's maiden name. And it works well as Dan or Danny."

"It's a good name, Sadie. Has his own book in the Bible. Daniel, wisest of the wise, counselor to kings. Noble and worthy, when thrown to the lions, even the beasts spared him."

"And can I choose Liam for his middle name?"

He considered for a moment and agreed, "Liam he shall be. Daniel Liam Corbett, born in the year of great hope and change. While thousands rush for land in Oklahoma, thousands more abandon farms in Kansas. From that irony springs a vast political movement. May the stars align for our son, Daniel Liam, and for us…"

XVIII. The Flower Fades

That's the picture framed in my mind, Hagan leaning to bless our son and still a prince to my eyes. Born in the age of princes, in the realm of lore and legend, he would have remained such. But he was just a man, subject to pride, ambition, one cause and another, from rally to rally in vain quest of a greater stage. For the play grew stale night after night without new faces, new lips and breath, and the lines fell flat, like wine to water. And Hagan lived for intoxication, not of drunkenness, but of spirit and ideal. All this I was yet to learn, though I had an inkling, as Maxie had warned, there were many chapters to Hagan.

My main chapter now was my baby. Having Daniel unleashed a deeper meaning and want, instinctual, subterranean, spawned from the earth, flowing from an essence as constant as gravity, compared to which gathering news and politics, all the far din and rivalry seemed but trifles, mere scribbles of ink, chaff to the wind. When he pressed his little lips to my nipple and supped, something more than milk flowed between us, old as mud and flesh, beyond conception. Yet I had conceived and cherished the gift of my baby before all else. Even Hagan.

Initially understanding, dutifully abstinent through a month and more, Hagan watched as I cradled and nursed our baby. Then he grew impatient, envious of my breasts as if our son came between us. One night after nursing Daniel and applying lanolin to my chapped nipples, Hagan tried to touch.

I slapped his hand away, "No! That hurts, they're too sore. Besides, they're for our baby to nurse."

Hagan took his scolding with a smile and persisted, gently tracing my skin, asking, "May I touch you here…or here…" then cupped the whole of my breast and moved his free hand lower, more insistent, caressing, tempting me till I relinquished. Unhurried, careful of my tender flesh, we shared a delightful night. And our lovemaking renewed, wonderful through a month, then he traveled to Des Moines for an Alliance meeting and other appointments, leaving the chore of the paper to Ian and me.

Returning in a week, fresh from his travels, he snatched up the current issue and gave it a quick look. "Nicely done," he said, then frowned, slightly perplexed, "but I notice you haven't written an item in some time, Sadie. Not since Daniel was born…" When I didn't answer, he urged, "You should keep writing, Sadie. You can make your mark, like Nellie Bly."

"Suppose I could," I answered doubtfully. "I read her little book, *10 Days in a Madhouse*, and I admire her ruse to have herself committed and share the plight of the poor desperate inmates. She was brave. The misery and cruelty she exposed made her mark, as you say, and perhaps did some good. But such concern is brief, another item, there a day then gone. Now she plans to round the world in 80 days. Live out the Jules Verne adventure and write another story. But she doesn't have a baby to tote, a home to care for. In that time I can grow a garden. Can our food. Hang sheets and diapers out to dry. Teach our son to walk, talk, and eat. Set type and print my husband's paper."

"But Sadie," he implored, "you can still have say. I miss your words, like your sweet flesh next to mine…" again using his charm, more in plea than admonishment. "Don't you have something to say?"

Empty of words until that moment, I sat down, dipped my pen and promptly wrote: *"Having seldom considered the umbilical before giving birth, since then I have thought daily of our common stigmata, the belly scar linking each to each through generations untold. Severed at birth, the mystic bond holds, pulsing in our veins, transcending wars, politics, nations, race and blood, rooting back to our primal womb, the good earth, where, in the chore of life, lies our lasting joy and duty. Now a wife and mother, that is my last word…"*

Signed Sadie Briar-Corbett, I handed it to Hagan. He furrowed his brow and read it through, taking his time, gave a sigh and said, "Subtlety defiant and succinct. Admirably so…" Then he smiled, "Methinks I've been spit on."

"Why?" I asked. "I'm your wife, Danny's mother, not 'The Last Spit Girl.' I simply don't want to write. My few words, like spit in the dust, soon dry up and blow away. I want to focus on immediate cares and concerns."

"Such as?"

"You, our baby, and my garden."

"And so you may," he agreed cheerfully. "But may I title this 'Sadie's Last Word' and print it?" Gracious and gallant in the moment, granting me my say.

Still, resentments grew. There was a deep reserve to Hagan, something distant and remote. While he kept his chapters hidden, his dalliances far flung, left alone so many nights, plagued by dreams, imaginings, I woke embittered, hurt. By summer's end, after several more trips, I mentioned my loneliness, not my suspicion, just his travels.

"Sadie, Sadie," he answered, partly cajoling but clearly annoyed, "the rails are my ocean. If I were a sailor, would you begrudge me the sea? Conventions, rallies, cities are my fisheries and harbor. I travel in currents of people, gather and pollinate to further a cause. To make a better and freer world. For you and Danny. You are my darling, the one I married. To you I return, always. I promise…"

Once more mollified, drawn to his embrace, happy for a time, his attentions genuine, gratifying, but never sustained. In a matter of weeks, a month, again called away, leaving me alone with my baby.

Daniel was a good baby, seldom fussy or colicky. Given a midnight feeding, he usually slept till dawn. And soon held his head erect, reaching and grasping for things. At six months he sat on my lap while I set type. Ever curious, he learned his letters even as he learned to speak — M for *Mom*, D for *Dad*, and G for *gone*.

Again left alone following Christmas, Danny on my lap as I set type for a tragic event in South Dakota, "Battle at Wounded Knee!" datelined

December 30, 1890, in which the Army turned mountain guns on a band of starving Sioux. I imagined running with my baby through the snow, family and loved ones slaughtered. Then I recalled the Callaways and their slaughter, and knew many had been so dealt. Yet a savage had spared my mother and me. Realizing this, my heart ached and I had no words. Put it out of mind, grateful to be safe and warm, and despite being lonely, I had my son, alive and well, and growing.

--------·◈·--------

Maxie was my constant, checking in most evenings after work. He'd take Danny like a big bear cuddling a cub and rock him to sleep while I finished setting type or pressed another page. So I endured Hagan's absences as I had vowed, for better or for worse. And eventually a good deal worse. Hagan, born to action, change, and travel, was off every month to another convention or meeting. Home from Dallas where the Cooperative collapsed due to lack of funds, then straight to St. Louis to help unite the Alliance north and south, which also failed. Then to Topeka in August of 1890 to join the People's Party and nominate John Willits for governor, a populist who also lost. But there were victories. In the same election populists won the state legislature and sent William Peffer in his foot-long beard and granny glasses to the U.S. Senate, the first populist to be so sworn; the former editor of *The Kansas Farmer*, like his slogan, proved "A Man Can Rise."

"The Torch Is Lit!" Hagan's headline proclaimed, "The Populist Fire Spreads!" And in Omaha on July 4th, 1892, he witnessed the party's official birth, there amidst the flags, marching bands, and cheering crowds. Watched and shared the fanfare and the enthusiasm caught like a fever, the greater number swept up in the thrill and promise. And I too for a time. That fall, along with taking the senate and apparently the house, Kansans elected the first populist governor in the nation, Lorenzo Lewelling, marking Kansas, as Hagan had predicted, the seedbed of change. And he at the very center.

No, you could not fault his will and energy. Even made occasional trips to Washington, D.C., to meet with Charles Macune, now editor of the nation's leading populist paper, *The Financier*, which featured articles by Hagan. Becoming known and he relished his notoriety.

Doubtless there were other women in these various chapters, but I put them out of mind, like Wounded Knee, and busied myself raising Danny and working mostly jobbers, for *The Advocate* lapsed in Hagan's absence. But he made amends upon return, madly working night and day to put out a double issue and seldom lost a customer.

Yet over time he was losing me. For it hurt, left alone, the thought of other women, though I remained silent and carried on, sustained by Maxie's gruff good humor, his fond blue eyes crinkling in smile, his large presence and manly scent. Seeing me silent, in a mood, he'd reach his rough hand and pat mine, but that was all, simply sharing a touch, a smile, a kindly word.

"Ah know, lass, ah know," he'd say, "Hag'll soon be home…"

And he was home for Christmas, on past the New Year. But in late January, the populist governor and senate sworn in, Hagan traveled to Topeka. A legislative war was brewing, Populists and Republicans each claiming control of the house. The Populists and Governor Lewelling accused Republicans of voter fraud. Both sides threatened violence. Hagan in the midst, I was sick with worry. The crisis continued into February. When Republicans tried to arrest the sergeant of arms, Populists occupied the house chamber and barred the doors. Next day a horde of Republicans bashed in the door with sledge hammers and the Populists retreated to the basement. Governor Lewelling called out the Militia to evict the usurpers, but the commander refused the order and surrendered his men to the Republicans. Guns drawn, the standoff lasted three days before a timely blizzard cooled tempers and a truce was called. Both sides agreed to let the Supreme Court settle the issue.

By a two to one partisan vote, Republicans gained control of the house.

Hagan returned home with a gashed forehead suffered during the break in. Now neatly stitched and bandaged, it recalled Glen's wound from the circus. Noting which, Maxie said, "Fisticuffs don' work agin' guns, Hag. Better wise up 'fore ya leave Sadie a widow 'n yer boy without his Da."

"You're right, Maxie," Hagan laughed it off, "next time I'll pack a pistol."

"Nay, not wha' ah meant," Maxie stood firm, unsmiling. "No joke, Hag, the boy needs his Da. You grew without one. Ah did too. Don' ya remember? Don' ya see? Each time ya leave he stands by the door on his wee wobbly legs 'n watches ya go. He needs his Da. Same as Sadie needs her husband."

"Yes, yes, of course…" Hagan nodded, "thanks for the reminder. I know what I need to do. I'll take care of it, I will…"

Next day he purchased a life policy through the ITU, the printers' union. When the confirmation letter arrived, he handed it to me and said, "Lock it away, Sadie, somewhere safe. It'll be there if you need it" — which was not what I needed, or what Maxie meant, but what Hagan did.

⸎

By the summer of '93 I was again pregnant, the nation in the grip of another panic sending over 100,000 Boomers in rush to claim the Cherokee Strip, bust out the sod, and plant crops. Yet the drought grew so dire that many farmers from Texas to Dakota had no wheat or corn to harvest, let alone market. And a good many rallied to Mary Lease's cry, "Stop planting corn and start raising hell!" Hailed as the People's Joan of Arc, her stern voice and visage held listeners spellbound. Still, prospects dimmed, with no relief as oft-vaunted plans to ease their plight joined the dust.

Despite the desperate news and endless heat, I skipped task to task, buoyant, hopeful that a second child would give Hagan anchor. Missing two cycles and barely showing, I had yet to tell him. Only my mother, who visited most Saturdays to trade, noticed. And of course, Maxie, keen to my cheery mood, guessed the reason.

"Aye, in bloom, ah see. Yer cheeks flush 'n rosy. A'nuther love child, ah bet…"

I merely smiled, keeping my secret for Hagan's return the next evening, Friday, the 14th of July, marking our fifth year of marriage. In anticipation, up at dawn to beat the heat, I baked a peach pie from canned preserves. Then midmorning, leaning over the washboard, scrubbing the last of my laundry while Danny took his nap, I felt a sharp pain in my belly and further spasms as blood started to flow, similar to a cycle, only different. Feeling faint, I stumbled through the kitchen to the bedroom and straddled the chamber pot, dropping more clots of blood. When the fetus came I instinctively caught it, tried not to look but felt a brief heartbeat then thankfully nothing. Shaken, trembling, I wrapped the lost life in the towel that had bound my hair and laid it aside. I removed my soiled undergarments and wiped myself clean then returned to the wash porch to leave them to soak. Wrapping a second towel around the fetus, I glimpsed Danny, awakened, standing at the kitchen door, looking on in question.

"Why are you crying, Mommy?"

"Ah honey, just a sadness came over me. It'll pass."

"What is that?" he pointed to the bundle I held.

"A mystery," I answered, "that breathes without breath and speaks without words. A secret blessing to all that lives and dies. And now I want to plant it in our garden. Will you help me?"

"Oh yes, I can help" — he loved to dig, especially in the garden. Now 4 years old and brimming with words, already reading Grimm's Tales and Aesop's Fables, each day an adventure, he reached for my hand and led the way. I steadied myself and followed, meandering to the center of the garden where we'd recently dug potatoes and onions. The spade still forked the ground; I laid my bundle nearby and began digging, careful of Danny's eager hands scooping out the dirt. Still bone dry a foot down, but at two feet the soil moistened and Danny found a worm. He held it to the sun then placed it back in the hole. And there we laid the little bundle.

Danny knelt by, touched it and said, "That's our secret blessing."

"Yes," I nodded then we quietly pushed in the dirt and covered it over.

Resting on my knees, again faint from the effort, I gazed down, silent for a time, then noted, "We need a rock to mark it."

Danny jumped up and ran to the edge of the walk path and asked, "This one?" pointing to a rectangular flagstone about the size of a skillet.

"Sure, that'll be fine," I answered, starting to rise as he said, "No Mommy, you stay. I can do it. Do it all by myself..." He dug in his fingers and jerked it free then huffed and tugged it over. We patted it neatly in place then he helped me stand and we walked to the cistern and pumped us each a cup of cool water.

Refreshed, I went inside to finish my tub of laundry while Danny romped with his imaginary playmate, Friend Wolf, whose ears perked like flowers in the morning and folded at night, and whose teeth never harmed Little Red Riding Hood or any other child. Later, I fixed him a slice of bread with apple jam. While he ate, I washed up and put on a clean dress. The blue one I'd worn the morning we were wed in Oakvale.

This was to have been such a special day, awaiting Hagan's return to celebrate the coming of another child. He'd left for Chicago the week of the Fourth to report on the World's Fair and the ongoing effort to unite rural populists with organized labor, grown even stronger since the hanging of the Haymarket Martyrs. In fact, in late June, the new Governor of Illinois, John Altgeld, pardoned the remaining Haymarket prisoners after determining they had been framed, wrongly convicted, and forthwith denounced police, prosecutors, and judges involved. For which he was swiftly vilified by papers coast to coast, many claiming "Altgeld should be gelded like is name!" Naturally, Hagan wanted to witness events first hand. And I, excited for him, awake that morning, so expectant, anticipating his arrival, hoping to reclaim our early promise and renew our love. But no, though drained and weakened by my loss, I dared not lie down and close my eyes for fear I'd see the horror play again.

In the print shop I occupied myself setting type. Danny tagged along clutching his favorite pillow, soon bellied on the floor, flipping through the pages of *Mother Goose*, humming an aimless tune. Ian, usually busy at one task or another, was off delivering photographs to one of his many clients, his sideline beginning to thrive. I gripped my type stick, composed a few words then simply stared, too sad and empty to attempt a thing.

There I sat, mindless of Danny asleep on the floor, bleak, despondent, as if posed for the madhouse, when Maxie walked in and rang the bell.

"Knocked off early for th' big day!" he brusquely declared, "Hagan's train due any minute! Aye, hear the rails a'hummin'. Hey thar, what's this…?" he quieted and walked forth. "Yesterday ya's pink as a rose, now pale as a ghost…" Hearing his gruff concern, my lips began to quiver and trembling I dropped my type stick.

"Dear girl, what has happened?" he asked, taking my hand in his to calm me.

"I…lost my baby," I managed to say before my eyes teared and I hung my head in sob. He eased me up and held me in his arms, softly patting my back, "Thar now, Sadie, say no more. Ye's wore to the nub. Les move ya t' the chair here 'n rest ye…"

After helping me sit, he took his red handkerchief and daubed my eyes. Then the steam whistle blew, announcing the train's arrival, and Danny shot up and out the door, off to greet his daddy at the depot.

I dried my eyes and caught my breath, smiled to Maxie, and he to me. We soon heard Hagan step lively to the boardwalk, jubilant, telling Danny of all the wonders he'd seen, carrying the boy in the crook of his arm as he strode in. He sat his leather grip to the floor and raised his hand in arc, depicting the famous Ferris Wheel — "A giant wheel, Danny, taller than the tallest tree, all lit up like the Milky Way, spinning people to such a height they could touch the moon. And here…" kneeling down, he opened his grip and fanned forth a dozen postcards, "See? The Pinta, the Nina, and the Santa Maria…the three ships Columbus sailed to discover America. And there's more…"

Danny gazed on like he held the winning hand, then rushed to me exclaiming, "Mommy, Mommy, look-it these Daddy gave me" — pointing to the pictured ships, the massive statues, the reflecting pool, and many grand buildings.

Hagan stood and slowly removed his hat, perplexed at why I hadn't stirred or spoken. Max leaned to him and said, "She lost her baby this mornin'. Been a rough day…" As Hagan came to me, Maxie called to Danny, "Hey Danny boy, les' walk up town with Uncle Max. Ah'll buy ya a soda 'n ya can show me yer cards, eh?"

Left alone, Hagan knelt, clasped my hand and said, "I didn't know."

"No, I wasn't certain till lately. I planned to tell you today. Then…"

"I'm sorry, Sadie, so sorry." Again my eyes teared as he stood and drew me to him. "I see you wore your pretty dress," he noted, brushing a strand of my hair and wiping my tears, "but you should lie down." He cradled me in his arms and carried me to our bed and lowered me to the pillows. He removed my shoes, went to the kitchen and returned with a glass of water and a damp cloth. He pulled up a chair and raised my head to help me sip, then wiped my brow and cheeks, his voice soft and soothing.

"My dear, dear, Sadie, I'm sorry, so sorry…perhaps if I hadn't been gone. But there's so much yet to do…so much pending. And I'd hoped for a glorious day as well. Our five years together. Anxious to share all the sights I'd seen. But now —"

"No, please tell me. I should like to listen."

Smiling, he caressed my hand and began to speak, describing the great columned buildings of pearly stucco in the splendid "White City" I'd glimpsed on the postcards. "Swarms of people and displays from all around the world," he said, "covering a full square mile, Sadie. An area equal to the Briar-Callaway Ranch…" And he touched on the marvels of electricity and scores of inventions, practical and fantastic, the crowds that stood admiring the massive gun built by Krupp, the German "Cannon King," that could hurl a shell the size of a tree 15 miles! Listening, I recalled what father said of the Civil War Springfield he'd carried and its grievous wounds — "Of little use 'cept to kill a man. Wouldn't leave enough rabbit to skin or eat…" And I wondered what this gun would do? And of all the other marvels, what would they lead to? Having seen one circus and its result, I remained skeptical and wary of things to come — even the machine I'd read of, which he mentioned, invented by a woman, said to wash clothes. Still, Hagan's voice and touch calmed me…dreamlike as he spoke of a new music being played in cafes by Negro musicians, wildly delightful and alive with unexpected rhythms between, before, and aside those known, and once heard, altered your pulse and step…imagining which I drifted off in a deep peaceful sleep.

On after midnight I awoke to a distant tap-tap-tap, intermittent, slow then rapid, pausing to start again. Seeing no sign of Hagan, I got up and peered into the print shop. He sat hunched over the new contraption he'd acquired in the spring — a Remington typewriter, at which he was steadily growing adept, an ingenious tool, efficient, precise, but cold and mechanical, with none of the fluid warmth and grace of pen and ink. When he urged me to learn, I refused. For it chilled my thoughts and closed them off the instant I touched the keys and heard them tap. I understood and accepted the need of typesetting for repeated press and printing. But the typewriter spoke more to service and use than to my heart where my words formed and flowed.

I returned to bed and left him typing into the wee hours, dauntless, in the froth of another essay or article on politics or economics, determined to reshape the world. Ever drawn to far events and future horizons, none of which matched the marvel of the tiny being I had buried. While I still loved and admired Hagan, from that night on I too grew distant and remote, seldom let him touch me in that deep and wonderful way.

XIX. Highs & Lows

"Sittin' on a crosstie, ah was, eatin' sardines. He comes shiverin' up outa the weeds…" Maxie stood inside the door, a cold winter day, snow melting from his boots, his face red from the bitter wind, cuddling a little black pup. "Starved 'n whimperin', he were, licked fish oil off my finger 'n th' can. Ate ever' cracker crumb. Could'na leave 'im for the coyotes. Poor lil' jinks got ringworm 'n mange. But give 'im soap, iodine 'n food, he may fur out 'n make ya a fine dog. What say ye, Danny, do you 'n Friend Wolf want 'im?"

"Yes I do!" Danny cried, reaching up, anxious to hold the pup as Maxie handed it down. "Yes, and I will name him Jinks!"

"Then he's yers. That is if yer Mum don' mind?"

All eyes turned to me, including the pup.

"Can I Mom, can I keep him?" Who could say no to that?

"Of course, you may. But you must learn to feed and clean him" — before I could say more, he was off to the kitchen, soon sudsing the pup in my washtub and stuffing him with table scraps, marking an auspicious beginning to year 1894. Within a week, Hagan once more home, the pup's ringworms had healed, his fur filling in, tail feathering out, daily running and frisking with Danny who never mentioned

Friend Wolf again. He and Jinks, best buddies, inseparable, they even slept together.

Through March and April, I planted my garden, all sprouted by mid-May. Hagan worked the paper with Ian, and life was good. Then another national crisis loomed, again centered in Chicago. Seeing their wages cut, rents frozen, all 4000 Pullman workers went on strike. Mr. Pullman refused to bargain and hired in scabs, including Negroes, further enraging the strikers. Eugene Deb, president of the American Railway Union, called for a general strike in their support. Overnight, trains coast to coast ground to a halt, leaving Hagan stranded in Mankato.

Maxie, a member of the ARU, laughed, "Gotta sit this one out, Hag. 'Less you wanna walk to Chicago…"

Hagan, frustrated, did his best to keep apace, rushing to and from the telegraph office at all hours, arguing for or against depending on the latest developments. The strike not only stalled passenger service, but delayed coal and iron ore shipments and threatened delivery of the U.S. Mail, which gave President Cleveland, a democrat, an excuse to act. In June he overruled Governor Altgeld, whose even hand had prevented violence, and slapped an injunction on Debs and ordered Federal troops to put down the strike. And they did, ruthlessly, in Chicago and other cities, leaving 30 dead and scores wounded. Such high-handedness got the trains rolling. But workers seethed. To soothe their wounds, one week after suppressing the strike, Cleveland backed a bill setting aside the first Monday in September to celebrate Labor Day. Granted a holiday but not their rights, angry workers marched and denounced Cleveland. Both major parties scrambled for the favor of disgruntled workers and farmers, but voters unwilling to forgive or forget delivered Cleveland and the Democrats a drubbing in the mid-terms. Yet the Populists rode high through the southern and plains states, particularly in Kansas, though Governor Lewelling lost to a Republican.

Beyond the far political thunder and rumbling, my life was relatively calm and pleasing as the air following a brief summer rain. For once I spent more time sewing on my Singer than setting type. Hagan home a greater part of the time, and following the November elections, he settled in and published the paper through winter and spring without a single impulse to leave. He even took Danny and Jinks sledding. And when the weather warmed, he taught Danny, now six, how to throw and catch a baseball. Seeing him act as a father, my bitterness waned and I again warmed to him.

Especially the day he overheard Danny singing and smiled, "Ever notice how he can mimic and remember any tune he hears?" While I had witnessed and marveled at this for several years, I'd never broached the notion of his talent.

Shortly thereafter Hagan surprised us with a piano, holding the door as Maxie and his crew carried it in and set it in our parlor — a brand-new Ellington Cabinet Grand of solid mahogany with fluted legs and ornately scrolled panel and trim.

Then Hagan triumphally added the seat.

"How…?" I gasped. "It had to cost four or five hundred dollars, at least?"

"Nay lassie," Maxie grinned in wink to Hagan. "Twas damaged in freight. A wee scratch, aye, but got ya a real deal, a dandy bargain. Right, Hag?" he winked again and called his crew, "C'mon boys, buy ya a pint for yer labor, eh?"

They all laughed, in on the scheme. For looking it over I saw no scratch. Another one of Maxie's connections, highjacked, I suspected. But thrilled, watching Danny plink out "Camptown Races," a tune he'd heard at a recent Chautauqua in the city park.

Hagan stood by, smiling proud. When Danny paused to admire the panel and trim, for the first time I saw not a boy but Hagan's son, tall for his age, the same dark hair and eyes, and equally determined, impassioned. Hagan handed him a book and several sheets of music and said, "That's a method book, Danny. It'll help you get started. Also a few samples of the new music sweeping the country, wonderful and lively, called 'Ragtime'. Ian has a young friend, Jonathan Elgin, from Kansas City, he teaches music at the high school. He's quite accomplished and willing to teach you, if you're willing to learn?"

"Yes, Daddy, I will learn everything, I promise!"

That was Hagan's finest day with Danny, his finest deed, the gift of music that Danny could savor and touch, that stayed with him always. For Hagan was soon off again, on the scent of a rising political star.

Willian Jennings Bryan — "the silver-tongued orator of the Platte" — at least he was close by. Hagan's trips were frequent but brief, traveling to Nebraska where the former Congressman was editor-in-chief of the *Omaha World-Herald*. But Bryan, less newsman than politician, had his eye on the coming presidential campaign and spent the bulk of his time crisscrossing the country, speaking in nearly every major city, gathering support and momentum. Hagan was keen to Bryan's rising prospects, not only for his oratory, but his political skill and instinct. As Hagan said, "He's too cagey to declare, but he's running. Tireless and astute, more and more people think he can win. But first, he needs to snatch the nomination from Cleveland, a stodgy Bourbon, and since the Pullman Strike, broadly detested, while Bryan is a people's Democrat, largely in sync with the Populists. If we can get him elected, we have a chance to actually change this country…"

Over the fall and winter and into the spring of '96, Hagan wrote weekly articles to that effect, eventually drawing father, Glen, and many others to the fold, voicing support. Maxie, however, held back, dubious of all politicians and leery of Bryan's high-minded smooth talk — yet sufficiently curious to join Hagan on a weekend trip to Lincoln to hear him speak. Arriving home late Sunday evening, they sat in the print shop while I set type and Danny practiced piano, each a glass of whiskey in hand and soon at loggerheads, of opposing will and view.

"Drat, don' trust 'im," Maxie shook his head, "rubs me wrong. It's ye should run. Taller, better lookin', can outtalk that prig any which way. He's a stuff shirt, Hag, quotes more Bible'n a Sunday preacher."

"That may be, Maxie, but I couldn't run for Mankato mayor. And you know why. The bastard son of a traveling actress, they'd find me out in a week and I'd be done. Best I can do is help pick and choose. Bet on a winner and cheer him on."

"Aye, reckon so. Still don' trust no teetotaler."

"But Bryan is anti-prohibition, Maxie. He's against banning alcohol."

"That's his say for now. But mark me, one day he'll be all in with 'em witches bashin' good barrels o' whiskey. Pities the poor man nailed to the cross 'o gold, he does. But nail us to the ol' rugged cross, he would. Claims ever' word in the Bible rings true. Not to this beer-swillin' railroader, it don't. 'N all his bi-metal talk twixt silver or gold, ain't buyin' that either."

"He merely wants to increase the money supply," Hagan said, trying to coax him to a fuller understanding.

"Bah!" Maxie took a swig and wiped his mouth. "Who don' want money? But bi-metal? Silver or gold is all money stuffed in yer pocket. A man's got enuff, he's fat 'n happy. If not, he goes starved mad or to crime. Bi-metal…bah!"

"Maxie, Maxie…" Hagan groaned, "bi-metalism refers to monetary policy. Deals with coinage, exchange values, ratios and the like, all very complicated."

"Com-plicated! Now thar's a word, com-plicated."

"Yes, Maxie, complicated, but it can be understood. There's a fine little book, *Coin's Financial School*, which lays it out in plain English."

"Hang it Hag, ah can read 'n write me letters. Knows me pasts, presents 'n futures, though mayn't speak 'em just so. Ah can read Bryan 'n ah can read you. When a man says com-plicated 'n tags *ism* to a'nuther word, he's stringin' a line 'n tryin' to hook ya. Bah! Bi-metal or bi-ism, ah ain't buyin'!"

"But Bryan's for the farmer, Maxie, and for the worker."

"Sure, he champs farmers out here 'n poor tradesmen wha' be Anglo-Saxon 'n Protestant o' like belief as hisself. But he'd ban any factory workers from a far shore wha' be Catholic. Me Mum was Catholic, Irish Catholic…me Da, same o' the German kin. Me, ah'm a blame heathen. Still, they's my blood. Aye, me Mum knelt 'n kissed the cross. But she kissed no man's arse. 'N if ya run Bryan for president, ya can kiss me vote goodbye!" He downed his whiskey and stood. "Thar, ah'm plumb tuckered 'n off to bed. Got work tomorrow…" With that he cast a nod my way and was out the door, not so good-humored as usual, leaving their friendship somewhat strained, partly politics, partly things unsaid.

———————— ·●· ————————

Hagan, disappointed in his friend but far from disheartened, redoubled his efforts on Bryan's behalf. Followed to Chicago for the Democratic Convention in early July and witnessed the "Cross of Gold" speech that won Bryan the nomination, slated to run with Arthur Sewell from Maine. Hagan, home briefly, then back to St. Louis for the Populist

Convention where they too nominated Bryan while choosing their own vice-presidential candidate, Thomas Watson, editor from Georgia who was even more anti-Catholic than Bryan. Populists fused with the Democrats for the coming presidential campaign with the question of which would be the running mate, Sewell or Watson? Bryan, left to decide, listened to arguments from both camps. And Hagan stayed on, in the thick of negotiations that extended into August.

Meanwhile, Maxie made up his mind — "Can stomach not one o' the three!" he stoutly voiced one Saturday, standing out front on the boardwalk with father and Glen, talking politics, each smoking a cigar. Ian and I worked in the print shop, enjoying their exchange through the screen, while mother sat in the parlor listening to Danny play "My Old Kentucky Home," her favorite song.

"Watson rails agin' Catholics worse'n Bryan," Maxie continued. "Sewell's jus' a'nuther millionaire banker. Swar, think ah'll vote McKinley, he's what he is 'n makes no bones."

"Well, gotta admit," father chuckled, "Glen 'n I been leanin' the same. Been a Democrat all my life, but something about Bryan, too cocksure 'n grips his Bible mighty tight. Just don't tell Sara, I'll hear no end of how she got me to vote Republican. But you're right, Max, more I hear of McKinley, he's a true-blue. Joined the Union Army, just a young private in '61. Fought all four years 'n made major on General Hancock's staff by war's end. Then studied law. Unlike me, he finished, now runnin' for President. But I wouldn't trade 'im, no sir. Got Sara 'n more land than I can walk in a day. And our cattle all vote 'yea' when we feed 'em hay, right Glen?"

"Right, but toss 'em sweet sorghum or a handsome bull, watch out...!"

The three men shared a good laugh, blowing smoke, finding consensus.

A consensus that steadily spread despite Hagan's efforts. Rarely home all that summer, he kept promising to set aside a day and take Danny fishing. With Labor Day approaching, things came to a head. This time Hagan strictly promised to make it home, Danny's second year of school set to start the following Tuesday.

Saturday morning Danny waited anxiously as the 9:05 bearing passengers from Saint Joe rolled in. No Hagan. Though the express office had a telegram saying he'd been delayed and would arrive that evening, Sunday at the latest. But evening came and went, as did Sunday. Still no sign of Hagan, and no telegram. Monday morning, frantic with expectation, Danny stood on the platform, I and Maxie on either side. Watching, waiting, till we heard the far whistle, then the 9:05, right on time, loomed up and chugged forth, hissing steam as it slowed to a stop. Took on several passengers then rolled on west. Danny stared at the empty platform, breathing hard, tears wetting his cheeks, but he didn't cry. He simply stood and stared, as if staring would conjure his father.

"Reckon ya know ain't no train comin' till this evening," Maxie softly allowed. "Reckon ya think that was yer last chance…" e paused, letting the notion hang. "But wha' ya don' know is Uncle Max's got a buggy hitched waitin' at the livery to take ya fishin'. That is if ya can con-vince Jinks to go?"

"You bet I can!" Danny glanced up, all smiles, off in a snap, calling for Jinks.

Maxie grinned to me and said, "Sadie, ya might pack a wee basket with bread 'n butter, plates, salt 'n pepper 'n such. We'll catch some fish 'n thar's ripe corn. Ah got beer 'n soda iced in a tin pail already loaded. Had hoped for Hagan, twas not to be…"

Within the hour we arrived at the White Rock five miles north. High noon, the sun bearing down, Maxie reined to a shaded area beyond a cornfield and we climbed down. Danny and Jinks off running towards the creek where it fed into a deep pool along a sheer mud bank anchored by overhanging trees, bare roots reaching to the water.

"Careful thar, less it caves off," Maxie warned as he bucketed water for the horse. "Here, over here it slopes safe. 'N look now…" they peered to the pool, "see 'em swarm 'mong the roots? Aye, jus' flippin' thar tails, lazy in the sun, hungry for a worm. Help me bucket this to th' horse 'n we'll catch us some."

Danny grabbed the handle and tagged along, asking "But how, Uncle Max? We don't even have a pole?"

Maxie set the bucket by the thirsty horse and said, "Thar, let 'im sip on that 'n we'll fix ya a pole in a jiff…" Returning to the creek bank, he opened his jackknife and cut a willow limb, knelt to one knee and started trimming the twigs. "See? Always slice away from yer hand, like so. Here, you give it a try…" Danny knelt beside Maxie, gripped the knife in awe and finished trimming the twigs and leaves. "Good job, lad. Got ya a pole. Now stab yer blade in that leaf rot 'n dig around. Bet ye'll find a big fat worm…" No more than said, Danny dug in, Jinks pawing alongside, and they soon unearthed a wiggly worm. "Aye, got a nice big fat one, ya did. Now hold tight 'n ah'll fix th' line." Maxie stood and plucked a leather coin case from his pocket, waved his hand and withdrew a hook and line. "Always pack this along, out on th' section, a stream nearby, catch me a fish for lunch, aye…" he grinned, tying the line to the pole. "Give it a double knot, so it don' slip, see? Now a bobber…" he reached down and snapped a thumb-sized stick and looped it an elbow's length above the hook. "All set, now hand me yer worm 'n watch close. We hook 'im smack through the middle, two or three times 'n leave a tad free to tempt th' fish. Got it?"

Danny nodded eagerly.

"So, ready to catch a fish?"

"I am, Uncle Max, I'm ready."

"Here then, take aholt" — both eyeing the pool — "Thar, see that 'un break th' surface? Now ease yer hook on down till th' bobber is afloat. Jus' hold tight a spell…" Maxie urged, laying his hand to Danny's shoulder. "Aye, see it start to jigger 'n bob? When he takes it under, give a wee jerk. Not too hard…jus' enuff to hook 'im. Steady now…got 'im!"

Maxie reached out and grasped the line as Danny's pole bent with a foot-long catfish flipping silvery spray to the sunlight. Man and boy both thrilled, dog barking, Maxie unhooked the fish and plopped it to the grass.

"Jinks, leave it be," Maxie warned, "ye'll git yer share in a bit." Then he grinned to me, "Sadie, might gather some rocks 'n build a fire. Cuz Danny's gonna catch a slew o' fish, right boy? Now dig ya a worm 'n hook 'im whilst ah clean this fish."

In a blink Danny had another worm and said, "I can hook 'im, I know how…"

Within a quarter an hour they had four more nice-sized cat fish. As Maxie tossed the last guts for Jinks to chew and roll in, I winced at the sight and said, "He's going to stink something awful."

"Aye, two things a dog canna resist, fish guts 'n horse lumps. But we'll swim 'im clean a'fore th' ride home," he assured, then said,

"Danny, you 'n ah best wash th' fish stink off our hands if we wanna eat. 'N this knife is filthy too."

While they washed by the creek, I rolled the fish in the cornmeal and eggs I'd packed along and set them frying in the skillet. Catching a whiff, Maxie called, "Sadie, yer a fine lass to bring all th' fixin's." Then he stepped up, wiped the knife on his pant leg, and said to Danny, "Looky here, when ya close th' blade, keep yer fingers clear else it'll snap 'n cut ya. Got it?"

Danny gaped at the knife, a trifle puzzled as Maxie held it forth.

"It be yers now. A big boy, fixed for second grade. Time ye had a knife."

"Really?" Danny glanced to Maxie, then to me in wonder if he should.

I nodded, "Yes, if Maxie thinks you're ready."

"Golly, Uncle Max, thank you. This is the best day forever and ever!"

Then Maxie handed him a pocket stone and said, "This'll help ya keep it sharp." Danny immediately sat down and set the blade to the stone as Maxie observed, "That's right. Jus' work in tiny little circles 'n add some spit now 'n then…"

While Danny honed his knife and the fish sizzled in hot butter, Maxie walked into the cornfield and shortly emerged with a half dozen ears.

"That farmer won' miss these few," he laughed. "Coons steal a wagonload most nights." Coming forth, he laid them by and said, "Hey Danny, ever et hobo corn? No? Why here, we jus' take a stick 'n scrape back th' coals o' yer Mum's fire, then lay 'em side by side, husks 'n all. Cover 'em over 'n let 'em bake." Then he asked, "What say ye, Danny? Like a soda whilst we wait?"

"Yes I would, yes please."

Maxie reached down and pulled a bottle dripping wet from the icy pail, popped the cork and handed it to Danny. "Thar ya go, lad. 'N ye, me lass, be wantin' a soda?"

"No, today I'd like a beer…if you have enough?"

"Always have enuff, ah do" — popping two bottles, he handed me one.

It tasted wonderfully bitter, fresh and heady in the shade by the fire, the sun dappling the grass. Soon we were all enjoying a plate of crisp fried catfish and hobo corn. And watching Maxie seated next to Danny, massive, joyous, and primal, I felt my love for him warm me in a less modest way. Especially when he showed Danny how to hold and eat his corn.

"Ye grabs th' stalk end, see? Aye, pluck th' curly silk 'n toss it. Then peel th' shuck down each side till she opens like a flower 'n shows her pearly ripe seed. Aye, then ya rubs on butter, sprinkle with salt 'n sink yer teeth…" And he did so with a big lusty grin as his eyes fell to mine and I imagined his hands undressing me, blushed and looked to my plate, now empty except for crumbs, and I wished this day, all itself, would shift to another time and never end. A wonderful day, just Maxie, Danny and I, and not a word of politics.

Finished eating, we slipped off our shoes and waded in the shallows while cottonwood seeds floated down and Jinks swam himself clean fetching sticks for Danny. And I delighted in fluffs of cotton forming bouquets in eddies, swished my feet and felt like a girl again. When we stepped to the bank Jinks caught us in a vigorous spray as he shook his fur and we jumped back, laughing, shooing him away.

Sated and happy, we loaded up and began our journey back to Mankato. The horse in slow canter, the buggy in gentle sway, Danny soon curled asleep with Jinks in back, I touched Maxie's hand and thanked him for the lovely day.

"Aye," he grunted, idly chomping his cigar.

"You can smoke that if you like," I assured him. "Really, I don't mind."

"Nay," he answered. "Smokes not good for ye nor the lad…"

He spat to the side and we rode on, silent, our urges unspoken as the south wind combed the tawny grasses, wafting warm scents to the air. In the near distance a small herd of deer, rarely seen by then, all but hunted out, raised their heads to our passing as the late summer sky blazed a glorious red above the golden sunset.

<hr>

Maxie helped me down and was hitching the horse front of the print shop when the 7:15 rolled in. Danny rose up rubbing his eyes awake and spied his father, grip in hand, a bag slung from his shoulder, in halting walk from the depot, haggard, unshaven, hardly his usual jaunty self.

"Hey there, Danny," he called in approach, "sorry I'm late. It couldn't be helped."

Danny stared silent, hurt, refused his greeting, jumped down and ran inside.

Hagan stood hesitant, caught off guard, at a loss for words.

"Ah took the boy fishin'," Maxie stated, "like ye had promised."

"Yes, I can see. And I thank you. I'm grateful…just couldn't make it."

"Aye…" Maxie turned away and carried my basket with the skillet and dishes through the door and set it on the desk. Hagan followed inside, dropped his grip and eased his typewriter bag to the floor. He looked around a moment, puzzled.

"Where is Danny? Why is he hiding?"

"Don' ya know? He wanted to fish with his Da. He's mad, angry."

"But I'm sorry. Said I'm sorry," pleading to Maxie and me, not to Danny. "You have to understand. We're on the verge…of electing Bryan President. I'm his advance man. I ride ahead and arrange ads, pamphlets, brochures for each event. It's either all in or all out. We're right on the cusp of making history. Understand?"

"Aye, off traipsin' after stuff shirt 'n leave Sadie 'n Danny alone."

"Now Max, this is not your concern."

"Then ah make it so. 'N wha' is this?" pointing to Hagan's hand. "Whar's yer ring?" Firm, unsmiling, he asked again, "Whar's yer weddin' ring, Hag?"

"Oh damn," Hagan slumped his shoulders and glanced to me, "I'm sorry, Sadie. Must have left it in my room. Typing late last night, I took it off. Sometimes, hitting the keys, it aggravates me."

"You typed for months at home and never took it off," I answered, my long bitterness welling up. "You swore, once swore to forsake all others, now you, you…" Ashamed I'd spoken and too ashamed to say more, feeling utterly forsaken and Hagan standing limp, silent, told me it was true.

"Aggravated, eh? Like a wife 'n kid?"

"You stay out, Maxie…this is between Sadie and me!"

"Out, ya say? Aye, les step out 'n talk this man to man."

"Damn right we will. And another thing," Hagan said, angrily following out into the darkening dusk, "from now on you stay away from Sadie. You've gotten too cozy!"

"So, Sadie it tis? That worry ya? Not ye stayin' away forever 'n anon…"

Hearing them cast fault and accusation I could not hold my tears, clutched my stomach and bent low in ache and fear of what they might do. Two jagged shadows beyond the screen, their boots stomped then planted hard.

"Stay out, Maxie, I mean it! She's my wife!"

"That she is, Hag. 'N know this, ah n'er touched her but to pat her hand as ya see me do. 'N held her once, th' day she lost her wee babe. Nay, n'er touched her in any way to shame her nor ye."

"Just stay out! Stay away! I'm warning you."

"Aye, ah'll stay out…if you stay in. But mark me, ya don' stay in ah'll take her from ya 'n make her mine, ah will."

"Damn you, Maxie!"

"Don' try it, Hag…"

Beyond the screen I heard their brutish clash, their harsh oaths, fists to flesh and bone, grappling back and forth, shaking the walls and lamps within, then the dull thud of a body fallen to the boardwalk. Amid the dread silence I imagined one dead from a knife or blackjack. Relieved to finally hear a low groan as Maxie said, "Pick yerself up, Hag. Go back to Sadie 'n yer son. Ah'll stay away. Aye, it pains me to see 'em hurt. Ye too, it pains me…"

More silence as Maxie stepped down and walked away.

Slowly Hagan roused and stood. I drew back from the door as he stumbled in, slightly off balance, holding a kerchief to his bloody nose, his right eye nearly swollen shut. He gazed vaguely and said nothing, walked directly to the darkroom in back and shut the door. Luckily, Ian was out, as on most Monday evenings, playing chess with Danny's music teacher, Jonathan, often till midnight or past.

I carried the basket of dishes to the kitchen then went to check on Danny. Found him still clothed, lying on his bed, staring at the wall; Jinks asleep in the corner on the cool bare floor. I sat on the bedside and stroked Danny's hair. He sniffled a few times, all cried out, breathing easy.

"Your daddy loves you," I said. "I know it's hard, him gone. But he's a busy man with important work. Hopes to make a better world…" Alluding to all at stake, I tried to convince Danny and myself. And perhaps did, partly, for he soon slept, still holding the jackknife Maxie had given him.

Exhausted, I went to bed, but couldn't sleep — hot, not a breath of air through the window, haunted by guilt, shame, and worry. Hagan and Maxie, sworn friends, once joined like brothers, now opposed, and I the cause. Loving both, I blamed myself. For I was woman, temptress, held the apple but saw no way to heal the heart.

Later, tossing in sweat, I heard Ian quietly enter the shop, then the murmur of him and Hagan speaking low. Finally, towards the cool of the morning, I slept and awakened to the gray dawn lighting the northeast window. I sat up and peered towards the depot. Beneath the overhang I saw Hagan, his grip in hand, typewriter bag slung to his shoulder, a dim shadow standing in wait of the eastbound train.

XX. Another Clime

Maxie stayed away as he said he would. Occasionally I'd see him walking to and from his work on the railroad. He'd nod and keep a respectful distance, each now shy of the other. Danny shared our bewilderment, though even more sad and confused. Many times he asked if the election was over and when his daddy was coming home. We'd received only one telegram early on that stated: "Found the ring. Give Danny a hug. Hagan…" Again I reminded Danny that his father was a busy man, and that he was working very hard to elect a new president. By October, Danny stopped asking. His silence more pensive than moody, he gradually immersed himself in the piano — played each morning before school and every evening until bedtime.

Trains passed daily, east and west, and none carried Hagan to us.

Judging from headlines he was undoubtedly busy, spearheading a campaign that visited over half the states in the Union with Bryan delivering hundreds of speeches in as many cities. Meanwhile McKinley remained on his front porch, politely greeted visitors, gave a few speeches with a nod to free silver, and rarely engaged the press. Maintained a dignified, respectful pose and thereby overwhelmed the eloquent, energetic upstart. As Maxie had signaled, Catholics went to McKinley in droves. But what doomed Bryan foremost was a column penned by a little-known Kansas newsman William Allen White, asking: "What's the matter with Kansas?" in which he cleverly ridiculed Populism's rude garments while dismissing just and vital claims. In one swift stroke of the pen he turned Mary Lease's rallying cry on its head, calling for farmers "To stop raising hell and start raising corn!" Words and sentiments echoed by Republican newspapers coast to coast, which overnight made White famous and Lease largely forgotten. Even at my far remove I could sense that, added to the might of banks, railroads, and industry, this single missive sank Bryan's chances. And so went the Populist cause.

Nearly Thanksgiving, a fortnight after the election, Hagan slipped in unexpected as the evening train whistled on west. Danny looked up from his piano and I peeked in from the kitchen as Hagan dropped his typewriter bag like a battered shield and stood defeated.

He glanced from one to the other and said, "Sadie, Danny…I've been gone too long, I know. Thought I could come home in victory and make amends. But we lost. And I…" He stared silent and grimaced, failed by words or explanation, knelt to his grip and took out a sheet of music. "This is a new piece being played," he said, handing it to Danny. "A fine little tune by Ben Harney, 'You've Been a Good Ol' Wagon, But You've Done Broke Down…' And a fitting title for a failed campaign," he added with a slight smile. Tried to shrug it off, but couldn't, not really. His face lined and weary, his eyes dark and sunken. Too many months and years of effort, of hope and promise, suddenly ground to a halt. Desperate for traction, like our marriage.

"I thought to bring you a necklace or broach," he said. "But they all seemed mere trifles, trinkets. Here…" again he reached to his grip and handed me a little book, "I got you this instead. Poems by a woman, Emily Dickinson…they remind me of you, Sadie. Especially in one where she speaks of 'a feathered thing that perches in the soul, sings a tune without words, and never in extremity asked a crumb of me…'"

With that he said he had some correspondence to finish and bid us "Good night."

Like an apparition briefly there then gone, back to the print shop, hunched over his typewriter, fixed to his task. Danny gazed on his absence, a moment forlorn, then turned to the new piece and played till he had the melody then let it rest.

"I'll do better tomorrow and make Daddy happy," he said as I tucked him in.

"I know you will. Now sleep…"

Later, in bed alone, while Hagan typed beyond the wall, I read the poem he'd quoted, "Hope" and others…*a certain slant of light that reveals differences, meanings, and death…that truth is best told aslant, in portion, else it blinds…that much madness is a divine sense.* And I felt her rise and mix within, like a sister. But hope eluded me.

Next morning I found Hagan stretched out on an army cot he'd packed along, its pegged wooden frame folded in canvas. From then on it remained assembled behind his desk in the print shop. Hagan home was the loneliest period of my life. We were cordial, but never touched. No, neither asked a crumb of the other. Both too proud to reconcile, we slept apart.

Suspicion and bitterness over his many chapters still gripped me. As for Hagan, I think it was a loss of desire, his long effort and defeat, and the hard blow from Maxie that felled him, left him wounded. You could see it in his stride and in his eye. Once proud, confident, straight as a soldier, now slightly bent, hesitant in glance and speech. He'd often pause, defer, seldom raced to conclude or grasp a thought. For long periods he'd sit listless and stare, then bestir himself to one print task or another, leaving Ian to direct the greater part of the business as he had for the past two years.

Myself, I was happy to skip typesetting and related chores, with Hagan home, no longer needed, nor did I volunteer. But one day Danny asked to help, for he was fairly accomplished. Hagan kindly dissuaded him, saying, "No, my son, spare your hands for the piano. Something special and lasting. There's a machine sweeping the country as rapidly as Ragtime, called the linotype, that will replace typesetters like the power loom replaced Ned Ludd and a host of weavers who vanished like ghosts. But music, nothing will ever replace music…"

Hearing him encourage Danny warmed my heart. The day after his arrival home, when Danny performed the new song, Hagan had actually lingered by and listened, then declared, "That's quite good, lively and flawless…" Thereafter, most evenings following supper, he'd sit and listen to Danny play awhile before returning to his labors in the print shop, always careful to leave the door ajar to catch the music as Danny practiced and explored song after song.

And later, after seeing Danny to bed, I'd peek in out of old habit and concern and find Hagan at his desk, rarely writing, simply gazing to the lamp and sipping whiskey, never drunken, but pensive, silent, perhaps reflecting on old chapters or hatching a new one. Drinking himself sober before he slept. One night when I started to slip away he glanced around and our eyes met. He beckoned me forth and casually spoke, as much to himself as to me.

"You know, I think Bryan will run again," he said. "But he will lose, and I will not help him. Once burned…" He slowly sighed and conceded, "Maxie was right. Bryan is a four-flusher, lacks that one vital card. Maybe the women's vote…" He tried to smile then sadly shook his head. "Like many I was swayed by his eloquence. But words don't win the day. Too bound by the good book, ensnared in the Bible, he lacked something elemental. Maxie sensed it, your father, Glen, and the greater number. McKinley from his front porch projected more strength and judgement. Delivered the telling blow and claimed victory." He took a sip of whiskey, licked his lips in brief thought. "But Bryan was right about one thing. The gilded few will continue to grab the greater share while casting a trifle to the many. The many will scramble for their speck of dust, blind to their folly. But you cannot rally people by calling them fools. I once thought it could change, but no longer. People hunger. Tossed a crumb and praised for their virtue, they struggle on, content with their meager lot and never throw off the yoke. Pity the fool who thinks otherwise…" He promptly downed his glass and doused the lamp.

Defeated, bereft of cause and ambition, Hagan clawed his way through winter.

While the election of '96 all but snuffed Populism, there were gains. Both major parties adopted policies once opposed. A majority of states began to regulate railroads and shipping rates. And most importantly for our region the wetter weather that came in latter '96 carried over into '97, ending the drought from Texas to the Dakotas, improving prospects for farmers, cattlemen, and people throughout the plains.

By mid-spring Hagan's posture improved, his eyes brightened, his speech grew more assertive and direct. One morning he called to Ian and said, "It's time we change the name of this paper, starting with that sign out front..." Ian merely raised his brow in question as Hagan, without further word, searched a ladder, climbed up and removed the sign. By the following morning he'd painted and stenciled a new one — no longer *The Prairie Advocate*, now *The Mankato Mercantile* swinging by two chains in the wind.

Hagan gazed up and observed with more irony than bitterness, "They say business wheels America forth. It's time we roll with it." Then he nudged Ian and added, "And it's time we make you full partner. I've noticed how your photo ads outsell editorials, in fact, pay for them. You've held the fort, you and Sadie, through my long absences. Held steady and never complained. It's high time you reap a fair share. From this moment I name you co-editor and co-owner of *The Mankato Mercantile*...Corbett-Winchell, which, if you are agreed, we will formally declare in our premier issue. Fair enough?"

Ian, surprised, stood blank a moment, then eagerly shook hands, stammering, "Why sure, but I...I need to change the header."

"Not so fast, young man," Hagan grinned. "First, let's draw up the papers and make it legal..." So said, before the day was over, the agreement was officially signed, counter-signed, and notarized. All of which I witnessed and signed as well, proud to see a flicker of the old Hagan shining through — active, forceful, and just.

The economy at large, still sluggish through winter and spring, threw off its doldrums in June, awakening to the cry of "Gold in the Klondike!" Overnight talk of silver ceased as thousands rushed north to Alaska to make the arduous trek, each packing supplies in relays over White Pass then descending to the Yukon and the destined placers. Hagan held no lust for gold, nor did he scorn the seekers, his sole attention merely ironic as he headlined the news "Stewards Folly Pans Out!"

But he did show more interest in our son, sparing time to play catch and encourage Danny's pitching. Until Danny caught one wrong, jammed two fingers and couldn't play piano. Hagan regretted the injury and set baseball aside. The very next Sunday he took Danny to the livery and they rode out double on Blood as Hagan taught him to rein and hold his seat. They continued the lessons over the following days on business errands to Oakvale, Otego, and others. And Blood, age 14 and not so spirited, was still a difficult horse to handle. But Danny, of smooth hand and lank leg, soon sat him well. Early one morning, as I later learned, they rode to the Limestone and returned that evening, Danny proudly riding my little mare Patches. After marriage and motherhood I seldom rode, seldom had time, and years prior, to save stable cost, I put Patches to pasture on the BC Ranch. She tossed her head, pleased to see me, and I her. Pleased to see her carry my son. Though Danny still preferred his father's tall black horse, Blood.

And there was a stirring in Hagan, considerate, attentive, but not content. Handing off half his business to Ian, grooming his son toward manhood, I'd read him too long not to suspect a new chapter forming. Bit by bit I began to discern its source and direction, far from Alaska, and of opposite clime, Cuba. For several years in setting type I'd read articles on the rebellion against Spanish rule. And during our recent election, while given mention, neither party made it an issue, much less a concern. Yet over winter and spring undercurrents surfaced with pamphlets and readings on "Cuba Libra" reaching even to churches and civic groups in Mankato, with more and more voices calling for Cuban independence, if not outright intervention — Bryan, although less militant, among them. Whereas McKinley urged patience and diplomacy, and pursued negotiations in hope that Spain would grant its far isle peace and freedom.

Through all this time Hagan remained silent on Cuba, said not a word. Then in late summer after skimming an article on recent negotiations, Hagan laid the paper aside and observed, "McKinley is right to show restraint. But I doubt Spain will relent. They've held Cuba for 400 years…see it as part of the mother country, merely separate by water. A vital province, a fertile Eden, rich in sugar, tobacco, cheap labor, bountiful crops year around. No, they will not let it go without a fight…" A brief comment made in passing, nothing more. He returned to his work, and I to mine, giving it little thought.

Perhaps a month later, Danny back in school, Hagan off on an errand, I chanced by his desk and glimpsed a map of Cuba, as well as several books on its history, a Spanish language text and a dictionary.

But I focused on the map, particularly a line drawn from Monti Cristo on the northern coast of Hispaniola tracing a journey to the easternmost tip of Cuba then passing under Cape Maisi to an "X" marked by the coastal town of Imias, beneath which a note in Hagan's hand read, "Jose Marti lands and joins rebel forces, May 11, 1895..." Then about halfway west along the southern coast, inland above Santiago Bay, he'd marked another "X" beside which was written, "Killed in Battle of Dos Rivas, May 19, 1895..." The poor man had lived barely more than a month after landing.

I felt the pang of knowing and wished I'd never looked.

But the question would not leave me. That night after supper, Danny at his piano, Hagan rising from his chair, I asked, "Who was Jose Marti?"

He gazed to me, mildly surprised, slowly stood and said, "He was a Cuban patriot. An altogether admirable man, unlike some of us."

"But he's dead. It seems such a waste."

"True. Many would think him foolish. But he was a revolutionary, willing to give his life for a cause. Freedom. And he expected to die. He was not a soldier. He was a writer, a poet, a thinker. He arranged his papers and left them with a friend before going to Cuba. I've read his various writings in eastern papers. Due to his activities he'd lived in exile for many years...in Spain, Valenzuela, then here, in the U.S. He admired much of our society, certain aspects, not all. As a young student he'd mourned Lincoln, the Great Emancipator. He hated slavery as much as any true man. Cuba did not end slavery until ten or eleven years ago. In truth it never ended. On grand plantations and haciendas the Spanish lords still rule with whip in hand and boot to the throat. The people, a mix of creole, African, and mulatto, are willing to fight and die to remove that boot. As was Marti, he laid down his pen to take up the fight. An admirable man, utterly..."

From that moment I was certain Cuba would be Hagan's next chapter. And while to me it seemed he were the author directing the sequence to his own ends, such storms play beyond our wishes, dreams, and fears. In October when Spain rebuffed McKinley's offer to negotiate, Americans of all stripes, rich, poor, colored, white, clamored to intervene, equating the Cuban rebellion to our own War of Independence. Sympathies increased to fervor upon learning of concentration camps, vast squalid prisons erected by the Spanish to suppress the rebels, where over 100,000 were rumored to have died.

Reading of which, I handed the paper to Hagan and asked, "Can this be true?"

He gave it a glance and answered, "Yes, possibly. I'd take anything printed by Hearst or Pulitzer with a grain of salt. They've staged crimes to make a headline. But even at half, or a third that number, these atrocities cannot be ignored. Not 90 miles off our coast. As McKinley says, such warfare is uncivilized and borders on extermination. Our action, our entry, only awaits an incident..."

XXI. By the Ocean

Vague and distant, the cruel drama played, one week to the fore, the next fading. Thoughts turned from autumn to winter, then to Christmas. Hagan gave Danny a new saddle, his initials "DLC" embossed on either swell. Deep brown leather richly tooled by "Chas.P.Shipley" stamped on an oval rosette with matching bridle and reins looped to the horn, and silver conches front and back. Danny was wholly surprised to find it straddling his piano bench that morning, knelt by and ran his hand over every portion.

"That's a man's saddle," Hagan said. "The stirrups are taken up part way, notched to adjust, so you can extend them each year. Before long, judging by your present height, you'll need the full length."

Eager to try it out, Danny grabbed the bridle and reins and ran to fetch Patches. He shortly returned, riding bareback, hopped down and lashed her to the hitching post where Hagan stood waiting with the blanket and saddle. But Danny insisted on doing the rest himself — steadied Patches, heft the saddle to his chest and shoved it up over the withers. Then he cinched the girth tight, jabbing a knee to the belly as Hagan had shown him. All set, he took the wool scarf I handed him and wrapped it twice around his neck against the chill wind, jumped to the stirrup, mounted up and rode. The happiest I'd ever seen him, Jinks trotting alongside as he reined west down the railroad right-of-way.

Watching, I reached and gripped Hagan's hand and said, "Thank you." He smiled and squeezed mine in turn, our faint gift to one another. Beyond that touch we remained separate, achieving a mild truce, if not peace.

Meanwhile, passing to the New Year, the far crisis deepened. Chants for war grew daily. Ultimatums issued and scorned. Spain would neither yield nor concede. Naval forces were sent forth, maneuvered and positioned. McKinley ordered the battleship *Maine* to Havana to evacuate American diplomats and citizens if necessary. Nightfall, February 15th, amid the glitter of harbor lights the *Maine* exploded, whether by accident or hostile act, whether the powder magazine or a mine, was only guessed at, never known. But 250 American sailors died, cast into the waters.

"That's our casus belli," Hagan said. "Once war is declared, I will go."

"Surely there's no need," I countered, startled by the grave shift of things.

"No, but I must." His tone firm and I said no more.

Weeks passed, both nations poised. In late March a naval investigation concluded that an explosion outside the hull had sparked the powder magazine, sinking the *Maine*. The report sank any bid for peace. My heart sank with it.

Awaiting the coming war, dreading the news, my one brief joy was Danny's birthday, April 16th, a Saturday. Hagan again surprised him with a gift, a new Spalding infielder's mitt he'd seen Danny eyeing in the Sears-Roebuck.

"That's the 6X, of tough buckskin and well padded," he said, handing the glove to Danny. "It should protect your fingers. That is if you ever care to try baseball again. If not, you can always toss it for Jinks to chew on."

"No!" Danny quickly fit his hand and fisted the pocket, as keen for the glove as he was for the saddle. "Can we go throw?" he asked, "Can we?"

Hagan pulled a new baseball from his hip pocket and grinned. Outside, they must have thrown for a full hour before breaking for a drink of cistern water. Then at it again, barely resting their arms. And like on the day Maxie took us fishing, I wished to freeze time, Hagan and Danny laughing and throwing the ball, at play beneath the sun.

But time sped forth, rapidly. Monday morning we learned McKinley had ordered army units to Florida while requesting 120,000 volunteers. Overnight as many signed up with more anxious to join. The following Monday, April 25th, Congress declared war on Spain. Hagan immediately prepared to leave, rushing to and from the express office in a flurry of telegrams. Friday noon, he announced he'd depart the next evening.

"For Camp Tampa," he said, voice and eyes alive with anticipation. "The Fifth Army Corp is forming there, training, gathering supplies, making ready. Major Reston on General Shaftner's staff granted me and several others permission to join, attached as war correspondents. They are to embark in a week or two. If I leave tomorrow, I should arrive the first of May. So I need to finish a few things and…" He began rustling through some papers and said nothing more, soon engaged with Ian over business and printing matters.

That evening he played catch with Danny until I called them for supper. After which he listened to Danny play several pieces on the piano, including their current favorite, "Harlem Rag." As the song ended, Hagan asked for an encore, saying, "That one puts a smile in my heart. But you, my son, make me smile even more…"

Later, Danny asleep, I found Hagan at his desk in the print shop, his grip already packed, his typewriter bagged along with a bundle of blank paper and journals waiting his words. Presently filling his pen at the inkwell, he tapped the tip dry and recapped it, reluctant to look up and face me and my question.

"Have you told Danny yet?"

"No, but I will," he raised his eyes to mine and added, "In the morning, we'll take the horses out for a ride. I'll tell him then."

"It's been good…for him, having you home."

"And for you?" he noted.

"Yes, for me as well."

He gave a wan smile and said, "Seems selfish, I know, me going. But I must," casting his eyes to the desk, then the room, as if trapped. "It's my last chance to stab at the heart of some act or deed beyond words.

Something that…" again he looked to me, struggling to explain. "We all bear a certain madness, or idiocy. Mine, a desperation borne since I was a boy, never knew my father, so I conjured him. Handsome of course, my mother would have none other. And likely a scoundrel. But in my mind's eye he was brave and true, fighting battles, righting wrongs to the ends of the earth. Always out there, somewhere. Foolish, I know. Yet something of that still draws me. And I need to bleed out all the wrong…to make it right. Then maybe —"

"But you can do that here, be brave and true, with Danny and me."

"That's kind of you to say, but —"

"But you are…Danny admires you. As do I."

"Yet I do not admire myself. Cannot. It's you who are true. Your quiet modesty and dignity become you, sets you apart from all the others I've known. You can't guess how many times, every day, I've longed to take you in my arms."

"Why didn't you?"

He gazed to me and slowly shook his head. "I had no right. You're so lovely, Sadie. Lovely as a rose. Faithful, caring, but can wound, and be wounded. Ever since that night, my row with Maxie, knowing I'd hurt you, I felt I had no right. None."

"My love gives you right," I answered, then offered my hand and said, "Come…"

He reached to me and followed. Cloaked in darkness, warm air wafting in from the lilacs in bloom beyond the window, we embraced, both tentative, slow to rouse. At my touch he softly stirred and strengthened, our love-making sweetly tender, more of regret and understanding than of passion.

At dawn I awakened, Hagan already up hustling Danny out for their horseback ride. Gone till midmorning, when they returned Danny leapt down and lashed his reins, hungry for breakfast, but more anxious to share the news.

"Daddy's going to Cuba, to the war!" he blurted, as if I hadn't known. "He wants me to ride Blood while he's gone. And I will. I promised…" — proud and excited, now part of the adventure. I smiled then looked to Hagan sitting his horse, staring southeast, somehow already fading from us.

But late that afternoon, accompanying him to the depot, he snapped alive to our presence, animate and joyful. Particularly when Maxie appeared around the corner, as if he'd been waiting. Hagan extended his hand in greeting then grinned to us, "As you can see, Maxie and I have made our peace since that night he rightly laid me low."

"Aw Hag, twas a lucky shot," Maxie said, slapping his back. "Caught ya tired 'n foul tempered else yer clever fists woulda cut me t' pieces."

"That's a lie, you loveable cuss. Not then or any day could I deck you." Then Hagan turned and said, "Sadie, Danny…I asked Maxie to meet us here. He's agreed to look after you. Check in each day and make sure all is well. So I won't worry."

Pleased to see them friends again, I merely smiled. In the awkward silence Hagan leaned close and we exchanged a brief kiss. Then he gripped Danny's shoulder and said, "You're growing fast, son. Soon be a man. I know you'll make me proud…"

Danny looked to his father, pressed his lips against the emotion of parting and said nothing. The conductor called "All aboard!" and Hagan slung his bag, lifted his grip and stepped onto the train. In his leaving, in his manner and words, I read something so final I could not bear to see the door close, turned my back as the cars clanked pulling away.

Danny stood by, watching the train roll east then disappear over the far hills.

Walking home, Maxie nudged my hand and said, "Go on 'n weep ye lass, tis sad to see 'im go. But he'll be back, he will…" — words as futile as tears in the dry wind.

Hagan gone, in another week school let out, and Danny like any boy ran happily free of lessons. For a day or two he threw the ball and played fetch with Jinks, then grew restless, moody, and would hardly speak. Next trading day father accompanied mother to town, and I spoke with them of my concern while Danny plinked at the piano, lately indifferent to that as well.

"Daughter mine, I wouldn't worry," he said. "Like every mother's son he's at that age he best be around men. Think I have an idea." We walked into the parlor and Danny turned to father's brisk voice, "Hey there, Danny boy. Swear you grow an inch each time I blink. Stand up here 'n let me see you…" At his grandfather's command Danny stood straight, raising his chin an extra notch. "My word, you're a half head taller than your Uncle Glen when he's a struttin' young buck. What say you come down 'n work with us this summer? Pay ya a nickel a day 'n all Grandma's fried chicken you can eat. There'll be chores 'n work to do. But once done there's miles of pasture to ride 'n catfish in the pond, bullheads in the creek. And the Limestone boys play baseball Sunday afternoons at your Mamma's old school. Now some of them boys are a mite older —"

"I'm not afraid!" Danny rose to the challenge, "I can do it!" Then he looked to me and asked, "Can I ride Blood down?"

"Sure," I said, "your father would like that."

His smile brightened then faded as he turned to the piano and tapped a lone note.

Mother tugged father's sleeve, and he softly chuckled, "Well now, reckon your Grandma would enjoy some evenings of music. Got the wagon here, bet we can rope it in 'n haul it safe, if you like?"

"I'll go get Uncle Max!" Danny shot out the door.

Within the hour Maxie and his crew had the piano loaded, covered with blankets and roped secure. Heading out on his father's horse, Jinks trotting behind, Danny leaned back and waved, off on a big adventure.

Left alone, I'd never felt so lonely. Only a single telegram from Hagan saying he'd arrived at Camp Tampa and would write more later. Husband and son both gone, that night I wept, wondering why I was put on this earth and let to live? Spared to love a man and bear his child, to what end? But I felt better by morning, having slept, grateful for sweet air and sunrise. Then Maxie walked past on his way to work, whistling a lively tune, waved and hollered, "Top 'o th' day to ya, Sadie girl!" Which cheered me, and I cast off my self-pity and stayed busy.

Late that afternoon, weeding in the garden, Maxie again surprised me. Heard the cistern crank and turned to see him drinking from the dipper. "Nay, thar's no sweeter water in Mankater," he grinned, droplets dripping from his mustache. "Aye, 'n no sight sweeter'n a lass in her garden." And there was a glint in his eye like the time he peeled and buttered the corn that again made me blush and look away.

Thereafter we greeted most mornings, I standing on the porch, he striding by with a broad smile and jovial gaze. Afternoons I worked in the garden, waiting, watching for him to come and drink from the cistern. Sometimes he offered a blossom from the lilacs in late bloom. We'd chat a spell, reclaiming our old familiarity and fondness. And if I was weeding, he insisted on helping.

"Tis no bother," he'd say, "done sweated through, a shay more won' hurt none."

He'd kneel down and edge alongside in grunt and snort, his hot breath, scent and shadow overlapping mine. Finished, he'd rise up and stand like a great horse, das Ross, give a keen nod and lumber on. Longing and want stirring in us both, expressed more in tone and manner than in words.

⸺ ◈ ⸺

Not until early June did I receive a letter from Hagan, written in a hurried hand, pages sweat-stained, ink-blotched, as he noted, "It's hot, damnable hot. Though I have managed to send several dispatches, typed in the early dawn before the heat becomes so unbearable you can barely focus amid the sweat, filth, and stink. Despite the general chaos, the disordered command and supply, you cannot fault the spirit. Nearly to a man our young soldiers are eager to meet and whip the Spanish. Given rank incompetence, the sheer effort, like the task, is staggering. An army of 28,000 two months ago now swollen to a quarter million, with 25,000 encamped here in Tampa, from the beaches backed up to the pines. They train and drill through the heat of the day then rest, mend, and grouse till taps. Adding to the misery, most still wear wool uniforms meant for the mountain west. A lucky few have kaki. Yet the greater part soldier on. As I heard one young officer scold another, 'If you can't stand the gruff, why did you come?'

"Indeed, many officers in the volunteers are green and clueless, mere appointees jockeying for a chance at battle, perhaps a wound or a medal, in hope to muster out and enter politics. Colonel Roosevelt to name one, a blustery opportunist, but he is brilliant. A bulldog with bark and bite, if not shot down, I predict he will rise.

"Then there's General Shaftner, overweight and over 60, who seems overwhelmed. Fortunately, among the regulars are many experienced officers of apt judgement, insight, and initiative. Selfless, resourceful, and sorely needed for there is a dearth of everything from fresh water to socks, even rifles. Barely enough Krags to equip our regular troops, while state volunteers, the 71st New York and 2nd Massachusetts, are issued single shot Springfields, black powder, the same as your father carried in the Civil War. What's more, many volunteers have never fired a shot, given a few rounds and brief instruction they stand dauntless, primed for action. No, you cannot fault their spirit.

"Facing dust, sand, and constant heat, a plague of flies, flees, lice, and mosquitoes, lack of latrines, little water, and bad food, the sooner we embark the better for the morale and health of all. Such conditions breed pestilence. Many already suffer from malaria common to these climes. Happily, transports are being readied and we may begin loading tomorrow. Perhaps engage the Spanish in a fortnight. Depending, for plans have been hatched and nixed thrice before. First, we were to seize Mariel to then attack Havana. Next, they aimed to invade Havana directly, but lacking timely transport, stood down. Then another shot at Mariel was canceled upon sighting the Spanish fleet. Now it seems we will target the underbelly of Cuba, round Cape Maisi, join with Mardi's rebels and hit Santiago. It's not the lack of will that delays us, only the deciding moment.

"No telling my part in all this. Witnessing a massed army prepare for war is like a great beast coming alive, where every man from commander on down is but a bit player in a vast drama set to unfold. Myself, a mere shadow flitting here and there like a ghost, writing what little I sense and glean as sweat drips from finger to pen, mixing with ink on the page. At times, thinking of you and Danny, I regret and wonder why I left. Miss you both terribly but must see this through. Your loving husband, Hagan…"

No promise of his return, not a word. It read to me like a final chapter, his life to conclude somewhere in Cuba. Hagan, the man my younger self once dreamed, his flesh now a figment vanishing in the dusk of war.

Next day when Maxie stopped by for his drink at the cistern, I looked him in the eye and asked, "Hagan told you something before he left, something more, didn't he?"

Maxie sobered. "Aye, he said a bit. Only to share if need be…"

My question left hanging. Before men and their loyalties, I had no say.

Numbness set in. Once more I helped Ian set type, formed the words but read not a line. A jumble of letters and spacing arranged, inked and printed then sent forth, heading a story I cared not to know.

On Saturdays, after mother finished trading, I'd return with her to the Limestone to spend the evening and most of Sunday. There, in the lull between wheat and hay harvest, I'd watch Danny romp and play through the orchard and creek like a scene from an innocent tale about to turn to a dark page. One Sunday in mid-July while mother and I washed the dishes, father shared the news from the *Kansas City Star*.

"By gad, says here they captured San Juan Hill 'n blasted Cervera's fleet. All set to lay siege to Santiago. Bet Spain surrenders any day 'n Hagan'll be home…"

I tried to answer his smile and Danny's hopeful eyes, but outside I saw only plow lines darkening the near field. And riding home from Otego on the evening train, each window mirrored a corpse etched in passing, his ghost image inked and pressed, faintly reflected, fading further and further until blinked away. Stepping down from the depot, the dim light cast my shadow and beyond I discerned Maxie's dark form pacing before the lilac bush, its blooms faded like my hope. At my approach, he tossed his cigar and stood waiting, thumbing a yellow envelope in his right hand.

"Got this yesterday after ye left," his voice hushed and husky. "Wha' Hag told me was…they'd let me know if…so you would not hear it from a stranger. Aw, dear girl," his voice choked. "Was the fever got 'im…"

I nearly fell as he caught me in his strong arms as I sensed that inked corpse etching through my flesh and his, draining life and blood till we would soon be nothing but bones on a black page and I cried, "Hold me! Hold me!"

"Thar now, lass, ah got ya…"

Faint and empty, I warmed to him and needed filled, "Love me, love me now…" I pleaded, pressing my lips to his, seeking life to cease from dying. Both anxious to claim the other and dispel the chill ghost between us, clutching, grasping, desperate, I led him under the lilac that shaded my window, unbuckled his pants and gripped him.

"Don' touch me, lass," he warned, "less ya mean it…"

I said nothing, already parting to him as he raised me up and peeled my underthings and soon knew me and I him as our flesh merged, relentless, locked in urgent passion and grief, sharing anguish, joy, and sorrow, pressed against the wall unto ourselves.

"Aw, Sadie, wha' have we done?" he gasped.

"We've found each other" — still embraced, would not let him go.

"Aye," he grinned through his tears. "But wha' will we do?"

"We'll wait a decent time. Then you'll marry me."

"That ah will, Sadie. 'N ah'll n'er leave ya. Promise…"

XXII. Shifting Tides

Was there ever passion in this old flesh? She casts her eyes to her blanketed lap in wonder. Or simply another life once dreamed like scores of others now shriveled to this? Bone stiff and blood thin like words inked with water. Speaking of what? A mere pulse of memory…?

She grips the moccasins next her heart in glance to the one drowsing off before the tree and calls, "Paul?" Her voice more feeble than she expected but it wakes him.

"Gram?" his eyes blink open in question.

"You were nodding off, it's late," she explains. "Before you go to bed, would you grab me that big black book on the top shelf? Yes…my Bible, thank you. And here…" she hands him the moccasins from under her blanket. "Hang these up near the top by the kitten doll, would you please?"

He lifts them to a near stem and gently dangles them by their laces as asked.

Gazing there he says, "Those were Danny's…" not certain why he knows.

"Yes, and Hannah, your mother, she wore them too."

"Did I wear them?"

"No, your feet were too big."

"Danny played piano."

"Yes he did. But listen…" she cups a hand to her ear. "That's Santa's sleigh bells. You better get to bed or he won't land."

"Really? You can hear?"

"Yes, he's coming down across the White Rock right now."

"How come you hear 'n I can't?"

"As I told you long ago, it's a gift the North Wind gave Gram so she can put Paul to sleep before Santa comes. Then Santa casts a spell and puts Gram to sleep."

"Oh…" he nods, puzzling a moment, then asks, "But you'll wake up, won't you?"

"Yes, in the morning."

"You won't leave with Santa?"

"No, Paul, I'll be right here."

"You promise?"

"I promise."

"Wish I could hear Danny play."

"I too, now go to bed. Even on Christmas the cows want milking at dawn…"

Reluctantly he turns and ducks through the dark doorway.

She breathes a weary sigh at thought of Danny. Does not wish to conjure such sad memories, but knows she will, and must. A final accounting, both dark and joyful, rises to replay through her long night. And she needs to use the toilet. No, cannot let Paul find she's soiled herself. But must wait till she hears him snore.

And waiting she opens her Bible. Turns to the Song of Solomon and finds the rose petal from her wedding day pressed next to the line "…*his hand doth embrace me…*" But the scent long faded, retaining perhaps a trace as she raises it to her nose, the white now aged to sepia. And two letters there tucked to mark the page — the one sent from Camp Tampa, and another stamped U.S. Army Hospital Corp addressed to Mrs. Hagan Corbett. Both envelopes browned and flaking. From the latter she carefully unfolds two pages, each written in a different hand. The first in Hagan's:

"My dearest Sadie," it begins. "What strength, clarity, and few words left me are meant for you. Words — I had filled notebooks in passage but lost them wading ashore. My typewriter as well. Strange, once freed of that cumbersome thing I felt free myself. So many tasks and needs faced us that I forgot words. If any are worthy, I may recall them, or not.

"They say I have the fever, Yellow Jack. But I suspect the canned meat from our Chicago packers that the boys have rightly tagged 'embalmed beef.' Tastes and smells like a rotting corpse. Gripped by hunger, I gulped some down. So foul you could not chew, only swallow, then chills and shakes soon set in, each wave worse than the last. Pure poison, I swear, and more die from that and the fever than by the Spanish Hornet, the rapid-fire Mauser that hit our boys in frontal assaults, foolishly ordered but bravely carried out, from the first landing to San Juan Hill. And reports that Roosevelt led the charge are damned lies. It was Lieutenant Jules Ord and his 10th Colored Calvary that took the hill. The very next instant Ord fell shot through the neck. Roosevelt and his Rough Riders were late to the scene. And not one rode a horse. A trivial note, perhaps, but should be known before the truth gets trampled underfoot.

"Now a week beyond the battle, the fever rages. Amid the filth and flies and foul sinks flooded from constant rains, hundreds of boys lay sick and dying. And thousands will die if not evacuated soon. Yet for all the death, blunder, bellyache and suffering, a spirit like a counter-contagion flows, uniting the sons of Rebs, Yanks, and former slaves alike. A blend of something uniquely American that fills my heart. Only wish I could bring my heart home to you..."

There the pen falters and dips away. She stares at the blank space, always wishing for something more. But there is nothing. She slowly folds it under to read the second page and notes the heading — "Wednesday, July 20, Siboney, Cuba" — not in cursive, but neatly printed as in the letter:

"Dear Mrs. Corbett, my name is Stan Barrow. I'm a hospital steward, somewhat like a sergeant in regular ranks. I came to know your husband on the transport to Cuba. Always friendly and down to earth, he moved among us, listening, gathering stories and such, writing in his journal for a book he planned, I guess. I tended him at the last and he asked me to send his letter on to you. Must admit I read it. To make amends I want to share a few things I hope will gladden you that he did not tell.

"For one, in landing at Daiquiri he did not lose his writing, he ditched it to save a boy. Navy tugs towed our boat close to shore then we had to wade. There was a wicked undertow that drowned two men. And there would have been a third if not for Hagan. When the boy went under, Hagan did not dally, dumped his duffels and dove after. They disappeared then surfaced about 30 yards out. Hagan grabbed the boy by his horse-collar pack and swam till they found footing. Then lugged him to his shoulder and on up to the beach where both dropped to their knees. The boy vomited a bucket of seawater, coughed and spat a spell, then caught his breath and rejoined his platoon.

"Hagan won our respect that day, did not look once for his writing. Right off he stood and lent a hand with one thing or another. We were terribly short of mules and horses. Hundreds had drowned forced to swim from a half mile out. A sad sight to see, but civilian transports would not risk Spanish guns. Anyway, from then on Hagan made himself a packhorse carrying food, water, and ammo to the boys then helped litter the dead and wounded. Tireless, cheerful, and rarely spoke in anger except for Roosevelt's claim to San Juan Hill. That and the rancid beef which we all quit eating and tossed to the sink. But he shook it off and continued to help with the sick and wounded. Cleaned up their blood and filth. Searched for clean water, a thing more precious than gold.

"And he started writing again, letters home for sick and dying boys. Helped them find a fitting word to lift their spirits. Then three days ago when the Spanish surrendered Santiago, the fever struck him. He tried to continue but collapsed and thankfully did not suffer long. Too weak to finish his letter, he told me your address and asked that I send it on. With that smile of his he said, 'Don't let them embalm me like that damn beef...' and asked that we bury him on the bluff just east of our tent.

"He died about an hour before dawn. We carried him, myself and two privates, to the bluff and buried him as the surf crashed on the rocks below. And you should know in his last breath he whispered, 'If there's a soul of me, let the wind and waves carry part back to Sadie and our son...'

"Hagan had a way about him that helped carry us all forth. May part of him now help carry you. My deepest regrets and sorrow for your loss…"

Reading the epilogue of a life ended 70 years ago her dry old eyes still shed a tear. She folds the letters and sets the Bible on the table. Rests her hand there a moment as if touching the bluff where he lies, hasn't felt so close to him since he left, perhaps because she will soon join him. She smiles, wishes his handsome ghost would take form and help her stand. But there is no Genie in her lamp, only the one asleep in the near room. She hears Paul snoring and knows she must summon the strength herself or he will find her soiled and she will not let that happen as long as she draws breath.

She drapes the blanket to the chair, grips the armrests and slowly rises. A bit dizzy as she stands, never quite erect these days. She grasps her cane set close by, takes a step then steadies. Her feeble legs painfully weak from her long trek to cut the cedar and visit the old grave. By the third step she strengthens and shuffles on to the toilet to leave the last waste of her before surrendering the whole. Not much left, each attempt difficult, the sitting and rising. Extra careful of the wipe paper, still she washes her hands, grateful for clean warm water, truly precious as gold. She dries her hands then goes to the closet for Paul's gift, new gloves and socks neatly wrapped in colorful paper, ribbon and bow. She carries it into the kitchen and places it under the tree for him to find.

On the counter Paul left a cup of milk and a cookie for Santa. She floats the cookie in the milk and carries it outside, anxious to see the stars. But first she kisses the air and calls for Bing, "Here boy, come Bing…" He soon darts out, wagging his stub tail while raising his hurt paw for her to bless. She gingerly kneels and takes it in her palm, "All better, I see. And Gram's got something for you…" She lowers the cup and he eagerly laps it dry, leaving not a crumb. "Good boy, now go curl warm in the shed. All is quiet, even the coyotes…"

He trots dutifully back to his cave as she grips the cane to help her stand. Again dizzy, only more so, always dizzy gazing to the starry sky. The moon somehow larger, stronger tonight, men orbiting there, and that gravity and light pulling her, and from the old grave on the hill and all around, a presence, sibilant in the wind and grasses, calling, drawing her till she feels herself slipping out and away, rising, but cannot, promised Paul she would not leave. She closes her eyes and takes a breath, holding still, and all settles, again grounded. She enters and shuts the door against the far chill.

Inside, quiet and warm, familiar and close, she calms, the tree blinking its lights, sharing her memories. She returns the cup to the counter then treads to the stove and adds two chunks of wood.

There now, she thinks, my last chores done. She leans her cane aside and slowly sinks into the chair and wraps her shoulders in the blanket. Her mind and flesh strangely numb yet focused, she gently rocks and waits…

Though Maxie and I would wait to wed, that night I would not be alone. Took his hand and led him in through the back door. Ian out for the evening, we quietly undressed as if the whole world leaned to listen. Next his massive bulk I felt like a fragile doll, but he embraced me tenderly and in bed shared his strength in a most apt way.

Later, while I nuzzled his chest, he whispered, "Aw, kitten, tis sorrow 'n joy all one. 'N shame for me joy. Poor Hag."

"There's no shame. Hagan left me and Danny. Now he's gone."

"Aye, but ah'll not leave ya. Since th' day ya snapped yer green eyes to me in th' Oakvale livery, ya owned me heart. Nay, not leave ya till th' Reaper nabs me…"

We slept naked to the heat and woke at first bird song. Maxie slipped out before dawn to ready for his work day. I washed myself and dressed in riding skirt and white blouse. Then grabbed my straw hat and entered the print shop, stood gripping the brim, afraid to speak for fear I'd break down.

Ian glanced up from setting type and quietly said, "I already know, Sadie. I'm so very sorry…" and so spared me. To his few words I simply nodded and left.

Walking uptown, the telegram tucked in my sleeve, I met the mute condolence of passersby and realized they also knew. The telegram arrived Saturday noon, and before it reached Maxie, had spread to others. Cuba was our first foreign war, and Hagan, the first casualty from our region. While others had volunteered, most had joined the 20th

Kansas, still training in California, destined for the Philippines. And I the war widow, examined by each gaze in part sympathy and pride, yet I felt exposed, pitied, and wanted to vanish.

At the livery I saddled Patches and snugged the cinch. Removing the halter to fit the bridle, I noticed her coat graying toward the nose. Showing her age, but still a trusty little mare, and over the miles to the Limestone her easy canter steadied my heart. For a time my thoughts gave way to the wind, the land and sun, again a schoolgirl riding home. Reaching the bridge before the lane, I let Patches slake her thirst at the creek while I wet my face and composed myself. No real thought as yet how to break the news, or what to say, simply mounted and nudged her on.

Halfway up the lane Jinks and my parents' little herd dog barked our arrival. Now high noon, I knew they'd be at dinner. Presently father stepped out followed by mother and Danny. For a moment all pleasantly surprised at my return. Then mother guessed my reason for coming, clasped her shoulders and winced. Father's face tightened as well. Only Danny stood in quiet wonder as yet unsuspecting, unknowing, as I swung down and lashed the reins to the near post.

"Come, Danny," I said, extending my hand. "Come take a walk with me."

Hesitant, he looked to father, who laid a hand to his shoulder and said, "Go on now, Danny. Go with your mother…"

We walked to the high hill west, to the old Indian's grave, both numb and silent, awaiting words we neither wished to speak nor hear. I thought to use the telegram to thread the moment, but left it tucked. Rising to the grave we turned and gazed southeast beyond the hills.

Finally I said, "You know where your father went" — more statement than question.

"Yes," Danny pointed and answered, "to Cuba, yonder a thousand miles beyond that rocky hillside. Uncle Glen showed me one day with his compass. And Dad's down there helping to fight for freedom."

That hopeful pride in his voice broke my heart for I had to break his.

"And this old grave…do you know who's buried here?"

"An old Indian, Grandpa told me…and said not to bother it."

"Right, an old Indian who snatched me from my mother when I was a baby. Then swapped me back and so spared me and my mother. But the world does not always spare us, Danny. Your father died in Cuba. He's gone and will never return."

"No! He's not gone! He's still out there!" And before I could reach to restrain him, Danny was off running down the hill, crying, "No! No, no…"

Nor could I see Hagan gone, a corpse shoveled under dirt, imagined him slashing through jungles, reaching through the far forever for some rare wisdom hidden in the high Himalayas. I'd been widowed to his feverish quests for many years. Now numb to his loss, like a sad ghost stumbling down the hill in lame fret for my son who ran the entire distance. The house stood forlorn and silent, far then near, like my sorrow, and I dreaded my approach, knowing I must face Danny and look him full in the eye. Eyes that might hate me for what I'd told him.

At the porch I paused, surprised to hear him playing the piano — music at once sad and beautiful, strangely familiar, yet new, born of the moment. As I stepped inside he continued playing, the tears that had streaked his cheeks now drying. Father and mother sat listening intently. Then father glanced up and quietly said, "It's that old Irish air from Derry County. Played it for him last night on my harp 'n here he's made it his own…" One of father's favorite tunes and he often joshed to mother, "It's a lad's lament for his lost lass 'n her lovely derry-air!"

But there was no joking today. Danny's solemn rendering, the melody slowed and given fuller play, made a fit requiem for his father — so beautifully sad it helped knit our grief. When Danny finished, he looked to me and asked if he could stay at the ranch until school started. Wanted to help with the third haying and still had a baseball game or two. Relieved to see no hate in his eyes, I kissed his forehead and gladly consented.

As mother gave me a fond hug father offered to saddle up and see me home.

"No, I'll be fine," I said. "I have thoughts to sift. Just keep Danny busy. That's the best you can do for him and me…"

— ● —

Now a widow but I would not wear widow weeds, the black dress and veil of mourning. Not on a hot summer afternoon. Still slender, I donned my blue wedding dress to honor my husband and walked uptown to submit the life policy he'd left me. Once certified and the claim wired, it came to a goodly sum, which I deposited in the bank. Then I walked home, mind muddled, a mix of grief and gratitude, and sat all afternoon at Hagan's desk.

That evening, off work, Maxie found me there and again took charge like on my wedding day when he supplied the beer and later our rings. Brusque and jolly, he roused me from my funk. Snapped his finger to Ian and said, "Come, lad, tis time we talk. Ah knows yer honorable 'n harbor no rude notions, but we canna have a young fella roomed under one roof with this comely widow. Tongues will wag!"

"But I never…" — Ian dropped his ink roller, utterly taken aback.

"Ah knows that. All th' same folks'll talk. Now listen, ah've a notion. Willum's old ice house 'n grocery's been empty since he moved to new digs a block west. Thar's th' place to hang yer Mankater Merc sign 'n grow yer business, jus' 'cross from th' bank, next th' express office, smack dab amid town merchants, eyewitness to all happenins 'n parades, folks duckin' in for photos 'n news 'o th' day. Wha' say ye?"

Maxie waited while Ian stood in blink of doubt, question, and possibility.

"Don't know…I need time and money, and —"

"Hey lad," Maxie walked over and gripped his shoulder, "Don' go limp, tis time to jump. Sadie here can buy yer half 'n thar's yer stake. Right, Sadie girl?"

"What about the presses, the type desk, and other tools?"

"They will be yours," I assured him. "And I'll buy your current half then you can start fresh. But I would still like to work half days and do the jobbers?"

"Sure, Sadie, of course, you're always welcome."

"Good! Tis done!" Maxie slapped his back and bulled on. "Aye, tomorrow ye two settle the monies 'n ah'll gather me boys 'n git 'quipment moved 'n set in place. In a day or two ye'll print th' news, eh?"

No more questions or delay, Maxie bade us shake hands to seal the deal and Ian leapt into action. Beckoned to his young apprentice, Bradley Jeffers, hired in Hagan's absence and already adept at typesetting, "Bradley, drop that type stick. We have a new task and no time to waste…"

Late into the night Maxie and I helped them organize material to prepare for the move. Ian grew more enthused each step of the way, and Bradley more so, bright and eager to learn every aspect of printing, constantly reading of new methods, of steam presses and linotypes, and knew the typewriter inside and out. Fascinated by its various parts and mechanics like most boys of bicycles then coming into use. And he had a bicycle as well, handy for deliveries and errands. He and Ian made quite a team and I was happy to step aside and help at the fringe of things.

Good to his word, in two days Maxie had the print shop moved and all set. Ian made his down payment and hung his sign. Meanwhile I stood facing an empty space that had once housed so many ambitions, thoughts, and dreams. Haunted by Hagan's loss and part of me gone as well. Hollowed out like that space, silent and empty, when Maxie walked in after work and caught me staring to the far wall.

"Aw lass, tis hard, but won' have ya mopin'. Come…"

He led me through the kitchen and out the door and pointed to the large white house directly west, bordered by cedars north, an orchard south, and a garden in back. Two full stories and attic crowned by tall shade trees.

"Aye," he nodded to my puzzled look, "Clyde Martin's place, me station master, 'n ye've long admired it, ah know. Ya see, Clyde's been bumped to th' big office in Saint Joe. Set to ship him 'n his family east. Ah bought it off 'im this mornin' in gift to thee. Mind, ah'll be wantin' this ol' print shop in trade. Tired o' labor in th' hot sun 'n mean winter wind. Aims to open Das Ross Beer Haus!" he announced with a laugh. "Nay, jus' call it Maxie's Chili House, with beer, cards 'n pool. Pay a wee tax to our city fathers 'n give 'em bourbon, they'll no mind me beer. All cards played, should make th' move by Labor Day…in time for Danny's school. Wha' say ye, Sadie, does that make yer green eyes smile?"

Not only my eyes, my whole body warmed to him. We skipped supper and went straight to bed and made love till after sunset. Whereas Hagan was ever poetic, deft of voice and hand, Maxie never made much ado, bulled his flesh to mine with ripe relish, full, firm, and satisfying

— "Aye, missed me supper to feast on ye…" — heaved a throaty gasp then laid back and stretched his great arms to the ceiling. I quickened to his sweaty bulk, his flesh quivering to my touch like a horse. Even favored his boozy breath, though less so his cigar which he then fetched. At least he took it to the window, standing in the raw, letting the smoke drift through the screen, some wafting back with his strong male scent to where I lay naked to the warm night air. Nearly asleep when he nudged me with his urge, "Ah sees me lovely lass 'n wants dessert…" And we embraced once more, him pleasing me in a whole other way, slow and steady in pulse with the gusting wind. So it went, under cloak of darkness, pleasuring one another many times over the remaining weeks of summer while Maxie painted his sign and acquired casks, kegs, and gaming tables for his roadhouse by the tracks. And many mornings found not only two, but three cigars stubbed out by the window.

XXIII. Wine Red Dress

By mid-September I was mistress of my new house, Danny in school, and Maxie had a bustling business, customers far and near shoving through the door day and night. Thirsty workmen, traveling salesmen, gamblers, and local toughs, all herded in and given a modicum of law and order amid beer and whiskey, raucous talk and laughter. A wheel of cheese wrapped in muslin sat on the bar next a jar of pickled eggs and another of pigs' feet. And the same fare morning, noon, and night — chili, cornbread, and eggs scrambled in bacon grease. Any who groused were shown the door and pointed to a cafe uptown that charged double and offered no spirits. To run the kitchen and help serve, Maxie hired Myrtle Shaver, and to any who sassed her she'd raise a fist or rolling pin and ask, "Say again?" then laugh it off, a stout lusty woman, accustomed to rough and tumble having run a saloon-eatery in White Rock, a dying town from the lack of a railroad, losing out better prospects in Oakvale and Mankato.

Naturally, with Danny home, Maxie and I grew more discreet, our trysts largely curtailed, seldom chanced, waiting a time when we could wed and put all above board. And there had long been murmurings and gossip during Hagan's absences, Maxie seen accompanying me. I always shed such talk and did so now. In a deeply personal way all but widowed since my miscarriage and hardly willing to wait the customary year or two for conjugal bliss. Felt six months would suffice, about midwinter, in February or March. Frowned on in any case for forgoing widow weeds, but unless confronted, vague talk and averted eyes did not concern me. Walked to my daily work at *The Mankato Mercantile* dressed as I pleased.

Nor did I fret of a baby, certain that the miscarriage had left me barren. But nature pushed things. In October I missed my period. Thought little of it at first, for it tended to fluctuate, ebb and flow with the moon. Even a brief phase of morning sickness I ignored as a passing bug. Then by late November, still no period, I knew I was pregnant.

Maxie beamed at the news — "We best wed quick a'fore ya show."

"But I'd hoped to wait awhile yet?"

"Wait? Bah! Me Mum always said only lame fools 'n rich snoots wait to wed. A poor widow is free to wed when 'n who she wants. By the Bible a woman is bound only so long as the husband lives. Why even the Musselman book says a wife shall mourn but 4 months 'n 10 days."

"How do you know this?" I asked, amused and curious of his assertion.

"Standin' back o' me Mum, a wee lad, ah was, heard it off Bristle Mullins. He'd eyes on Mum since they sailed from Ireland. But me Da wowed her 'n when he died, Bristle shows up some weeks on, pounds at the door 'n says, 'Ah've waited a righteous spell, ah have, 4 months 'n 10 days as th' Musselmen say a widow should mourn. Tis a fact!' Stands by his word, he does. Same as ye, Sadie, me Mum asks, 'Jus' how d'ya know this?' Bristle puffs up 'n says, 'As a young lad four years at sea ah sailed through th' Bosporus to a port o' th' Ottoman. Aye, Musselmen sailors tol' us if they drown at sea, by law thar widows do mourn 4 months 'n 10 days then wed. Tis time this day, so ah'm here to have ya for me wife…' Me Mum glared hard in answer, 'Bristle Mullins, ah tol' ye once 'n tell ye now, ah love but one man 'n will have no other. Now scram!' She slammed the door 'n none dared ask her agin.

"But Bristle was right o' th' Musselman law, heard it some since. Tis now last 'o November, 'n by th' telegram, Hagan died July 20th. Today tis Wednesday, let's wed Saturday when yer folks come t' town…" pausing to count his fingers, "one, two…aye, Third o' December marks 4 months 'n 10 days plus 5!" — affirmed by the spread of his hand —

"All done proper by th' Good Book! Wha' say ye, Sadie, then ya can proudly show yer baby bump 'n none can talk, eh?"

Maxie never one to tarry, staunch, convincing, and contagious.

I smiled and said, "I'll need a new dress…"

"Then make it red…to show yer green eyes."

"Red…?" I answered skeptically. "If red, people will surely talk."

"Not but once, ah'll shut thar yaps good! 'N no need to sew yer dress, Sadie. Ah'll buy ya that red velvet one in th' shop window uptown" — for he'd noticed me gazing one day, quietly admiring it, but far too lush and expensive for my taste.

"No, don't," I insisted. "Velvet is too fussy and hard to clean. I prefer to sew my own and suit myself."

"Aye, but make it red, eh? To please me eyes 'n soft to me touch like yer warm breasts" — he cupped me with his large hand and squeezed.

"Very well," I agreed.

While Maxie went to the courthouse to find the judge and arrange our marriage, I walked uptown and purchased a dress pattern and wine-red corduroy of fine wale, soft to the touch. Passing by the newspaper, I stepped in and asked Ian for a few days off, didn't tell him why. He merely nodded and said, "Sure…"

Once home I spread the material on the floor, pinned the pattern and cut out each piece. Working the treadle, sewing the first seam, when Danny walked in from school, he glanced my way, vaguely curious, then called to Jinks and ran out back to gather the eggs and feed the chickens, his daily chores. That evening Maxie joined us for supper as he often did. All eating, speaking casually of the day, I caught Danny's eye and chanced to mention, "You saw me sewing earlier…my new dress." He stopped chewing, slightly puzzled, and I added with a hopeful smile, "It's a wedding dress, Danny. Maxie and I are getting married Saturday at the courthouse."

He dropped is fork and stared at his plate.

"Aye," Maxie chimed in, "aims t' wed at high noon. Would ya hold th' rings?"

Danny tensed, breathing hard as he looked to Maxie then me.

"But he…he may be out there, still alive," he answered, his voice desperate.

"Nay, lad, we showed ya the telegram. Yer Da's gone, buried in Cuba."

"No, not him! They mixed up, buried someone else. Hundreds of soldiers still lay sick and wounded in hospitals, the newspaper says so. Some have lost their memory. He could be one…" His eyes met mine, pleading that it be true.

And yes, many men were trapped in limbo; newspapers carried their stories along with patent medicine ads claiming to cure malaria and other tropical diseases as well as rheumatism, lapsed memory, and ill effects of poisoned meat eaten in the camps. Now fresh casualties being shipped home from the Philippines, Kansas boys of "The Fighting 20th" hailed as heroes for routing the very rebels who'd helped defeat the Spanish, and I wondered what Hagan would make of such irony. Then I looked to our son.

"Danny, there's something I should show you…" I walked into the bedroom and returned with a cigar box, set it on the table, opened the lid and handed him an envelope. "It's your father's last letter, and another by the man who tended him. I was holding it back until you were older, but I think you should read it now…"

Danny's hands trembled as he carefully unfolded the pages. He read, taking his time, one page then the other. Finished, he sat quietly then folded them in the envelope and held it as if the words still spoke.

"He was brave…wasn't he?"

"Yes, your father was a brave, good man. And I loved him very much. But I also love Maxie…and wish to marry him."

Again Danny looked to me, his eyes glistening, warm and acceptant.

Maxie laid a hand to his shoulder, "Aw Danny, ah loved 'im too, yer Da. Hagan was the best man ah ever knew. 'N he gave th' world th' best son. Nay, ah can never fill his shoes, but loves ya like a son, aye. Would do me proud if ya stand 'n held the rings when ah wed yer mum."

Danny gave a faint nod of consent and handed back the envelope.

Saturday morning Maxie covered my red dress with a black wool coat he'd bought me, crowned my head with a new fox fur hat, tucked my arm in his and accompanied me uptown with Danny and the rings in tow. We stopped by the newspaper at half past 11 and Maxie shouted in, "Be at th' courthouse, high noon! We're to wed!"

Taken by surprise, they dropped their work and Ian bade us stand for a photo.

Back outside, our eyes blinking from the bright flash, we stood in the warming sun and brisk air, waiting to hail mother and father. They soon arrived with their wagon and mules. And happily, Glen had ridden along.

Father whoaed the mules and hollered, "This a funeral or a Christmas hangin'?"

"Jus' haw yer mules 'n foller," Maxie directed with a big grin, keeping our secret till they all stepped down front of the courthouse. Father lashed the reins and stood.

"Now what's this all about?" he demanded, acting pugnacious, playing along.

"Ya come in nick o' time, Pat Briar. Ah ask yer daughter's hand t' marry."

"By heck 'n hell, you hear that Sarah, Glen? But when, where?"

"Here 'n now. Danny holds th' rings. In a blink we go meet th' Judge, say th' words 'n wed. 'N yon comes our master newsman Ian 'n his young devil Bradley to spread th' word."

"Bless this day 'n bless you both" — father gave Maxie a hearty handshake then turned to Glen, "A dern shame you can't ride 'n fetch Holly, have us a double-hitchin'."

"Say no more, Uncle Pat," Glen warned. "If Holly hears of this, we risk a double-hangin'. Like you, she's some set in her ways."

"Well, it is a ways to ride. Guess we'll settle for a single-hitchin'."

In high spirits we all proceeded up the steps. Once inside I removed my coat to show mother my new dress. "Oh Sadie," she said, admiring the style and color. "It fits you so nicely. And your eyes have never looked so green…" which made Maxie smile.

The ceremony took only a few minutes, vows exchanged and sworn on the Bible, rings set and all sealed with a kiss. As we stepped out into the sunny day I removed my fur hat and draped the coat over my arm. Father, conspiring to give Maxie and me our wedding night, winked to me and stopped Danny at the bottom step.

"Got an idea, Danny. Nice weather 'n all, how about we finish our tradin', fetch a quick meal at Maxie's, then you saddle up Blood 'n trail us home. Stay the night 'n ride back later tomorrow. Make school Monday. Heck, your mother did the same each week to Oakvale."

"Can Jinks come?"

"Sure, he can help ya hunt. A flock of geese done landed in that cornfield beyond the creek to feed on the leavings. Take my shotgun out at dawn, might sneak up 'n bag ya one. Tie it to your saddle, take it home 'n let it hang a couple weeks. Have a sweet fat goose for Christmas."

"Uncle Glen? Will you hunt with me?"

"Might, if you promise not to shoot 'em all."

"I promise…!"

So arranged, Danny rushed home to change his clothes and saddle Blood while mother, father, and Glen did their trading. Within the hour we rendezvoused at Maxie's place. Myrtle served us her pork-pie special with warm cider for mother, Danny and I, and stout for the men. Then Maxie stood and ordered, "Beer 'n chili on the house!" as his former crew and others crowded round. To spur the moment he snapped his finger and called for music from "Ornery" Andre Sokolac, a Czech immigrant who habitually dropped in on Saturdays to play his accordion for tips and beer — round and stout as a beer barrel, his music, warm and frothy. Maxie made the first request for "Beautiful Dreamer," and we slow-waltzed while others watched and cheered.

He held me close and whispered, "List unto me, oh Queen o' me song…"

Finished, Glen cut in and said, "Got to dance the bride once before we go," then flipped Andre a silver dollar and demanded something lively. As "O Suzanna" roused from the bellows, he clapped his hands and said, "Ready, Duchess?"

Hesitant, uncertain of the step, I said, "It's been years since I've really danced."

"Bah!" Maxie scoffed, "Take a big swig o' me beer, yer feet'll remember all."

True, I chugged the last of his mug, licked my lips and let go, dancing in glee to the spry old rhythm. Mother and father high-stepping as well, but not for long, Danny soon tugged his grandfather's sleeve, anxious to head to the Limestone. The day waning and miles to go, they bid a quick "Good-bye" while Maxie and I danced on and on. And I admit, after a full beer or two, I loved Andre's wild Bohemian polkas, felt free and light as a feather in Maxie's strong arms and certain stride. Amid one swift turn he swung me off the floor for a long passionate kiss.

"Watch it, Mister," I laughed as he set me down.

"That's me trouble," he grinned in answer, "watch ya swing to 'n fro 'n grow dizzy in want o' ye."

"You can want and not always get," I teased, enjoying our game.

"Aye, so reads many a sad chapter 'o me lonely life. But turn a page 'n hope to read one better. A secret scene 'o love we paint 'n dare not tell no other…"

With that he helped me into my coat, tipped his cap to the rowdy crowd, and we exited arm in arm, hurried on by the chilling wind. Once home, the stove stoked warm, we painted many a lovely scene. And I awoke next morning feeling whole and blessed, at ease for the first time in years.

Returning to work Monday and on through the week walking uptown, I ignored distant stares and gossip. Warmly clothed for winter, my baby bump would swell in spring and ripen by summer. Meanwhile I had a home and a husband. And Danny had proudly returned from the Limestone having bagged two geese that he promptly hung to cure on the back porch. But Friday evening as I prepared supper in the kitchen, Danny, usually at his piano by then, came in late and went directly upstairs to his room. I thought little of it, only puzzled at why he hadn't called to Jinks, pawing at the back door, whimpering till I let him in. Then he too disappeared upstairs.

Awhile later, Maxie home, table set, food steaming hot, I called Danny to supper. No answer. Maxie leaned to the doorframe and hollered up, "Hey, Danny boy, come eat! Got chuck stew 'n baked bread! Put meat on yer bones!"

This time Jinks came bounding down to greet Maxie and have his ears and fur mussed, then told, "Go lay by the stove." Soon we heard footsteps shuffle across the upper floor and slowly descend. Danny entered, eyes downcast, cupping his right hand in his left. Maxie reached out and said, "Hold up here, lad…" then peered to his face, "Say, ya got a fat lip. Had a fight, eh?"

Danny nodded.

"That hand thar, lemme see…" Danny slowly held it forth and winced as Maxie examined the swollen ring finger. "Aye, hurts don' it? Bashed it good, but don' think it's broke. Hit hard 'n jammed it, ya did…" Then he turned to me, "Sadie? Fetch yer scissors, some gauze 'n tape. Ah've fixed a hunnerd busted hands, me own 'n yer Da's. Aye, we'll splint it to yer pinky…" In little more than a minute Maxie had it neatly wrapped and said, "Thar, hold it safe till th' swellin' goes. In a week or two ya can play piano. But no fights, nay, not for a month or more, hear? 'N when ya do, make a tight fist, like so…curl yer fingers under 'n hit 'em with yer knuckle, see?"

Danny stood by, listening, watching, then made a hard fist with his left hand.

"Good," Maxie affirmed, "a man needs to fight in this world." Then he leaned back in question, "Now, what o' th' other boy?"

"I bloodied his nose good. Had him down and…" Danny stopped, tense, as if back in the moment. "But Mr. Bartleson, the head teacher, pulled me off and sent us home."

"More'n a scuffle," Maxie observed. "Ye be angry yet. Why is that?"

Danny's eyes darted side to side then he blurted, "He called you a barkeep!"

"So ah am," Maxie chuckled, "in me own tavern. Ah'm not ashamed, are ye?"

"No, but…" Danny stammered and stood silent.

"Go on, lad, spit it out."

Danny raised his troubled eyes to me and I knew what was coming.

"He also said…that my mom was…" he stopped abruptly, "I won't say it. It's a bad word…" Tears of hurt and shame strained his eyes.

"So that's it," Maxie's voice firmed. "Tell me, lad, who is this boy?"

"Phillip…Phillip Chester."

"Ah know his Da," Maxie's eyes hardened, "E.Q. Chester. Runs th' land office. Ah'll pay 'im a visit first thing in th' morn, ah will."

"No, please don't," I finally spoke, trembling, ashamed for the shame my son felt. "I'm the one that's slandered. Others are talking as well. If I don't face them, talk will never cease. Like the Chesters, many are staunch Methodists. They'll be in church Sunday. I'll go and face them."

"Then ah'll go with ya."

"No, I'm your wife, proudly so. I'll stand by you, not behind you. And I can never stand proud again if I don't face them myself."

By now my tears were streaming to match Danny's, and his fight had entered me. Maxie read it well and said, "Aye, go then, Sadie. But mark, any more talk on ye, ah'll burn thar blame church t' th' ground…"

———————————————

Sunday morning, in long black coat, fur hat, and gloves against the cold, yet I felt utterly naked walking alone toward the Methodist Church, gray winter clouds lowering from the northwest, wind scuffing dust and leaves. I stood before the large white-framed structure, staring up at the spired steeple, the tallest point in town. Then I mounted the steps to the double doors and quietly entered to the final refrain of "Onward Christian Soldiers." I removed my hat and right-hand glove, clenched them in my left and slowly unbuttoned my coat as I walked down the center aisle. Approaching the pulpit, I stopped and faced the minister.

"I have been slandered and ask your permission to speak."

He raised a brow to my abrupt request but warily nodded consent.

Turning to face the massed host, Mankato's largest congregation, my coat fell open to reveal my red dress. Many eyes widened, expressing surprise, curiosity, or reproach, depending. Alone, frightened and angry, I called on all my instinct and courage to defend my son and husband, my kin along the Limestone and those buried above the White Rock — summoned their spirit to defend their honor and my own.

"My name is Sadie Briar-Corbett-Ross," I began, my voice quavered slightly but sounded amazingly strong in that vast interior. "Most of you knew my late husband, Hagan Corbett, who died this past summer covering the war in Cuba. Word has reached me that some here count my period of mourning unseemly brief. Such talk prompted my son to fight another boy just two days ago, Friday, after school, leaving both of them hurt and confused…" I looked to the Chester boy — a blackened eye, nose swollen, he lowered his head. His parents stirred uncomfortably and I let my eyes drift on. "This angers me, two boys fighting for no good reason. I'll have you know I loved my first husband and will hold him dear to the end of my days. But the Bible states that a wife is bound to her husband only so long as he lives. That when he dies, to avoid slander, she should wed again, care for the home and raise children. Last Saturday, December 3rd, legally before judge, God, and man, I wed my new husband, Max Ross, who I also love and will joy in as I vowed till death does us part. An old religious law states that a widow should mourn 4 months and 10 days. As Hagan died July 20th, my mourning has exceeded that period by 5 days!" Stressed by my raised hand and spread fingers, then I finished:

"Therefore, I will thank you to say no more of this. And I thank you for listening. But I warn, if any further word reaches us, the parent of such talk will answer to my new husband, Maximus das Ross" — adding his full given name for good measure. They sat hushed and solemn as I rebuttoned my coat and walked up the aisle. In my passing there arose a low murmur and question. At the door I donned my hat and glove and left them to ponder what old religious law I'd cited.

Outside, I took a breath of fresh cold air and felt clean and free. Reached out and cupped my hand to the large snowflakes floating down, dusting all in a swirl of wonder.

By Christmas a foot of snow blanketed the town and surrounding plains. We feasted on baked goose, apple crisp, and all the trimmings. Then feasted again, traveling to the Limestone in an open sleigh, huddled warm in mufflers, coats, and an old buffalo robe. To Maxie's delight we entered the New Year with the baby bump starting to show. But heavily clothed, no one noticed. Even working at the newspaper I wore a long wool sweater, moving from task to task, you could see your breath beyond radius of the stove. And fingerless gloves were a must handling the metal type, frame, and press.

February turned fiercely cold. An Arctic mass dipped down covering all the states east of the Rockies. Known as the Great Blizzard of 1899, though not so bad in Kansas as the Blizzard of '86, still it brought record cold, freezing temperatures reaching even to Cuba. One night, opening the stove door to add some wood, in the dark cavity above the blinking coals, I imagined Hagan asleep in his ocean cave where sea-nymphs swam to watch him wake and dip his pen in ink then sleep once more…

XXIV. Ragtime

*S**kin within skin, tumbling, wrapped in agony, kicking to break free, reaching for light and air…ripped inside out, weighted, submerged, draining into darkness, limp bone and earth…*

"Wha…!" she gasps for first or last breath, uncertain which. Hands folded on her lap, blanketed in her rocker, capsuled like those brave men tumbling through space, she too tumbles in mind and eye and realizes she's been dreaming. As if her soul or spirit briefly left her like when she birthed Hannah, a dream she's dreamed many times and again this night. Seated motionless and still tumbling like those dear men in dire hope of return. She wonders if they'll make it, safely reenter and land. But knows she'll never know, time and question, everything distant except for death. Her flesh, cold and stiff, barely pulses will or warmth. Wishes she still had her old house cat Reba to warm her lap, lost her in early autumn, like herself finally too weak to stand, and she hadn't the heart to choose another. No, time is not a friend. The clock reads a quarter past three. Paul will wake at rooster crow. She gazes at the flames through the isinglass flickering like moonlight off the waves below Hagan's grave, no nymphs or pen in ink, only bones. No, she cannot forget, but remembering, forgives all…

Late night, June 5th, 1899, Hannah, named for Maxie's mother, nearly died of a breeched birth, the umbilical noosing her neck as Dr. Sudlow pulled her forth, her face purple, body motionless. He quickly cut the cord, dangled her by her heels, delivered several sharp slaps, and she cried out. I too caught my breath, feeling life return to my exhausted limbs.

Madalene leaned down and said, "A difficult delivery, my dear. For a moment I feared we had lost her. But my husband says she will live."

"Yes, amazingly strong," Dr. Sudlow observed, handing the baby to Madalene. "Scarcely six pounds...I'd say two months pre-mature," he added in a confiding tone. "But given warm summer months and mother's milk, her chances are very good..."

Thereby Dr. Sudlow and Madalene helped scotch waiting rumors. Said the baby was born at 7 months, but "a fighter, like her mother, likely to thrive..." So quoted and printed in *The Mankato Mercantile*. Soon returning to work, walking uptown, my baby in her carriage, women who had scorned me now met my eyes and smiled. And I was ever grateful to Dr. Sudlow and Madalene for their kind ploy and forgave their prim ways. While Glen had lost out with Madalene, he was happier with Holly. And Madalene seemed content, if not entirely happy. But who was?

In such manner our lives raveled and twined to weave anew.

Danny ushered in the new century playing "Maple Leaf Rag" from the sheet music gifted him by Maxie, Christmas, '99 — "Snagged it off a salesman headed for Denver, ah did. Says, tis hottest tune in Kansas City, he does!" And it rapidly spread coast to coast, by summer popular in all the major cities of America and Europe, marking the theme and spirit of the time. The happiest years of my life with Maxie, our baby and Danny, rolling season to season like a festive carriage ride, witnessing wonders and changes utterly new and unexpected.

Of course there were bumps in the road. In September, 1901, President McKinley was shot while shaking hands and sadly died a week later. Our leader struck down, the nation mourned. But Teddy Roosevelt swiftly took the reins and nearly overnight proved popular as a ragtime song. Buoyant, energetic, and ruthless, used "Gunboat

Diplomacy" to snatch Panama from Columbia and forge the canal connecting two oceans. And later brokered an end to the Russo-Japanese War and preserved vast swathes of the American West. I doubt the great trustbuster who wielded the big stick ever spoke softly, full of bluster as Hagan had warned, but he delivered. A man fit for the times and most voters. Father and Danny devoured his books, and he even gained a nod from Maxie, "Ol' Teddy's a fighter, he is…"

As was our daughter, Hannah, fiery red hair like her father's, willful and scrappy from the start. Fussy being picked up, fussy being laid down. "Aye, 'minds me o' me sis, Polly. Tiny slip o' a thing, but fierce, oh…any boys as teased her she went at 'em tooth 'n nail…" And little Hannah grew beautiful as a doll, adored by her daddy who did little to temper or soothe her rages.

One day, not quite 3 years old, she was playing in the yard, and a neighbor boy, a year older and bigger, shoved her to the ground. He stood laughing as she sat hurt and confused, about to cry. But only for a moment. In a snap she also laughed, stood and shoved him down, then picked up a big rock while he lay stunned and raised it high, set to bash his head. I'd glimpsed them through the window and rushed out in the nick of time, imagining the headline: "Girl Murders Boy!" Though it may not have killed him, it would have surely left him brain damaged. Enough of a moron as it was, yet wisely never bullied her again.

Those early years of our new century I would gladly live again. But we took our lumps and bruises. The summer Hannah turned 4 Jinks got caught in the spokes of the first car in Mankato, a Toledo Steamer. Broke his neck, as father declared, "Tryin' to herd the dern contraption back on the tracks where its kind belongs. Scarin' our horses, killin' our dogs, s'pect we're next…"

In any case we buried him in the back yard, a sad event. Danny solemnly dug the grave and filled it in, then stepped back as Hannah placed a bouquet of weedy dandelions and patted the mound, murmuring, "Poor, poor Jinks…"

And Danny, about to enter high school, nobly deferred to his little sister who now pined for a little dog named Toto. For *The Wizard of Oz*, set in Kansas, had swept the country like the "Maple Leaf Rag," enchanting young and old with its magical tale and fanciful drawings, a copy in nearly every home that housed a child. We read the story to

Hannah so many times she knew it by heart, reciting each line and never tiring — a Kansas girl, certain it was meant just for her. At least the pictures remained fresh at each turn of the page. And that it spoke of witches good and bad, minus religion, helped as well.

Jinks gone, Maxie put out word, and in a week or so came home cradling a little wire-haired terrier, brindle with black eyes and nose, still a pup, which Hannah instantly named Toto. Every bit as smart and devilish as she, and soon proved a wily car-chaser, nipping at the tires, sent rolling to the ditch to shake it off and chase another. Till Maxie swore the dog had more lives than a cat — "Or a wee good witch to watch o'er 'im…"

Happily, over time, Danny and the boy he'd fought, Phillip Chester, became fast friends. While they still sparred and wrestled like boys will, never again with rancor. Though their rivalry turned serious each summer when Danny pitched for the Limestone Boys against Phil and the Mankato lads. Maxie umpired most games, always hotly contested, played on Sunday afternoons under a scorching sun, fields laid out on scrub and sticker patches, surrounded by folks standing on benches, wagon beds, carriages, horses tethered by, men cursing, spitting tobacco, some drinking and all heckling either the pitcher, batter or each other. Tempers often flared over a close call, a mean slide or wild pitch, the crowd jeering, "Kill the umpire!" To which Maxie would holler, "Come 'n try it!" and swiftly checked most disputes short of fists, though that too, then the dust settled and the game resumed with his sharp command, "Play ball!"

The summer I gave birth to Hannah, father surprised mother with her own piano. No longer needed to haul Danny's and her evening lessons continued apace. Though never tempted by the snappy ragtime rhythms, she handily played Stephen Foster tunes and others she loved — even Danny's version of "The Derry County Air," which always quieted the listener.

And my little mare Patches, long since put to pasture, finally died in the winter of '04, just shy of 30 years. I didn't learn of her passing until spring when father handed me a brown and white horsehair robe and said, "She had such a fine winter coat, hated to see it go to waste…" So he and Glen had skinned the hide and sent it to a tannery, returned supple, soft, and neatly trimmed and backed with felt. "Always a faithful little horse," he added, "she'll make you a fine lap robe."

***

While Danny and Phil battled each summer, come fall they teamed up for football, a new rough and tumble game that began with a coin toss and of which I could never make heads or tails. But it kept Dr. Sudlow busy setting fractures, supplying casts, crutches, and slings while sternly admonishing each casualty for playing such a foolish game. Nor did Danny escape injury, proud of his broken nose. "Matches the one you gave me!" Phil laughed, daily joshing one another, talking sports and certain girls. And the good times carried forth to the autumn of 1905, marking their senior year.

By then Phil was dating, while Danny, tall and handsome as his father, drawing many a girl's eye, held firmly apart, determined to enter the wider world and taste every scene and clime — out there, *"somewheres east of Suez..."* like he pictured his father. Often quoted Kipling's "Mandalay" and the beautiful Burma girl *"By the old Moulmein Pagoda, lookin' lazy at the sea...a neater, sweeter maiden in a cleaner, greener land..."* Even put the poem to a spirited march, or "Drinkin' song!" as Maxie called it: "But mind ye, lad, the maids at hand, not all beefy-faced 'n grubby. Nay, not yer mum, sis, nor many a'nuther. N'er drop thorns on the primrose path ye aims traipse one day..."

Danny just smiled and continued to dote on his little sister, teaching her piano. And she loved to sing along, always great fun hearing her sweet angelic voice express the raw soldier sentiments of "Mandalay." Having entered first grade, little wonder she was sent home one day for refusing to sing "Mary Had a Little Lamb" which she termed "A silly song. But Miss Florence said I should like it because it's about a little girl. But I'm not Mary, I'm Hannah, and I don't like it..." I tried to explain that there were different songs for school than for home and suggested that it was sometimes best to sing along. She knit her brows and answered, "I don't care. I like Danny's song best..."

That same autumn, his tavern thriving, Maxie bought our first car, a Model C Ford with a 2-cylinder engine and a canvas top. Known as "The Doctor's Car" and purchased the previous year by Dr. Sudlow who sold it to Maxie for $500 upon the arrival of his new $2000 Ford Model B, a posh touring car with polished wood and brass trim and a powerful 4-cylinder engine. Still, we felt well set, apace with the times. Oddly enough, by some strange means, Danny already knew a deal of the workings and how to drive. But Maxie soon got the knack and one bright Sunday afternoon in October we made our first trip to the Limestone with Toto clasped warm in Hannah's arms. Luckily, we had Patches' lap robe for the air was quite crisp cruising at nearly 20 mph, a much faster clip than by mule or horse. When we rolled in, father stood as wary as the horses shying back from the fence. He frowned and said, "By gad, I'm with Jinks, the blame thing belongs fixed to the tracks, not let to roam. They'll soon lay claim to every road 'n field…"

An apt prediction had he included the sky above, for since Kitty Hawk machines climbed there as well, though that would be a few years. Later that day, Glen joining us for dinner, Max and Danny convinced father and him to go for a drive. They all climbed in and set off while I washed the dishes and mother engaged Hannah at checkers, both clever players and neither gave quarter. Three games to two Hannah's favor when the men returned. Father stepped down and said, "Sarah, I have to admit, the dern rattle-trap would make a fast trip to town. Be there 'n back in the time it takes to do the milkin'."

"Or the washing," she prompted, "if I had me a Maytag instead of them old wood tubs…" The Maytag washer was another noisy machine, but mother and I, and every other woman wanted one. Nor was father about to chuck his McCormick reaper, mower, or corn binder. And in '08, beef and grain prices holding steady, father bought them a brand-new Model T Ford, driven home with a Maytag loaded in back. But again, that would be awhile yet — like the telephone connecting town to town, appearing in banks, newspapers, and other businesses, even to Mankato, but wouldn't reach the Limestone or most rural townships for another decade or more. Same with electricity then lighting up major towns and cities, but in between still sporadic, intermittent, a mere flicker spoken of or witnessed from afar. Despite our druthers, we adjusted to the various changes ever subject to the old verities: who, what, when, where, why, and how you landed.

Winter coming on, done with football, Danny voiced his desire to attend the University in Lawrence. Not surprisingly, he wished to study journalism, now a full-blown profession, with many schools, including the one in Lawrence, offering degrees. Plus the nearby draw of the *Kansas City Star*, among the nation's leading newspapers.

For Christmas Maxie gave him a Remington Standard No.6, like the last model Hagan had owned. Much improved over earlier versions of the "infernal machines" as Mark Twain had cursed them. Once again, when offered to try, I declined, still preferred the quiet cursive flow of words. But Danny's piano fingers quickly adapted, found the tempo and rhythm amid the click and clatter, ding and clang, soon producing a music of words — his essays featured in the school paper and he even landed several columns in *The Mankato Mercantile*, lauding Populist policies being brought into play by both major parties. Fiercely proud of his father and the ideas Hagan once championed, as was I.

A year following the war with Spain, congressional hearings were held on the "embalmed beef" supplied our soldiers in Cuba, at which Roosevelt himself testified to its foul quality, claiming he'd rather eat his hat. This and other rumblings, particularly Upton Sinclair's *The Jungle*, a muckraking novel that exposed the horrid filth of Chicago meatpackers, helped spur The Food and Drug Act in 1906. And I took heart in Danny's pride, knowing that Hagan had made a ripple on the wave of change. Obscure, but not forgotten, not by Danny, myself, or Maxie, who'd point to the Wiley Act and other laws protecting child laborers and limiting the work week, and say, "Aye, Dan, yer Da, Hagan, done that. Fought for farmers 'n workers, he did. Fought with words 'n fists…"

In April when Danny turned 18, Maxie took him to the tavern, poured each a beer and as they tapped glasses, said, "Ya be a man now, Dan. Look me 'n all others in the eye 'n ne'er back down. Aye, now chug it…!" Danny drank several more that night, eventually rubbing shoulders with a trio of musicians traveling to Denver who regaled him with tales of ragtime clubs in Kansas City, further feeding his fever to taste all the sights and sounds. Next morning when he descended the stairs in moan, Maxie marched him out back and doused his head under the cistern while pumping the handle, laughing as he tossed a towel and said, "Shake it off, lad. Look me in th' eye. Good, now go eat a big plate 'o pancakes. Got a'nuther great day a'waitin'!"

After graduating in May, Danny and Phil shared pitching chores for the Mankato men's team. Again over summer Danny worked with father and Glen on the Limestone, but seldom stayed the week, every few days driving the "rattly beast," as father called it, into town for baseball practice or a game. Among other activities. Several times, doing laundry, I found lipstick on his collar and realized he'd finally discovered girls and even sampled a nectarous lip or two.

The morning after Labor Day, gathered at the train station to see Danny and Phil off to Lawrence, Hannah, who idolized her big brother, clung to his pant leg, loath to let go. He knelt down and gave her a long hug, then pinched her cheek and said, "Keep singing, little nightingale. Time will fly and I'll soon be home for Christmas."

"Promise?"

"I promise. And we'll sing all the carols and Hot Time in the Old Town —"

"And Mandalay too?"

"You bet, hot and loud as '*the dawn comes up like thunder outer China 'crost the bay…*'" Then he laughed and stood, grabbed up his bags, and turning his back to board the train, it reminded me of Hagan. Watching him go, Hannah and I both wept.

XXV. Ute Theater

Our lives dulled with Danny gone, days vaguely empty, evenings more so. Not a week later, father in town with mother for trading day told me Blood had died, "Found 'im in the far pasture already bloated 'n left 'im be. Always was a proud horse, liked to graze off alone…" Sad news but long expected, shared in my first letter to Danny.

No, time did not fly. Especially for Hannah who grew mopey, listless, sometimes went to the piano and plinked a song then sat staring out the window, counting the days to Christmas. Week to week, on into October, I'd expected her to snap out of it, but her lone refrain was "How long before Danny comes home?"

Hoping to cheer her, for Halloween I sewed a Little Red-Riding Hood outfit as she loved touching my wedding dress, carefully stowed away, only worn at Christmas; it still fit, though I had let the waist out. We chose the same material for her outfit, and Hannah took interest, helping pin the pattern, learning to thread the needle and stitch. Seemingly pleased when I adjusted the hooded cape and sent her off to school with her little basket where she and other kids would gather and play and later scatter out to trick-or-treat.

That evening while fixing supper, the sun setting golden red in the great blue west, she came skipping in, her basket filled with apples, nuts, and various candies. I noticed the sparkle had returned to her green eyes. Toto saw it too, jumping for a treat, begging more till she snapped her finger and said "No!" Then placed the basket out of reach and sat at the table, hands folded under her chin, mulling one thought or another.

Presently she caught my eyes and asked, "What does *conceived* mean?"

"Well…" I slowly answered, slightly puzzled, though she often asked of words, "conceived means to think of something…to hatch an idea or possibility…perhaps a song or like when a woman conceives a baby before giving birth. As do all animals."

"Marion Thomas says only tramps wear red. And said I was born too soon and conceived in sin!" Boldly stated, yet sounded more assertive than ashamed as she waited, her green eyes searching mine.

"No, honey," I carefully chose my words, "you were not conceived in sin, but in delight and love between your daddy and me. And you were born precisely when nature prompted, neither too soon nor too late. So if this Marion Thomas says anything more, just ignore him."

"Oh, he won't say anything and better not!"

"Really? Why is that?"

"Because I kicked him right where Daddy told me to kick a naughty boy!" And she smiled quite satisfied that she'd done as her daddy wished.

"Well then," I offered, trying not to smile, "let's hope Marion learned his lesson. But let's keep this our secret, okay? Some things Daddy does not need to know or hear."

"Oh, I won't tell," she answered, flush and confident, as if that kick had settled things. It saddened me knowing there was still talk of Sadie Briar and her red dress, of her baby born too soon. But our town and its people were no better or worse than any other. Of my sins, such as they were, I could not amend a thing.

Happily, Hannah was finally herself again, up each morning, spinning like a top, she and Toto running and laughing amidst the swirling autumn leaves. While she still asked of Danny, not so often, and always in eager anticipation. And apparently Marion learned his lesson, for she mentioned it no more, and thankfully never told her daddy.

Though one night not long thereafter, Maxie and I making love, rather loudly I fear, when the door cracked open and we looked up to see Hannah and Toto peering in. Then heard her little voice ask "What are you doing?"

"Why dear…" I gasped, a bit breathless, "your daddy and I…are delighting…like when babies are made…or conceived."

"Oh, delighting," she giggled as if in that instant conceiving the very notion. Then she eased the door shut and we listened to her and Toto trot back upstairs. We waited till they'd settled then quietly resumed delighting.

Finished, Maxie laid back in chuckle, "Con-ceived? De-lighting? Wha' in devil's that about?"

"Just a little talk between mother and daughter about the birds and the bees."

"A wee talk, eh? Birds 'n th' bees…ain't that a stinger." With that he slapped his belly, sat up and grunted, "Believe ah'll have a smoke…"

A cold night, he took his cigar to the kitchen and cracked the window to let the smoke drift out. I hugged his pillow, inhaled his scent and thought of Hannah, fierce and innocent, full of wonder and curiosity. What arms, what delight and pain awaited her?

In 1905 the Ute Theater opened in Mankato, seating over 300 people on posh red cushions before the velvety stage curtains drawn open and held in place by silken ropes. Various theatrical productions passed through, including *The Wizard of Oz* then touring the West, though sadly it never stopped, slated for the bigger places. Yet others played to hungry audiences in our little town, packing the theater, enrapt, enthralled. Except for Maxie, who seldom went, saying, "Ah got theater ever' day at th' tavern…" Whereas Hannah and I, and Danny when home, attended nearly every show, and now and then a film — a new fascinating spectacle of actors and action cast on a flickering screen. Most of which dimmed, easily forgotten, compared to live performances.

But not so *The Great Train Robbery*, in graphic black and white, full of violent drama from beginning to end. In the opening scene a railroad dispatcher is overpowered and bound by the robbers who then secretly board the train. Some miles on they commit the robbery, during which they murder a crewman and shoot a passenger, leaving the rest stranded and penniless. In the meantime, back at the station, a little girl, about the age of Hannah and dressed in a black cape, discovers and frees the dispatcher who immediately alerts authorities. A posse rides forth and overtakes the culprits in deep timber. The robbers, caught counting their loot, are dealt swift justice, shot down to a man. Brutal, fast-paced, thrilling, and the heroine was a little girl. Hannah absorbed all and reenacted every detail for weeks on end, staging scenes and characters with sticks and rocks, tracing the train tracks through the dirt, shooing Toto back before the bloody climax when the robbers fall before her blazing pistol finger.

Still in thrall of the film, talking of little else through Halloween, past Thanksgiving, then shortly before Christmas we heard of an amazing French film coming to Mankato. Danny soon arriving home, she begged him to take her. We sat in front row, center seats, waiting as the curtain opened and the screen filled with *A Trip to the Moon*, based on the Jules Verne adventure, and not at all realistic like *The Great Train Robbery*, but magical, operatic, and dreamlike with brilliant-colored costumes and fantastic backdrops. Unlike the novel, in the film the voyagers actually land on the moon and battle lizard creatures that eerily tumble forth in threatening dance and when struck vanish in puffs of smoke. We watched riveted, spellbound, especially Hannah who barely blinked. We saw it three times and on the last she even convinced her daddy to "Come see!"

So enthused it eased Danny's departure at the station. Though she shed hot tears and hugged sweet goodbye, once home she dashed to her crayons, watercolors, and paper and began recreating all the fantastical creatures and scenes. The same through the dark winter months, each evening on the floor coloring the wondrous celestial figures, and her favorite, the lovely Venus sedately seated in the cusp of the moon. All the while Hannah sang her own narrative with fresh words and melody, drawing line to line, defining form and space, the latter filled with stars, asteroids, and ringed planets. Each page of which her daddy would deem better than the film, "A beauty like me wee lass," then swing her to his broad shoulder and prance her around like a circus princess on a grand horse.

When Danny returned home for Decoration Day, it was he who swung her high at the depot, then gave me a hug, smiling to all, eager to share the news — "I'm to work this summer at the Kansas City Star, answering directly to the city editor, Henry J. Haskell. He said he'd known my father. That they'd met during the '96 campaign..."

Apparently the man had read an article that Danny landed in the Lawrence paper, recognized the name and admired the writing — which in essence bemoaned Roosevelt's pledge not to seek a third term while commending him for keeping his word, concluding, "Of all the President's worthy deeds, this act of honor may stand foremost..."

While we shared the general regret of Roosevelt not running, our greater regret was Danny's brief stay, particularly father, who gripped his shoulder seeing him off and said, "Gonna miss ya, Danny boy, but I expected as much. Also expect to see your name on a byline or two. So go for it, all the way to the top!"

For once we had a happy farewell.

As the train threaded to the distance, we returned to our patterns and routines — father, mother, and Glen at the ranch, Maxie at his tavern, and I busy with Hannah and jobbers at the newspaper. Thankfully no more typesetting as Ian had acquired a linotype, which Bradley quickly mastered. Another election year upon us, we were soon churning out posters and pamphlets at a frantic pace in political battles for city, county, state, and national offices, including the presidency, contested by two Williams: Taft, Roosevelt's chosen heir, and Bryan, making his third run and it would not prove a charm. Despite Bryan's eloquence and the ascendency of progressive ideals, voters delivered his worst and final defeat, electing William Howard Taft president.

Hardly the focus of our lives, more a distant clamor, and the political season soon faded with the autumn leaves. Our present anticipation was Danny coming home for Christmas like a conquering hero, for he'd gained several bylines over summer reporting on the Kansas City Blues baseball games, only a farm team but avidly followed by area farmers and townsfolk. Moreover, there was "A big surprise!" he'd promised Hannah, which had us all wondering.

Gathered at the station, we watched him step down, a large box heft to his shoulder, beautifully wrapped in glittery gold paper, red ribbon and bow. Phil followed jaunty at his side carrying their satchels, both grinning to Hannah as Phil announced, "I know one little girl who's going to love Santa this year…" Then he handed Danny's satchel to Max and skipped away, heading home.

As did we, all enjoying a festive reunion that evening. But still two days before Christmas, Hannah could barely contain herself, bursting with curiosity and questions, "Oh, what is it? What could it be?"

"Just have to wait, little sister," Danny mildly teased, "till Santa comes and taps it with his magic…" Hannah glanced to the clock reading half past nine, minutes ticking like hours and her wait seemed forever. She sat with Toto on her blanket, staring at her present till she finally nodded off and Danny carried her upstairs and put her to bed.

Next day we went to the Ute Theater to see *Skyscrapers of New York* that showed harrowing scenes of men erecting massive structures to dizzying heights. A film perhaps more breathtaking to an adult than a child, for Hannah sat only vaguely engaged, at the end she simply said, "Those men look like workers at Daddy's tavern."

But a short while later, following supper, Christmas Eve, she joined Danny at the piano where they sang song after song, never tiring, till Danny reminded her, "Time for bed, little sister, else Santa won't come and work his magic…" So convinced she did not tarry, scampered off to bed, no doubt to dream, not of sugar plums, but of what magic wonder Danny had gifted her.

Christmas morning found her trembling in her nightgown beside her present which she dared not touch as Danny had warned her not to jiggle for it contained a rare, fragile treasure. At last yielding to her quiet appeal, he knelt by with my scissors and let her cut the ribbon then helped her peel back the paper and open the box from which he lifted an oblong object wrapped in plain brown paper. Setting this aside, he reached in and pulled forth a polished mahogany cabinet, about a foot and a half square by one foot tall, at which Hannah joyfully screeched, "It's a Victor!" having seen and read of them in our Sears-Roebuck catalogue.

"Yes," Danny answered, gently placing it to the floor, "it's the Victor IV disc gramophone. And all yours, Hannah…" Complete with the emblem of a little dog like Toto peering to the sound horn — the mystery object which Danny now unwrapped, also of mahogany with brass flaring, and shortly affixed to the cabinet.

Hannah crouched down listening intently as he explained the workings.

"First, we turn the crank to wind the inner spring…but not too far, only until it feels firm. See?" At her nod he pulled a black disc from its cover and said, "Always grasp the edge, handle carefully and never drop. They are brittle, made of slate, and will shatter. Also try to never scratch the surface, for these tiny grooves hold the magic of the music. Easy now, we center it over the silver prong and lower it to the felt table, like so. Then here," pointing to the front edge, "we flick this switch. Ready?" Her eyes widened with a quick nod and the table and disc began to turn. "Now, most important," he cautioned, "the very last thing. We must carefully lift the arm and set the needle in the outermost groove. Then voila! The magic happens…"

The music arose like a genie through the horn to our ears as we listened to the first song, "Sweet Adeline." When it finished, Hannah jumped up and hugged Danny's neck, crying, "I love you, love you, love you…" Laughter and music filled the day. Next, they played "Hot Time in the Old Town" then "Give My Regards to Broadway" and several more of a dozen stacked aside until Danny picked a new one we'd never heard but were destined to hear many times, "Take Me Out to the Ball Game!"

Standing by, listening, Maxie nudged him and asked, "Jus' how'd ye lay hands on that jimdandy music box?"

Danny nudged him back and said, "Like you, Max, I've got my connections." Then he grinned, "Just say some fellas in Kansas City like the way I play piano."

Maxie slapped his back and laughed, "Aw, ye be Hagan's son, no doubt. Bet he's proud 'n smilin' down…" For love of his mother, Maxie gave nod to the old faith and when asked, would answer, "Aye, Catholic, born 'n bred, Irish 'n German both!" Stoutly asserted but held at arm's length, never went to church except to light a candle for his "Mum 'n Da" nor questioned other views, including my heretic family. Embraced life, like music, and let it play.

Father, mother, and Glen arrived shortly before noon in their Model T and they too marveled at the music. "That Victor is one machine I can abide!" father vouched. The song winding down, he swept Hannah up and set her at the table, scooting his chair by to check her protest, "Like the Good Book says, there's a time for all things 'n now it's time to eat!" Winning her smile, he winked, "That's my girl," then barked, "Gol-dern it, let's pass the food!" And we dove in, passing hot bowls of meat, potatoes, gravy, and bread, sharing a hearty Christmas dinner.

Afterwards the men slipped off to the tavern for mugs of beer, cigars, and pool, while mother and I cleared the table and washed the dishes. But Hannah jumped down and returned to the Victor, sorting through and playing all the songs. Without question her most joyous Christmas. And her delight did not wane, not with Danny's departure or through the dark months of winter. Every evening found her knelt by the Victor, Toto perched before the horn while she gaily sang along, mimicking each singer, gradually finding her own voice and inflection.

XXVI. Distant Thunder

Blanketed in her rocker, she sits listening to the flames battle up the flue against the timeless wind and hears the child's bygone voice singing to her inner self and even sees her sitting by the Victor. She flexes her hand and knows she's not asleep, only paused in transient dream, her mind like a bee alighting here and there, gathering nectar to sweeten the moment before facing the bitter things to come. The girl and song now fade and she hears only the wind and ticking clock as she stares through the darkness to the stove. The bejeweled tree, its bubbly lights and reflective spheres, the single prop in a fated play that she alone must witness…

⁕

From then on Hannah's love of singing held strong, fixed like the North Star, determining her path. A natural performer, fearless, exuberant, she sang in school plays, for social gatherings, and even on occasion in church. People soon forgot or at least forgave her being conceived in sin. Voice of an angel, they readily conceded. And beautiful, her long red curls, her green eyes and cupid smile charmed every audience, winning new admirers.

And each time Danny visited, he delivered another armload of discs, or records as they came to be known. Hannah astutely listened to and memorized each, ever careful not to scratch, yet fervent, anxiously selecting one then another. Likewise, father scanned the pages of the *Sunday Star* for any article with a byline that read, Daniel Liam Corbett, and seeing which he'd slap the paper and shout, "By gad, Sarah, that's our grandson!" then beg her scissors and snip it out.

By early summer of 1910 when Danny graduated and went to work full-time for the *Kansas City Star*, father had filled one scrapbook and started another. And Hannah had a collection of over a hundred records and a brand-new Edison diamond-needle phonograph to play them on. A magnificent tall cabinet with filigree doors softly curtained to frame the horn under which a large sliding drawer slotted to neatly file her favorite records with a matching side cabinet to hold the rest — all purchased by her adoring daddy. The clarity and volume easily surpassed the Victor, while the turntable housed four feet off the floor spun the records safely beyond reach of Toto.

Hannah was ecstatic and exclaimed, "Papa, I love you to the heavens!"

Later that summer a hint of romance drifted our way, a trifle disconcerting for it concerned Danny in the *Kansas City Star* and sparked considerable gossip among women and no doubt envy among the men. Not a byline to an article, though father promptly cut it out and added it in his scrapbook, but a photo of Danny "Ivory Hands" Corbett, as the caption read, seated at the piano in a swank uptown nightclub, gazing to a silken-clad mulatto beauty, her hand draped to his shoulder, and their smiling eyes told a story that could not be printed. I read all at a glance and knew his hands favored ebony as well. Quietly proud, I admit, truly his father's son. Still, it saddened me, thinking of Hagan's haunted lineage, all the ill-begotten sons and daughters unwittingly bequeathed this life, seduced by want and need. Roused from my sadness, I reached to Maxie and led him to our bed…sweet moments, indeed.

In my brief life the world had witnessed constant progress in science and industry, and improved political and social conditions. Even our conflicts, for most part colonial affairs between rising and fading powers, brief and passing, seemed to bring betterment to many. As if the Age of Reason reached every shore in warrant of fair seas and endless prospects sailing to a glorious future.

On April 9, 1912, Danny's 23rd birthday, the *Titanic*, a new ocean liner hailed as unsinkable, struck an iceberg on her maiden voyage from England to New York, taking 1500 passengers to the depths of the cold Atlantic. A tragic tolling that hushed previous hurrahs in doubt and question. Designed and built by bold intelligent men, how could this happen?

By that time faith in the Progressive Era had also dimmed. After Roosevelt's matchless vigor, Taft's more conventional approach, while competent, seemed as staid and dull as his corpulent self, more suited to an office chair than the Presidency. Hopes and expectations dashed as with the film of *Ben Hur* that came out during Taft's first term, billed as "16 Magnificent Scenes!" yet never made it to Mankato, canceled over a copyright issue. Danny had caught the film in Kansas City and said it should have been canceled for boredom — "Worse than Phil's wedding rehearsal." A grave disappointment for Hannah, for I'd read her the story and she so wanted to see the chariot race.

"But what of the chariots?" she asked, awaiting a thrilling description.

"Sorry, little sister, there's more action uptown on trading day. They just lined up four chariots, horses abreast, then set off and flashed by four or five times while a crowd of toga-clad citizens lamely waved like greeting an unwelcome visitor. Then a big 'The End' lettered the screen."

Hannah gazed up and sighed, "Is that all…?"

Which was pretty much the view of Taft by the spring of 1912.

Roosevelt, former friend and patron, felt betrayed by his successor for opening public lands to mining and timber, again siding with railroad, bank, and industrial interests over farmers and workers. Finally so fed up he denounced Taft as more a Gilded Age Republican than of the Lincoln brand, shucked his vow not to seek a third term and threw his hat in the ring. The old Rough-Rider, still popular with the voters, surged through the primaries only to crash against Taft's hold on the party machine. Denied the nomination, claiming it was stolen, he stormed out of the convention and formed the Bull Moose, or Progressive Party.

Always ready to fight, Roosevelt took his cause to the people, crisscrossing the nation in a fierce campaign. At a rally in Milwaukee a saloon keeper shot him point blank — the bullet, slowed by an eye-glass case and a speech folded in his breast pocket, lodged in his chest muscle. He even helped subdue his attacker then shielded him from enraged onlookers while police whisked him away. After which Roosevelt mounted the stage and delivered an hour-long stem-winder.

When I read Maxie the account from the newspaper, he clenched his fist and declared, "Thar's a bull o' a man! Got my vote, he has…" Like father, Maxie usually leaned Democratic, but did not care for Wilson, calling him, "A'nuther protestant priss like Jennings. Least Taft, all be a fat-cat, n'er spit on Catholics. Give 'im that…"

True, Taft dealt favorably with the growing Catholic population, but less so with others — Negros, or Coloreds, in particular. As Danny reminded us during his Labor Day visit, his remarks directed foremost to mother, still a staunch Republican, Taft had vowed in his Inaugural Address not to appoint Negros to federal positions. In fact he proceeded to remove Negros from such positions throughout the South.

"Don't you find it strange," Danny patiently noted, appealing to his grandmother, "that after fighting a bloody civil war to free a people, 50 years later we deny them work and positions rightfully theirs?"

At her smile I knew he'd won her over, rejecting Taft for Roosevelt at least in voice if not in vote. While the suffrage amendment in Kansas did pass on Election Day 1912, our right to vote for president still waited. However, mother and I did cast a vote for governor. As both candidates supported suffrage, we happily split our vote — I, for the Democrat, Hodges, who won, and she for the Republican, Capper, who lost by a mere 23 votes, the narrowest margin in Kansas history.

Nationally, Roosevelt and Taft also split the vote to factions left and right, leaving Wilson to sweep the center and gain the Presidency. An eloquent, highly intelligent man, now captain of our Ship of State, I only hoped he fared better than those who'd steered the *Titanic*.

<hr>

The election over, our concerns shifted close to home, the newspaper noting crops and weather, various school and local events. Ian had married a young woman, Elizabeth Hansen, her class valedictorian in 1908, who like myself forwent college to work at the local paper. Like Ian, Liz was quiet, prompt, and efficient. They had a two-year-old son, James, and a baby on the way. At their wedding I'd spoken with Ian's sister Shannon, who smiled like she hadn't since that horrid night in Oakvale. Now a widow, she ran the hardware store with her oldest son, her youngest a barber in Denver. Sometimes death did not cast a shadow, but opened a window to sunlight.

The following spring, crocus and phlox in bloom, Toto went missing. Often gone in hunt overnight, but usually home in a day or two. After three days of calling for him and searching along the tracks, Hannah feared he'd been snatched by coyotes or poisoned by a neighbor, for he was invariably digging in one garden or another. At last, losing hope, she sat down and wept, face in hands, inconsolable.

Maxie stepped in and quipped, "That lil' imp, why a gust 'o wind prob'ly spun 'im clear to Oz!" Hearing which she moaned all the louder. "Aw now, lassie…" he sat down and drew her close, "ah know tis hard, Toto gone. But know wha' ah bet? Always down to th' depot, waggin' his tail, beggin' pets…bet a good tramp picked 'im up for a travelin' buddy. Bet ol' Toto's headed west, his red tongue lappin' th' breeze…"

This did cheer her as she choked back her tears and leaned to his shoulder.

But I bet her daddy had found the little dog and buried it to spare her feelings.

To further distract her we went to a film, *The Unseen Enemy* by D.W. Griffith, starring the Gish sisters, Lillian and Dorothy, who Hannah resembled, more so the latter, though prettier than either to my mind. Another melodrama featuring two damsels in distress, sisters held at gunpoint by their wicked maid while her partner in crime blows the safe to steal the modest inheritance their deceased father left them. The theft thwarted by their good brother and a boyfriend who arrive in the nick of time to nab the thieves. For Hannah and me the poignant moment came far earlier when the boyfriend, soon departing for college, tries to lure the younger sister into the cornfield for a kiss, which she modestly refuses.

Afterwards, walking home, Hannah abruptly broke her silence, "That's just silly, her not kissing him. I would have. Well, maybe not him. But someone cuter I would…"

Of which I had no doubt. An immediate and deepening concern, for Hannah, soon turning 14, had blossomed into a fetching young woman and expressed no qualms of her budding breasts, in fact proudly showed them off, "See, Mother, how fine they are?"

Not to mention other changes in our midst. That summer we acquired a telephone, the lines having reached the Limestone, and seeing father and mother age, their hair gray, gimps and pains, though both still stood and walked straight, they'd slowed, time nipping at their heels, so it was good to call every few days and stay in touch. Our phone was the "candlestick" style with the ringer box set by, theirs had the ringer box and phone all in one fixed to the wall. Aside from checking on mother, the phone was more a novelty, an occasional convenience, and to reach Danny required so many connections, it was easier to send a telegram. But Hannah, never shy, had no trouble reaching her friends, and our phone, which initially rang no more than once or twice a week, began ringing several times each evening. Maxie shook his head in aggravation, like father, refusing to touch the "blame thing" and would not have one in his tavern.

"*Con-sarned* cling-clang, a man needs one refuge from th' curse o' things…"

Still, the world reached out and tapped us, events so distant and foreign that you could not pronounce their names, yet soon grew dreadfully familiar. In late June, 1914, an assassin killed the Archduke Ferdinand in Sarajevo, which within a month unleashed the Great War. Father, in town with mother in early August, letting her drive due to his failing eyes, stepped from the Model T, fisting the front page that headlined war, slapped it with the back of his hand and said, "Don't like this business, not one bit! A madman shoots a damn duke 'n got all of Europe…Russia, England, Germany, Austria, France, Italy itchin' to tear each other's throat. Thinkin' it'll be over by Christmas, fat chance! Most thought the same in the Civil War, be done by summer's end. Bull Run changed that. Once the shootin' starts 'n blood spills, all the massed men, cavalries 'n mighty guns grind to a halt. Dig in 'n trench, fight 'n die till one or the other runs out of bullets. All the bold tactics 'n battle plans are just fools playin' toy soldier. Hope Danny steers clear of the whole mess 'n keeps playin' piano…"

Until hearing it voiced, the implications had not struck me and suddenly the far battles opened close up like a film in my mind. Fear gripped my heart and I secretly wished Danny a score of mistresses if that would keep him safe.

Far easier to grant casual romance to a grown son than to a young daughter — Hannah, now 15, entering her sophomore year and more assertive than ever, no longer wished to attend movies, as films were now called, with her mother. So I stepped back and let her go accompanied by two or three friends, young girls like herself anxious of life, awaiting their first kiss. Gradually, no doubt, they sat closer to the boys and even chanced to sit beside one. Finally, about midwinter, a boy came calling, gangly, not bad looking, and polite enough as Maxie greeted him with a powerful grip and bid him "Step right in, lad. Give me a big smile. Aye, fine set o' teeth ya got. If ya wanna keep 'em, ya'll behave a gentleman, hear?" The boy's smile vanished in solemn vow and Maxie nodded, "Good!" slapped the boy's back and saw them off.

Not surprisingly, that very evening, aiming to keep an eye on the boy and his daughter, the tavern in good hands with Myrtle and her burly son Clyde in the kitchen and a trusty former railroader, Jerome "Jar" Harlan, to man the bar, Maxie offered his arm and said, "Sadie, tis time ah see me a picture show…"

That night the Ute featured Charley Chaplin in *Tillie's Punctured Romance* and Maxie loved it. In fact, forgot about Hannah and her beau — until afterwards, making certain they walked straight home.

Films improving year by year, many running to an hour or more, telling a fuller story, that spring we saw Mary Pickford in *Cinderella* and Cecil B. DeMille's *Squaw Man*, among others. Between movies and tavern, school and newspaper, we shared a cozy little world of mildly amusing drama and pattern. Our tranquility shaken by the ominous news of May 7th when a German U-boat torpedoed the British ocean liner, *Lusitania*, claiming nearly a thousand lives, including over a hundred Americans.

"Be like the Maine blowed up, th' bastards!" Maxie cursed. "Bet we go to war!" Something neither of us nor few Americans wanted.

Yet Roosevelt roused from his near-fatal adventure in the Amazon to call for "Preparedness!" He and others demanded that Wilson start building up the army and navy. Wilson fired a stern protest warning Germany away from all civilian and neutral shipping. The Germans countered that the *Lusitania* had been carrying munitions, which the British denied. Wilson held firm. Finally, Germany issued a pledge to respect our neutrality and in the future allow civilians and crews a chance to disembark before they torpedoed suspect ships. But food fed the hungry and munitions fed the guns and as the blockade tightened there were further incidents. And casualties in France rose from tens to hundreds of thousands into the millions. While Wilson kept the peace amid shouts for "Preparedness!" no matter how many movies we saw we could no longer ignore the war drums drumming.

Nor could we ignore the most popular song of 1915, "Danny Boy," famous near and far, especially among British soldiers fighting in the trenches. The old Derry County air had been given voice and lyrics, an ode to sad partings in our tragic, mortal lives. Yet I winced hearing Danny's name therein. Maxie bought the record for Hannah who within minutes had it memorized, joining with the fine vibrato voice, ironically of an Austrian-German immigrant named Ernestine. And when we all gathered for Danny's Christmas homecoming — including mother, father, and Glen — after dinner Maxie placed the record on the Edison and Hannah sang along.

Danny listened with a wry smile and once she finished gave warm applause and said, "Nicely done, little sister, wonderful. But that song," he shook his head, "people shout out and ask for it every night I play."

"Why heck, why not?" father glanced in frown. "I love that song."

"It's a fine song, Grandad…if you don't have to play it a dozen times a night."

"Why, I'd gladly listen a dozen times…" and he sang a favorite passage, "*I'll be there in sunshine and in shadow…*" and swore, "What beautiful words. And once I'm planted under Sarah's apple tree, hope you'll come visit me, Danny boy."

"Oh pooh," mother lightly scolded, "you'll outlast me."

"No Sarah, that won't happen."

"It would if you slowed down."

"Slow down? Heck, if I slowed any more may as well stand me next a post in the pasture 'n have me grip the wire, least I'd be of use."

"Horse manure, Uncle Pat," Glen chimed in, "you're spry as a jackrabbit."

"I wish…only wish," bemoaning his lack of strength.

"Don't listen to 'im, folks. Just the other day he out-horsed me on the hay lift."

"Cut-a-hay!" father snapped genially, "you always could tell a good lie."

We all laughed. But in truth father had slowed, a halting walk, hesitant in manner and speech. Not only had he given up driving, his eyes so poor and rheumy even with glasses he seldom read more than a few minutes. Still, he kept apace of things and slyly noted, "The fates hold the cards 'n we get dealt…" as we put concerns aside to enjoy our time together. Danny looked to Hannah and requested an encore.

"Hearing it from your sweet voice, sister, I actually enjoy the song…"

Entering the dark months of winter, the initial phrase, "*Oh Danny Boy, the pipes, the pipes are calling…*" kept playing through my mind. In late February the big guns at Verdun opened up and thundered on for months. War raged beyond the ocean and below the border where the Mexican Revolution had blazed and smoldered the past 10 years. Lately, Carranza held sway, sending his former ally Poncho Villa into the hills where the rebel-bandit continued to fight. In early March Villa led a raid into New Mexico, burning the town of Columbus and killing over a dozen Americans before fleeing machinegun fire from nearby Camp Furlong. Next day, amid howls of outrage and vengeance, Wilson ordered General "Black Jack" Pershing in pursuit of Villa.

"Hope they catch the bastard!" Maxie spat, echoing the common view.

But hunting Villa in his own haunts proved as futile as tracking dust in the wind, leading to endless halts, skirmishes, and senseless deaths until the mission became more an embarrassment than anything punitive. At least it kept Glen busy helping Holly provide fresh mounts for the U.S. Calvary. And farmers and ranchers prospered like never before with fertile lands of Europe left fallow, shell torn, and littered with bodies, yet armies and people still needed fed.

Wars and rumors of war loomed over and wove into everything, even the movies.

Birth of a Nation, D.W. Griffith's epic film of the Civil War, reached Mankato in mid-May. The three-hour spectacle had sparked considerable controversy, both praised and condemned, even banned in a number of places for inciting White violence against unfortunate Negros. Reading of which, father was prime to see and judge the movie for himself. We were all curious, Hannah particularly excited as it starred the Gish sisters and Mae Marsh, though she sat apart from us with her current beau. And we watched riveted from beginning to end, for the action, drama, and battle scenes were compelling even as the story tilted heavily in favor of the "Lost Cause."

Outside the theater Maxi arched a brow to father and said, "Sure paints a dainty picture o' th' South, don' it, Pat?"

"Yep, like they were all fine gents who only fought to preserve their women's virtue 'n not their blame plantations, but I know better."

"Why, they show that devil shoot poor Lincoln in the back," mother protested, "yet paint abolitionists black as all evil and hardly bat an eye at the evil of slavery…"

Instead, the central drama framed the plight of an innocent young girl who leaps from a cliff rather than submit to ravaging by a lustful Negro, the rogue shortly dealt his due by gallant knights of the Ku Klux Klan. While many teared and cheered, we were mostly sobered by the old battle, its continuing strife and question.

Once home, awaiting Hannah's return, Maxie admitted, "Ah did feel for that poor lass, or any done th' like. But 'em KKK boys as soon stomp Catholics as Coloreds. Been barns burned hereabout. Protestant snoots like th' damn Brits who'd make us all slaves if ya let 'em. Like with th' Easter Uprisin' last month, stood our Irish lads up 'n shot 'em down. Fool Germans too, some gone back to fight for th' Kaiser. Damn 'em, what they done to Belgium, rape 'n murder, makes me ashamed o' my name, das Ross. Like yer da says, thar's rot in th' whole blame mess. Some bad things comin'…"

Maxie, seldom morose and never for long, paced the floor briefly then checked out the window and spied Hannah and her beau in full embrace just beyond the porch. He stormed out and yelled, "Ya young whelp, takin' liberties with me daughter!" and sent the boy packing, at least he didn't bust his teeth.

Hannah rushed in crying, "It was only one kiss!" then disappeared upstairs.

Maxie stood doubly perplexed, did his duty but hated to displease his daughter. "One kiss, my hat!" he scoffed. "If so, that boy got a dollars' worth…" He grabbed his flat-cap and tugged it low in disgust, adding, "Believe ah'll go have a pint…" No doubt off to the tavern to spill his woes to Clyde and Jar.

While Hannah resolved her frustration in a fit of tears and pillow flops, I sat up writing a long letter to Danny concerning the romantic impulses of his precocious young sister. Several days later, in lieu of a letter, Danny, expected home for Decoration Day, sent a short telegram: "Will arrive on noon train Saturday. Do not worry. I have an idea. Daniel…"

Hannah remained in a sulk all that week, refused to sit at the table with her daddy, so Maxie took his meals at the tavern. And she'd barely speak to me, saying, "You're no help. Both of you, always watching everything I do."

"That's because we love you and don't want to see you hurt."

"Well I don't like it. I'm not a little girl…" then stormed back up to her room.

However, she did accompany me to greet Danny at the station, doubtless seeking a heart more sympathetic than her stodgy parents. In truth, the passions that birthed her had waned, my flesh no longer burned in want, mostly plagued by the flush and sweat of inner changes and somewhat eased by tincture of snakeroot or dram of whiskey. But no palliative can cool the ardor of youth — Hannah bursting with want I could well recall but dare not urge, only fear for her and hope she would not be consumed.

Hannah still in a pout as Danny stepped down and she did not rush to meet him. He carried two bags, his usual grip and a carpeted one which I suspected held his typewriter, packed along to do some work. Yet it seemed rather light as he set it down to give me a warm hug. Then turned to his moody sister, "What? Not even a smile for your brother?" At which she perked up a bit and offered her cheek for a brief kiss.

He winked to me, grabbed up his bags and once home he set them by the door, grasped her hand and coaxed her to the piano, "Come now," he said, "let's sing a gay tune and make me happy to be home."

"I don't want to sing. I don't feel like it."

He shrugged it off, sat down, plinked a lively tune then abruptly stopped and flashed a grin, "Would you feel like it if I asked you to come to Kansas City for a couple weeks?"

Stunned and silent, Hannah and I both taken by surprise as she looked to me in question, while Danny, still grinning, pointed to the carpet bag and said, "See that fine valise? Inside there's a new dress. Both are yours. You might want to make sure it fits you nicely for when I take you out to all the special places."

Hannah gasped, "Mother, can I go, please?"

Maxie had just stepped in and asked, "What's this? Go where?"

"Oh Daddy!" Hannah blurted brightly as she snatched up her valise, "Danny is going to take me to Kansas City!" She dashed up the stairs to her room in sudden glee and bustle, singing, humming bits of songs while trying on her new dress and deciding what else she'd need and how to pack it.

"Ah dunno…" Maxie hesitant, speaking for both of us, "she's awful young."

"Max, Mother, don't worry," Danny assured, "I'll watch her like a hawk, chaperone her everywhere we go. Except for the ladies' powder room," he noted to humor us along.

"Aye, maybe so…" Maxie actually warmed to the notion sooner than me.

"Listen, there's nothing to worry about," Danny leaned forth, speaking with greater earnest, "Hannah's always been a ball of fire, hard to handle. Full of spirit and talent that you cannot and should not restrain. But feed her ambition and she will take hold. Trust me. I've already arranged voice, dance, and etiquette sessions with some very refined young women. Polished, respected theater professionals. They play in the arena she can aspire to. And I'll introduce her to several accomplished and charming young gentlemen who'll be delighted to meet her. Once she's danced in their arms she'll abide no clubfoot from Mankato."

"Jus' keep 'er from th' likes o' me."

"I'll hear no such thing, Max. You're a true knight. Albeit more roughhewn and battle worn than shiny. A true knight nonetheless," then added soberly, "good and true. That's what my father told me…before he left for Cuba."

Maxie lowered his head a silent moment then cleared his throat, "Aye, yer Da. Ah thank ya for that. Bless 'im, ah'm but a lucky lug is all…"

Just then Hannah descended the stairs in an elegant sky-blue summer dress replete with bowed waist, ruffles, and matching hat and handbag of the latest fashion.

"Wha'?" Maxie exclaimed, "Has me wee lass become a beautiful woman?"

She blushed in smile to him, presently reconciled as Danny offered his hand and said, "Stunning, fits you perfectly. First thing when we reach Kansas City, we'll find you some dainty shoes then you'll step out and dazzle them all…" Hannah flashed her green eyes and twirled round and around beneath his raised hand.

Again a happy family when we saw them off at the station Monday morning.

XXVII. Over There

High summer in late July before Hannah returned. Her two-week visit grew to two months and would have lasted all summer except Danny needed to focus on the pending presidential campaign. In June Republicans had nominated Charles Evans Hughes, the esteemed former governor of New York and Supreme Court Justice to lead their newly united party. Prospects for Wilson's reelection steadily dimmed. Meanwhile, Hannah, mindless of politics and in thrall of all she was doing, sent a weekly letter pleading to lengthen her stay. And Danny assured us all was well. When Maxie caught me stewing over her long absence, he said, "Don' fret. Danny gave 'is word, trust 'im, he's his father' son …" which hardly eased my concern, recalling Hagan's lost ring and frequent philandering. Yet again I accepted what I could not change. If I said no and demanded her return, she would have balked and likely never come home.

As it was, when she finally arrived amid the shimmering heat, I met a modestly dressed, poised young woman who smiled warmly and said, "Thank you, Mother, for letting me stay. And I do have the best brother ever…" A sentiment she extended to her father when she entered her room where he waited to surprise her with a tall three-panel mirror. She leapt into his arms, again his little girl, and cried, "Oh Daddy, you're the best Daddy ever!"

He beamed proudly and swung her around then pointed to the far corner, adding to her delight — "Aye, tis the new Victor Victrola! The best they got. Now ya can dance to yer music anytime ya like…" From then on records played in her room nearly nonstop as she sang and danced, practicing her daily poses and movements for hours on end.

Near and far, politics continued to play as well, more so following Labor Day when the presidential campaign ramped up. Headlines and odds makers still favored Hughes. "Would be my bet," Maxie allowed, judging by the fellows in his tavern, many leaving their wagers in his hands to divvy up come Election Day. Holding all bets like he did for the Johnson-Jefferies fight in 1911 that focused the nation, laid his money on Johnson, a Negro, claiming, "Big Jim's day is done," and raked in over $300. This time he stayed neutral, saying, "Don' care which or who wins. Hughes is jus' Wilson with whiskers but says straight out, be ready for war whilst Wilson stays mum 'n th' Bull Moose blasts his trumpet to charge, a mite too eager in my book…" roughly echoing the yeas and nays of the two campaigns. Some claimed Wilson had put America first and kept us out of war, others said he'd left us unprepared and wanted Hughes to take the reins.

Mother favored thought of war no more than me and urged father and Glen to vote Wilson. The election so close they still had not declared a winner by morning. At the tavern Maxie held the wagers through one day, then two, and not till the third day when California cast its lot to Wilson did he slap down cash to the victors and ordered drinks on the house — "Shake hands 'n drink up, damn ye! 'Lections over, we're all one…!"

And the country fairly much followed suit, steadily bracing for war while Wilson held his cards close. We watched, waiting, uncommonly subdued through Thanksgiving to Christmas, Danny's visit less joyous with thought of the coming storm. Still, Hannah eagerly sang him a new song she'd learned while he accompanied her on the piano. Then she pranced about, showing off fancy dance steps, spins and leaps.

"Impressive," he smiled, "you've come a long way, all on your own."

"Aye, drills like a trooper, she does," Maxie declared proudly. "Next summer she aims to learn more."

"Indeed, I'm so looking forward to Kansas City."

"As was I…" Danny answered, checking her enthusiasm as she asked, "Was?"

"Yes, Hannah, war is coming," he spoke directly. "We cannot wish it away. And it will change all our lives…and plans."

Hearing this from her brother, she did not fuss or object, simply lowered her eyes.

It was I who stammered hopefully, "But…surely they'll need war correspondents?"

"Yes, I suppose they will," he answered, his tight smile offering no assurance.

———————•❖•———————

In January, 1917, Pershing and his "Doughboys" caked in desert dust from their vain search for Villa headed home as seed to build an army. On February 1st, German U-boats resumed their attacks, sinking seven American merchant ships in short order. This coupled with the exposure of a German plot to subvert Mexico to their cause left Wilson no choice. Friday, April 6th, a fine spring morning, jonquils and tulips in bloom as I walked to the newspaper, America declared war.

Wilson's critics were right; we were in no way prepared to field an army and span an ocean. Germany gambled that before we could amass the will and achieve the task Britain and France would fold, as had Russia, and sue for peace. Long reluctant, once roused, America rallied — Uncle Sam "I Want You!" posters went up everywhere on courthouse, bank, post office, and depot walls. Young men poured forth and answered the call. Even those more dubious and wary like our family felt the surge and pull.

Within a month Washington announced formation of the Rainbow Division, spanning coast to coast, comprised of guard units from many states, including Kansas. Father read an article in the *Kansas City Star* headlined "Call for Men" written by Daniel L. Corbett, reporting on Lt. Colonel Frank Travis' request for volunteers to join the 177th Kansas. He showed me the paper and shared his concern, "Heck, Sadie, he's 28 'n world wise, surely he won't jump in?"

"I so hope you're right…" I answered faintly, remembering Hagan was nearly 40 when he left for Cuba.

And father gripped the very paper rolled in his left hand, anxiously awaiting Danny's arrival home at the station in late May. Glen there as well, our whole family gathered in hope to hold him back. After the customary round of handshakes, Danny gave Hannah a hug and said, "You look so fine in that dress."

She'd worn the blue one and tentatively asked, "This summer, do I get to come?"

He shook his head, "No, Hannah, sorry. In a week I leave for training."

"But they'll be wantin' correspondents, won't they?" father asked hopefully as had I at Christmas. "They'll need…need you fellas to write the story?"

"They want journalists, sure. Already they clamp down on what you can and can't say. That's not for me."

"But your dad, Hagan, he went to Cuba a correspondent, not a journalist."

"Yes, but he quit writing. Dropped his duffel to save a man then joined the fight to free Cuba and died. And I'm proud of him. You told me long ago, Grandad, that there's a time for everything…for harvest, sowing, work and rest. Now is the time for war. My writing is done. Besides, I've already given my word to Colonel Travis. In a couple days I'll stand with others and swear my oath."

"Well," father grimaced, "if you gave your word, it's settled," then working toward a smile, he fondly added, "You'll make a damn fine soldier, I know…"

Danny's stay was brief. He caught the morning train to Kansas City, and the following day swore his oath and commenced 90 days of officer training. And he was right about the government keeping tabs on what was written and printed. Hovering like a hawk even in Mankato when the Committee for Public Information, the CPI, issued guidelines for positive, patriotic, pro-war sentiments while urging all to plant "Victory Gardens" and purchase war-bonds and the like. Of course, there was little chance of Ian and *The Mercantile* printing otherwise. Yet I'm certain

Hagan would have railed against the lockstep as did others less enthused with our march to war, claiming it was in large part to secure Morgan's big bank loans to Britain and France. Voiced by Eugene Debs and other socialists, mostly Catholic Workers pamphlets and publications far removed from Mankato that mysteriously wound their way to Maxie's tavern.

At times he added his own rants, "Ah fear tis war like none a'fore, damn Brits wan' our money 'n blood too. But th' Boche, hang 'em, they got it comin', they do…" From breath to breath his old conflicts and contradictions battled within. Through the nation at large, skeptical views and voices were quickly snuffed, silenced, and shouted down by the patriotic fervor from newspapers, newsreels, movies, brass bands and massed crowds of flag-wavers chorusing "Over There" — a song that swept the country in midsummer, soon familiar to every ear.

Hannah had it memorized from a recent recording, ready for Danny's return on Labor Day. His summer training ended, he walked tall and straight in his uniform and officer hat. "Aw, if yer Da could see ya now!" Maxie proudly shook his hand and we rushed him home and stood admiring his lieutenant bars, brass buttons, Sam Brown belt, riding boots, and trousers. His uniform so tightly tailored he seemed even taller, smiling to us as we patted the "Rainbow" patch stitched to his shoulder.

Then father noticed the crossed-rifles pinned either side of his collar and said, "Why, that's the sign for infantry. Thought you were in supply, the ammunition train?"

"Was, but in mid-training I requested transfer to infantry. Next week I'll join my platoon at Camp Mills on Long Island where the AEF is mustering before shipping out. Some, the First and Third Divisions, are preparing to embark as we speak. Others, like my group, are scheduled for mid-to-late October. Until then we'll drill and train. Once we reach France, they say we'll continue training through winter. Not likely to enter the trenches until spring."

"Don't hurry to the trenches, Danny," father said, grasping his shoulders, "just hurry you home to us."

"Just you be here when I come."

"Oh, Danny boy, in sunshine or in shadow, I'll be here…"

As father's smile faded, Hannah tugged Danny to the piano, anxious to sing the song he most assuredly knew after marching and singing to it daily in recent weeks. Spirited and lively like a show tune, oddly gay considering where and to what it pointed: *"Over there! Over there! And the Yanks are coming…"* Danny flexed his hands and found the keys, grinning to Hannah as we all joined in singing, tears flowing from my and mother's eyes, and father's too, as I noted.

Seeing Danny off a day later, he and scores of other young men, some in uniform, many headed for boot camp, all leaned out the passenger windows, laughing, shouting goodbye to family and friends, town and country folk, hundreds gathered waving hands and flags to the long train receding from my eyes, losing color and sound, vanishing like autumn leaves to a distant swirling wind.

———•———

Autumn came, then winter, Christmas quiet and lonely without Danny. Hannah still harbored dreams of theater and music, yet fixated more on her handsome soldier-brother, each week writing three letters to my one. Like a fever you could feel it drawing young men by the millions to the gaped maw of iron ships waiting to deliver them to the fiery fields of war and death, everything from train to harbor and ocean, of monstrous size and murderous intent.

Danny had landed in France at Saint Nazaire. Trained briefly at Vancouleurs, then directly after Christmas made the winter march to Rolampont where the 42nd "Rainbow" experienced "Their Own Valley Forge" as newspapers noted. Confirmed by Danny in a letter received somewhat later.

"Reminds me of winter along the Limestone," he wrote in a firm hand like his father's. "Stark black trees etch snow-encrusted hills and valleys. And bitter cold, men and horses suffer with little shelter, scant food and supply…" echoing Hagan's words of the chaos and stressed conditions at Camp Tampa and in Cuba, only of opposite clime. "Pity the Texas units and others from the South, poorly clothed, few have overcoats and their shoddy boots shred in the icy snow. Poor devils, many lost toes and feet to frostbite and a sad few succumbed to pneumonia and were planted in the frozen ground. Though lately it has warmed and the thawed surface adds to our misery. The boys call it 'Camp Mud' and laugh it off. To grouse does no good and there's little time. Each day, when not training, is a mad scramble for food and a place to dry and warm our feet. Fresh socks and cigarettes are prized items and a dear comfort.

"At present no major offensive, though Boche snipers and artillery spit lively fire, as do ours, all along the front. You run at a crouch and dare not show your head. At any moment a bullet cracks the air, or a shell explodes. We hug the trenches despite the filth. Men snatch their sleep standing up, wrapped in ponchos, palm a cigarette, watch and listen. It's best to stay active. Most nights I detach with a French unit to reconnoiter and probe German lines, maybe chance on a prisoner, while they do the same, sometimes passing so close you hold your breath. A deadly game, and must admit I find it thrilling. Once you've touched the vital heart of things it's hard to pull back. Something I sensed in reading Father's last letter. I think he found it, a deeper act beyond thought and words that both frees and captures you.

"In another week they hand this sector of Lorraine, all 26 kilometers off to us, just us Yanks facing the Germans, waiting summer to see what plays. And I know it sounds strange, Mother, but I sense my father's spirit here among us. If I fall, think of me as I do of him. He's still out there, somewhere…" signed, "Your loving son, Daniel…"

This the lone somber letter out of the score he sent to Hannah, father, and me, the others crisp, lighthearted, full of humorous anecdotes and banter. I folded it away and showed it to no one. Dreaded the thought of summer, a dread that gripped heart, mind, and dream.

But the dark premonition struck sooner than expected, and close to home.

A Friday morning in late April, Maxie still abed and Hannah off to school, the telephone rang. I lifted the receiver and heard mother sobbing, "Oh Sadie, it's Patrick, your father…he's gone. Glen is here…can you come…help us?"

Her voice faint and muted as I answered, "We'll be right down…"

Maxie had awakened to the ringing, stood in the doorway and knew by my manner and tone even before I told him that father had died. Soon dressed, we took Hannah out of school and arrived in time for Maxie to help Glen dig the grave. They marked it out where mother pointed, in the orchard between two apple trees in bloom. The ground thawed, they worked at a quiet solemn pace while father's two cattle dogs, Buck "the younger" and Shag "the elder," as he'd come to call them, watched and whimpered just beyond, but staying where they were told. Father lay in his cedar coffin, the lid thereby, his hands folded, his body cleaned and neatly dressed, his face gaunt and pale in long sleep. He'd built their coffins, his and mother's, several years before, ever prepared like he readied his wood for winter.

Glen paused in smile and recalled, "Uncle Pat swore he'd have no man blister his hands over his bones. Said he'd dig his own grave too if he only knew when..." They shared a brief chuckle and resumed digging as the warm wind stirred the trees dropping rosy-white petals to the fresh black earth.

Standing, watching them work, mother told us what had happened:

"There by the window...glimpsed Patrick coming up from the barn, carrying two milk pails. I turned back and filled the kettle. Then set it on the stove. Been a minute or two, him still not in, I checked and saw him flat on his back, the pails set on either side. Funny thing, he hadn't spilled a drop. Just lay clutching his chest, breathing hard. As I knelt down, he managed to speak, said, 'Was a bushwhacker, Sarah. Saw 'im across the creek. Thought it was Glen...odd him ridin' from the east. Then he disappeared 'n come up swift through the trees, horse 'n rider one dark form, no color, all shadow. Reined by in blur of smoke 'n struck me down, Sarah, right here...' He tapped his heart and dropped his hand. And that was all. I just knelt there, could not move him. Thank goodness Glen did come riding up, helped me carry him in and get him ready..."

She glanced to his body. By then the men had finished the grave. We all took one last look before Glen slid the lid over and nailed it shut. He laced two ropes underneath and we each lent a hand and lowered it down. We stood silent for a moment, gazing to the grave and the darkness therein. Again, mother spoke:

"I have no words, not really. He was a good man, my Patrick. He lived his mortal span and enjoyed life. I loved him so..." Her lips quivering, her eyes moist, she looked to Hannah and asked, "Will you sing the song he loved? The old Irish air, Danny Boy..."

And Hannah sang it beautifully as the wind hummed in chorus and our hearts grieved to the plaintive melody and lyrics: *"And I shall hear, though soft you tread above me…and all my grave will warmer, sweeter be…for you will bend and tell me that you love me…and I will sleep in peace until you come to me…"*

While the men filled in the grave, Hannah and I caught and killed a chicken, dipped it in a bucket of scalding water mother set out, then plucked the feathers. Mother soon had it cut up and frying in the skillet. Within an hour, potatoes baked and biscuits and gravy ready, we shared a hearty meal. Finished with the dishes, I asked mother if she'd like me to stay.

"No," she answered. "Patrick's nearby. And he'll always be here," she pressed a hand to her heart. "And Glen comes each morning to help chore. I'll be fine…"

So we waved goodbye and returned to Mankato, leaving so much and so little changed — father beneath the earth in the orchard, the old Indian beneath the rocks on the hill, and mother in between.

That evening Hannah went to a movie she'd been waiting to see, *Hearts of the World*, the latest from G.W. Griffith, starring the Gish sisters in a story about a small French village and two young lovers torn apart by the Great War. Maxie and I stayed home and quietly shared a glass of whiskey in memory of father. The kerosene lamp turned low, he put on a favorite record of piano waltzes. We danced slowly in gentle sway and I leaned to his chest and wept, shifting images of father, young and old, then lying in his coffin and covered over, muffling even the music until there was only that distant wind and Danny and the others silently waving, being carried away as darkness swept forth and all were gone, like father, from flesh to nothing…

XXVIII. Home Front

*F*og *on a silvery surface…like the gray morning sky…*then she slowly discerns her withered features frozen in the speckled rot of an old mirror. Her portrait briefly framed before his large hand folds it away and lays it on the table.

Paul has checked her breathing as she recently showed him and finds she's still here. Only just waking, blinking her eyes. She glances about in question, time and thought atilt and scattered…sees Paul standing by the tree, tapping the tiny moccasins. He taps once more then looks to her.

"You fogged the mirror good, Gram. You're still here. I'm glad."

"I too, Paul…I too."

"But Danny's gone."

"Yes, long, long ago."

"He died in the war, didn't he?"

"Yes, the Great War in France."

"At Cattle Terry, right Gram?"

She does not correct him. Many mispronounced Chateau Thierry as they later said "Sam My Hill" for Saint Mihiel — another French village that marked a bloody battle and like Chateau Thierry sounded so quaint like a fine place to visit, or sleep.

"Yes," she answers softly, "he lies there with many others."

"Buried like the old Indian?"

Reflecting on which, she simply nods.

"Does he also watch?"

This surprises her — "I have no idea, Paul. Perhaps he does."

"Is France far, like the moon?"

"May as well be…far across the ocean, he and thousands of boys, all fallen."

"How did he fall?" he asks as she expected he would. The old question she's asked herself nearly every day since. *Did he drown in gaseous vomit that filled his mask? Was he vaporized by a shell, bits of him splattered in the mud? Did he linger for hours with a grievous wound in no man's land until he hissed his last breath?*

She prefers to think he died in an instant and says, "Cut down, Paul, by machine gun or cannon fire. Like a sickle mows wheat, they fell in a cruel way, threshed and planted."

"Will they grow?"

"Now there's a thought…" she ponders a question never asked.

"Maybe Danny is a tree, Gram? A Christmas tree…over there in France?"

"That's a fine notion," she answers. "Thank you, Paul…"

He stands proudly smiling to her like their tree might be part Danny too. Then he puts on his wool cap and coat and lifts the pail to do the morning milking. As the door closes, a breath of wind stirs the tinsel and moccasins amid the glittering lights and orbs as if the tree is coming alive…

In mid-May, following Hannah's graduation, nearly every boy in her class fit to serve joined the Army or Navy. Several had quit school in dead of winter to sign up, either gaining their parents' permission or lying about their age. One, Andrew Farley, a former paperboy for *The Mercantile* had died in training at Camp Funston of influenza. The disease rapidly spread from Fort Riley to other military camps and adjacent cities, wreaking much sickness and death through the spring. Soon termed 'the 3-day fever,' frightfully virulent and strangely it targeted heretofore healthy young men and women. Many soldiers shipping over were infected and died, buried at sea while others landed. By May there were outbreaks of deadly influenza in all the armies entrenched in France. Despite which the Germans pushed forth in late May, straining Allied lines.

Summer arrived and I feared for Danny night and day.

Hannah still planned to attend university in the fall, but out of concern for her brother and other boys she too caught the war fever and wished to play a part. Her new role, nurse assistant, a regular little Florence Nightingale in white cap and apron as she worked diligently alongside Madalene and Dr. Sudlow tending various patients bedded in their grand three-story mansion that served as home, hospital, and clinic. Good to see her busy and thankfully the epidemic subsided in June without a single death in Mankato.

Hardly relieved, however, when word of the war played daily on every lip, bringing its painful throb to my ear — "By gosh, our boys are gonna get it done right soon, you can bet!" To which I'd smile politely and nod. All proud of our boys and their doings "over there," I too, of course, but dreaded each headline, fearing the worst.

July saw the launch of a big German offensive led by General Ludendorff on the Marne, just north of Danny's sector, which within a week threatened to break through. At the newspaper I avoided headlines and any report of advance, retreat, or casualties, simply focused on jobbers and ads. Each night I lay in sweat, staring into the darkness, imagining every horror, finally lost in fitful sleep to wake in fear of what the day would bring. Then one night in haunted dream near dawn I heard a voice, Danny's, clearly call, "Mom?" — in mild question, as if saying, "Here I am..." or "I'll be going now..." And I knew he'd come to say goodbye. But I said nothing of this, simply waited.

The following evening Maxie came in from the tavern full of beery bluster, anxious to share the news, "Did ya hear, lass? Th' Boche been stomped on th' Marne. Twas our Rainbow boys, Danny 'n his bunch..." He stood smiling proud, awaiting my answer. But I sat silent, hands folded in my lap, tears brimming my eyes.

"Aw, Sadie girl," he patted my arm, "ya worry, ah know. But he'll write soon..."

We hadn't received a letter since June, now late July, with news of the mighty battle on the Marne, I held no hope against what I sensed. Hannah grew anxious as well, off to work each day, staying late, hoping her earnest efforts here would protect her brother over there. Maxie no longer tried to cheer us.

"Aye," he said, pacing the room, shaking his head, "tis a worry, near to August 'n n'er a word. A worry for us all…" Another week passed — I at the newspaper, Hannah at the hospital, Maxie at the tavern, daily checking the depot dispatch — we slept, woke and shared our meals, mostly silent, afraid to speak our fear.

Again it was Maxie who first got word, sitting slumped in his chair, the yellow envelope in his hand as Hannah and I entered the door, arriving home together in late afternoon. His broad red face cringed in tears, he rose from his chair and said, "They got Danny, damn 'em…" We crumpled in the spread of his arms and shared our sorrow as daylight turned to dusk.

All was darkness thereafter, an inner darkness borne each day.

"We must wear black, Mother" — Hannah insisted, her devotion to her brother carried into mourning. We purchased black cotton cloth with simple patterns. Cut and sewed our dresses, barely speaking, as if a vow of silence settled over our doings — she her brother's widow, and I bereft mother of a lost son. When Hagan died, Maxie held me and I still had our son. But Danny gone, left me staring into an open grave that would not fill in. My heart beat but there was no music.

We drove to the Limestone to grieve with mother and found her standing in the orchard by father's grave. Still peering down as we walked to her, she shook her head sadly and said, "Only glad Patrick never lived to hear this," then raised her gaze south and added, "and now Glen's gone off God knows where…"

I'd called to let her know the night we received the telegram. Of course she told Glen first thing next day. He took it hard. Mounted up and rode off, disappearing on a week-long binge that only ended when Holly found him passed out in the Ionia tavern. Two hired men helped her cart him home where she cleaned him up and kept him busy, and mostly sober, though he was never again so carefree or prone to laugh.

Myself, for a time too numb to notice, I finally glimpsed in the mirror one morning and saw my hair had grayed to nearly matching mother's.

My face more lined, I raised a hand to my chalky skin. Maxie caught me staring there in frown, snapped a suspender in place, lately of larger girth and no longer wore a belt, winked to me and said, "Still a fine looker, Sadie…" I smiled to please him. But our better days were past — he now 60 and I pushing 50. Somehow my gray hair and black dress seemed more fitting.

Nor did Hannah resume plans for university. Her dancing had lapsed through the summer till she no longer practiced or even mentioned it. But she still sang, mostly to the patients to lift their spirits. They called her "The Mankato Nightingale" — ever earnest and punctual in her nursing duties. A somewhat surprising transformation, and admit I was relieved to keep her home and not send her far away with no guardian or protector.

One lazy day in late summer, between our usual tasks and routines, she asked me to go for a walk and I readily agreed. My heart calmed close to my daughter as we strolled hand-in-hand past trees and houses, down one street then another in leisurely meander. Until she abruptly stopped in front of the Catholic Church, Saint Theresa, an impressive red-brick structure with white stone trim. We stared up at the tall bell tower that stood like a sentinel next to the grand facade with fine rosette window set in the gable end above the arched entrance. Hannah had attended several services, or "mass" as they called them, with a friend, intrigued by the mysterious ritual and Latin chants and especially admired the organ, choir, and "Ave Maria." But finding the chants and music rote and repetitious, her fascination soon waned. Presently, however, she urged me forth, saying, "I want to go in…" Curious, having never been inside, I accompanied her.

The heavy door, left slightly ajar, perhaps to catch a breeze, creaked at our entry to the shadowy interior, cavernous and a pleasantly cool from the August heat. Gradually our eyes adjusted in gaze to the vaulted ceiling, the stained-glass windows and statuary along either wall, the hushed rows of empty pews, and above the altar a life-sized Christ on the cross, and lifelike, of painted wood, I supposed. And to the lower left, tending an array of devotional candles, a tall young priest in black robe, new to the parish, somewhat tentative, reserved, still finding his way and only now noting our presence as Hannah whispered, "I want to light a candle for Danny…"

I stayed back and watched her descend the carpeted aisle, quiet as a shadow toward the waiting priest. Amid their muffled greeting I heard her ask, "May I light a candle for my departed brother?"

He nodded graciously and took a long match from a silver canister, struck the flame and handed it to her. She reached and lit the tallest candle on the upper row then returned the match. He snuffed the flame and laid it aside then extended his hand to the carpeted step in front of the altar and said, "Let us pray for your brother..." And Hannah and the priest knelt side by side and prayed, he in Latin, she silent.

Listening, discerning a word or phrase, I hoped some essence of the Holy Spirit might flow to me. Or perhaps I'd feel a brushing touch of the Sacred Mother, however brief and fleeting. But I felt no blessing by word or hand and sensed nothing of the one hoped for, no evidence of my son forever lost to me, just mumblings of a dead language through the solemn empty space. Yet Hannah seemed comforted and reassured, smiling warmly to the priest when they finally stood. He bade her wait and disappeared into the antechamber and shortly returned, handing her a small black book and a string of beads. They spoke briefly then she came to me clutching the gifts to her breast as if she'd been touched through and through.

From that day forth, in every spare moment, Hannah studied her catechism and learned to pray the rosary, up at dawn for early mass and made every Sunday service, anxious to earn confirmation so she could sing in the choir. The young priest, Father Marcus LaMarche, particularly attentive, tutored her along. No doubt they shared a mutual infatuation. For Hannah was ever charming and no less so wearing black against her white skin, green eyes, and red hair. And Father Marcus was a rather nice-looking man, tall, broad shouldered, with neatly trimmed black hair and deep brown eyes. His voice a fine baritone of practiced cadence, musically attractive even when he spoke. He visited the paper from time to time to print an announcement or bulletin, politely deferent and respectful, yet always wary of me as if I read thoughts he dare not confess. Knowing my daughter, I knew I could not dissuade her, only hope that her path of mourning would run its course.

Oddly enough, after a month of such, it was Maxie who expressed concern and bluntly said, "Don' let that priest talk ya to be a nun, Hannah. Thar's more to life than clutchin' pearls."

"Why?" she asked, shocked at his rare disapproval. "You're Catholic. Didn't your mother pray the rosary?"

"Aye, for a wee time after me Da died. Clutched 'er pearls 'n prayed sunrise to sunset. Nay, did not bring 'im back. One day she tossed 'er beads 'n n'er prayed agin."

"Don't you believe in God and heaven…faith, hope, and charity?"

"Ah see heaven in ye 'n Sadie. O' God, tis or tisn't, ain't mine to know, nor any man. O' charity…aye, help th' least, 'em as lift a hand, 'n do yer best with wha' each day gives. But daughter, ye are meant for this life. Don' go hide in no church…"

Hannah was not dismayed, continued to recite her "Hail Marys" and "Our Fathers," though did so upstairs in her room with the door closed. Soon adding "The Song of Solomon" to her recitation as her tutorials went from two to three or more evenings a week. By then a delicate golden crucifix laced her neck, a further gift from her adoring young priest. Or "Marcus" as she referred to him, using the familiar, though only at home and only to me — "Mother, I never imagined a man like Marcus, so handsome, kind, and true. Of highest reason and spiritual depth…"

Echoing my early sentiments of Hagan, and I knew Maxie needn't worry of her becoming a nun, nor would Father Marcus likely remain a priest. Within a month, her impassioned mourning had turned to love, a torrent you can neither dam nor direct, only witness its inevitable rise and ebb.

Though in thrall of faith and love, she did not neglect her nursing. The influenza had returned with a vengeance, infecting a number of area youths, soon claiming several lives. Dr. Sudlow, Madalene, and Hannah all wore surgical masks to reduce the risk. Each day she went bravely to her patients, tended their fevers and fears, trusting in the cross and faith to protect her. One morning in a rush, she left her rosary beads, usually carried along, on the table. I picked them up and held them in my hands, wondering of the beads, the why and meaning of their use. Variously arranged and strung in pattern like a strange abacus it seemed to cipher price and payment in our mortal scale. From life to death, from flesh to spirit, then what? More spirit? No, from flesh to dust, I saw only shadow and more shadow.

Maxie suffered as well, in the years of raising Danny more often there than Hagan and became as much a father to him as he was to Hannah. Like Glen, he drank in grief, returning from the tavern to sit up late with a bottle of Old Grand-Dad. I'd wake, see him sitting there and sometimes join him for a glass. One night he shoved back his chair and spat the whiskey out.

"Bah! Does no good," he said, turning his bloodshot eyes to mine, "could drink a river 'n not drown th' ache…" He stood and grabbed his cap and coat then went outside to smoke a cigar and stare at the night.

I poured another glass and awaited another dawn.

Each day brought more news of battles and casualties, leaving other families to grieve as the war continued through Reims, the Somme, Saint Mihiel, then slogged on through the Meuse-Argonne from late September to the end. How I tired of patriotic songs, brass bands and flag-waving parades, and Wilson's grand speeches on "The fight to save democracy" and "The war to end all wars" that left our sons stacked like sardines in their distant, dark graves. Until I didn't want to hear or feel anything and nearly every night when Maxie left off drinking to have a cigar, I'd fill another glass, letting the fiery warmth fill me with rapt sorrow, staring on as the bottle slowly emptied of liquid amber like a low, dying flame. I'd raise my glass to the old man on the label, tipping his to me, smiling like father, and I imagined him there amid the whiskey, alive in the lamplight, sharing memories of Danny, shedding tears and humming the old Irish air.

Then Maxie would return and gently take the glass from my hand, cork the bottle and say, "That's e'nuff, lass, else th' water o' life be yer death…" He'd carry me off to bed, many times still sitting there when I woke, patting my hand, offering me a glass of water, "Thar now, drink it down, ye'll feel better…"

Numb and groggy, I'd drink it, but no, didn't feel better. Didn't feel anything except the want of whiskey, just a bit to warm me, then another and another to reclaim fond memories and finally sleep, sweet sleep, till again I awakened and all was lost, the emptiness and pain compounded by the sober light of day.

So we drifted, Hannah, Maxie, and me, in various ways and phases, from night to day, from sunlight to shadow. Then came that fateful Monday they signed the Armistice and the bells rang out in France and all around the world, even to Mankato. People lined the streets, gathered on porches, waiting the first tolling, then the band struck up, voices cheered, boys and girls danced, hurrahing the grand victory — the excitement and clamor as infectious as sunlight dispelling darkness and I tried to smile and join in but could not. Only relieved the war was over. And having learned from Hagan, asked, what victory? Morgan and Rothschild still held and dealt the cards; Carnegie and Krupp still forged ore, steel and cannon while poor boys on every side paid the pound of flesh, gave their hearts and very lives. No, I could not bear the high-toned sermons echoing Wilson and others that took a grain of truth and sowed a field of hate and left the many to suffer the reaping. Given a gold star for the loss of my son, I returned home, exhausted, numb, wishing only for silence and peace.

But the hateful reaping had not ended. Late that afternoon, amid the revelry, a young man, Rawley Hogue, an itinerate butcher prone to drink and thrown out of the tavern earlier that day for brawling, stumbled back in and hollered, "*Das Ross!* That's German, ain't it?"

"Aye," Maxie answered coolly as the tavern quieted. "Me Da was German born, died American…in a Skullkill coal mine. Me Mum, Irish born, she too died American. Now scram 'fore ah toss ya twice!"

Rawley pulled a pistol and cried, "No German gonna toss me nowhere no how!"

"Why, ya sorry pissant, come in here 'n say that. Lost me dear lad Danny, killed fightin' th' Kaiser's bunch. Now gimme that pistol, damn ye…"

All this I soon learned when Clyde came pounding at my door, shouting, "Maxie's been shot!" Hannah, home from the clinic, heard all and rushed on ahead. "Gun went off," Clyde gasped, running at my side, "Jar 'n the boys wrestled Rawley down, but too late. I'm sorry, Sadie…"

We reached the tavern as the sheriff and deputy hustled Rawley into a car and off to jail beyond the angry crowd howling to hang him.

Inside, I found Hannah prone over the body, crying, "Daddy, oh Daddy, no, no…" And Maxie, a primal, robust bull of a man who always seemed somehow mythic, and again that morning lying next to me in bed, his great chest heaving, alive, invincible; but struck down, sprawled on the floor, utterly still in hopeless stare, he appeared sadly shrunken, diminished, mortal.

"Shot bad 'n went fast but swear he said your name…" Clyde vouched as I knelt to lift his huge hand in mine, heavy, lifeless, and already cooling to my touch. Through the drift of tavern smoke and smell of beer, like a shadow Dr. Sudlow crouched to check for a pulse and confirmed him dead. I gently pulled Hannah away while Myrtle covered him with a table cloth.

"Don't worry yourself," Clyde said, "Jar 'n I'll get him to the undertaker…"

Unlike in the country, in town due to health law and ordinance, we could not bury our own and delivered him to a stranger to prepare and embalm. A strange and unnatural thing, preserving the dead, but I said nothing. Could not speak, simply hugged Hannah and walked her home where we sat and wept, clutching one another late into the night till thoughts, words, and feelings succumbed to darkness and fatigue.

I awoke in bed with no idea how I got there. Hadn't drank, and never drank again, just lay there clutching Maxie's pillow, inhaling his scent. Nearly 8 o'clock, Hannah up, having prepared breakfast and brewed coffee, stood at the door and announced, "Good to see you awake, Mother. We must get busy…" I'd expected her to list and flounder in grief, instead she stepped forth firmly determined on all we must do. Walked straight to the closet and laid out my spare black dress then shuffled through the hangers, declaring "We need Daddy's good suit. Ah, there it is…" Actually his only suit, which he'd bought for our wedding and thereafter seldom wore, finding it too snug and fussy. Though I imagined the undertaker would rip the back to make it fit.

"Come now," she said, "let's get dressed" — like I was a patient and she in charge. More so than I thought as she turned and said, "At early mass I told Father LaMarche to arrange the funeral for noon Saturday."

"Father LaMarche?" I asked, puzzled by the formal address in lieu of "Marcus."

"Yes," she answered, skipping on to other matters. "After breakfast we'll take the suit to Bryant's Funeral Home…then select a casket and a vault."

"All this," I cautioned, reminding her of practical concerns and prior dreams, "the funeral, casket, embalming…will cost every dollar set aside for your university."

"I don't care. If I have to empty bedpans and clean up vomit the rest of my life, I want Daddy to have the best casket and the biggest Mankato funeral ever!"

She chose the finest that Bryant's offered — silk-lined, solid mahogany with polished brass handles and a cast-iron vault guaranteed to last 100 years. And Maxie, felled by a butcher's pistol, shrouded on the embalming table, soon to be gutted, boxed, and buried, had no say and rarely said no to Hannah. Nor did I.

Walking away I thought of his murderer, Rawley Hogue, eldest son of the Hogue clan, dropped out of school in 5th or 6th grade to help his father butcher. Lately the boy had taken over the task, roving the countryside with wagon and mule to butcher a hog or steer while scavenging old farm equipment and harnesses which he carted home for his father Eldon to sort, repair, and sell. Or often simply junked, left scattered through the perimeter of their place on the east edge of town, cluttering an acre or more, as if every broken, unwanted thing for miles around ended up at the Hogues.

There were a dozen more kids, boys and girls, all younger than Rawley, and "Ma" Hogue so often pregnant people joked she'd soon have more kids than chickens. Since the turn of the century there'd been numerous articles in newspapers and magazines on the "menace of morons," decrying the idiots and imbeciles let to breed, threatening the healthy blood of our nation and race. "Worse than the Coloreds," people would grouse, pointing to the Hogues in proof. I'd long pitied the poor family and their broken lives. Now they'd broken mine and I felt no pity. None for the boy, drunk, caught up in the fervor, and wanted to kill a German. They said that once he sobered, he sorely regretted the deed. Bawled a full night and day then sat quietly accepting his fate. As his father Eldon said, "He done it certain. Now he's a goner…" No doubt of his guilt or sentence. After a brief trial he'd be sent to

Leavenworth and within a year face the noose. Yet I took no solace in thought of his hanging. Nor solace at Maxie's funeral.

Hannah insisted we both wear store-bought dresses of black satin with matching hats and spidery veils. Adamant, extravagant, theatrical, and wholly against my instincts, but I numbly complied, a shadow to her will. That morning mother and Glen drove in and we sat together enduring an hour or more of the Holy Mother Church, its language and ritual as incomprehensible as the act that set us there. At last outside, each relieved to breathe the air of a beautiful Indian summer day that Maxie would have loved. At graveside it seemed nearly the whole town had gathered, none too surprising as Maxie was widely known and liked. And many were likely drawn by the drama of his murder, the final curtain about to close.

As the incense and benediction dispersed to the wind, they lowered the casket and I gripped a handful of dirt and let it crumble into the grave. Hannah stepped forth and did the same, then paused and cast her rosary as well. The young priest, standing opposite, blanched and raised his palm in faint appeal. But she was not finished. She removed her hat and veil, passed them to me, then reached behind her neck and unclasped the crucifix, dangled it before the priest then dropped it to the vault while casting a look that stripped him bare and hissed, "Lies, all lies. And you, a liar..."

Then she shook out her long red hair and rushed away.

The priest and those thereby shocked by her act and accusation and the crowd hushed as clouds from the west swiftly darkened the day. I had no words and offered no apology, merely raised my veil and glanced to mother. She said, "Go..." and I hurried after my daughter. But she raced toward a young man waiting in a fancy car — another particular she'd apparently planned. He opened the door, she hopped in, and they sped away in a plume of dust.

XXIX. Another Heartbeat

She sits and stares, sees her life a rush of scenes through a maze of sorrow and so many dead ends…like the breath left her. Yet she smiles at Paul's joy in bringing a fresh pail of warm milk into the kitchen. He hangs his cap and coat then looks to his presents under the tree. Squats on the floor by the stove and slowly unwraps the socks and gloves like they're the magic gifts he's long wished for.

He pulls on a glove and grins to her, "See, Gram? It fits!"

"Hope you wear them this time."

"Yes'um, when it gets cold, I will…"

Reluctant to wear gloves even in winter, like a boy shucking shoes in summer, did little good to remind him. Every winter she ordered him an extra-large pair only to find them stashed in some corner, seldom worn except in the bitter cold. His hands so rough and calloused from work and weather he has to rub them with lanolin each time before milking the cows else they will kick, though he's careful of them and uses a gentle grip. A losing proposition getting him to wear gloves, but he enjoys unwrapping them. Now pulling on the other, he pats them together, pleased at how they fit.

Suddenly he stands and says, "Sorry, Gram, almost forgot…" Still wearing the gloves he goes to his bedroom, reaches behind the door and brings forth a new cedar cane he's secretly whittled. He leans by and proudly tenders it to her, "Found one with a good burl knot to fit your hand..." She grips the whorled nub so finely shaped, smoothed and oiled it warms her palm as if part of her.

"It fits perfectly, Paul," she says. "The best cane ever..."

Maxie gone, there was no warmth. The thought of whiskey left me cold. The days shortened, the sun dying. I stood sober, empty, hollowed out. Alone — and understood the word like never before. Alone except for Hannah.

Watching her disappear that day from the funeral, I recognized the driver, or the scoundrel lurking by. Marion Thomas, the very boy she'd once kicked for calling her a tramp. The banker's son, rich and spoiled, wore the finest clothes and drove the fastest car around; a cad and slacker, avoided the draft thanks to his father's favorable loans to members of the board — a lively rumor and likely true. Marion, a large young man even larger than Maxie, a star athlete in high school, had scorned college and other prospects, preferring his immediate ease and status. King fish in a little pond. He caught for the Mankato men's team and hit an occasional homerun, otherwise bounced between hard drink and leisure. A dissolute dandy with slick black hair who Maxie had recently ran out of the tavern for boasting of ruining a young girl's reputation — "Use a poor lass for fun then wave yer stinky finger like a prize! Ah oughta bust it off..."

Seeing Hannah with the wretch, my heart wept.

Father and Danny dead, now Maxie. So limp with grief I wished to drop to dust and never rise again. But there was Hannah spiraling off as if the poisoned act that took her father entered her, carousing nightly in a desperate dance that could only end badly. No, I could not despair, nor clasp my hands in prayer, not for her, myself, nor for Maxie who'd sworn by the good earth under which he lay. Having wallowed in grief a week, I braced myself and stood. Could not lose my daughter.

Hannah, out each evening, up at dawn, not to mass but off to tend her patients. Then briefly home and out again with Marion in his swank Buick Roadster, royal blue with bright chrome. I could not lock the door or rope her down, only hope to rein her in. One grey afternoon when she arrived home from the clinic I pulled our funeral dresses and veiled hats from the closet and said, "I want to burn these, any objection?"

"Of course not," she answered, "I tire of black and those hats are silly."

"Well, they do hang there and haunt me and…"

"And what, Mother? What is it?"

"I just…wish you'd see someone besides Marion Thomas."

"Someone?" she smiled, more amused than offended. "Perhaps I should, but who? Most young men are still in the service, far away. Marion's hereby and fun to see."

"You should be careful of him."

"Should and am, Mother. I know him well enough. And once kicked him where it hurts. He behaves, mostly…"

What she hinted at I did not ask. But knowing my daughter, her impetuous, willful ways, I had to wonder how she behaved. "Just be careful," I urged her, "please."

"Don't worry, Mother, we're only going to a movie. And I promise to stay home for Christmas and help bake candies and cookies and make a big meal for Grandmother and Glen…"

At least she reacted pleasantly. Having expressed my concern, I took the hats and dresses outside and burned them. Watched the fabric flare and crimple to ash and smoke carried off in the wind, while overhead a lone leaf tossed and swirled, reminding me of Hannah's erratic shifts and turns, and wondered where life would take her and if she'd ever safely land.

We shared a joyless Christmas. Like shadows going through the motions, ate, quietly conversed, but no one sang or laughed, mostly relieved when it was over, each turning inward to face the dark months of winter. Temperatures fell with the first big snow and howling wind that drifted the roads and locked the land in a cold grip, making it difficult to even walk uptown. Yet the day before New Year, Hannah rushed in and stomped her boots, excited with news of a big barn dance that evening.

"At the Kubleck place!" she gushed. "They have a huge haymow with a smooth floor and there'll be a Bohemian band and maybe even a traveling jazz trio and I so want to go! Can I wear your red dress?"

All in a rush and the question left hanging as she paused for breath.

Not since Danny left had I worn the dress and said, "With your slight waist, I doubt it will fit…" But she was already racing to the closet and returned pressing it to her.

"It's so gorgeous, Mother, I can take it in. May I wear it, please?"

"I imagine you're going with Marion."

"Yes, of course," she looked to me as if nothing else mattered but the dress, herself, and the dance that evening.

"Listen, Hannah, I must speak plainly. I don't trust Marion, fear he will hurt you."

"Oh Mother, I know he's a rake and a bit of a devil. But he's honestly so. Marcus only pretends to the virtues he preaches. Cowers inside his robe, afraid of life. Believe me, I know…" And I realized there was more to the drama staged at the funeral than I'd guessed. "Besides," she added, "Marion makes me laugh and dances wonderfully."

"There's more to life than dancing and laughter, and more to a man."

"Didn't you dance with Daddy?"

"Yes, we danced at our wedding."

"And never before?"

"Well yes, several times. We even danced at my first wedding. He and Hagan were best friends and Maxie often cut in."

"Cut in? Is that all?" she teased in sly smile. "Mother, I can count. You and Daddy were married in December and I was born in June. Not long ago Doctor Sudlow let slip that once he unlaced the umbilical, I was the most vociferous child he had ever delivered. I wasn't born early, was I?"

"No, you were a fully formed, beautiful baby girl…"

Naturally, I let her wear the dress. Given a few stitches at the waist, it fit her perfectly. Within an hour I draped my black wool coat to her shoulders and kissed her goodbye. She dashed out to the waiting car, eager to embrace the night, the music, and dance in the arms of a brash young man I still did not trust.

Nightfall, the window blackened in full darkness of winter. The wind roused and groaned, spewing a dust of snow beneath the door. I scooted a rug to seal the threshold, brewed some tea then sat at the table and stared at the lamp. The low flame fluttered as if in sync with my breath, attending my heart. How I missed Maxie, his huge flesh and laughter. His scent. From the bureau I fetched his cigar box, returned to the table and opened the lid. "Hambones," he called them, large and thick like him. I pressed one to my nose and inhaled the dark rich aroma. I licked the tip, recalling the taste of him, his lips on mine, his massive strength filling, warming me, and the many times we danced. Remembering brought a smile and I laid the cigar in the box and closed the lid. Again I stared to the lamp, the door and window, wondering of Hannah dancing in the arms of a large young man of bold presence and lax manner.

The night lengthened, the clock ticked past 11 while the wind howled on and I lowered my head to the table beside the lamp...through the gauzy haze perceiving only the flame indistinct as myself flickering between thought, memory, and the wind. Then something vague and intermittent, like the ding of a bell, far and near, suddenly strident, piercing the moment and I awakened in sharp scream — "The telephone!"

I rushed over and grasped the receiver, it was Madalene.

"There's been a wreck," she said. "Out west of town. Hannah was hurt...but Marion carried her in. Doctor Sudlow is tending her —"

"I'll be right over..." I said nothing more and hung the receiver, filled with dread, panic, and fear...my dear daughter, jewel of my life, her precious blood slipping away. No, I dare not think it! Pulled on my coat, scarf, and overboots and headed out through the deep snow and swirling wind. The Sudlow place stood only three blocks south, still I trudged painfully slow as in a frozen dream. At last the tall house loomed, the porchlight on, Madalene waiting by the door.

In the parlor Marion sat hunched in a chair warming his hands by the radiator. He glanced up, his left jaw swollen black and blue, just a large boy, fragile, concerned and by now utterly sober. Painful to speak, he tried to explain, "Going out...we busted through the drifts... piece of cake. But coming back, they doubled in size...we skidded off, hit a post, I guess, so much snow. Then Hannah, I'm sorry, Mrs. Ross…" he raised his hands in futile gesture and I made no reply.

Anxious to see my daughter, Madalene led me to the surgical room where Hannah lay lightly sedated. Her eyes barely open, dazed, confused, she took little notice of my entry. Now and then she'd wince or moan as Dr. Sudlow shushed her and continued stitching a long gash on her right temple, a nasty wound that reminded me of Glen's that night at the circus. They'd shaved a swath of her hair as well. Blood soaked her dress and coat and still oozed a trifle, but daubed once more, soon fully stitched and bandaged.

Finished, Dr. Sudlow wiped his hands and stood.

"The cut looks bad," he said, turning to me, "but should heal fine. And her hair will grow back and cover the scar. More worrisome are her internal injuries. Some bruises in her lower abdomen, and I suspect, several cracked or broken ribs. As with the cut, given rest and care…she should heal. However, we need to monitor her closely and watch for internal bleeding. And there's…one other thing…" He paused, unusually hesitant.

Until then more or less relieved, I tensed and asked, "What…other thing?"

"Rather delicate, I fear. In examining her, I discovered…another heartbeat."

"You mean…Hannah's pregnant?"

"Yes," he nodded, "about three months along, I would say." Then he shook his head in weary sigh, "Sorry to add to your troubles. As you know, Madalene and I think highly of Hannah. If you like, I can speak with Marion's father. Benjamin Thomas and I are well acquainted and I believe he will see that his son does the right thing."

"No…" voiced quietly yet clearly as Hannah stirred, her eyes fully open and directed our way. "No," she repeated more firmly. "Marion is not the father. It's Marcus."

"You mean the priest?" Dr. Sudlow paled and asked again, "Father LaMarche?"

"Yes, he's the father," Hannah affirmed. "Marion never touched me in that way." She gazed past us to Marion now standing by the door, listening in. "We laughed and danced, but Marion has always behaved a gentleman."

Dr. Sudlow looked from one to the other, pressing his hands to search a solution, and said, "To be honest, Hannah, in light of your injuries and trauma, you will likely lose the baby. For the sake of your health and all concerned, perhaps we…" he caught himself suggesting something more and simply stated, "Yes, you may lose your baby. And if so, it may be a blessing."

"No, a life spared is a blessing," Hannah countered. "My brother was taken, my father was taken, and I'll die before I lose my baby."

Her defiance foreclosed any further option. Seeing which, Dr. Sudlow reluctantly conceded, "Very well, Hannah, but there's still the danger of influenza. Especially here, and in your weakened state, you're even more susceptible. For the sake of you and your baby, we should get you home tonight. But with the snow —"

"I'll carry her," Marion offered, "if it's okay with you, Mrs. Ross?"

Having carried her from the wreck, I trusted him to carry her home.

As he stepped forth, Dr. Sudlow warned, "Be mindful of that jaw, Marion. It's likely broken. I strongly urge that you drive to Salina tomorrow and have it x-rayed. They may need to wire it shut."

"I'll be alright," Marion answered indifferently, looking solely to Hannah. Helped wrap her in a warm blanket then deftly cradled her up to carry her home. Contrite and dutiful, didn't say a word as he marched through the snow, up the steps and through the door. Then laid her gently on the bed and she softly moaned, drowsy from an added dose of laudanum, as we covered her over and left her sleeping. I followed Marion to the door where he stood a moment, waiting to speak.

"I'm sorry, Mrs. Ross…sorry for what happened."

"You actually care for her, don't you?"

"She's a special girl…" Then he turned and walked into the night, a considerably less selfish and more humble young man than heretofore witnessed. And I realized I'd misjudged him, at least in part.

But we're all of parts — part greed, part envy, part callous, meddlesome, churlish, and yet often selfless and caring. One thing certain, Hannah, however changeable, was always willful. And the part she now played was expectant mother. She knew that Dr. Sudlow had alluded to an option to relieve her of her burden, or "predicament" as it was commonly known. And he did so directly several evenings on as she suffered sweats and delirium, having succumbed to the influenza, then in her second day. After checking her pulse and temperature, he placed a cool cloth to her brow and noted, "With your injuries and the fever, Hannah, you may miscarry any moment. I therefore urge that we induce the very thing and so control the bleeding and any other complications."

"No!" she clenched her blanket protectively. "You'll not take it! I'd rather die!"

Futile to press further, he once more acceded, "As you wish…" and abruptly left her to my care. No matter the quandary, I loved and cherished my daughter and stood by her stubborn determination to have her baby. Next morning the fever subsided and she began sitting up, taking soup and tea. Within the week she was walking about, impatient of her hair bristling forth.

In short order the errant young priest was recalled by the St. Joseph diocese and assigned to a small parish thereby. Promptly replaced by a staid, middle-age fellow, aptly plump and pompous, named Father Edward J. Mertz. This given brief mention without explanation or further detail in *The Mankato Mercantile*, reading which, Hannah laid the paper aside and glanced to me in pained smile.

"You know…Marcus swore he loved me. Swore by the cross that he wanted to leave the priesthood and marry. But it would kill his mother, his poor mother…" she scoffed. "He held her pure as the Virgin…me the lost lamb, and he the fallen. Like a good shepherd he wished to send me to a nunnery. To be cared for by the flock, he said. And our child given to an orphanage…" Her eyes teared and she said, "I was foolish, I know. But he was handsome and kind and also a virgin…strangely innocent, frightened of my touch. I thought being with him would somehow bring Danny back, alive, risen in the Church. But Danny's gone…now Daddy too. Just lies, all lies…"

She came to me and we wept, clasping our truth, her flesh and mine.

Marion stopped by twice. The first time she was still bedridden and did not wish to see him. A week later when he returned, she ushered him in and they sat and exchanged pleasantries. After an awkward silence he spoke right up and asked her to marry him.

"You need someone, Hannah," his voice earnest, pleading, "and I want to take care of you, be your husband."

She thought a moment then smiled, "No, Marion, it would not be fair to you."

"But I...what will you do?"

"I'll have my baby," she stated flatly — as far as she cared to look or answer.

Reading her well enough, he politely excused himself and left. Within a fortnight we learned that the chastened son had taken his father's advice, or ultimatum, and entered a business college in Lincoln, Nebraska.

XXX. Fallen Flower

No, Hannah did not wish to be cared for, relieved of her burden, or sent to a nunnery. She wanted to love and be loved passionately. As she strengthened, she grew restless. Beginning to show, she could not return to the clinic, or nursing, no matter how favored by Dr. Sudlow and Madalene, simply out of the question, worse than a contagion, an unwed mother in the midst. Yet her burgeoning child, her very condition, rose from a yearning long evident. As Danny had rightly observed, Mankato could not contain her, whether wayward or willful, she would reach for something more. To what or where, she gave no clue. But once her baby came, I knew she would go.

For now she went to the Limestone. Winter soon in thaw and spring coming on, mother welcomed her company and could use her help with the chores and garden. So we loaded her Victrola and favorite records and drove her down. Hannah relished the change, having seldom stayed more than an afternoon or evening, quickly took to her grandmother and Uncle Glen.

I visited each weekend then returned to my lonely life in town. Talk resumed of my long ago rush to marriage, my red dress, taken even into a church — a veritable Jezebel, they'd say, and what's more, the mother of a Jezebel. Yes, they readily agreed, the fruit never falls far from the tree…then it spoils and rots — Hannah's scandal so ripe that few could resist dipping a spoonful and lapping their tongues. I ignored all and replied to none, closed my ears and walked straight. Hid in task and routine, spending full days at the paper, busy at editing and layout, helped clean and maintain the printer, laid my hands to anything that needed doing. At night I read, mostly from father's books, returning again to Plutarch and others, recalling what he'd told me, "Them old Greeks will make you wary of all things current…" with that gleam in his eye while quoting Bobby Burns on how our "best-laid schemes gang aft a-gley…" I'd think of Wilson, our righteous leader, off to Europe to fine-tune the Treaty of Versailles and concoct the League of Nations, redrawing borders like a clever boy at play with a map. He soon returned and traveled the country speaking with eloquent fervor of world peace and other high notions that few favored as much as he. Weary of such I returned to the Greeks, taking solace in old words till I found my sleep.

While Wilson failed to win support for the Treaty, or the League, over winter Congress did pass the 18th Amendment outlawing the manufacture and sell of alcohol; shortly ratified by a majority of states, including Kansas. Having no desire to keep the tavern in any case, I sold it to Ma and Clyde for a modest sum, thereafter named, "Ma & Clyde's Pancake 'n Chili House." A considerably less spirited place, though they sold boot-leg on the side and openly served a cereal beverage known as "near beer," which Glen judged so weak and blank, "Ain't fit for a church picnic!"

"Just when did you ever attend a church picnic?" Hannah promptly teased.

"Once, I surely did. Took that doctor's wife, Madalene. Yep, took 'er dancin' too," he winked, "then she got savvy to my ornery ways!"

"Then she missed out!" Hannah chimed in, sparking our first real laughter since the passing of father, Danny, and Maxie. From the sale of the tavern we purchased Maxie's stone, as Hannah insisted, of polished black marble with his full name broadly chiseled: "MAXIMUS DAS ROSS" and below that, "Beloved Husband & Father" — finished and set in time for Decoration Day.

By then late May, Hannah near to term and looked to have quite a large baby for such "a spry slip o' a thing," as Maxie had often fondly declared. "A big baby certain, full as the moon," affirmed Mabel Kranston, a friend of mother's from nearby Ionia who'd been checking in on Hannah. "My guess a boy, 'cause he seldom kicks, none active, content to ride in her belly till she bursts..." Mabel, an old-time midwife, had delivered hundreds of babies over the past 30 years up and down the Limestone and small towns beyond, often clashing with Dr. Sudlow and other "Docs" as she called them, concerning modern methods.

"Best get her to Mankato quick," she advised, "if you want the Doc's hand in this. Those back pains are a sure sign, no time to mess, but you've got a good hour or two..." Then she wagged her ringer in final warning, "Birthin' is a battle, girl. That's nature's way and God's too, takes all your strength and muscle. Them Docs and their morphine, not all they're cracked up to be. Knock you half out then yank your baby. Them forceps are just big pliers. Can injure the head and leave them half dumb. I've seen it..."

Such talk did little to ease Hannah's worry, having heard lurid tales and several times witnessed the agony of childbirth she preferred the "twilight sleep" induced by morphine, a common practice of late. Mother shared her concern, "But given a large baby as you say, Mable, she's bound to tear if not cut right? And there's the danger of her bleeding and infection setting in?"

"True, I won't argue that," Mabel folded her arms as if washing her hands of the matter. "Mayhap best to bide the Doc, he may have a trick or two. And he may have to do the Caesar thing and cut it out."

"No!" Hannah shot back. "I'll not be skinned open!"

"Suit yourself, girl, I'll not lie, it'll be a struggle. Just beware, that morphine will sap your strength, it will..."

On that grim note we loaded Hannah in the car and drove to Mankato.

We'd called ahead and Dr. Sudlow and Madalene, due to lingering cases of influenza at the clinic, were waiting at our house with their medical bags when we arrived. They followed inside as we hurried

Hannah to the back bedroom. Madalene helped me undress her while Dr. Sudlow readied his medical instruments and mother boiled water in the kitchen. We eased Hannah back on a clean sheet and covered her with another. Contractions quickened and her water soon broke. Her knees now raised and spread, Dr. Sudlow held his lamp close for a brief examination.

"Fetal macrosomia…" he sighed, handing the lamp to Madalene. "It invariably complicates things. At least it's coming headfirst, but abnormally large. In this instance, for the sake of Hannah and the child, I need to perform a caesarian."

"No-NO-NO!" Hannah cried, utterly opposed. "I don't want a big ugly scar, I can bear it, I can…" she gasped, her contractions growing stronger and more painful.

"Nevertheless," he replied, perturbed at her obstinacy and dousing his hands with alcohol, "I must make a vaginal incision. Of that there is no question, no debate. Now let's get you sedated…" So resolved, he took the needle and vial from Madalene.

"No!" again Hannah objected. "You'll hurt my baby. I need my fight."

"You've been talking to Mabel Kranston, haven't you?" he glared angrily. "That woman's caused more needless pain and suffering than I care to count."

"But I need my…*AH!*" she shrieked amid another sharp spasm.

"No, young lady, you need to listen."

"But the forceps will hurt my baby. Promise you won't hurt my baby…don't hurt my baby," she pleaded.

"I can't promise you that," he stated frankly, preparing the needle. "But I can promise if we don't get the baby out, it will die and so will you. Now give me your arm," he insisted. "Trust me, Hannah, it will relieve your pain and facilitate the delivery…"

At that she consented and extended her arm. The effect was nearly instant, she relaxed, her eyes half closed, now and then a wince, a deep breath or moan. I held her hand and stroked her hair to soothe her as Dr. Sudlow worked the baby forth. Mother stood to one side, holding the lamp, Madalene to the other, passing whatever instrument requested. Seeing him grip the forceps, I focused on Hannah, dreading the results as he grunted and pulled to free the baby. Then Hannah screamed in final shove and the baby gushed forth. Mother flinched and by her expression I knew my dread was real.

The baby gave a faint gurgled cry then silent as I turned to see the red mass placed on a towel, the umbilical cut and tied. The curled legs barely moved, nor did the hand or arm. Then Dr. Sudlow stepped aside and I saw why mother had flinched. It stopped my breath — the temples and forehead scraped and dented, the cheeks badly bruised. And the eyes unfocused, as are all babies, but these bulged in dark bloody stare.

"A most difficult delivery," Dr. Sudlow concluded. "And unfortunately required more force than is optimum. But given his size, easily two foot long and eleven pounds or more, it's a miracle he even breathes. And we're extremely fortunate that Hannah has not hemorrhaged…" He looked to her then, first checking her pulse, her ordeal over, now deeply sedated. While she slept, he proceeded to clean and stitch the incision.

Finished, he stood back and knit his brow. "I admire her courage," he offered in sober assessment, "but sadly it was for naught. Observe…" He turned to the baby and tapped its foot then lifted its hand. "See? There's no reaction, none. To kick and grip is the first instinct…that and to sup. Now here…" He touched the lips and again, nothing, not a quiver. "Yes, I fear she has birthed a defective…a mental defective. If it lives, at best it will grow into an imbecile, or idiot, a torment to itself and others. Therefore, in my medical judgement, if it stops breathing, there is no blame. My recommendation, if it's indifferent to nursing, why feed it? Let it go, that is the truer mercy. Release it from its frightful existence and return it to the hallowed earth…"

Succinctly reasoned, convincing, and left to myself in the dire moment I may have agreed. But mother, standing silent till then, gently cupped the wounded head and lifted the baby to her. "Perhaps he's only hurt and not defective," she quietly observed. "Many animals on the farm, injured at birth, are slow to stand and nurse. During spring calving there's always a few we have to help along. Same with horses, pigs, sheep, or any animal yanked from its mother. This boy might be damaged, but if he can nurse, he will live…"

Mother, who once faced an Indian warrior to spare her baby, could certainly stare down a smug medical man to save another. Dr. Sudlow, clearly disgusted, said nothing more as he and Madalene, more pitying, packed their bags. Services rendered, I paid their $50 fee and they left.

***

That afternoon while mother tended the baby and Hannah slept, I purchased a fine nanny goat fresh with milk from a neighbor then walked uptown and bought three rubber nipples. Returning, I poured the last of the Old Grand-Dad on the ground then rinsed it in scalding water. Outside, I squatted by the tethered goat, washed her udder then milked directly through a tin funnel into the bottle. Shortly half-full, nearly a pint, I went inside and capped the bottle with a nipple. Mother helped me cradle the baby, so limp and long, difficult to position. Its battered head lay to the side. I nudged the lips, no response, and recalled the doctor's words, "Why feed it…?"

Mother went to the kitchen and returned with a jar of honey.

"Here," she said, dipping her finger to daub a portion on the nipple. "I've used molasses to tempt calves, piglets, and lambs. See if this won't help…"

Sure enough, given a taste, the lips twitched open and latched the nipple and he eagerly turned his head to sup. Raised both fists as well and did not leave off till he emptied the bottle. As I lifted him to my shoulder to burp him, a soft breeze wafted in through the window. Nearly three hours since his birth and Hannah only now awaking, still groggy, propped to her elbow, curious of her baby as mother sat beside her and pointed proudly, "A big baby boy, and he just fed…nursed the bottle dry."

Hannah echoed her smile, but when I walked over and leaned him forth she winced in horror at sight of his head and cried, "He's a monster…it's like The Black Stork! What have I done? What have I made…?"

Her anguish so deep and immediate, mother hugged her close and assured, "No, honey, not a monster, only a poor hurt baby. It was a hard birth, for you and him. In a few days he'll be better, you'll see…"

Hannah's shock to be expected, the head a hideous sight, but her fear rose from a movie by the notorious Dr. Haiselden, titled *The Black Stork*, widely talked about over the past two years. Shown throughout the country, even came to Mankato, mandatory viewing for Hannah and her classmates at the high school as a cautionary tale. Though I never saw it, she'd told me the story, written and starred in by Haiselden himself as the kindly doctor who fails to euthanize a defective infant that grows into a degenerate and returns to kill the very one who'd foolishly let him live. While offering modern shadings of Frankenstein, it focused on the rising threat of idiocy and promiscuity and promoted the moral right to eliminate the ill-suited and so protect the general health and well-being. This a fashionable notion named eugenics, supported by many leading persons, including President Wilson. Locally, Dr. Sudlow and Madalene were staunch advocates, arguing that it was not only sensible but more humane to relieve defectives of their accursed fate and others of their burden. And admit, in light of Maxie's murder, I felt some sympathy. Yes, if indifferent to nursing, why feed it?

But I had held the baby and he had fed.

With mother's gentle coaxing, Hannah soon calmed, sniffled briefly and wiped her tears. Still tentative, doubtful, she reached to the baby and touched his chest. "Poor little thing," she smiled sadly, "hasn't got a father. But he'll have part his father's name…Paul, from Marcus Paul LaMarche. And Daniel, for my beloved brother. Paul Daniel Ross…"

Having named him, Hannah laid back and softly hummed herself asleep.

That was Sunday, and through the week Paul improved. The bruises faded, his flesh pinkened, and his eyes cleared, no longer ghastly red, simply remote, dim, as if no one there of will or intent except to feed. Never cried nor fussed, and only woke when cleaned and diapered. But when nudged by the nipple he latched and supped with a vengeance, easy to care for, but also worrisome, for he seemed to lack any sense or desire beyond hunger. Nor did Hannah take to him as I dared not hope, let alone offer to nurse him. Like many young women, reluctant to breastfeed, fearing I suppose that it would spoil their shape and charm. Although natural, such was considered socially primitive, unsightly and obscene, particularly in public. Since bottle-feeding was all the fashion and Paul readily taking goat milk through a rubber nipple, why press her? Besides, Hannah was severely weakened from giving birth and likely sapped as Mabel warned by the morphine and needed to convalesce and strengthen. When Madalene called midweek to ask if Dr. Sudlow should stop by and check on her, Hannah shook her head. I felt likewise. Faced with our dilemma, we did not want any further lectures on how-to or whether one should or should not live.

Yet as I held baby Paul in ponder of his fate, I was haunted by the thought and question, was I to blame? Had my prideful bearing, my quickened marriage and red dress unwittingly cursed my own flesh? Had my moral idiocy murdered my son and Maxie? No, it was a drunken fool that shot Maxie. It was Hannah's desperate sorrow that drove her to the arms of a trifling priest and begat this misshaped child. And it was rabid wealth and power, trains and troop ships that gathered up our boys by the tens of thousands and sent them to slaughter. Not meager private acts, though we all shared in the reckoning. Seeing my daughter a fallen flower, I wanted to rend my flesh and fling my heart. Instead, I embraced the baby and wept.

Saturday noon when mother returned to town for trading day, Hannah brightened and climbed out of bed. Still recovering, weak and wobbly, mother held her arm and walked her around the room till she steadied and found her balance. Anxious to freshen up, first thing she asked for was a bath. While mother drew a couple buckets of water to heat, I checked Hannah's vaginal incision, had done so daily, well-knit, healing nicely, the catgut nearly dissolved, no infection, a slight itching, but ready to move freely about. She stepped into the bath and knelt to her knees as mother and I helped suds and sponge then rinse her clean. Toweling off, she was appalled at her slack belly skin.

"Don't fret, dear, it'll firm in a jiffy," mother assured with a slap to her bottom, "up and at it, you'll soon be fit and trim for dancing."

"Dancing…?" Hannah repeated in smile. "That would be lovely."

Wrapped in the towel she marched upstairs and returned neatly dressed, her red hair curling dry. We sat at the table for a modest meal of buttered bread and potato soup. She ate about half then glanced up and said, "I wonder if there's a movie. I haven't seen one since the wreck last winter."

The Ute Theater showed a matinee every Saturday afternoon at 2:30.

"I'm sure there is," I answered. "But have no idea what's playing."

"Why don't you take her," mother urged. "I'll tend the baby. It'll do you both good."

A hot day with a fine breeze, Hannah and I strolled uptown beneath the shading trees and drew many an eye as we entered the theater, which happily soon darkened as the screen lit up. Titled *Broken Blossoms*, the latest from D.W. Griffith, again starring Lillian Gish, a moving story, grimly tragic, about a poor flower girl in a London slum befriended by a Chinese immigrant. Their love, although chaste, is frowned on if not forbidden by the old taboo of racial mixing, and once exposed the girl is beaten to death by her drunken father.

A somber exit from the theater into the blinding sun and accusative stares and we hurried away. Walking home Hannah gripped my hand and said, "I can't bear their eyes on me, Mother. I can't stay…I cannot. I'll die like that poor girl, trapped in a dark space, the walls closing in" — for that's where the father had found her, hiding in a closet.

I gripped her hand in turn and said, "I know. And I won't make you…"

No, I would not make her stay and be what she was not. She had birthed the child, given him a name, but she could not mother what she did not love. Had yet to even hold him, though day by day less hideous, the skull taking shape, the baby lay limp, insensible, except to sup.

"But won't you stay awhile yet?" I asked. "And let yourself strengthen?"

"No," she answered. "It will only be harder to leave…"

That evening after mother left, and all day Sunday, I helped Hannah pack and make ready. Monday morning I walked to the bank, and Marion, now working with his father, secured me a loan against the house for $800, deposited in her name to be wired for once she settled. Of the remaining $200 in her college fund, I withdrew $50 in ready cash, the rest in traveler cheques. Finishing up, Marion, naturally curious, asked of her plans and where she was going.

"Honestly," I answered, "I have no idea."

"Well, that would be like her, always a mystery," he said, betraying a note of regret then cracked a smile, "But hope she skates all the way to the top!"

I thanked him and walked home. Stepping inside, I saw Hannah gazing out the window, her two bags set by the door. When she turned I noticed she wore the blue dress and matching hat that Danny had bought her years ago. In an awkward moment I handed her the envelope with the cash and cheques and the information she'd need to wire for the deposit.

She quietly slipped it in her purse and said, "Thank you, Mother."

"The money…won't last long," I cautioned. "Please…be careful."

She stood silent, her lips beginning to quiver, mine too as I finally asked, "Do you have any notion where you're going?"

"Not really," she answered, turning again to the window. "I'll take the train west and decide on the way…"

We heard the far whistle drawing near. She walked over to where the baby lay in vague stare, apparently awake. Once more she laid her hand to his chest and said, "Poor little Paul…" Then she leaned down and kissed him for the first and last time.

XXXI. Return to the Limestone

"Gonna walk today, Gram?"

"Don't believe I can, Paul."

"But you got the best cane ever…you said?"

"Yes, it fits my hand nicely," she smiles, gripping the cane leaned to her lap. "And it will soon take me to the moonlit world, the magic world of Aladdin."

"And Genie?"

"Yes, if you and he grant my last wish…"

He turns away as she knew he would and busies himself making breakfast.

"There's no hurry, Paul. I'll make the day, I think. Close to moonrise…"

He ignores her and continues mixing the pancake batter, soon frying eggs and bacon. Her hands long failing her, in recent years he's become a fair cook.

"Will you eat some, Gram?"

"No thank you, Paul. It would only pain my stomach."

"Want some tea?"

"Why yes, that would be fine. With a dab of honey, please…"

He pours a cup and stirs in a spoonful of the magic amber then carefully sets it on the table. Still steaming, she lets it cool a moment before cupping it in her shaky hands to take a sip then sets it by.

"You know," she says, savoring the warmth with a memory, "when we returned to the Limestone, you were only a month old…and already 16 pounds."

"At the feed store I weigh 360."

"Yes, but you were a big boy then too. And funny thing…" she pauses as he looks in question. "At first, we were worried you wouldn't eat."

"Not eat?" he gazes at his full platter of pancakes and eggs in wonder of such a thing and repeats, "Not eat?"

"No, you wouldn't even nurse. Then Gram-Gram, my mother, smeared some honey on the nipple and you took it in a blink…"

———————•❋•———————

After Hannah left that day, hearing the train whistle fade, I cradled up the baby and walked west of town to Maxie's grave. Drawn to the past, I guess, had to go somewhere, see someone. But kneeling there, tracing his name, there was no one, nothing. Returning home, I gazed toward the station where I'd said goodbye to Hagan, then Danny, and now Hannah. Alone, except for a mute, unwanted child, my world listed this way and that till I could hardly stand. And decided I too must leave.

At Maxie's funeral mother let me know that I would always be welcome on the Limestone. Within a month I sold the house and furnishings, keeping only my clothing and personal items, Hagan's and Danny's letters, and Maxie's cigar box to retain a scent of him. Danny's piano and our grand Edison I gave to Ian and Elizabeth for them and their two boys to enjoy. Thanking me, they expressed their regret at my going and asked that I stop by when in town. I assured them I would, ever grateful for their kindness and friendship, Ian and I having worked together for over 30 years.

At the bank, settling up with Marion, he said they'd wired Hannah's money to a bank in Los Angeles, grinning as he added, "Guess the City of the Angels has gained one more…" That made me smile, having half expected her to try her luck in Denver, perhaps the more sensible choice, but nonetheless proud she'd reached for her greater dream of landing in the movies.

After paying off the loan, I pocketed $100, and later that day with the goat loaded in mother's car, baby Paul and other items in mine, we headed for the Limestone in the high August heat. By the time we turned up the lane the road dust had colored both Model-T's a ghostly gray. And unloading, I felt like a ghost, burdened with a flesh all but dead, that merely breathed, slept and fed, not alive in any real sense.

Mother and Glen had arranged another bedroom on the main floor so I needn't climb the stairs, and we quietly settled in. I helped with morning and evening chores, milked the goat, cleaned and fed the baby, and though growing, through another month he simply lay, rarely grasped or kicked, and never with intent, eyes blank, apparently without being or soul. Like Hannah, I could not take to him, not really, even reluctant to say his name, referring to "he" or "him" or more often "it."

As with most people, my life was framed in my youth. I dreamed of and met my prince and lived happily for a time. And when Hagan died, I wed his faithful warrior, Maxie. I bore a son and a daughter and watched them grow then leave. There was much I mourned, wondered of and questioned. Now at half a century, I held an infant fated to be an idiot, a moron, or fool, and felt myself a fool to look ahead. Although home, at a loss, and looked to the ground in wish to fall there and never wake. But did so each day, crawled out again at dawn to clean, feed, and fret for one I dreaded to hold.

Mid-September, still hot with no rain since July, the grass a dormant brown, the leaves a dull green that flaked at a touch and the roiling wind hurled dust past door and window. I sat and listened to the howl as if my whole life circled in haunt to claim me. Stripped of husband, daughter and son, I thought of Liam finding his family massacred then tracking his sister to find her hung. Again I saw him standing, staring off, alone unto himself, his nights gone drinking and fighting, returning even more silent and sullen. Finally taking the red skull and stomping it to angry bits on the tavern floor, and I too wanted to take something, stomp and smash it.

Mother gone, I grabbed up the baby and rushed out, my eyes tearing in the gusty wind. A mindless plunge without thought or direction, found myself climbing, stumbling toward the old Indian's grave. I sat on the mound and idly grasped a rock, the baby limp on my lap, my hair swirling in the wind, tears streaming down my face as I gazed to the distant hills in answer to a further haunt. A tale told while I was in high school of two sisters found dead north of Arcadia in the adjacent county due east. Old maids in their mid-thirties left destitute on a pioneer farm, their parents deceased — a neighbor found them drowned in a shallow lake nearby. By their tracks in the mud it appeared one sister had dragged the other to her death, both found floating face down in the shallow water. And I thought, yes, I could drown myself in father's pond, end this pain and find peace. But first I gripped the rock to bash the baby's head.

At that very instant I felt another hand, not heavy and solemn like the old Indian's, but lightly insistent, tapping my own. I glanced down and saw the baby reaching for the rock, grunting, "Uh-uh-uh…" until he too gripped it.

I clasped him to me and whimpered, "Paul, Paul…" so ashamed at what I'd nearly done, yet grateful he'd finally awakened and my heart filled as if my soul too had been missing. Clutched him to my breast and rocked us both till my panic ended, now certain he was wholly alive and real to me. At last I caught my breath and stood. Seeing that mother had returned, I hurried down, careful of baby Paul and my step.

When we entered the door, mother glanced up mildly surprised.

"There you are," she said, "thought you were napping in the back room."

"No, we were out. But look, Mother," I gasped, sharing my joy, "Paul's alive, awake and alive!"

"Why, he surely is," she smiled, pleased to see his eyes move to her. Then peering to his hands, she asked, "What is this?" Only then did I realize he still gripped the rock.

"We found it at the old Indian's grave," I answered without further explanation. "And he carried it down all by himself."

"Well, he certainly has a strong grip, don't you, Paul?" she patted his hand proudly then said, "Look at this…" pointing to a hole eroded at the edge. "That's a fairy stone, he has. Remember? Liam used to find them for you…"

In my mind I saw Liam kneeling down to show me a rock, saying if I looked through the hole I'd see another world, one full of magic and wonder. In those rare moments Liam did smile, and I smiled in wistful memory, "Yes, Liam and the fairy stones…" then brightened, "But Paul's alive, Mother, fully awake and alive. Gripping things, looking to us…he's really here."

"Of course he is, and always was," she nodded fondly. "Just a little slow and maybe always will be. But he's alive and ready to love. Live, love, and endure…"

From that day on I loved Paul truly, began to cuddle, talk and sing to him, "In the Tree Top" and other nursery rhymes, not as a mother, but a grandmother, more abiding and circumspect, like an old cedar shading a frail stem in hope it will bud.

Later that fall, a warm sunny day, Glen and I in the creek timber, readying wood for winter, the buckboard and mules hitched nearby. Baby Paul lay on a blanket in a spot of warm sun, golden leaves twirling down to his blink and wonder. We worked a salmon-belly crosscut saw, I at the far end in guide and pull, Glen providing most of the muscle, sectioning a long hackberry limb fallen in a recent storm.

"That sap smells like wild plums, don't it?" he noted, taking a breather. "Then again, always catch a whiff of whiskey cuttin' ash or oak."

"You wouldn't be working up a thirst?" I teased.

"Just might be…" he grinned to where our two dogs yipped after a rabbit.

Tuning back to the saw, in a shard of sunlight I glimpsed the cattle had circled around baby Paul, all facing in like spokes of a wheel, and he the hub. I made a mad dash in fear they'd harm him. But my panic eased as they parted to my shove and I saw Paul reaching to a big wet nostril to feel the hot breath sniffing and tickling his hand. For the first time I heard him giggle while behind me Glen laughed at my foolish alarm.

"You been too long in town, Duchess…forgot them cows are good mothers too."

True, I'd forgotten many things. Be that as it may, I picked Paul up, didn't want him stepped on, his head further bruised or damaged. And he reached back to the cattle, giggling as I carried him to safety. Laying him down in the wagon, I said, "See how his head has nearly taken its proper shape. You can barely tell he was ever injured."

"Yep," Glen agreed, "just a big handsome boy…"

Had dark hair and brown eyes of his father, but from his mother he bore Maxie's broad features and shared his big smile. Though slow, still not in full control of his neck and head. Seeing him reach and grasp, to help him along I fashioned a carrier from a pair of father's old denim overalls. Snipped off the legs and sewed them shut. Adjusted the straps to harness my shoulders, set Paul in the deep pocket and went forth each morning to gather eggs and milk the goat and cows. Same again come evening, and Paul, witness to every task, began reaching his hands to mimic mine.

His biggest thrill was milking the cows. "Loves them cows, don't he?" Glen laughed, watching him lean to pat a swollen udder. I'd twist a teat and shoot a stream to his mouth. Licking which, he'd grunt for another. By Christmas, the goat gone dry, he was happily supping cow's milk. And mushing butter-honey biscuits and anything else within reach, growing by the day, and I soon had to cut holes in the carrier for his legs to poke through. Yet the weight of him became such a burden my back gave way. Finally, by mid-April, Paul sitting up, holding himself steady, Glen made us a rolling cart out of a wooden wheel barrow then fixed a seat with a leather belt to hold him in. Which greatly relieved my back.

But not my worry for Hannah, entering summer, still no word from her, mother shared my concern. She caught me staring off one day and said, "Hannah's a prideful girl. And left feeling shamed. Let's give her time and hope no news is good news…"

Paul turned one in June, sitting up strong and taking solid food but slow to crawl or stand. Lifted to his feet, his legs would wobble briefly then he'd plop back down to sit or roll to his belly. Content to stay put and watch bugs cross the floor while flies buzzed at the window screen and summer crawled on.

———————•❦•———————

July, 1920, another political season upon us, and Wilson, though ailing, angled for a third term. But time had passed him by and Democrats nominated Governor James Cox of Ohio. While Republicans chose to run another Ohioan, Senator Warren Harding — a large affable man who promised to put "America first" and return us to "normalcy," plain words that pleased many an ear. The country fed up after a decade of fancy phrases and foreign entanglements wanted a President that stayed home, which Harding certainly did, campaigned from his front porch like McKinley and trounced his opponent, gaining my and mother's nod as we cast our first vote for President.

In proof of normalcy, the political news was largely overshadowed by the White Sox-Black Sox scandal — 8 Chicago players indicted two weeks before the election for throwing the 1919 World Series. Glen who followed the game related and updated the story to us each Sunday. The Chicago 8 as they came to be known, though eventually found "not guilty," were thereafter banned from baseball, including the great and popular favorite, "Shoeless" Joe Jackson, who'd slammed a Series record 12 hits. Many, angered by the harsh ruling, suspected a legal fix and collusion by the owners, as did Glen.

"Damn big shots," he chafed. "Pack the stands 'n make millions sellin' peanuts, then pay the boys peanuts. What the hay, leave ol' Joe 'n the other fellers out in the cold. Though reckon they did cheat…"

At least they weren't left dead and buried in some far war…my thoughts as the clutter of headlines and news on baseball and politics faded amid daily chores on the Limestone where my cares centered on Paul…and more and more on mother.

While autumn skies grayed to winter, I watched her rapidly weaken. Embarrassed to accept help, one evening she leaned to the stanchion and confessed she could not carry the milk pail up from the barn. And soon she left off milking altogether. Eating less and losing weight by the day, and each night taking laudanum to ease the pain in her stomach so she could sleep. Early one morning I found her standing out in the orchard by father's grave, clutching her side, her face creased in pain, and suggested once again that she see a doctor. She waved me off.

"No, don't want the bother, Sadie," she sighed through frosted breath. "There's nothing they can do. Besides, I miss Patrick, gone four winters it's been. Doubt we'll meet in the great beyond. But I can join him right here beneath the apple tree. Yes, do believe I am ready…"

No use arguing the matter, I simply helped her back to the house.

Yet Christmas was a surprisingly joyful day. Paul took his first step, urged on by Glen extending his hands and clicking his tongue like training a colt. Moving forth, one step then another till Paul finally reached Glen's knee and offered a big grin. Mother brightened and struggled on through the winter, pleased to see Paul walking and proud she'd taught him his first word, "Gram" for Graham Crackers, about the only thing she cared to eat by then. She'd dip one in warm milk to share with Paul and say, "Want a Graham…?" From that it became her name and mine. She held her brave smile and most days managed to get out of bed and do a few kitchen chores, otherwise she sat in a rocker by the stove with her old house cat Matilda to warm her lap.

By the Ides of March she declared, "Believe I've seen enough…" and took to bed her last three days, taking no more food, only a little water and laudanum. The night she lay dying, I sat beside her as she gazed to the ceiling, mostly silent. Then she looked to me and asked for the kitten doll.

"You'll find it there stored in the trunk…"

Utterly forgotten in all these years until I took it out and handed it to her. She held it intently to her eyes then spoke, her voice calm and pensive, "Ever since that night the old Indian reached to you, I've puzzled, asking, what did it mean him returning with the kitten doll? He'd lost everything and gave us a kitten he'd taken in returning you to me. First my baby, then the doll, to somehow square things, I guess. Sparing you, you were part of him, the only thing left. That's all I know…"

She handed me the kitten and I gently cupped the matted fur and looked to the turquoise eyes. Again they seemed to stir and it frightened me like I beheld another fate. Had the warrior taken me I would have died long ago as had the kitten. Then I glanced up and mother was gone, still gazing to the ceiling, but gone. Her old cat Matilda curled quietly at her side, watching. Paul had toddled to the door and peered in like Danny had that day I wrapped my miscarriage in a bloody towel to bury in the garden and told him it was a secret blessing. Presently, I said nothing, merely smiled sadly, not certain whether I held a blessing or a curse. I returned the doll to the trunk, covered mother with a blanket and put Paul to bed.

Next morning Glen and Holly drove over, two hired men followed in another car. The men helped Glen dig the grave while Holly helped me carry the coffin up from the barn. I'd already cleaned and clothed mother and combed her white hair to wreathe her withered face. Her flesh so thinned in her last month, light as a sheaf of corn as we lifted her in, tucked neatly with the patchwork quilt from her bed. Then the men carried her out to her orchard grave.

Glen knelt nailing the lid shut as Hiram and Ruth Holland, our neighbors to the north who I'd also called, came walking up the lane with their tow-haired boy trotting alongside. An older couple in their mid-forties, they'd given up having a child, then surprised with a baby boy, they named him Isaac. Little Ike, born the same month as Paul, was as small and active as Paul was large and slow, saying words and walking at eight months, and now approaching age two speaking full sentences and running circles around everyone, especially Paul. But promptly quieted when told and stood politely by his mother as all gathered at the grave.

The men, paired on either side, gripped the ropes and eased the coffin down. Looking on, I took comfort seeing the roots reaching from father's side towards mother. Finished, the men coiled up the ropes and dusted their hands. Then Hiram cleared his throat, opened his Bible and read the Apostle Paul's "Hymn to Love," mother's favorite passage. Listening, I caught the phrase "Face to face…" and thought of mother and father joined again in the good earth.

While the men filled in the grave, we watched the boys play — mostly little Ike running hither and thither, fetching a stick to show Paul or pointing to the trees about to bloom. "They will make apples, big red apples!" his voice rang out, speaking clearly of many things. Paul stood mostly mute, eyes fixed on his little friend. Finally he turned to where the men tapped their shovels, shaping the mound of mother's grave. He raised his hand toward them and said, "Gram…"

"No!" Ike countered, pointing to me, "that's your Gram, right there!"

Paul tottered over, took my hand and smiled. And that was a blessing.

Their grim task done, Holly's hired men offered condolences and drove on. Hiram and Ruth did the same, expressed their regrets and high regard for mother, then returned up the lane toward their farm. Little Ike ran on ahead, ever curious, stopping to examine a rock or tuft of wild onion sprouting green, then off to a further discovery, truly a bright precocious child.

Holly joined Glen and me in walk back to the house to fix a noon meal. Along the way Glen hunched his shoulders and choked up, something I'd never seen him do. But he soon recovered, took a deep breath and gasped, "Awful sad day…Aunt Sarah, more a mom to me…" Then he cast his eyes to the old Indian's grave and said, "When my time comes, plant me up on the White Rock with my first kin. That would do."

"Hold on, buster," Holly linked his arm, "that'll be a long while yet."

"Just might be," he turned in ornery grin, "and might be the only day your horse whups mine…" Joshing her over a recent race he'd won.

XXXII. Ike & Paul

Mother gone left an emptiness I had not expected, I'd wake to a far train passing east or west, the fading whistle only compounding my ache. At sunrise and sunset I'd stare to the horizon in wonder of Danny and Hagan and where they lay amid rock, roots, and mud. And of Maxie and our dear restless daughter. Anxious and forlorn in glum of dusk, I'd kneel and give Paul a desperate hug. As spring warmed, most days I worked in the garden, back bent hoeing and planting, then straighten and glimpse the mounds of my parents' graves and sense their presence. Still I ached. And when I suggested to Glen that he move back to the home place, offering to cook and do his laundry and spare him the daily ride over, he jocularly declined.

"Don't think so, Duchess, too old 'n set in my ways. Besides," he winked, "hate to miss my surprise visits from Holly. She slips by a time or two most weeks, then skips off 'n flat disappears. But I don't press her 'n she don't press me. She's my darlin'…"

Lived their lives together and apart and I was happy for them. Wished I could call Maxie up from the grave and simply hold hands. And if wishes were horses, I'd beg him to stay. At least I saw bits of him in our grandson, mainly in Paul's red-cheek smile.

Shortly thereon I did convince Glen to take mother's Model-T to ease his travels back and forth. Always stubborn of "auto-mobiles," he took one glance, kicked a tire, and reluctantly agreed, "If you insist, Duchess. Suppose it'd spare my ol' hoss in foul weather…" And within a week he traded it for a 1920 Model-T truck. "Good for haulin' grain sacks, calves 'n such," he said, invariably cussing "the danged ol' T," as he called it, from first crank to rattly halt. Though I noticed he drove it more and more, increasing his trips to town and likely to Holly's.

One morning he pulled in and stepped out, set Paul up behind the wheel and said, "How 'bout it, Bud, wanna go for a drive?" Paul gripped the wheel and burbled his lips, making motor noises, one sound he knew besides *Moo! No!* and *Gram!* "You too, Sadie, hop in. Wanna hit that land office in Mankato 'n get things in yer name." When I started to protest, he said, "Listen, Duchess. No doubt you'll outlast this ol' cowpoke. Though I aim to poke along a spell yet, show ya the ropes of the cattle trade so you can rein the BC Ranch midst Mother Nature 'n the markets. Of tough Briar stock, you'll pan out…"

That said, we drove to Mankato and settled things "Legal like," as Glen declared.

Gradually over summer I felt life renew and fill again. It helped having Glen school me daily, though as apt to trip me up to test me and make me laugh. In such manner we carried on and seldom spoke of our loss. Following father's death, our neighbor Hiram, who owned a Fordson tractor, had plowed and planted for mother, basically farming our tilled acreage on shares. Glen didn't balk, never cared for plowing, but still hitched the mules to mow and rake our hay.

Hiram and Ruth were good people, religious, but not terribly so. Pleasant and practical, down-to-earth, they often visited to let the boys play. Utterly different, Ike keen and quick, Paul quiet and slow, being the only children proximate they became fast friends, saw themselves in the other like all young animals, puppies, kittens, calves, or colts, new to the world and its wonders. Most Sunday evenings we'd gather, they and Glen, and sometimes Holly, to enjoy homemade ice cream and cake. Later we'd sit and talk, watch for falling stars or signs of rain while Ike romped and chased fireflies, Paul shuffling along behind. Ike would catch one and show it to Paul then let it go — never mean, always generous and considerate, an admirable little fellow.

Naturally our rhythm changed through autumn and winter. Instead of ice cream we'd share a supper of oyster soup or a big kettle of chili, then have popcorn and play pinochle, hearts, or pitch while the boys lay on the floor by the stove, thumbing through pages of old picture books such as *Grimm's Fairy Tales*, *Aladdin's Lamp*, or *Wizard of Oz*. Ike, already reading, sounded out many words to Paul, who as yet could say little more than "Gram…"

Life ambled on through winter to another spring, then came summer and the boys turned 4, Ike avidly learning piano from their church choir lady. Many days, sharing our canning chores, I'd venture to Ruth's place or she to mine, we'd peel and slice vegetables and fruits, boil and seal jars, the boys at the piano, Ike plinking out a song, "America the Beautiful" or "Amazing Grace" or the local favorite "Home on the Range," now and then adding the lyrics, singing to Paul. One day we heard another voice join in on "Amazing Grace," strong and melodic though slurring the words and wholly different from Ike's. Ruth and I quickly toweled our hands and rushed in as Ike looked to Paul and blurted, "You sing good! Real good!" Paul's smile spread full to his cheeks, realizing he could do something good. A wonderful voice, a gift from his mother, and that's how he came to learn his words. Once he sang something, he could say it — "*Amazing Grace, how sweet the sound, to save a wretch like me…*"

Felt my heart rise in that moment, grateful for whatever grace fell to Paul. Next day I told Glen what had happened, how Paul was singing and saying words.

"Ain't that somethin'," he answered, none too surprised. "A mite slow, that boy, but ain't stupid. Like with a horse, just gotta figure a way to learn 'im. As Aunt Sarah would say, 'Once you thread the needle, it's set to stitch…'"

Thereafter, nearly every day, I put a record on the Edison and the boys loved to listen. Ike immediately curious of the workings and soon both boys up on a chair, Paul turning the crank while Ike carefully set the arm and needle with big smiles each time the music sounded forth. And of course in their eagerness they dropped and chipped a few, playing everything from Stephen Foster songs to Souza marches and "Hot Time in the Old Town…" Then they found "Danny Boy" and at shock of hearing it play I went to stop them but checked myself. *Once you thread a needle*...Paul learning new words by the day, I dare not interfere and so endured the song as they played it over and over, especially loved that it sang of a boy...

———◦●◦———

Beyond Labor Day came murmurings of another presidential campaign, which I mostly ignored. Harding had died the summer before on a train trip through the West, unexpected, only 57 years old, of rather mysterious causes, though they did mention a bout of pneumonia along with bad heart and immoderate drinking. Replaced by a flinty-eyed teetotaler out of New England, Calvin Coolidge, who looked as stern as a school proctor and who tersely claimed, "The business of America is business." So it seemed, and I left the business of politics to others and focused on raising Paul.

To thread the needle I added sing-song lyrics to many tasks: "*Off to the barn we go, where the ol' cows moo and low, then gather the eggs the hens have laid, always careful, kind, and slow...*" Mostly silly rhymes soon tossed. Though there was one limerick Paul favored, or "Gram's Song," as he called it: "*Here stands an old woman beneath the sky of blue, left one child and don't know what to do. I scrub him and tub him and put him to bed, fluff a pillow for his dear sweet head. He grows tall and wide as the old barn door, eats all I cook and sings for more...*" Oft-recited to his quiet glee, though at times I was tempted to end with "*more straw than thought where such is stored...*"

But if his thoughts fell short, his heart beat true.

The following summer Paul turned 5 years old, stood over 40 inches tall, and was proudly gathering eggs on his own. We had one old hen prone to peck your hand when guarding her nest. More so if you hurried, but given patience and sweet talk she would generally yield. One day she pecked Paul's hand so deep it bled. Early next morning, determined to put an end to her mean ways, I wrung her neck, plucked and fried her up for noon dinner. Told Paul as he hungrily bit into a leg, "That old hen won't bother you anymore. You get to bite her now."

Stunned, he stopped eating and looked up, tears brimming his eyes, "No, not Henny!" he cried. "Not Henny's fault, Gram!"

Having thought he'd be pleased, I slapped my forehead and swore, "Oh darn, my mistake. It's the coyotes got Henny last night. I found her feathers behind the henhouse this morning" — which was where I'd plucked her, thinking to surprise him.

"Coyotes?" he asked.

"Yes, those darn coyotes got poor Henny."

"Coyotes got Henny..." he repeated, then looked at the leg he'd been eating.

"That's just Carnie," I said, "that old barn rooster. Thought he best feed us before the coyotes got him. He's the one I fried, Ol' Carnie, the barking rooster, crowed day and night and finally gets to rest. And he won't mind if you eat his leg."

"Carnie crows real good...Paul sings real good!"

"Yes indeed, and I bet he's in rooster heaven right now crowing about how good his leg tastes to Gram's good boy Paul." Hearing this, Paul forgot about Henny and ate both legs and a thigh.

By fall Paul had grown nearly to my shoulder, slow and clumsy, but strong and steady at his chores. Helped Buck drive cattle up from the creek for milking, boy and dog faithfully paired to the task and one another. Shag, old and weak, had disappeared over summer, likely lured and killed by coyotes. When Paul asked where he went, I said, "Over the hill, where all good dogs go..."

But I soon faced a tougher question: "Gram, do I got a dad? Ike's got a dad."

This caught me off-guard and I had to puzzle the notion.

"Yes, you have a...a father," I answered slowly. "A special kind of father who speaks with old words and ritual and must answer to many children. So many that he cannot see or speak to all."

"Can I see him?"

"No, I doubt you ever will. Long ago he was called far away to bless his many children and offer prayers to the Holy Ghost."

"Ghost...?" his eyes widened at the word, having heard tales of such from Ike. He stared as if in a spell then blinked and asked, "Do I have a mom?"

This I had expected, seeking the answer myself, plagued night and day by thoughts of Hannah. Was she well? Alive? Happy? Each morning after breakfast I'd walk to the mailbox along the road and often greet Ruth checking her box about 50 yards east of mine. She knew my concern and read my dejection each time I opened the box to find nothing but a newspaper, farm journal, or an intermittent notice from the county or state. Over five years gone, still no word from Hannah, as if she had taken the vow of silence. Weary, disappointed, I'd return to the house and busy myself through another day.

Presently, I smiled to Paul and said, "Yes, you have a mother. Young and beautiful as the princess in Aladdin, only her hair is a glorious red. And she sings like an angel."

"Where is she?"

"In the far magic land of California…where they eat fresh fruit every day and sing and dance on a big silver screen and make dreams come true."

"Where is…*Cowl-for-ya?*"

I pointed west and said, "That way…over the hill."

"Oh…" he paused in wonder then said, "where good dogs go…"

Always tricky explaining things to Paul, and often brought a question or mystery back to the fore. There I stood an old woman beneath a sky of blue, gazing off over the hills through thousands of miles to mountains and oceans, imagining millions of people inhabiting the earth, waking, eating, sleeping, and toiling to what end? Each asking a question none could answer.

Another Christmas came and went of little note excepting snow. Though Glen carved the boys each a wooden horse, and I sewed them red flannel shirts, one large and one small. To which Ruth added matching sweaters and stocking caps she'd knitted. And Santa left each a candy cane, an orange, and a bag of apples. When we gathered for Christmas dinner, Ike brought along his new crayons and a coloring book of the world with its various continents, people, mountains, oceans and sailing ships. Eager to explore each page, he immediately lay down by the stove and began deftly outlining and coloring in, while Paul sat by content to scrawl and scribble on an old newspaper, adding his cryptic note to the word of all doings.

Recently I'd read an article in the *Star* noting a new movie soon to premiere. Hadn't seen one since *Broken Blossoms* with Hannah and didn't much miss them. But the title caught my eye, *Ben Hur*, proclaimed the greatest film ever, costing over four million with a cast of thousands, featuring a naval battle and the death-defying chariot race. Intrigued, I mentioned it to Glen and asked if he recalled the chariots at the circus.

"Oh yeah, biggest thrill of all 'n all I remember 'fore I got clobbered…"

We shared a chuckle and gave it little thought, saved the paper for kindling and other use. Then in mid-January, walking to the mailbox, my face double-scarfed against the fierce north wind, so bitter cold I nearly turned back, but spying the tiny red flag that signaled mail, I forged on. Reaching inside, I withdrew a single envelope addressed to *Sadie-Briar-Corbett-Ross* written in Hannah's hand then glimpsed her name in the upper left corner. I wept for joy, clasped it to my breast and let the hard wind hurry me to the house. Paul stood back as I rushed in and cast off my scarf, mitts, and coat, and told him, "We've gotten word from your mother…" Then I stoked the fire and sat down, carefully opened the envelope and unfolded the letter:

"Dearest Mother," it began, "sorry for the long silence which I imagine caused you grave concern. But I was so ashamed in leaving and frightened of what was to come that I could not bear to write until I had something worthy to say. I dare not ask forgiveness, nothing can atone for abandoning my child. Only cross my heart and hope he survived and is not a monster or too terrible a burden for you.

"I am well, love my life and would not trade it. I have a good man, JB, who I met one night while singing in a club, which I do on occasion, though less so of late. He was standing in a far corner, listening with a quiet smile, and we locked eyes. When finished, I walked to him and he said, 'You sing right pretty…' We've been together ever since. JB hails from Montana and horse wrangles for the movies. Trains and rides and performs dangerous stunts for the stars, falls from the saddle, fistfights, and the like. Tall, athletic, and handsome, but does not care to act, happy to do action scenes. Fun and lively, yet shy, reminds me of Uncle Glen, only much younger, of course.

"We have a modest place up Topanga Canyon where the mountains meet the sea. Just a small stucco cottage with stalls, corrals, and a few acres for his horses, but it's our heaven. Riding through the hills, we can see the ocean a few miles distant and every day brings a mild coastal breeze. We have orange, avocado, and lemon trees, and a kitchen garden year around. He added my initial to his and hung a sign over the entrance that reads JBH Ranch!

"I work in the movies as well. At first as an extra and common set work, now fulltime in wardrobe and costuming. Though in my recent and most featured role I wore hardly any costume at all, merely a skimpy little leafy thing to cover my loins, otherwise naked, one of three dancing girls leading a triumphal parade through pagan Rome in the new movie Ben Hur. Fearing they might cut my part, I waited to see the premiere before writing to you. Only a brief scene, lasting a few seconds, but I appear in full color.

"When they called an audition for dancing girls willing to bare their breasts, JB dared me and I walked in that very instant, shed my blouse and got the part. My scene comes about one hour into the movie, right after the great naval battle where Juda saves the Roman admiral, Arrius, to become his adopted son and soon the most famous athlete of Rome. Acclaimed in a grand march, and I appear in the first minute or so, the middle of three dancing girls, a dozen more behind us, all baring our breasts, skipping, laughing, tossing flowers to the cheering crowds along the way. Lots of fun and we had a gay time. So if you see the movie, I hope you don't blush and think too badly of me. Like they say, 'When in Rome…' Anyhow, we did our best, and I'm really quite proud.

"JB also appears briefly. He drives a chariot in the big climactic race. And it is spectacular, swift and dangerous, on the fourth turn his chariot spins and crashes, tossing him and the horse, one of which, impaled by the yoke, had to be destroyed. JB suffered a broken leg, which they promptly set, and has nicely mended. Already back in the action, he laughs it off and says it was just deserts for wearing a skirt and sandals and swears he'll stick with boots and jeans from hereon.

"Give Grandmother and Glen my love. Wish I could hug you all, but sadly cannot reach that far. With much love, your happy-sad daughter, Hannah…"

Only words, but ever so welcome, tears warmed my cheeks as did my smile, as Paul looked to me and asked, "Why Gram cry?"

"The letter, your mother's words and voice carried all the way from the City of the Angels…" Paul slowly returned my smile, tentative, puzzled by the notion of words or a voice scribbled on paper. I sat silent for a time, savoring what I long awaited and hoped for. That night I replied, thanking her for the letter and breaking the news of mother's death. On a happier note I spoke of her strong healthy boy, though said nothing of Paul's slow grasp and scant thought. Yet he looked normal enough, neither dull-eyed not slack-jawed, simply large for his age. Though seldom used, we owned a box camera and I had Glen snap a photo of Paul and me and one of Paul alone. Then I convinced Glen to pose. Reluctant, he pulled his hat low, shading half his face. Still, I caught a twitch of his smile at the corner of his grizzled mustache. Once Ian developed the photos, I sent them along with the letter and awaited a timely reply. A month passed, then spring, summer. Each day I checked the mailbox, thinking surely by Christmas, but again no word, nothing.

We lived, loved, and endured…in ache, hope, and question. And it was nearly two years following Hannah's letter about her part in *Ben Hur* before the movie was released to the nation. Not coming to Mankato until December, 1927, the week before Christmas, Paul's first movie, and I told him that we'd see his mother on the silver screen. Sharing details of Hannah's role with Ruth, she blushed in surprise then smiled excited to see for herself, though swore she'd keep it secret even from Hiram. Of course I told Glen who coaxed Holly to come. We all sat together in a middle row, lights dimming to darkness, Paul and Ike side by side, riveted as the film opened with the mute roar and majesty of the Metro-Goldwyn-Meyer lion.

The theater packed, yet utterly silent, every eye entranced on the flickering action and images. In an early scene of Joseph seeking lodging for his young wife with child, the camera focused on the face of Mary. Paul suddenly tensed and said, "Momma…" I gently shushed him and warned he must be quiet. Although Mary appeared several more times, it was a similarly lovely young woman, Esther, daughter of Simonides, that Paul followed thereafter, murmuring "Momma…" so softly I neither hushed nor corrected him. Having found his mother on the silver screen, I let him believe as he wished.

When Hannah did appear I nearly cried her name at sight of my lovely daughter smiling brightly, flinging flowers, the scene so brief and natural that the dancing breasts went largely unnoticed amidst the lavish procession and pageantry, eliciting scattered awes of surprise and delight. The greater response awaited the chariot race that proved every bit as dramatic and spectacular as Hannah had promised.

Exiting the theater, Glen said, "Amazed her man only broke a leg 'n not his neck. Bet they killed more'n a few horses in doin' that race. Though it was some deal to see. 'N our Hannah up there to boot…"

Beyond the crowd, Holly nudged me aside and said, "I'm proud of your daughter, making it all the way to California and into films, all on her own. She's a very brave and beautiful young woman…"

Yes, we were all proud of our Hannah, though we didn't bruit it about. Never told Marion or Ian, and other than Glen, Holly, Ruth, and me, I doubt anyone recognized our bare-breasted girl among the cast of thousands, happy to let Paul see his mother in Esther, her lovely image borne forever in his mind's eye.

That Christmas I wrote to Hannah and told her we'd finally seen the movie and enjoyed her part in it. This time she did answer, again apologizing for her silence and said the shock of seeing Paul's photo and what a fine-looking boy he appeared made her feel doubly guilty she wasn't there to see him learn, play, and grow. Knew she'd cheated him and burdened me, yet felt she could never be a worthy mother.

And I suppose she feared I'd send him to her, which was hardly the case, would rather have her haunted by his absence than see him a curse. To spare her feelings I sat down to explain more fully Paul's mental skills, or lack of, and wrote: "Please know that Paul is not a burden, but a blessing. My joy against all I've lost. Only hope I raise him well enough to survive once I'm gone. Although his head healed, taking a natural shape as good as any, damage remains deep within. He's what doctors term a 'defective,' and what others call an idiot, imbecile, or moron. It's difficult to fathom. He learns, but only in part. At practical things like dressing, using the slop jar, and keeping clean, he does remarkably well. But at language, common reason, even children's games, he's painfully slow and limited. Still, his kind heart and goodness make up for all he lacks and I would not trade him. So do not worry yourself, we fare quite well…"

Paul did struggle, especially at school, every day difficult and would have proved impossible without Ike at his side, tutoring him along. Their teacher, Miss Ryder, a young woman from Elim, while politely tolerant, could spare him little time or patience, given others students and all eight grades to teach. Paul was often mocked and teased, called a dummy, a big oaf, or worse. That he could sing became his salvation. When surrounded, he'd fold his hands and sing "Amazing Grace" until his tormenters quieted and withdrew. And Ike was a scrappy little guy, quick to Paul's defense and never gave up, determined to make him learn. By spring of 2nd grade he had Paul printing his name and counting to 20. Even taught him to add and subtract minimal amounts by using his fingers, as I had tried many times, but Ike had better luck.

"Paul, hold up your hand," he cheerfully prompted then asked, "If you gather five eggs and Gram fries you three to eat, how many eggs are left in your basket?"

Paul curled down three fingers of his spread hand and said, "Two."

"That's right! Now you gather five more eggs and put them in with those two…" Ike raised his full right hand and two fingers on his left as Paul did the same. "Okay," he asked, "how many do you have?"

Paul, stumped a moment, slowly counted his fingers out loud, "…three, four, five, six," until he stammered, "Se-seven…?"

"Right again!" Ike clapped and cheered him on. Not always successful, Ike never grew irritated or tired, made every lesson a game, coaching Paul to read and recognize a few nouns and verbs, most other printed words seemed beyond his grasp.

One day I watched and listened through the kitchen screen while they sat on the stoop, hunched over *The Wizard of Oz* laid open on Ike's lap, when Paul asked, "What is 'the'?"

Ike tapped the book in answer — "See *the* book?" Paul looked down in nod as Ike continued, "*The* is a pointing word," he said, "like our finger. Out there are many rocks, and some rocks have mica that catches the sunlight…like we saw the other day."

"*The* shiny rock?"

"Yes, not a rock or any rock, but *the* shiny rock that you picked up and put in your pocket. And that tree beyond the henhouse," Ike pointed, "that's *the* tree we swing on!"

"Oh…" Paul paused in gaze, still puzzling when a bird swept past and he pointed and exclaimed, "*The* bird!" Then pointed to the sky and shouted, "*The* cloud!"

"That's right!" Ike cheered — "Like *the* mean boy at school who teases you."

"Yeah," Paul answered quietly, "Freddie Chambers…" I knew the Chambers, they farmed a mile east beyond the school. And the son was a rotten apple just like his father, the loutish boy I once outran.

"Yes, the mean boy," Ike affirmed, again tapping the book, "and that's the word right there, *t-h-e*. But poo on Freddie Chambers, think of Lindberg and the plane he flew clear across the Atlantic, not any plane, but *The Spirit of Saint Louis!*"

Listening, I had to smile — only a month before Charles Lindberg had braved the ocean and made our nation proud. Likewise, Ike made me proud. Generous, exuberant, but sometimes his ardent curiosity led them into Dutch.

Later that spring, school let out, still waiting Decoration Day and full summer, a blustery south wind scattered apple blossoms over my parents' graves as I hung laundry on the line, thinking to make a rose wreath to honor Maxie. Turning to hang another sheet, I glimpsed the boys on the high hill west, silhouetted against the sky, tossing rocks from the old Indian's grave, I gasped and screamed, "NO!" My voice drowned by the wind, they heard nothing and persisted. I dropped my laundry and ran, knees pumping against my skirt, my lungs bursting in ache and anger. Not until my last staggered steps did the boys see me coming, yet clearly read my rage and dropped their rocks, stunned as if I shook the earth.

"What are you two doing?" I shrieked, "You bad, bad, naughty boys…" spitting my words and slashing the air then bent hands to my knees and simply glared, breathless.

Given silence, Ike meekly answered, "Just hunting Indian stuff."

"Stuff…?" I scowled. "This is a man's grave! What a horrid thing to do!"

Only then realizing what a horrid sight I made, like the Wicked Witch of the North looming over them. By now Ike's soft blue eyes brimmed tears, his lips quivering as he blubbered, "I'm sorry, Mrs. Ross…" while Paul stared at me aghast, arms limp at his side, hands grasping for something to grip like he always did when anxious or upset.

"Fold your hands, Paul…" I urged, easing my tone, ashamed of myself like on the day I nearly bashed his head with the rock. "Boys…" I knelt to one knee to gather them in, "come, I don't mean to sound mean. I know you're just curious. But there's only an old man buried here. A tired, worn out, old man who traveled here one day long ago and laid down on this very spot. That evening we gave him some tea and watched him die. My father buried him in the cold wind and snow. Next morning I helped cover his grave with these rocks. Now…" I said, pressing a hand to my knee to help me stand, "let's put the rocks back where they belong…" And they set to work, fixing what they'd wrecked with such care and attention that you could hardly tell the grave had been disturbed.

When they'd finished, I smiled to them, "Well done, may he rest in peace."

The boys nodded, relieved to see my anger gone, themselves reprieved. And Ike's curiosity quickly reclaimed as he asked, "The Indian? Who was he?"

"We never learned his name," I answered, "though my mother thought he was Cheyenne…" Then I cast my eyes to theirs in deeper wonder of him and said, "For certain he was once a boy like yourselves, curious of the world and full of questions. And he grew to be a tall warrior who once came to our cabin when I was a baby and briefly took me captive. But for some reason he returned me to my mother and left us unharmed. Why, I cannot answer. Such things are a mystery, like all before and all to come. For many ages his people and others roamed these very hills hunting the buffalo. Then they watched our people come fill the land and kill the buffalo, leaving them to starve and mostly die out. Like this man and his family. But his spirit remains, I think, still watching…part in the grave, part in the wind and the grass hereabout. So we should be respectful, for he is watching…"

From then on the boys referred to the old Indian as "The Watcher."

XXXIII. Bootleg & Bullies

Paul stands at the sink, his back to her, washing the dishes, rinsing and drying each then carefully placing them in the cupboard like he once replaced the rocks on the grave. She revisits that moment of her and the boys and her tale of "The Watcher." She looks to the tree and the kitten doll — its mute turquoise eyes tilted to her. No, she thinks, he did not return you to square things, but to plant a memory, you were all he had to prove he ever was…his tribe and family, his wife, daughter, and grandchild all wiped out. Like myself, my world and people, those I loved, dead and gone. Except for Paul…

She waits till he's done then says, "You know something, Paul," raising a crooked finger to the west window, "the Watcher's been watching and waiting for me to return the kitten doll. When it's time, you will help me, won't you?"

Paul stands silent gripping his hands at his side, then slowly folds them in nod to her and says, "Yes'um…"

The boys never again bothered the grave, though they often visited. Natural pagans like most children, over summer they bore offerings to the mound, a special rock or a rare cactus flower. And a horny toad they captured one hot day, a quizzical little creature they called "the magic lizard," carried it there and set it free among the rocks.

As Ike said, "To keep the Watcher company…"

In such a manner they ranged and roamed and indulged their imaginations. Soon back to school, another grand adventure for Ike, less so for Paul. One rushed eager for the bell, the other tagged along dragging his feet in glum shuffle, enduring daily taunt and ridicule to be with his friend.

Likewise, Glen endured the pain in his knee, dragging his leg from chore to chore. During the final summer haying, while hitching the mule to the mower, the mule kicked. "My own dern fault," Glen moaned upon reaching the house, "hurried the ol' cuss 'n he clipped me…" his knee so swollen by then I had to snip his pant leg with my scissors to relieve the pain. Then he couldn't stand. For a makeshift crutch I doubled a towel over the bristle broom and drove him to our horse vet near Ionia, Wilbur Riggins, the only Doc he'd agree to see. Wilbur, shoeing a horse as we drove in, walked over and knelt by as Glen eased his leg out the door. "Looks nasty," Wilbur grunted, gingerly checking the knee. "Bet that sharp hoof tore some ligaments. About the only thing you can do is stay off it a good spell 'n hope it heals some. Though you'll likely limp."

"Heck with that. Done sat half a day as is."

"Suit yourself. But if you don't ease up it's bound to get worse…"

Glen wouldn't listen. We drove on to Cotter's Leather Shop in Mankato. A good man, Randal Cotter, put a harness repair aside to fit and stitch Glen a leather support while we waited — fixed with two straps above the knee and two below, with notches to tighten as the swelling went down.

Next day Glen tossed off the crutch and hobbled through his chores using father's old cane, but grimacing, chary of that knee. Held his leg out straight as he sat the milk stool, cursing through more tasks than not — "Dern thing pains me to work, pains me to sit 'n pains me to sleep…" And Glen, who never passed up a drink, began taking a nip now and then every day, keeping a half pint in his hip pocket. Bootleg, of course, from a moonshiner he trusted and never named. Then one night the sheriff and deputies found the still in a far pasture. While the shiner escaped, it left Glen high and dry. Within a week so desperate he bought a gallon from a stranger passing through. "Smelt a little off, but priced right," Glen later confessed. "Dern rotgut near killed me…"

Whether laced with iodine, creosote, eye of toad or lizard tongue, it proved toxic and the following afternoon Glen stumbled to the house, clutching his stomach, so sick he willingly took to bed. Holly and I took turns nursing him through two days and nights while he retched and spat blood, rolling his eyes in delirium. Paul looked on from the doorway, pale and silent. We all feared he'd die. The third day Glen sat up and shooed us away, swore he stunk too bad to be around. Somehow managed to dress himself then fastened his brace and walked outside.

He took a deep breath and sighed, "Sure could use a drink…" half teasing us but truly needed it to ease the pain. His stomach messed up, poor vision, dizzy spells, "Here I am," he spat in disgust, "half-blind, half-lame, they shoot horses less worse off."

"Don't you even think it," Holly warned.

"Well, kind of you to care," he grinned. "But some thoughts can't be helped…"

Luckily, his old bootlegger was soon back in business, which lifted his spirits some.

October came and went, then November saw Hoover elected, but I hardly noticed, focused on Paul, the ranch, and Glen's decline. Approaching Christmas, he seldom made it over unless I went to fetch him, too lame to ride and couldn't see to drive.

"Leaves me plumb discouraged," he said.

Watching him steadily weaken and losing weight, I urged him to ease up.

"You may do better if you drink less?"

"Ah Duchess, could be you're right," he shrugged then squinted a watery eye at me. But ya really wanna help me out," he said, reaching in his vest pocket, "take this Double Eagle, keepsake from my Colorado days 'n 'bout time I spent it. They say Clyde up to Maxie's old place has got a stash of Canadian Club. That's some fine whiskey 'n I'd like to sip some whilst I still suck air." Then he placed it in my palm, patted it softly and said, "Would you kindly do that for me, Sadie…?"

A bittersweet moment and think I knew what was coming but I could not deny him. Drove that day to Mankato and while Paul and I shared a soda, Clyde disappeared in back and returned with an odd-shaped package wrapped in butcher paper. Handed it to me and winked, "Ma's special honey-cure…"

That was Glen's Christmas present — "Mighty sweet of you," he said, but didn't open it. Ate a meager portion of his meal then tucked the bottle under his arm, smiled goodbye and Holly drove him home.

Not two weeks later, a cold gray dawn in early January, Holly called…they'd planned to join me for Sunday dinner. "Found him just now," she said, "door and windows braced open, the stove fire dead. Already laid out in that pine box he built, dressed in his white shirt, blue jeans and boots. That bottle of whiskey, nearly empty, still gripped in his hands. Guess he sipped himself to final slumber…"

And he'd left a note: "Holly, hope you find me with a smile on my face. Tell Sadie I hate to skip out. But I'm all done in. Time they laid me down. So long…"

He did look peaceful, lips and eyelids sugared with frost, not exactly smiling but free of pain and disheartenment…a good sweet man gone to his long cold sleep.

Holly's hired hands, Conroy and Evert, arrived shortly and nailed the lid shut and loaded the coffin in Glen's truck. They drove ahead while Holly, I and Paul followed to the White Rock. Along with spade and shovels, they packed a chipping bar and pick-ax. Good thing they did, for the ground was frozen rock-hard the first foot down. Thereon they dug without much hindrance, only pausing to warm their hands on a fire we'd built. Paul, unaware that his uncle would not wake, enjoyed feeding the flames and scanning the unknown pasture, a whole new experience, in part an adventure. And I walked him briefly to each grave and named his distant kin buried there, sparing details of their death. Finally, we helped lower Glen down and watched them cover him over, then stood a silent moment and walked away.

Though Paul was a comfort, I faced a long lonely winter. Missed Glen's daily joshing, never lost his wry humor even as he failed. In February, reading of the Saint Valentine's Day Massacre, seven gangsters shot dead in Chicago, I could imagine him laughing, "Dern temperance fools, dump liquor in the gutters 'n now the blood flows. Next thing they'll outlaw the air we breathe!" Often scoffed at do-gooders and their fancy notions — sometimes we agreed, sometimes not, but he never angered. Always fond of my brother Glen, his only fault was leaving too soon.

Slowly, over many days and nights, my thoughts and memories warmed. By May, when the apple trees blossomed and Glen's stone was set, Holly had sold her ranch.

"With Glen gone," she said, sharing a wistful smile, "there's nothing to hold me. Plus the horse market keeps fading, each year more cars and tractors and the Army needs fewer mounts." When I asked what she planned to do, she gazed off and answered, "Oh, think I'll travel for a time, like I dreamed of when I was a girl..." I wished her well and saw her off at the depot. But my desire to travel had died long ago in waving goodbye to Hagan and Danny, then Hannah. Come what may, dearth or plenty, content to remain on the Limestone.

H.L. Bolton, an oilman out of Wichita, had bought Holly's ranch, renamed the Bar-B. He hired a manager, Jim Swanson, who wisely retained Holly's two men, Conroy and Evert, both proven hands. They took up lodging in Glen's old house. In turn they helped me during calving and hay season, and later shucking corn. A beautiful Indian summer that fall and the boys, now 9, helped as well — Paul, thrilled to have a week out of school, given his size and strength, he out-shucked Ike two to one, soon matching the men.

"By howdy," Conroy declared, "best boy cornhusker I ever seen!"

"Daggum right," Evert seconded, "that boy's plumb dogged..."

Hearing their praise, Paul swelled with joy like when he sang.

But harvest soon ended and he slouched back to school, to the maze of words, numbers, and torment. "You big dumb Scarecrow!" they chided on Halloween, stuffing straw in his shirt collar and sleeves. Ike told me. This time Paul didn't cry, came home and sat quiet and sullen, and never asked me to read *Wizard of Oz* again.

Weather cooled in early November when we heard of happenings back east. The stock market fell in late October, on Black Tuesday and again Black Thursday, wiping out millions of investors overnight, headlined in the *Sunday Star*. Further rumblings followed, causing folks to pause and draw breath even in our remote little valley. Farm prices tanked after the Great War and whatever roared through the Twenties it certainly wasn't corn, wheat, hog, or beef markets. Like Holly, many folks had sold out and left for better prospects in the cities, while those who'd mortgaged and borrowed to hang on were in sudden peril, caught in a vise and squeezed to the last red cent.

Fortunately, I owed no debt, mostly bartered with neighbors, sharing threshing cost or trading a calf in fee for a good breeding bull. What cash on hand when Hannah left, I added to mother's savings kept in a lockbox hidden behind fruit jars in the cellar. Any ready cash, egg and cream money, kept in a coffee can on the kitchen shelf. With the "Crash of '29" as it came to be known, Paul and I faced no imminent threat, but you could sense uncertainty settling in, the jazzy good times drawing to a close. While no one jumped off high buildings like they did in New York, the coming months saw a number of sheriff sales and two suicides in our valley, one by hanging, one by gunshot, both poor broke farmers too proud to face defeat. We shook our heads in mutual regret and carried on.

Another winter turned to spring and sadly no more word from Hannah, though I'd written to her of Glen's passing and at Christmas sent another photo of Paul. Perhaps the photo shocked her — it sure shocked me, seeing myself just shy of 61 years, still standing straight, but nearly a full head shorter than Paul, him smiling big, mine worn thin. Ever since corn harvest, finding his strength and rhythm, Paul fared better at school, not at his lessons, but began to stand his ground against the usual taunts and dirty tricks. Freddy and other boys often had their brattish fun, one crouching behind Paul while another gave a shove, toppling him backwards to their collective glee. All great sport until he shoved back and tossed Freddy rolling through a sticker patch.

"You should've heard him wail!" Ike laughed, sharing his joy in the bully's fall — "Had sandburs in both hands and knees. Not so mean now!" Paul stood back of him, smiling slightly, not sure he should, but pleased none-the-less, nearly 10 years old, six foot tall, and school almost out. As expected, I got a call that evening from his teacher, Miss Ryder, expressing concern over the incident.

"He's twice their size," she said, "doesn't know his own strength. He might hurt someone. You should talk to him."

"They shouldn't tease," I answered.

She gave a long sigh and confessed, "I know, but there's little I can do..."

True, a slight young woman amid a scrap of boys, one a scorned giant, mute and angry. Yet I wasn't about to chastise Paul, only urged him not to start a fight.

"No Gram, I won't..."

But a bully will have his way, and there's none more vengeful than a hurt bully. Early May, the final week of school, out hoeing the garden when I glanced up to see Buck rush out to greet Paul striding down the lane, pumping his arms. The dog, sensing something wrong, shrank back, whimpering, the boy red-faced, tears streaming from his eyes, the dog circling us both as I led Paul to the cistern and filled the dipper. He gulped and gulped then caught his breath.

"Don't let 'em cut me, Gram!" he cried, heaving his words. "Like Hiram does his boy pigs 'n they squeal. They tripped me down. Freddy had a knife...then Ike comes 'n bites his hand 'n they let go 'n got on him! I pulled up my pants 'n throwed 'em off Ike 'n grabbed Freddy's arm. It snapped like a stick. He yowled, 'My Dad's gonna cut you sure...' I run home fast. Don't let 'em cut me, Gram!" he pleaded.

"Don't worry, Paul," I tried to calm him, "Gram won't let them hurt you..."

Then I glimpsed dust trails on the road east, several cars already heading our way, and hurried Paul to the cellar, raised the door and said, "Go on down there, that's right. Now light that lantern like we do during a bad storm..." He did as told, struck a match and lit the wick then lifted the lantern in question. "Good," I said, "now sit you in that back corner and don't say a peep until Gram comes to get you..."

Paul gave a hopeful nod and entered. He liked it in the cellar, surrounded by colorful jars of canned fruits and vegetables, sacks of dried onions and potatoes, and cured hams hanging from the ceiling. A quiet magical place guarded by the Genie.

I eased the door down, shutting out the day, walked to the porch and waited.

Within a minute the lead vehicle roared in followed by two others. Before the dust settled, several more came rattling down the lane, turned about and cut their engines. For a moment the drivers sat hunched in shadow beyond their windows, headlamps perched in blank hard stare. Merle Chambers was the first to emerge, his brother Curtis from the opposite door. Followed by their neighbors Clarence Phillips and Josh Morgan while a dozen others gathered around behind.

"Know what your damn idiot done?" Merle snarled, jabbing his finger at me. "He broke my boy's arm! The wife's got him to the Doc in Mankato. What you say to that?"

I folded my arms and answered straight to his glare, "That's because your boy tried to cut him like you would a hog."

"Well he oughta be cut!" a far voice hollered, egged on by others.

I ignored their shout and continued, "And when Ike Holland tried to stop them, they turned on him. That's when Paul broke your boy's arm. Rightly so, I'd say."

"Don't believe one word," Merle spat. "That idiot don't know squat, don't learn 'n don't belong in no school. We're here to demand you yank him out or we go to the judge this day 'n see him put in the nuthouse. Or by God I'll cut him myself. You hear me?"

"Oh, I hear you quite well…" I said, unfolding my arms to reach inside the door and grab father's shotgun always leaned there and always loaded. Then I leveled the barrels and cocked both hammers. Merle's face twitched from anger to apprehension as others stood hushed, uncertain. I tensed as well, not holding as steady as I wished, and warned, "Now you hear me, not a month ago I dropped a coyote at 40 yards with one barrel. And I'll drop the lot of you if any tries to lay a hand on Paul…"

Suspended between their rage and mine, violence set to break out like on that long ago night after the circus, when we heard Hiram's tractor charging down the lane at full throttle, belching black smoke. Ike crouched at his side gripping the seat and fender — must have found his father in the field, the corn lister still hitched when Hiram wheeled in and jerked the clutch to kill the engine. They hopped down and Hiram shoved a path through the crowd. None tried to stop him. A stout six-footer, he'd played early football at the turn of the century and several there had suffered his bruising.

Hiram stepped up beside me and guided Ike front and center.

"This stops right here and now," he commanded, his voice rumbling with anger. His commonly genial face, stern and rough as his whiskers, only shaved for Sunday church or social visits. "You men should be ashamed, crowding a woman like hounds out for blood. You listen good," he said, "and I mean you, Merle Chambers. It's your son as caused this. He cut my boy's arm today." Then he turned to Ike and said, "Go ahead 'n show 'em, son…"

Ike pulled up his sleeve and revealed a fresh bandage of gauze and tape, blood still oozing through, then spoke in a mix of anger, hurt, and fear. "Freddy, he did it…slashed his knife when I tried to help Paul. They meant to castrate him. Then they knocked me down and they…but Paul saved me…"

As Ike's voice broke Hiram gripped his shoulder and said, "That's enough, son. Good job." Then he scanned his eyes to Merle and the others like a judge weighing the facts and declared, "I think it's time for you men to go."

"The hell I will!" Merle, stomped the ground, determined to salvage his pride. "That damn idiot don't belong in our school among our kids. If he don't go, I go to the judge 'n get him gone!"

"Merle's right, he don't belong…"

"And I got a daughter, they comin' to that age…"

"Breaks a boy's arm, what'll he do a girl…?"

"NO!" I cried and raised the barrel to silence them. Holding steady as sweat wet my brow and trigger finger, I lowered my voice but not the barrel and said, "Paul will harm no one, neither boy nor girl. From this day on, you have my word, he will not return to your school. But my aim is as good as my word. And if anyone comes and tries to harm him, or take him away, I will shoot them dead, I promise…"

Amid some grumbling, they shuffled back to their cars and headed out. Only then did I lower the barrel, my hands shaking so badly from the weight of the gun and tension I feared to lower the hammers. Hiram quietly took it from me, eased the hammers down and set it back in the kitchen.

Much relieved, I thanked him for coming. Thanked them both for their help.

"You were very brave," I said to Ike, "to stand up there and face them."

"Aw, I just told the truth, Mrs. Ross. But Paul, he's the bravest boy ever…"

While they went to start the tractor and return to the field, I went to the cellar to retrieve Paul. As I raised the door and laid it open, I didn't hear a peep. Descending the steps, I noticed the faint glow of the lantern and expected to find Paul curled up in the corner, trembling in fear. But he sat cross-legged, utterly content and unaware of my entrance until he glanced up startled, caught slurping from an open jar of peaches — the one fruit strictly rationed as the trees only produced every 2 to 3 years.

He licked his lips and sheepishly answered, "Genie said I could."

"Oh he did, did he…?" I tried not to smile but found that quite clever.

"Yes'um. I sat here by the lantern…like you told me. Saw the peaches 'n wished I could eat some. Then Genie come up all around me 'n said I could. Can I, Gram?"

After all he'd been through, I could hardly deny him.

"Sure you may. But only this once without asking."

He nodded, raising the jar, eager to finger another slice to his mouth.

"And Genie has granted you another wish," I added as he paused in wonder. "Yes, something you've wished for many times, Paul. You never have to go to school again."

A big smile lit his face as he stood nearly floating to his feet.

"Now watch your head," I cautioned, leading him out. And he rose from that cellar like a boy reborn. Like all the trouble in his world had vanished in a day.

Two days later school let out and Ike rushed over bearing a gift for Paul — a little black and brown Shephard-Collie pup with white paws and a curly tail. "On my way home," he said, handing it to Paul, "Darlene Sattler showed me their new litter and gave me first pick. I chose the frisky one."

The puppy just weaned that morning licked Paul's face as he grinned, "Frisky, Frisky…" amid the kisses and asked, "Can I name him that?"

"Sure you can," Ike answered, "he's yours." Then he tagged Paul's arm and said, "Let's go show the Watcher…"

They were off, soon topping the hill to the old Indian's grave. They stood in sharp contrast — Paul twice as large with dark hair, Ike slight and wiry, his hair wispy blonde in the sun and wind. And while they shared a golden summer in jaunts to the pasture and creek, they were reaching that age when they and their world changes. At summer's end Ike returned to school and Paul remained behind. Many times that fall he gazed toward the school, no doubt missing his friend. At least he had Frisky, boon companion at his side through every chore and herding cows. More and more, old Buck, his hindquarters crippled, lay by the house.

XXXIV. Rising Storms

The Depression deepened despite claims from Washington that the "Crash" was merely a dip. The market bounced but did not rebound. Business stalled, banks failed, and farms foreclosed. Grains prices fell till it hardly paid to harvest, though corn made fair stove fuel and fed Hiram's hogs which kept us in bacon, hams, and roasts. Grateful for our plenty shared at Thanksgiving and Christmas while many faced dearth.

Shortly into the New Year, 1931, I received a letter from Hannah after a lapse of three years, having recently written expressing my concern for her and JB given the state of things. She answered promptly and assured me everything was fine — in fact movies were booming with the advent of talkies. She further explained that JB worked mostly in Westerns with Tom Mix and others. "I'm still in costuming," she said, "but jump at any extra role that comes, usually a dancehall girl or the like, and always in the background. However, we both appear in *The Big Trail* with the new star John Wayne, an extra good movie that I'm proud to be part of. And no worry, I'm fully clothed this time in frontier dress and bonnet. You can't even see my face or figure, just one of many pioneer women bustling about in an early scene, packing provisions in a covered wagon, preparing for the hard journey west…"

Before signing off, she added a cheery note on their horses, garden, and orchard and wished me good health. Never mentioned Glen's passing nor asked of Paul. Perhaps for the best as it likely pained her to think of them. I was simply relieved to know she was happy with her man and working in the movies. Even happy to be an extra.

Folding the letter away, I looked out the window on the wintry land and supposed we were all extras in this life, like Paul and I on the Limestone, moving through our days unseen except perchance by the Watcher and those of the wind, grass, and dust.

The following summer we did see The Big Trail, and no, I could not spy Hannah among the many, but thoroughly enjoyed the movie, only wishing mother, father, and Glen could see it for they had lived the story. But I took Paul and Ike as well though he only joined us that once, busy playing baseball with the Limestone Boys, shortstop and lead-off batter. And Freddy's arm had healed well enough to make him their star pitcher. We attended several games. Paul stood back confused by the odd flux and flow, the boys now standing, now running, but thrilled each time Ike cracked a hit. They still worked together at hay and harvest time and met up most Sundays for dinner, but their friendship, while never stained, grew more distant.

<hr>

Hard times continued through '31 and '32. We seldom hit town except to trade our milk and eggs for coffee, flour, salt and pepper, and a chocolate bar for Paul. Our needs were few, mostly sufficient unto ourselves, but millions of men had been thrown out of work and we'd see them riding the rails or hitching along the road, haggard and hungry. In the cities "Hoovervilles" sprang up, mere shanties roofed with tarpaper and tin where entire families lived without proper water or latrines, their children half-naked, begging for food. Charity and relief agencies could not keep pace and the general unrest sparked concern of a violent revolution, like happened in Russia. Even William Allen White who once roundly denounced populism had changed his tune and proclaimed Russia "The most interesting place on the planet…" While Will Rogers joked, "Them Red rascals along with their cuckoo stuff have some mighty good ideas. Just think of everybody in a country going to work…" And Huey Long, the firebrand Governor of Louisiana, further stirred the pot, calling for "A chicken in every pot!" But Hoover stoutly maintained, "We have passed the worst," and kept promising prosperity "just around the corner…"

That summer thousands of veterans from the Great War formed the Bonus Army and marched on Washington to demand their bonus money — not legally due them until 1945, but due them nonetheless. Hoover stubbornly refused, denied them a hearing and would not budge. Nor would they yield. They camped in peaceful protest and waited. As public sympathy soared, Hoover angrily ordered them removed. In late July, on his high horse, General MacArthur led cavalry and tanks into the camps and forced hundreds to flee, burning and trampling their tents, leaving a baby and two veterans dead in their wake. I could only think of Danny — was this what he died for? And I never cared a spit for Hoover or MacArthur thereafter.

More and more I and others turned our ears to the hopeful message of Franklin Delano Roosevelt, Governor of New York, now heading the Democratic ticket. His jaunty manner and frankness won the favor of many. Affable and optimistic like his theme song "Happy Days Are Here Again," wore a crumpled hat and a perpetual smile, held his head high, neither humble nor grand eloquent, spoke plainly and directly of challenges ahead. Offered a "New Deal" for the "Forgotten Man," vowed to serve the many, not the privileged few, said he'd try and do, and if that failed, he'd try and do again. Which gave people hope, and Roosevelt won in a landslide — the largest popular vote ever.

That Christmas Santa gifted Paul and I a brand-new RCA Cathedral Radio, a fairly pricey item that a majority of folks found the means to acquire. Used sparingly in our case due to the cost of batteries. And once the novelty wore off, Paul preferred to crank the old Edison, playing his current favorite "Whistler and His Dog" over and over to the point of annoyance, claiming, "It needs no battery, Gram." True, but in my isolation the radio brought the pleasure of another adult voice, an occasional story, and fresh music. Plus I liked to catch the weather report and tidings of current events. So when Roosevelt gave his brief Inaugural Address in March of '33 and said, "The only thing we have to fear is fear itself," I took heart. For he promised to act.

Over the next 90 days listening in on his radio chats, I heard echoes of Hagan's old populist ideals coming to the fore. Some proved out while many would fail, the country so vast, the needs so varied, bound to have mixed result. Like the CCC, the Conservation Corps that put an army of desperate men to work building dams, ponds, and terraces, and planting trees near and yon. A fine thing, laudable, but they also planted trees in regions west where they were never meant to grow. The saplings dried up and blew away with the land itself. While Roosevelt touted his Rural Resettlement program in '33 and '34, severe drought scorched southern and plains states, sparking a further exodus of farmers to the California and Oregon coasts.

Looking on, listening in, I shook my head at thought of rural resettlement, perhaps in some quaint green vale, but not on the Limestone. Late that fall a pleasant young man drove in towing a big CAT dozer on a trailer and offered to rebuild father's pond.

"A water conservation deal," he said, "won't cost you one shiny dime."

I thanked him kindly and said, "It's held this long, believe I'll leave it be."

"That might be best," he admitted, "with so little rain, most new ponds just stand there dry…" He smiled politely, bid me "Good day," eased his rig around and drove out.

For the past two summers, due to drought, Hiram had grazed his Herefords with my Shorthorns. We kept our bulls penned and made do, sharing the meager grass and water.

The next spring, wanting, waiting rain, we watched as the red dust rose up from the Texas-Oklahoma Panhandle. Then that devil sky rolled in darkening the day, fouling the air so that Paul and I pressed damp washcloths to our mouths and escaped to the cellar till those horrid winds passed. Frightful, like Last Judgement, all of us damned, and spooked the horses and mules like they'd seen a ghost. But in a day or two the sky cleared and we cleaned up the mess. Many folks prayed for rain, couldn't blame them, but may as well spit in the dust for all the good it did. Rain seldom came and the drought lingered on till by '36 nearly one in every three farmers hereabout had loaded up and moved on. Often overnight, simply leaving land, house, barn, and stock abandoned.

Always welcome when the sun breaks through and the dark clouds pass. The skin warms; the heart gladdens. Yet we saw less and less of Ike, busy attending Mankato High School by then. A stellar student, president of their FFA, and a good athlete — in fact he set the school record in the mile that spring. Certainly no Glen Cunningham, but he trained hard and in his coming senior year hoped to compete in the state meet. When school let out we did see him most days, running the roads morning and evening. He'd dash up our lane and splash his face at the cistern. One day he paused briefly and said, "Wish we had you at school, Paul. You'd be champ at shot-put!" Paul had no idea what "shot-put" meant and no desire to find out. Just smiled vaguely and waved as Ike raced on. Like the Pony Express, nothing seemed to slow him, not heat, wind, or dust, had his heart set on next year's state meet, then to the University, definitely headed places.

That summer Republican's nominated Kansas Governor Alf Landon to run against Roosevelt. Not a bad man, Landon, nor a bad governor, but advocated return to the same sorry path that led us over the cliff in '29 — a free market and tax cuts championed by the wealthy few to undo what good had been done. If Huey Long had headed a 3rd party and not been shot dead in '35, the election may have proved close. As it was, Landon lost by an even greater margin than Hoover, carrying only Maine and Vermont.

No denying things had improved. Corn, having fallen to 10 cents a bushel in '32, bought 70 cents a bushel. Banks reopened, trust renewed by the FDIC insuring deposits. Work and relief programs were up and functioning — the WPA alone employed several million men on hundreds of projects in every state, including our new stone bridge over Limestone Creek. They'd even repealed Prohibition in late '33, though too late for Glen and other victims of poison liquor. Not much had changed in Kansas, still mostly dry. In '34 a bootlegger was found murdered just east of Ionia. Late that fall a young man went missing in Elim, Miss Ryder's hometown, his body found a few days later at the bottom of a well. Again foul play was suspected, another murder unsolved.

Law and politics seldom play to our druthers. It had taken nearly 4 years to get the veterans their bonus. The bill not passed till January of '36. Even then Roosevelt vetoed out of concern for the budget, which I thought a dirty shame. But his veto was promptly overridden and he did not fight it. No, I did not always sing his praises. Still, seeing him re-elected eased my doubts, and shortly after Christmas I took the strongbox from the cellar, drove across our new bridge and deposited the Briar-Callaway savings in Marion's bank in Mankato. A tidy sum of slightly over $5000.

Finishing up the paperwork, Marion arched his brow and said, "Think I saw Hannah in a recent Western."

"Uh-huh," I noted. "Wasn't the little chorus girl dancing beyond the bar?"

"The very one!" he snapped his finger and grinned. "And she still has her figure!"

That she did, flashing her thighs and dressed like Betty Boop, a popular cartoon character, though Paul's favorite was Popeye. We caught a movie now and then on Sunday evenings, preferring that time for the smaller, older audience, most kids kept home for school Monday. The previous winter, leaving a Saturday matinee, a rude boy had shouted, "Lookit that big oaf! Looks just like Bruno!" He and his buddies laughed and ran while Paul stood hurt and ashamed, like he was back in school with no one to defend him, Ike having run his senior race, long gone to the University. Futile to seek their parents or protest, we chose to avoid them. To others an oaf, but to me Paul was simply large, having reached his full height of 6'7 and weighed 270. And truly not bad looking, many girls glanced his way as their mothers hurried them on. Paul held shy, seemingly innocent, perhaps that part of him blunted, damaged at birth. In any case I guarded him closely, like an old duenna, for they now routinely sterilized, or cut, those such as he deemed defective, insane, or otherwise unfit.

Notions of purifying the race, common enough in America since the turn of the century, had grown to a plague in Europe. Hitler clenched his fists and screamed in fury, vowing to rid Germany of gypsies, cripples, idiots, and Jews, along with others unwilling to march in step with the frenzied throngs that raised their arms at staged rallies to hail him Fuhrer. A storm of rage and hate set to engulf the world as if evil snaked to the heart of man choking any goodness. In Asia the Japanese raped Nanking, seized Manchuria and turned the red eye of the Rising Sun towards Indochina. After a bloody civil war in Spain, cities bombed and burned by German planes, Franco ruled with an iron fist. As did Mussolini from Italy to Ethiopia, while Hitler continued massing a vast army to threaten his neighbors and expand his borders.

Much of this I witnessed in newsreels until it often seemed best to skip the movies, leave the radio silent and keep Paul safe on the Limestone.

❖

During the hot summer of '39, Reb, the last of father's old mules, named for his gray coat, died, having seen 35 years, half the lifespan of a man. Finally put to pasture. Hiram chained his hindquarters to the tractor and dragged him beyond the south gulley to join the dust of others from bygone times, signaling something, I suppose...*our hallowed past, etched in trial and struggle, oft fondly savored.* This jotted in my journal, for I had not lost my love of words, nor of reading, though both lapsed at times. On a recent trip to Mankato, Ian asked me to write a monthly column titled "News from the Limestone" — just observations on the crops and weather, a coming card party, a wedding or funeral, or even an old mule's passing. In lieu of pay, I gladly accepted complimentary issues of *The Saturday Evening Post, Harper's, Atlantic Monthly, National Geographic* and others, so I kept abreast of things.

And I took great pleasure in novels; my spectacles perched to my nose most evenings. Read everything by Dickens and Twain, Willa Cather's prairie stories, and Margaret Mitchel's *Gone with the Wind,* as well as the current best-seller, *Grapes of Wrath,* by John Steinbeck — a story that caused quite a stir among the well-healed, their injustices exposed in the dire plight of the Joads and other poor migrants fleeing the Dust Bowl for California. I often read aloud to Paul, passages and stories he might enjoy such as *The Red Pony,* whereas *Of Mice and Men* was voiced solely to myself. Lately, I'd discovered the stories of Katherine Anne Porter, loved her tales from "Maria Conception" and "Virgin Violeta" to her recent novella, *Pale Horse, Pale Rider.* Like Hannah, Porter had nearly died of influenza — another comely, ambitious country girl who had ventured into the wider world. While Madalene and myself made it only to Mankato. I widowed early then re-wed. She the devoted wife of Dr. Sudlow, and now lay beside him in the Mankato Protestant cemetery. Her death also noted in my column. For her sake, I hope she loved him at least a little.

On September 1st, Germany invaded Poland, and two days later England and France declared war. The full news hit us on Labor Day. Although expected, more dreadful to hear it named. Borne home in headlines, over the radio, and again at the movies where many sought escape, war footage filled the screen. By early 1940 Poland lay gutted by Germany and the Soviets who'd joined in the slaughter. Both licked their paws as snow fell quiet as death. Many hoped that the winter lull boded an end to the war. But in May Germany blitzed France and forced the British evacuation at Dunkirk. In mid-June Paul and I seated in the Ute Theater witnessed a newsreel of desperate men boarding vessels of every make and kind to cross the Channel while Nazi planes strafed and bombed the beaches.

Tense, breathless, relieved once the movie played, swept up in the action and color of *Gone with the Wind* — of dubious history like *Birth of a Nation*, but a splendid cast and wonderful story, immense, dramatic, and thrilling. I admit, the lead man, Gable, minus his big ears and thin mustache, reminded me of Hagan, same forceful manner and built. But Maxie remained a whole other animal, tough, bullish, yet kind, and I never saw his like presented. Carried his memory home with me, wrapped my arms around his pillow and tried to forget about the war.

A week or so later we saw Ike, briefly home to help with harvest, bright and smiling, soon back to Lawrence and University. His promising future clouded by war. For at the very moment they finished threshing, the Battle of Britain raged over the skies of London where a handful of valiant young pilots in Hurricanes and Spitfires fought off the powerful Luftwaffe. Ruth expressed their concern that the war would snatch him up. I could only press her hand in mine and say, "Let us hope not…"

Few Americans wanted war and fewer still wanted Hitler and Tojo to succeed. But there were others, among them American Firsters like Lindberg, Hearst, and Henry Ford, who preferred to look away, remain staunchly neutral if not sympathetic to Fascist views, urging partnership, peace, and profit — particularly Ford who held more in common with his counterpart Krupp than with his own union workers. Amid the swirl of question and debate Hollywood released the movie *Grapes of Wrath* — a gritty portrayal of common struggles told in stark black and white that filled theaters through summer into fall.

Not surprising, perhaps, that Republicans choose a most unlikely candidate to deny Roosevelt a third term. Wendell Willkie, an up-by-the-bootstrap Indiana farm boy who became a prominent New York lawyer and business man and who had never run for nor held office. And until recently, a life-long Democrat, yet emerged from the shadows to capture the nomination. Certainly not the choice of American Firsters, for he supported aid to England and the peacetime draft, and actually favored the New Deal, in part, only decrying the waste and failure of certain ill-conceived programs. A well-informed man, articulate and altogether admirable, if you ignored rumors of his womanizing, though the same was whispered of Roosevelt. Not especially handsome, Willkie, but had a strong manly face and a shock of dark wavy hair and apart from his age looked much like Paul, which caught my eye but did not win my vote.

While Willkie fared better that Hoover and Landon, the election was never close, and Roosevelt secured a third term. Willkie immediately pledged his support and helped sway the public to speed aid to England — and Americans answered the call of the island nation, besieged but holding strong, inspired by Churchill's fervent vow "to fight them on the beaches, the landing grounds, fields, streets, and hills…and never surrender!"

Blocked by that stubborn will, over the coming winter Hitler changed plans, turned about and attacked east in June of '41 with over a million troops and thousands of tanks, rapidly rolling up Soviet forces in a lightning invasion code-named Barbarossa, one devil to another dealing Stalin his due. A funny world, in short order we made a pact with the lesser devil, soon supplying the Soviets along with England, known as the Lend-Lease Act which put the whole country back to work. Factories ramped up, churning out war material night and day, week after week, month after month.

At last farm prices reached parity and long disgusted with Henry Ford's Fascist leanings, I got rid of our Fords and bought a 1935 Dodge half-ton pickup. Powered by a 6-cylinder engine, it suited our needs quite handily, and Hiram often borrowed it to haul grain or hogs. Likewise, Hiram shucked his Ford tractor for a newer Farmall, going from a one-bottom to a two-bottom plow. So politics extended even to our machines.

Earlier that year in his Third Inaugural Address, Roosevelt had offered the Four Freedoms — freedom of religion, freedom of speech, freedom from want, and freedom from war. Succinct and laudable goals, but there would be no freedom from war.

On Sunday, December 7th, the Japanese bombed Pearl Harbor, as Roosevelt grimly proclaimed, "A day that will live in infamy..." Congress convened and declared war on Japan and Germany. Overnight millions of young men, women too, flooded Post Offices and recruiting stations, clamoring to sign-up. Ike, soon home for Christmas, promised his parents he'd wait till he finished his studies and graduated in May, granting their anxious hearts a brief reprieve.

Meanwhile the country braced and mobilized, massive, awkward, chaotic, yet amazingly rapid and determined. Spirits buoyed by Doolittle's daring raid over Tokyo in April, serving proof we could strike back — as did our two naval victories, at Coral Sea in May, and the Battle of Midway in June. By then, instead of law school as once planned, Ike had entered Marine Corp officer training at Quantico, Virginia. Commissioned a 2nd Lieutenant at summer's end, he took further training at Camp Lejeune. After which he received orders for Camp Elliot in San Diego.

Crossing the country by train, he paid a brief visit home. At the depot, stepping down to greet his mother and father, Paul and I there as well, he wore his new dress-blue uniform funded by Hiram's sell of three spring calves. What a handsome sight, slim and tailored in the black-blue jacket belted at chest and waist, light blue trousers with blood stripes down the side, and the white dress hat that featured the eagle, globe, and anchor emblem. And his blonde hair so closely cropped when he removed his hat to kiss his mother's cheek, you could hardly tell that it had thinned. Impressive, standing straight and strong like I remembered Danny…then cast the thought aside to savor the moment. He and his parents so proud, and rightly so.

A tight schedule, he could only stay one day. They rushed him home and asked us to share the evening meal. Paul barely touched his food, eyes fixed on Ike, listening as he told of his training, the amusing pranks of his buddies and of adventures to come. All the while Paul sat silent, spellbound like a little boy, envious of the uniform and the grand excitement and rush to war.

When we stood to leave, he looked to Ike and asked, "Can I come too? Can I…?"

Ike kindly laid his hands on the shoulders of his giant boyhood friend and said, "Sorry, big fellow. But you're needed here, on the home front, to soldier on the farm, to help Dad in the fields and with the cattle and hogs. Napoleon, the greatest general of all, said an army moves on its belly. We need food. Corn harvest coming up, you're the best cornhusker ever, right? So promise me you'll stay here on the Limestone with Dad and your Gram and be a good food soldier…"

XXXV. Home Soldiers

"**G**oing to pluck a chicken…for your Christmas dinner?"

"No Gram. Don't wanna kill no chicken. Don't want nothin' to die today…"

He leans down and shoves a split log in the stove, stokes the fire then latches the door and stands staring off. She notices the package of hamburger laid out to thaw, the last of last year's butchering, the blood-melt pooling on the counter. Then looks to her last letter yet to read and understands his reluctance. But feels she must for some reason recall that knowing, if granted time and strength, read the words there present and made known again before she releases self and knowing.

In no hurry, she'll wait awhile yet. And waiting, she asks, "Do you remember that little fellow? His name was Marv…no, Monty, I think."

Paul slowly turns to her and smiles, "Monty was my other friend. Monty 'n Ike…"

———— •❦• ————

Hannah wrote that she and JB both served part-time in Civil Defense, Ground Observer Corp. They and others took turns manning a nearby tower to spot for enemy planes and boats along the shore. Though after Coral Sea and Midway they sensed little threat — "Rattlesnakes," she said, "are the main worry. But we pack pistols loaded with birdshot which ends their rattle right quick…" Seldom a letter, yet always a treat to hear from her and know she was safe.

But elsewhere through '42 and '43 the war raged in a serious way. Every week brought more casualties in new battles with strange names, from Casablanca and Tobruk to El Alamein as the Allies, mostly the British, drove Rommel from North Africa and across the Middles East. Then our American boys landed in full force to take Sicily and lead the thrust up through Italy in a long series of battles that lasted for months, costing thousands of lives. While half a world away in the Pacific our Navy and Marines quickly cleared the Aleutians of the enemy, but the far-flung island campaign proved a different story, requiring bloody beach assaults against the entrenched Japanese who often as not fought to the last man.

Ike and the 2nd Marines initially deployed to New Zealand. Trained through the winter then shipped to Guadalcanal, primed and ready for the Solomon Island campaign set to launch. His letters invariably cheerful but spare of detail which we mostly gleaned after the fact from newspapers and over the radio. November brought word of heavy American actions in the Gilbert and Marshall Islands, the 2nd and 3rd Marines both engaged in the brutal battles for Tarawa and Bougainville.

No wild guess that Ike was involved, and Hiram and Ruth, no letter in two months, naturally shared their concern. Hearing which, Paul grew anxious, gripped his hands and said, "Ike needs me. They might hurt him. I can fight…" Again, Hiram reminded him of what Ike had said, "You're needed here, Paul. We're smack in the middle of corn harvest 'n you're the best shucker in the valley…"

Calmed for the moment, Paul turned to the task at hand and soon had Hiram's and our field picked clean. Then they hired out to others, Hiram driving tractor and wagon, Paul shucking tirelessly alongside, tossing two ears to other men's one. And Hiram made certain they paid him top dollar, clearing over $60 the first week. Paul proudly showed me his earnings — "Three Jeffersons, one Lincoln, and two Washingtons…" Counted his paper money by the faces and his coin by "Big silver, little silver, and copper…" always stumped by how one thin dime equaled two fat nickels. Finished counting, he folded his money in his leather wallet and tucked it safe in his bib pocket. Pleased with himself as he stood to make as much or more over the next two weeks — farmers desperate with the harvest running late due to bad weather.

A cold mist falling by noon that Friday, I fully expected them home early. Still, I was surprised to see Hiram coming down the lane in road gear, minus Paul, and shaking his head as he idled to a stop.

"Feelin' awful bad, Sadie," he said, stepping down. "I should've known but —"

"What happened?"

"Paul, he's gone off, God knows where. We was workin' Jim Elway's field there along the state road east of Ionia. Paul been eyein' those trucks passing by all morning, ya know how they cut down 'tween Highway 36 to 24. Well, we just finished that field 'n rain comin' on, Jim didn't wanna chance wet corn in his crib to rot 'n spoil. Made sense to me, I took the wagon to next field on over the hill 'n unhitched there for an early start once things dry up. Paul, he fawns on that ol' bitch dog of theirs about to pup, said he'd just stand by 'n pet Sally. So I drove on. Wasn't gone but 5 or 10 minutes. Headin' back down the hill saw nothin' but ol' Sally gazing off. Figured Paul had ducked into a cornrow to take a leak. Waited a minute 'n called a couple times. No answer. Then Jim stepped out 'n hollered, 'Why, he was there a minute ago. Must've moseyed on towards the road…' And I bet that's what he did. Hitched a ride off some trucker headed north or south. I'm sorry, Sadie, sorry as all heck."

"Not your fault, Hiram. But will you do me favor?" I asked before fetching my coat and keys. "While I check in Mankato, will you drive down to Cibola? I don't know that town. But please don't call the Sheriff."

"I understand…" he answered, mounting his tractor to head for his car.

He knew my fear that Paul would land in court and wind up committed. Facing my 74th year, if he got in trouble they'd likely take custody, claiming I could not control him. With that in mind I sped north to Mankato. First talked to Ian, then to Clyde, neither had seen him but promised to keep an eye out and corral him if they did. My head spinning in panic, I rushed on, wondering where, where? Even stopped briefly at the Ute Theater, *Casablanca* showing that evening and didn't care to see another movie or newsreel again, in good part the cause of Paul running off, sowing vainglory and war fever to our mutual idiocy and ruin. With such thoughts I drove in circles and slowly searched the streets. No sign of Paul.

Approaching sundown, I drove home and milked the cows. Didn't fix a meal, just sat and listened to the thrum of my heart and the ticking clock. Hiram called along past 8, said he checked the bus stop, train station, and drove the main streets. Knew Paul had money and was bound to be hungry, he also checked cafes, groceries, and pools halls.

"Never mentioned his name, Sadie," he assured me, "or say why, just asked if any of them had seen an extra big fella that day. Expect a few knew who I meant but they all shook their heads no. Thing is…there's that big recruitin' center down in Salina. Some trucker may have driven straight through 'n dropped him there…" He paused and again apologized, "I'm so sorry, Sadie. Wish I knew more…"

I thanked him for trying and hung up. So sick with worry and fear for Paul, I laid awake all night, could not sleep. Next morning, sun not yet up, I rang our local operator and asked to put me through to the Army recruiter in Salina. Only 6 o'clock, she doubted they'd be in, but at my urging she rang for several minutes and could not rouse a soul.

I thanked her and went to morning chores, gathered the eggs, fed and milked the cows. Fixed a pot of coffee then sat and waited till 9 o'clock. This time my call went through, answered by a Sergeant Campbell.

"Yes mam," he said when I asked if he'd seen a huge young man dressed in blue overalls and red plaid shirt. "Was waiting outside when we arrived, I and Chief Nelson, our Navy recruiter. He followed us in and I asked him his name and business. Said his name was Paul Ross and he wanted to join and fight. Said he needed to help his friend, Ike. And he looked and sounded most earnest."

"Hope you didn't sign him up, he's my grandson," I pleaded," damaged at birth. He does not belong in the Army."

"No mam, I gathered as much. Asked him to write his name, he gripped the pencil in his big hand, leaned down, struggled a bit, but did manage to scrawl it out. Had the 'R' reversed. Then I handed him the induction form and asked him to read the top line. He held it close and mumbled 'the' a couple times then laid it down and said that Ike did most of his reading."

"Yes, they grew up together," I explained. "Ike's in the Marines, fighting in the Pacific. Paul sees newsreels and hears his parents worry and wants to join up and help fight. But please, you must not let him."

"Yes man, I understand. Though sad to say there are some who would. No, I just focused on those big rough hands of his all scratched and calloused and said, 'Looks like you've been at some hard work?' He nodded and said, 'I help Hiram, we shuck corn. I'm strong...' And I answered, 'I don't doubt you are. So why don't you go home and help Hiram. Bet he'll be glad to see you.' At that he kind of angered and said, 'Ike needs me, I can fight...' And he sure looked like it, his face red, shoulders tensed, those big hands flexing to grab hold of something...or someone. Chief Nelson started to rise from his chair. I told him to stay put. The Chief 'n I are pretty stout fellas, but your grandson, big as he is, at full rage, doubt we could handle him. I just thanked him for coming in and calmly suggested he go back home. Not at all happy, I could tell, but he said nothing more, turned about and left."

"Did you see where he went?" I asked.

"Yes mam, he crossed the street to the Greyhound Station, circled a couple buses loading up. They pulled out about a half hour ago. He may have boarded one."

"Any idea where they might be going?"

"Well mam, this time of day, either east to Kansas City or south to Wichita. And I'm truly sorry, mam, but I got recruits lining up here. Hope you find your grandson..."

My hope fading, I thanked him for his bother and hung up the receiver. Stood a moment wondering where Paul was and where he might be headed. Knew I'd have no luck chasing him down, and to call the State Patrol risked losing him forever.

Around noon, the sun out, a mild breeze from the west, Hiram drove in, curious of any news. When I told him what I'd learned, he grimaced and said, "Sadie, I know you don't want to. But might be you should notify the State Patrol."

"I know..." I answered vaguely. "I'll give it till tomorrow and hope he shows up."

"That would be a blessing," he said, looking off and away, "to have at least one of our boys home..."

Hiram drove on while I returned to the house. Sat all afternoon clutching my arms in my rocker, silently thinking, "There was an old woman in a lonely room, she lost her boy and stared in gloom…" Saw my whole life just spilt milk. And I didn't get to the milking till late that day, our three bossies waiting in their stalls rightly complained as I appeared with the lantern and relieved their swollen udders.

Exhausted, that night I slept soundly, woke refreshed, mind free of trouble until I remembered Paul gone and wished I hadn't wakened. But at the next rooster crow I got up and dressed. Tied back my hair and washed my face, brushed with salt and soda then rinsed my mouth. Still had most of my teeth, lucky for my age, but would have traded them to have my boy back home. Wondered how I'd live if he stayed lost. To calm my thoughts I went to chore, and it helped, the company of cows and hens. But Frisk shied from my hand and sniffed the air in want of Paul, like I had somehow failed them.

Back at the house I ate a slice of bread with a glass of milk which helped settle my stomach. Then I fed the stove a chunk of wood and turned on the radio to catch the 9:30 weather report. They predicted another good drying day, saying, "It should put most of our farmers back in the fields by tomorrow or Tuesday…" — a Nebraska station, lots of corn up their way as well. After the weather I turned it off to avoid the war news. Early December and no snow as yet, I sat listening to the wind whistle through the bare limbs, a lonely sound. Presently a male Cardinal fluttered to the window sill, perched briefly then flew on. A brilliant mote of life, perfectly plumed, it made me smile.

Next instant Frisk let out a husky howl at a car's approach. A smooth, quiet engine, definitely not Hiram or Ruth, their muffler shot and no replacements due to war shortage. Curious, I went to the window and spied a dusty blue Ford coup pulling to a stop; a little man in a derby hat at the wheel, dwarfed by a huge passenger. I rushed out as the driver hopped down from the running board. And I saw he was a dwarf.

He stepped up, extended his stubby arm and said, "How do, I'm Monty Flynn. You must be Paul's Gram?"

"Yes," I answered, shaking his hand, "I'm Sadie Ross, pleased to meet you."

"Whelp, I brung 'im home," he nodded toward Paul emerging from the far side. "Him 'n me had us some night, didn't we big guy…?"

Paul stood waiting, still hadn't rounded the car, wary lest I scold him. But he brightened to my smile as I said, "Welcome home, Paul," then asked, "Why don't we invite Mr. Flynn in and share some of that apple pie left untouched since Friday night? That is if he doesn't mind?"

"Apple pie, you say?" Mr. Flynn rubbed his hands in delight. "Give me that 'n coffee, I'm pleased as punch…" He strutted on in the house alongside Paul, a regular little bantam, hat cocked, chin up. He doffed his hat and hopped to a chair as I served each a slice of pie and poured them coffee. Mr. Flynn fisted his fork and dug right in, took a slurp of coffee, smacked his lips and began spinning his tale.

"We met up late yesterday, right Paul?" he waved his fork to stab another bite and continued, "Just finished my shift, work there at Boeing Aircraft. Saw him out front of The Fish Net, a bar me 'n my pals hit most Fridays after work. They have dancin' girls, but we's just wantin' beer. Anyhow, I see our big guy standin' there all alone. Now I been a stranger a time or two myself 'n lots a' folks ignore my kind like we're too short to bother with. But Paul cast me a look like he needed a friend 'n I says, 'Hi-ya, big guy, how ya doin?' And he says, 'Dunno, I'm lost…' I winks to him, 'Not now you ain't, I done found ya…' He smiles at that 'n I ask his name 'n he says, 'Paul.' Then I shake his hand 'n says, 'I'm Monty. C'mon in 'n join us for a beer…'

"So we goes in 'n take a table by the door there. Enjoyin' our beer, mindin' our business, couple wiseacres at the bar start crackin' about him a giant 'n me a runt. Tried to ignore 'em till they call me a 'Pug' 'n I says somethin' back —"

"You said your pug was bigger than theirs…"

Mr. Flynn quieted a moment, swallowed his current bite and nodded, "Sorry Mrs. Ross, guess I did say some such. Then they said worse."

"Called Monty a little rat, Gram. Made me mad."

"Sure 'nuff did. His eyes darkened, he clenched his fists 'n starts up. I says, 'No, I'll handle this…' Then ventured over to offer a friendly gesture, didn't wanna cause our big guy no trouble 'n says, 'How 'bout I buy you fellas a drink?' They gawked down 'n one sneers 'n says, 'How 'bout I stomp you like a bug?' Now I pack a ball-peen work hammer hitched to my belt when I enter a bar, call it my equalizer. Swung 'n slammed his foot, broke it sure. He yipped 'n yowled 'n I spun workin' my hammer like a baton, bashin' through a forest of legs in retreat to our table. Then Paul rose up like a mountain partin' the sea 'n tosses bodies ever' which way, bustin' heads 'n noses, left the whole bunch sprawled in less'n a minute. Saved my runty arse, then we scram. Sirens blarin', we had to lay low. Went to see some workin' girls —"

"Oh?" I blinked in question, "Working girls?"

Mr. Flynn again paused, took a sip of coffee and continued unfazed:

"Just friends a' mine, Mrs. Ross. Nothin' happened. Told 'em about our big scrap 'n wild escape 'n drank more beers is all. Headin' to the wee hours, gettin' hungry, they fried us a batch of eggs 'n sausage. Sure tasted good. Then guess all that beer got our big guy a little weepy."

"I was sad, Gram. Wanted to see you."

"Yep, he wanted to see his Gram, wanted to go home. So I ask, 'Where, what town?' And he says, 'Ionia…' That rang a bell. I know this area from my circus days, hit through Cibola, Mankato 'n all around. So we gulped down our coffee 'n heads out. Girls kinda sorry to see 'im go, I think. But he insisted, so we come on. Got a dandy little '39 Ford V-8 with raised seat 'n extended pedals, custom-fit thanks to my pals in the fab-shop there at Boeing. Left Wichita right at sunrise. What's it now…" he checked his wristwatch and said, "a wee past 10. Heck, we made it in 4 hours. But I gotta scoot, my shift starts at 5 'n I ain't slept a wink…"

That's when I tried to pay him for bringing Paul home, but he wouldn't hear it.

"Nope," he said, "it's been my pleasure, your coffee 'n pie will do. We all gotta make sacrifices for the war, right big guy? Now gimme your hand…" He reached across to Paul and said, "You saved the best blame tail-gun riveter on the whole bomber fleet. Us home soldiers gonna help whup them Japs 'n Nazis like we whupped them fellas last night…" Then he hopped down, fetched his hat and waved at the door, "So long, big guy. You're 'bout the best pal ever…"

Paul and I leaned at the window and watched him spin around and tear up the lane in a trail of dust. Paul said nothing, still reluctant to look at me as I grasped his hand and said, "You had me awfully worried, Paul. But glad you're home and hope you'll stay."

He hung his head and muttered, "Won't go off no more, Gram. I promise..." Then he turned away and sat down, the mass of him collapsing in his chair. Doubt he'd slept in the two days he'd been gone, his eyes blank with fatigue, tears soon streaming down his cheeks. "Monty lied," he said, gazing to the floor. "One girl did something. She washed my thing 'n asked, 'Want to see my puppies?' I did then she took my money and Monty come 'n said, 'No, you give that back...' He gave her one Jackson 'n left the room 'n she did something to me...and I...did too..." his voice choked and he sobbed in shame.

It seemed he'd had him quite a fling thanks to Mr. Flynn. I softly patted his back and said, "That's okay, Paul. Let's get you to bed..." I led him to his room and helped him off with his boots. Then he leaned back and I covered him with a quilt. He closed his eyes and within seconds he slept. I quietly closed the door and smiled, happy to have my boy home, ever grateful to Monty Flynn.

XXXVI. Toll of War

Welcome news by Christmas, Hiram and Ruth received a letter from Ike, in good spirits having survived the battle for Bougainville, though not unscathed. Ruth shared particulars with us over Sunday dinner. He wrote: "Don't worry, just shrapnel wounds, actually bled less than that knife cut from Freddy. Shrapnel is as common on a battlefield as stickers and thorns on a Kansas creek. Nearly everyone gets a scratch or two, yet they gave me a Purple Heart. Lucky, I guess, but hardly feel deserving when others lose an arm or leg. And a good many lost their lives. Don't mean to dwell, I'm proud of my part in our victory and we need to press on. But war is a hard, ugly business and the sooner it ends the better…" Ruth paused at the sobering words and skipped to a brighter note and read: "Tell Paul, Hi! Hope he's soldiering alongside father with the crops and cattle to keep us supplied with good food…" Paul smiled to hear his named mentioned by a real soldier far away at war. While it cheered our hearts to know Ike was well, we braced for the many battles to come, turning to or from the news in hope or dread, depending.

Our big news in early '44 was pleasing and local. Jim Elway's bitch dog had weaned her pups and with Frisk growing old and lame, Hiram drove Paul over and Jim gave him first pick. He chose a little brown and white female with flop ears and feathery tail and brought her home cradled in his arms, fed her warm milk then sat cuddling her to his cheek. Wanted to keep her inside that night but our grey cat Clementine, a stern housemistress, gave a scowl that did not approve.

"No," I said, "she belongs in the woodshed with Frisk. He'll keep her warm and she'll learn to guard our hens…" So he carried her out and she snuggled with Frisk on his old blanket in the straw. But first thing each morning Paul would fetch the pup to carry her in his coat pocket as he gathered eggs and milked the cows. She soon outgrew the pocket, and watching Frisk, sniffed her task and began trailing along, herding the cows right to their stalls then sat by while Paul squirted warm milk to her mouth. Spoiled that dog and named her Stella. Had my suspicions, but never asked why.

Later that winter my old friend Shannon died, peacefully in her sleep, they said. Hadn't seen her in years, still it hurt when Ian told me his sister was gone. Once such a golden girl, a hopeful flower faded, fallen to the snow. This noted in my journal.

Ever grateful to see the spring — the tender green shoots above the sullen browns, pink and white blossoms puckering to the sweet warm air. We planted our gardens and fields and carried on. So did the war.

D-Day, June 6th, '44, left thousands of our boys dead on the beaches at Normandy. Paid a heavy price to secure a foothold but opened the Western Front, marking a turning point, though far from the end. And our attention shifted to the Pacific, to the Marines engaged in battle on the Island of Guam. All through July into August, Hiram and Ruth waited word. Finally, a week before Labor Day, they received a letter. This time Ike came through with barely a scratch — "But command took my platoon," he joked, "Your son is now a Captain in charge of a company…" Naturally, this made his parents proud, yet dreading news of the next island, the next battle, awaiting the next letter.

While the war slogged on in Europe, MacArthur made his promised return to the Philippines, wading ashore at Leyte in a photo featured in magazines and newspapers. Hailed a hero by many, but for his vile treatment of the Bonus Army in '32 I could not much credit the man, his fame borne aloft on the blood of others. Yet admit his island-hopping strategy proceeded apace.

As did the '44 presidential campaign, more weighted by rumors of Roosevelt's failing health than any question of the outcome. Republicans ran yet another New York Governor, Thomas Dewey, with the usual result. Americans, not about to trade horse in mid-stream, again voted strongly for Roosevelt and his vow to "Stay and finish the job!" — beginning to sense an end to the war, especially in Europe. But just before Christmas the Germans mounted a surprise counter-offensive, penetrating Allied lines in a lightning thrust through the Ardennes. Soon named the Battle of the Bulge, the outcome hung in balance for weeks, particularly for American troops cut off and surrounded at Bastogne. To the German demand to surrender the American Commander answered, "Nuts!" By such stubborn fight McAuliffe and his men held on and broke the siege and the German offensive ran out of gas, literally. With the Russians pounding from the East, it was only a matter of time.

Prospects in the Pacific were less sanguine, or more so, depending on how you meant the word. The Japanese having fiercely defended every island to the death, the pending invasion of Japan itself was expected to cost a million American lives. A fear written of, spoken of, and a constant heartache for Ruth and Hiram. In February of '45 the 3rd Marines stormed the beaches of Iwo Jima, the Japanese dug in and ready. From the first day the casualties were reportedly heavy and weeks of bloody fighting lay ahead. By the time the American flag raised over Mount Suribachi, American dead and wounded numbered in the thousands. Hiram and Ruth hung by the radio morning and evening and scanned the weekly casualty lists. Hoped, prayed, and waited.

March bled into April with no word of Ike, when we learned that Roosevelt had died. Not unexpected, still a shock, after so many years, his familiar voice now silent. Overnight we had a new President, Harry S. Truman, heretofore a relatively unknown man, said to be plain-spoken, direct, and honest. Also stubborn, from Missouri, once plowed behind mules and like Danny had served in the Great War along with other boys of his generation. And he took his education not from Harvard, Princeton, or Yale, but the Public Library, an uncommon, common man. I recalled Hagan saying, "Choose one of your own. One you can trust to see and speak the truth…" While no few scoffed at his rise and ability, I found much to favor and in time grew quite fond of the man.

Our attention remained riveted on the war with the Battle of Okinawa where the fight raged week after week and where Hiram and Ruth feared Ike and others had been sent as reinforcements. Then in early May they received a letter from a Navy surgeon in Honolulu, informing them that their son, Captain Holland, had been badly wounded at Iwo Jima. "Expected to live," he assured them, "but his right arm and leg were shattered by a shell blast. While we hope to save both limbs, he faces extensive surgery and a long rehabilitation…" Hiram and Ruth took heart — at least he was alive and no longer at war. Strong and athletic, surely he would recover.

A few days later Germany surrendered, or more truly collapsed in ruins. Hitler dead; reportedly shot his mistress then himself, their bodies blown up and burned. Good riddance and hallelujah…had it rid the world of evil. But what was, is, and lives on in and all around us. In June the desperate fight for Okinawa ended and American forces began massing for the invasion of Japan. Hiram and Ruth were grateful Ike would not take part, but their distress grew through July, receiving no further update or letter from their son. They could not fathom why he hadn't written. Surely he could use his left hand?

Then the dread war suddenly ended. On August 6th, the Japanese city of Hiroshima all but vanished from the face of the earth, as did Nagasaki three days later. Each gone in a tremendous blast produced by a new weapon called the Atomic Bomb. To think of an entire city, nearly every life therein, consumed in an instant, took your breath. At once a horror and a joy, for it saved a million American lives. No, I did not fault Truman for his decision. Would have wished the same on a dozen more cities had it spared my Danny. Still, I wondered what evil had been born with those two bombs. I thought of Hagan returning from the World's Fair, extolling the marvels of science and engineering and the endless promises to come. And in my mind, I saw the glorious White City he'd depicted reduced to ashes.

But Japan had surrendered and Ike was coming home.

Hiram and Ruth received the letter of notification not from the Navy surgeon but from an Army psychiatrist who said that their son had made remarkable progress and could now walk, dress, and feed himself, yet would be accompanied home by a medical orderly. Then explained that while Ike's physical condition would continue to improve, his mental state was less certain, and cautioned that they must be patient — "For…" as he clarified, "along with significant hearing loss, which impairs his balance, Ike suffers from what is commonly termed 'shell shock' or 'battle fatigue,' and consequently his mind has regressed…" Reading this to me, Ruth looked considerably bewildered, as was I, trying to conceive what a mind 'regressed' could mean. Then the doctor closed on a brighter note and suggested that "Given care, time may restore your son to his normal self…"

Gripped by that hope, Hiram and Ruth fetched their son home from the Mankato train station shortly after Labor Day. A full week passed before they invited us over, Paul excited to see his friend. When we entered the door, Ike rose from his chair and said, "Hi Mrs. Ross, hi Paul…" with the eyes and voice of Ike at age 9 or 10. And not the trim straight young man we'd sent away to war, but hunched and skeletal with faint tufts of hair like a baby bird. He stutter-stepped our way, his right side crippled, leg stiff, arm curled under, his hand frozen in a claw. He reached for Paul's hand with his left in eager greeting, "Paul, Paul, where have you been so long?"

Paul answered, "On the Limestone, waitin' for you…"

They shared a big grin while Hiram and Ruth looked on and silently wept. Their dear son returned to them in great part broken, brittle, his mind clearly regressed.

"Want to go outside?" Ike asked like when he was a boy. "Maybe find something?"

"Sure," Paul answered, lumbering after Ike hobbling out the door.

Hiram just turned away, lowered his head and went to chore. Ruth's lips began to quiver and I walked over and held her for a long, long while.

XXXVII. Uneasy Peace

A hamburger patty the size of a pancake sizzles in a large black skillet, spitting bacon grease as Paul stands by with a spatula, likes to fast fry both sides and leave pink in the middle. In the popping grease he stirs a pile of sliced potatoes and onions then pokes the hamburger. Deemed ready, he takes the hot pad and scrapes the whole lot onto an oval carving plate. Places it on the table beside a quart jar of fresh milk, likes a quart jar as it fits his hand.

Smell of cooked meat makes her dry old mouth water. Although not hungry, she savors the memory of driving her father's Shorthorn herd from the White Rock to the Limestone so many years ago, briefly sees all again, even their trail dog. She watches Paul uncover a loaf of bread she baked just yesterday. Senses her taste buds awaken as he slices a good chunk and asks, "Want some, Gram? You like bread."

"Yes, but only a pinch, please…"

He breaks off a small portion, walks over and lays it on her tongue. She rolls it in her mouth, letting it slowly mix and melt, remembering sunshine and ripe fields of wheat, golden sheathes from grain to flour, summer harvests and winter feasts, baked loaves wafting sweet as honey, and straw stubble rotting in the dark earth.

She swallows and asks for a sip of water, "Just one would be fine…"

Paul fills a cup and holds it to her lips. She takes a brief sip then smiles and closes her eyes. Folds her hands and recedes into the past…

Strangely, Ike now seemed more damaged than Paul, having lost so much, once made music, ran with the wind, and learned at a blink, his flesh and mind tattered while Paul held steady, like a guardian shadowing after his fragile friend. The one thing that held constant was Ike's curiosity, evident the day Paul greeted him home and followed him outside to find something. Mostly bugs and rocks, but also leaves and wildflowers pressed in a heavy book then glued to a page of a Big Chief tablet, common and Latin names painstakingly printed with his left hand. Likewise with insects, butterflies, and moths — chloroformed and carefully pinned to large squares of cardboard, their respective names etched in ink on white tape till he had hundreds of various types arranged in row after row neatly stacked in his room. At the foot of his bed sat a chest filled with fossils and shells chipped from rocks, and he spoke of little else except bugs, leaves, and rocks. Daily in search, delving — in fair weather he collected, in foul he sat at his desk working on displays and labels. In winter he used a magnifying glass to sketch butterfly wings, a moth's antennae, a cicada shell, the veins of a leaf, and other intricate patterns that caught his eye. To no other end or purpose, tireless in his singular endeavor, and at peace, never spoke of the war nor prior ambitions, intently focused on his boyhood fancy, as if his mind sought an eternal summer at age 10.

Ever curious and cheerful, Ike helped Ruth with lighter chores, tucked a basket in his crippled arm and gathered eggs with his left. Morning and evening he enjoyed milking with his father, often joking, "I'm only half the milker Dad is…" And by and by his parents began to smile again.

As Ruth confided one day, "It is a blessing he's alive and home…"

And in the fall of '47, following a bumper wheat crop and in prospect of a good corn harvest, Hiram blessed his aging body and traded up to a Farmall H. With rubber tires front and back and more powerful engine, he could work more ground with greater ease and less jolt. Proud of his "Row-cropper" as he called it, could shift to 5th gear and top 15 mph while roading to another field or neighbor.

Once more we settled in, our lives relatively content on the Limestone.

———••———

But post-war soon became the "Cold War." As Churchill, clear-eyed and pugnacious as ever, declared in a speech in Missouri, "An Iron Curtain has descended across Europe…" Behind which Stalin's Red Army poised ready to threaten the peace. In spring of '48 when Truman launched the Marshal Plan to rebuild Europe, the Soviets slammed a blockade on West Berlin, choking off the city. Truman promptly countered and ordered an airlift to resupply the hostage city over the coming months.

By mid-summer Truman angered his domestic foes as well by ordering complete desegregation of our Armed Forces. The Dixiecrats, already riled for his daring to honor the Coloreds and speak before the NAACP the previous year, rose up and chose a third-party candidate, the staunch segregationist, Senator Strom Thurman from South Carolina. Republicans, seeing the Democrats split, smelling blood, again ran Thomas Dewey. And Dewey, a respected moderate, campaigned with confident reserve and care, all but certain of victory. So declared by most major newspapers and over the radio the morning after the election, right up until noon when the tally tilted toward Truman and the uncommonly common man pulled off an historic upset.

This gave us a chuckle on the Limestone and helped soothe the vagaries of winter. Wet, freezing weather damaged much of the young wheat emerging in the fields. Then the air warmed, the snow melted, and our spirits lifted with the spring. And in June the Soviets lifted their blockade of Berlin, marking a minor victory but no thaw in relations. Their belligerence swiftly affirmed with an A-bomb of their own. Nor did prospects of wheat harvest improve, struck by hot winds and mosaic followed by the worst hailstorm in memory wiping out any chance of a "Miracle Crop" like the previous summer. Hiram barely harvested enough to make seed. But in farming you take the good with the bad and plow on in hope for the next year.

By October, with the ground worked, recent rains and fair skies, Hiram itched to plant a new crop. "Here I am nigh 70 years old," he grinned, "and still makes me giddy as a kid fixin' to shoot marbles…" Ike liked to ride the footboard attached behind the drill and make certain the seeds descended to the fresh-cut furrows. If a tube plugged or the trough needed filled, he'd yell up to his father.

They'd planted a full week, nearly finished, had only one field north of our place left to do. We could hear the tractor chugging beyond the trees that morning, Paul and I out in the orchard gathering the last apples, many fallen, half-rotted and wormy, but once pruned and crushed they made good cider. Paul liked to crank father's old cast-iron press and watch the juice flow from the spout. We'd just topped off a jug, hadn't heard the tractor for a spell and figured they'd shut down for lunch. Paul and I fixing to do the same when we heard a distant cry and looked up to see Ike lurching down the lane, his left arm reaching forth as if to swim the air and speed his approach.

We met him at the orchard edge, his face desperate in panic.

"They got Dad!" he gasped. "A Jap mine blew the tractor and pinned him under. Mom and I can't pull him out. Come Paul…" Ike tugged his sleeve, "come help, you're strong…can do it…"

Paul didn't linger, off running up the lane like a charging bear. Never guessed he could move so fast, he one-handed the corner post and leapt the fence, barely breaking stride and outdistanced Ike double in rush across the field. Other than Glen, Hiram was the only man Paul had truly known. Loved him like a father. I too loved Hiram and Ruth like kin, but lagged far behind. At age 80 a brisk walk was the best I could do.

Upon reaching the road I spied the tractor upended at the north end of the field, the planter twisted at a sharp angle. In summer the ditch bordering the road overflowed with purple cockle flowers, lovely to touch, but by autumn their tender cones turned to mean brown burrs that clung to my skirt and pricked my skin as I waded through, anxious to lend a hand. Then cut my hand in threading the barbed wire and trudged on across the cloddy field. In catching my breath, I saw Paul bend down by the big back tire, grip the fender then slowly rise, lifting it a good two feet as Ike and Ruth pulled Hiram free. For a moment my heart beat with hope, but walking closer I saw Ruth cradling her husband's head, his chest caved in, his eyes blank, blood pooled in his mouth. Pinned under the steering wheel, I only hoped he had died in seconds.

Ike knelt by, rocking on his knees, wailing, "Japs got him…damn Japs…" had never referred to the war until that cruel day. Paul stood in shock, gripping his hands, gazing to the ground. And given a closer look the ground told what had happened. Rising up over the terrace to make a turn, the nose wheels cocked sideways in a badger hole that Hiram likely failed to notice in reaching back for the lift-lever, and it flipped the tractor.

Presently, the sheriff and ambulance sirens sounded in the near distance, called by Ruth while Ike ran to fetch us. Ruth glanced up so stricken, having seen her son torn by war, now this. She cast a look like Job's wife cursing the Lord. And she held that look as they loaded Hiram for delivery to the funeral home. Held it through the church service and again at graveside, never once bowed her head, utterly forsaken. Nor did Ike retain his lively curiosity, from that day he bitterly mourned his father and cursed the Japs.

That month's "News from the Limestone" was the saddest column I ever wrote. I sat for the longest time, the question burning like the spines in my flesh. What can you say of a man's life in a few words or in many? Once a flower of kindness and strength, now a corpse, a burr that gnaws in your heart and memory…

Ike's cursing steadily worsened. Initially sporadic, it grew more violent and vulgar. When Paul would ask him to go outside, he'd shout, "No! Japs are out there, the dirty bastards!" Then describe mutilations and other unnatural acts he'd do them. Ruth could not restrain him nor could he console her. And neither one nor both could work the farm. With Hiram's death, something had snapped — Ruth, soul weary, in constant mourning, and Ike either silent or rabid. Paul and I went over daily to help cook and clean and tend the chores. Some days better than others, but nothing improved. Past Thanksgiving and Christmas, into the New Year, more and more tasks left neglected on their place and ours. Honestly, I didn't know how to carry on or what to do.

Then one night in mid-winter Ruth suffered a stroke. When Paul and I arrived the next morning, Ike met us at the door, more his old self and anxious for his mother. "She can't walk," he said, "or hardly speak. Her mouth's all twisted…"

Her whole left side, face, arm, leg, numb and paralyzed. With help she could stand but shook her head at trying to walk. Easing her back in her chair, she moaned, "Wha um ah goin' do?"

I gripped her hand and said, "How about I call Doc Hofner?" a respected surgeon from Elim who she'd doctored with ever since her hemorrhoid surgery following Ike's birth. She leaned her head and nodded. And Doc Hofner, not only a wealthy surgeon but the biggest landowner in the county, having acquired scores of foreclosed farms in the 30s, said he'd be right down.

Within the hour his long black Buick pulled up next to the house. I met him at the door and once inside he shortly confirmed that she'd had a stroke. "Yes, it's apoplexy," as he called it, using the old term. "And I won't lie," he said, "There's no real treatment. You may improve, you may not. One thing certain, you will need considerable care…" Then he gently urged that she consider the Sunrise Rest Home in Mankato, of which he was part owner. "They handle stroke victims better than others I've known."

"Wha uh th farm…un Ike?" she asked.

He pondered this briefly then answered, "Of Ike, I'm not certain. They may take him in. But your farm…I can and will buy, if you wish. And I'll pay a fair price, won't cheat you one dollar, Ruth. Buy lock, stock 'n barrel, land, cattle, machinery, and ease your worry. I know a young farmer eager to take on a large rental. Have your banker meet with mine and get it all drawn up and settled in a week's time. All you need do is raise your good hand and sign…"

Ruth, defeated, cornered, simply tilted her head in nod. And Doc, amiable and decisive, followed through, within a week owned the farm and had moved Ruth to the rest home in Mankato. But not Ike, he could not be calmed, saw Japs at every window, masked in every face, coming for him. In short order he was judged incompetent and sent to the Veteran's Hospital in Topeka. It pained my heart seeing Ruth and Ike gone, their place sold. Relieved on one hand, forlorn on the other, at age 81 realized I could be next. And what would become of Paul? No doubt committed, handed over to strangers, likely drugged. I thought of Ike as if taken captive, straight-jacketed in some dark cell, awaiting shock treatment, his torment total and deep.

In seeing Doc to his car the day he checked on Ruth, he asked about the BC Ranch

"Ever think of selling?"

"No," I answered and told him I wasn't interested.

"Well…" he chuckled in a rather annoying way, "if you ever change your mind, Sadie Ross, might give me a call…"

Later that spring, a land agent for the Wichita oilman stopped by. Seems he'd caught wind of the Holland place selling and wanted to add our mile of pasture to his own. He offered a fair sum for my 1000 acres. I said no dice. But time and gravity closing in, and Holly's old hands threatening to hang up their spurs and move to town, finally had to admit we could no longer manage our land and cattle. Next day I phoned Doc Hofner and said if he could match their price and leave me the 60 acres surrounding the house that included the old Indian's grave, father's prairie meadow and the swath north of the orchard to the road, I'd consider selling.

"Consider it done," he answered, did not dicker. "You've got stout fences, good water, and fair stock. I'll match their price and get a surveyor out tomorrow to step off the portion you wish to keep. Plus I'll throw in my '46 Buick, got the Dynaflow drive they call automatic. Piece of cake compared to a stick shift. Runs fine but I want the new model, the Electra, and they won't give me but $700 in trade. And it's yours…that is if you'll toss your old Dodge truck to my renter. He could put it to good use and serve us all…" — playing one card after the other, the old Doc a sly wheeler-dealer.

"Fair enough," I said. "You get that in writing and we've got a deal…"

XXXVIII. Keeping Faith

So I sold the BC Ranch in early summer of 1950. As with others, my pioneer inheritance gained by hazard, blood, and long toil passed to the hands of the wealthy few. But it had served us and I hoped the money would one day serve Paul.

I'd written to Hannah, offering to forgo a will and send her half. This time she promptly answered and graciously declined, saying she would not take money from the son she'd once abandoned. It made me proud to know she cared. She ended saying not to worry on her account, that she and JB were well set and happy. That settled, Paul and I in good health, we had few concerns beyond the garden and orchard, our milk cows and chickens. Content with our quiet life.

Then in late June the North Koreans attacked across the 38th parallel. America rushed troops from Japan to reinforce the South Koreans. Soon other countries, Britain, France, and Australia, joined in the oddly named "Police Action." The combined forces, mostly funded and manned by the U.S. and commanded by MacArthur, fought under the blue banner of the United Nations, an outgrowth of the League of Nations, hatched postwar to maintain the peace that no one quite grasped the will or workings of.

And no one was truly prepared for war, except the enemy. U.N. troops, scattered and disorganized, fought a desperate retreat to the tip of the Korean Peninsula and were encircled at Pusan, trapped, their backs to the sea. That's when MacArthur showed his genius with "The Miracle Landing" at Incheon and cut enemy supply lines, killing and capturing the greater number while sending the rest packing north.

Flush with victory, MacArthur vowed to have our boys home by Christmas and proceeded to mop up. Had he stopped at the 38th parallel as Truman wished, the war may have ended then and there, sparing thousands of American lives. But MacArthur ignored orders and pushed on, routing the enemy all the way to the Yalu River, waving his saber, itching to cross into China. And the majority of Americans shared his desire for total victory. Headstrong and full blind to the quarter million Chinese troops hidden in the snow that sprung up in mid-October, delivering MacArthur a counterblow, slaughtering and capturing thousands of American and U.N. troops who fought a bloody retreat all through that long, cold winter. Each week bore news of rising casualties and I remember standing out back, gutting a chicken and thinking of our poor boys over there dying, only pieces of them ever sent home, if that.

By spring the fighting had largely stalled at the 38th parallel. Yet MacArthur continued to lobby and bluster for total victory, threatening to A-bomb Chinese cities. By then Truman, having long suffered the famed general's arrogance in deference to his prior service and popularity, had had enough, and never one to mince words fired "The Five-Star SOB" forthwith and replaced him with Matthew Ridgeway, the keen-minded young general who had steeled the men and solidified the front.

While fighting continued, MacArthur came home to a hero's welcome, cheered by millions in a miles-long tickertape parade through New York City. Many people wanted him for president. And Truman, deeply unpopular for firing the revered general amid the ongoing war, now choosing not to run and return to Missouri, odds favored a Republican. But given a closer look the public quickly soured on MacArthur's grand self-regard and rallied behind another 5-star general of a more common touch, Dwight D. Eisenhower, who'd commanded the Allied victory in Europe. Ike, as he was popularly known, was considered honest, level-headed, and trustworthy, and the Democrat, Adlai Stevenson, although capable and appealing, stood little chance. In November of '52 on his promise to go to Korea and end the war, Eisenhower gained the Presidency and MacArthur aptly faded away.

After the election Paul continued wearing his "I Like Ike" button proudly pinned to the left strap of his overalls, certain that his boyhood friend was now president. Which may sound foolish, but most folks believe what suits them, and I never told him different. Sadly, Ruth had died by then. Suffered a second stroke her first summer at the rest home and couldn't move or speak, just lay there and blinked once for yes and twice for no. We visited each trading day for an hour or two, Paul always eager to see his other Gram. And she enjoyed our coming, I think, as I sat by and told her of the crops and harvests, of fields rotated between wheat, corn, and alfalfa, others left fallow. And depending on the season, I'd mention the clover or buttercups in bloom, or a blue bird I'd spied along the creek. And the big story in July of '51 was the 10-inch rain that flooded the Limestone, topping our bridge, uprooting trees, and drowning livestock. Waters nearly reached the cellar and house before receding. What a mess.

She especially liked to hear of Doc's new renters, Odie Nietenthall and his young family. Ode, as he preferred, was earnest and attentive, a good farmer. His wife, Sara — same as mother without the 'h' — was pleasant and mindful, kept careful records on the cost of planting, number of new calves and the like, as her husband noted, "To keep ol' Doc honest…" Ruth rolled her eyes, amused at that.

Ode and Sara had two sons — Albert, about 10, serious and quiet; and Dickie, age 5, a little dickens, active and ornery. "Up to the devil," his mother cautioned, "if I don't keep a close eye…" But they were good boys and respectful of Paul. Heard their father warn them one day, "Don't you ever tease that man or make him mad. Big as he is, he'll toss you clean over the moon…" Though Paul would do no such thing, perhaps it was best they were cautioned.

That first year Paul helped them in corn harvest, easily out-shucking Ode, which impressed the boys and their father. An extra good harvest and with cash in hand Ode bought a corn picker, a new machine that eliminated a load of labor along with the need of cornhuskers. But Paul still helped them put up hay. No longer in loose stacks, like most farmers, Ode now baled his alfalfa as well as father's prairie hay. The twined bales weighed 60 pounds and more and Paul would grip one in either hand then toss them to the boys to stack, stepping in at the top like a pyramid. Once they reached 8 or 10 feet, he'd stab a bale with a pitchfork and fling it up and the boys were always amazed at his strength and could well imagine themselves being tossed over the moon.

Ever in awe of Paul's giant size and feats, but their hero was their "Uncle Rye," a Marine fighter pilot who descended from the clouds to buzz haystacks and trees to their wild cheers and delight. Major Ryan Wales, Sara's brother, had flown in WWII and remained in the Marine reserves to supplement his farm on the White Rock. Called to war in early '51, he made a low pass over the Limestone, dipping the wings of his Corsair left and right in wave goodbye. A cold blustery day, we all stood waving him off, hoping for his return. Happily he did, shortly after Christmas of '52, wholly intact, a gift to all, still spirited though bitter at the loss of buddies, the stalemate, and leaving his wife and newborn son alone a year. And he'd lost three planes, though safely landed, too shot up to fly again, evident by a shrapnel scar above his brow. Paul and I were visiting the day he regaled his nephews with tales of the flak he'd encountered in missions over the North — so thick at times he swore you could have walked on it.

Little Dickie gaped and asked, "Wha' d'ya do all them bullets flyin' at cha?"

He grinned and said, "I just caught 'em with my teeth…" Dashing and handsome with a razor-sharp mustache and that wry bravado that lures boys and men to war and in part sustains them, you couldn't help but like him. Glad he made it home. Many didn't, like Danny, left frozen in the ground, and Ike, maimed beyond knowing.

Such thoughts and talk of war I spared Ruth on our visits, too upsetting, but of the hay-stacking and the boys' other adventures she'd listen and roll her eyes, pleasantly amused. In late winter of '52 she closed her eyes forever and we laid her to rest next to Hiram in the Ionia cemetery. Paul stood extra sad and silent that day. Shortly thereon, when we first heard news of Ike running for president, Paul smiled and repeated his name. And no, I never cared to correct him.

Our visits to the rest home never lapsed for Paul enjoyed seeing the other Grams he'd come to know. He made his first acquaintance early on when leaving Ruth's room as a hunched little woman crept our way. Her eyes widened at Paul's huge presence and in a childlike voice she said, "Father…" then reached to him and asked, "Will you bless me?" Paul stood uncertain what to do.

I said, "Go ahead, Paul, raise your hand and say, 'Bless you…'" And he did so.

She smiled and answered, "Thank you, Father," then gave her name, Jenny Thorp. From then on, often as not, Jenny sought him out with the same request. A blessing from Paul, good as any I suppose.

After Ruth died, my old high school roommate Caroline moved into the room. The same bright eyes and pleasant manner, but she didn't recognize me or any of her children who seldom came to visit. So demented she did not speak, simply sat knitting doilies day in and day out. Paul liked to sit quietly and watch, fascinated by her stitching. They'd trade smiles and now and then she'd hand him a finished doily till he had a score hanging like giant snowflakes on his wall.

By then Paul claimed at least a dozen Grams. Mostly just women at the rest home, seldom more than two or three men, or Dads, as he called them — currently Dad Hollings and Dad Campbell. He'd listen to them talk of the old days, the good and bad, the same tales over and over, and never grew bored. And if they couldn't speak, he'd listen to their silence and somehow seemed to understand. Mr. and Mrs. Arlen who managed Sunrise welcomed Paul's visits and said he cheered the old folks. As they didn't mind, it cheered me to leave him there on trading days and take time for myself at the library and browse through the books. One day I discovered Isak Dineson. Sounds like a man, but her real name was Karen Blixen, a Danish woman admired by Hemingway, no less. I loved her *Seven Gothic* and *Winter Tales* — strange to say, her old-world settings laced with myth, violence, and chance reminded me of my early prairie life, timeless, basic, and real.

So our lives carried on like characters in a quaint tale, quiet and uneventful.

Until one hot afternoon in July of '56, shortly after our neighbor boys and their cousins had fired off their last firecrackers, a little black-gray wire-haired Scotty came trotting down our lane directly to Paul who snatched it up, laughing as it licked his face and said, "See the puppy, Gram?"

Beneath the wiggly stub tail I spied its ample balls and answered, "No, he's full grown I'd say. Just a little tyke."

"Then he's a forever pup!" Paul exclaimed. "Can I keep 'im, Gram?"

"Oh, I expect so…" From that moment he was ours. Showed up out of the blue, perhaps run off, but likely dumped, for he was a persistent little cuss, constantly after Stella till she'd snap and nip him. For what good it did — he'd yip, blink, then bounce right back. At her again, and had no chance, we'd had her spayed years before else she would have birthed a litter of half-coyotes. They'd courted her too. In any case Stella didn't last long after Bing arrived. Think he wore her to death, poor thing.

While carrying his new pup to the house, Paul named him "Bingo" from the old children's song, *"There was a farmer had a dog, Bing-o was his name, oh…"* But soon shortened it to "Bing," for if he heard "go," he was off running and you had a devil of a time calling him back. What's more, when Paul set him down on the kitchen floor and poured him a bowl of milk, which he lapped right up, in gratitude he pissed on the table leg and got a piece of my mind and the broom as I chased him out the door.

Bing certainly stirred life into things. And Paul loved the little guy.

For the first time in years he cranked up the Edison and played "Whistler and His Dog" then hummed along to a dozen more records. He hadn't sung since the war came and Ike left and returned, like music had broken as well, but soon started singing acapella to the Grams and Dads at the rest home as they gathered round, "Amazing Grace, Danny Boy, America the Beautiful, Home on the Range…" and other favorites that flawlessly flowed to and through him.

Another presidential season gearing up, Paul sported a second "I Like Ike" button on the right strap of his overalls. On Election Day, while he sang to the old folks, I went to the courthouse and cast my vote. I too liked Ike but did not trust Nixon standing in the shadows, of dour aspect and little sympathy. So again I wasted my vote on Stevenson, bound to lose. Riddle love or politics, you can seldom cipher why or who we choose.

But that day I did solve the puzzle of what to do with Paul. Found him still singing to his Grams and Dads, who aside from the Hollands were the only people he'd known by whom he'd been accepted. Since the days we first visited Ruth, I knew Sunrise was my one option, but held it like a hole card, fearing he'd be refused like Ike and sent away. Then and there I went directly to Mr. and Mrs. Arlen and asked if I paid extra due to his size and appetite, would they take Paul in upon my death?

To my great relief they readily agreed — "Why, off course, Sadie…" the Missus assured while reciting that old refrain, "Heaven forbid that day ever comes…"

Having found a place for Paul, I merely smiled, for that day surely comes.

— ◦ —

Recent years, along with Hiram and Ruth, had seen Shannon, Caroline, Madalene and others gone, Clyde and Ma as well — Maxie's old place, once my home, boarded up and used for storage. And the previous winter Ian had died of a sudden heart attack while walking home, found frozen stiff an hour later — his face powdered white as snow at his funeral three days later. Shortly thereon his wife Elizabeth moved in with their oldest son James, who now ran the paper.

Their youngest son Jacob had studied law, as Ike once planned, then returned to Mankato to hang out his shingle at an office next to the bank. By now an established, reputable young man who I trusted to manage my estate and draw up my will, he placed my money in a trust that paid out quarterly and would fund Paul's care upon my death. At which time Jacob, who charged a modest annual fee, would gain title to my remaining 60 acres. In discussing this, I quietly offered him my dust-black Buick as bonus.

Caught off guard, still sorting papers, he glanced up, noted my grin and laughed, "No thank you, Mrs. Ross, that's one gift horse I'll pass on…"

The old Buick, only washed when it rained, served Paul and I well enough, but carried a deal of rust and rattled and shimmied from hitting ruts like that new rockabilly music. Some songs not so bad, I guess.

Returning to matters at hand, in conclusion my will declared that after Paul's death the trust money would go to the Oakvale and Mankato libraries and the county historical society. Once signed and stamped to our mutual satisfaction, I handed him two copies of my final wishes, which I'd typed out as I did my monthly column due to my poor cursive of late. Yet my signature held firm and I asked him to please read and countersign each copy, one for his safekeeping and one for mine.

"Most certainly," he smiled, taking the papers in hand, and no more than began reading, he balked, "But this, Mrs. Ross, I don't..." shaking his head like a horse wary of a wood-plank bridge, "this...is highly irregular."

"Perhaps so," I conceded then asked, "Do you judge me of sound mind?"

"Why yes, but...there will be questions."

"Likely so, and you will answer that such was my wish. That Paul did his duty and no blame fall to him, or to you."

"But Mrs. Ross, Sadie, please...won't you reconsider?"

"No, we Briars and Callaways have always tended our dead in our own way. That is my final wish and my final word..."

XXXIX. Hourglass

Copies of her will and last request lay open on the table for others to find. She felt her breath weakening…not much time now, little to do except say goodbye to Paul.

Catching his eye, she asks, "Remember Sputnik?"

He blinks in question and shakes his head.

"That slow-moving speck in the night sky," she reminds him, "there shortly after Stella died. We stepped out to see it and you said it was Stella going to the stars. What a nice thought. Then I said, 'No, it's Sputnik, a Russian satellite…' Remember?"

"Oh yeah, Spud…Nick. Not Stella."

"That's right, Paul. Stella found a star higher up near the Big Dipper that always holds true and steady. The North Star. Sputnik sailed on for a time then fell to earth, burned up and gone. And I'll soon be gone, Paul, only minutes now…can feel the cold numbness moving from my legs to my chest. You know what you must do."

"Don't want to, Gram. Don't want you gone…" he kneels by and takes her hand.

"I know…" she says, faintly gripping his in turn. "It's hard to say goodbye. And a hard thing I ask. You've been so good. But will you do this for me…please?"

"Can't they do like Ruth? Put you in a shiny box with flowers?"

"No, Paul. They'll pluck my clothes and gut me like a store-bought chicken then put me on display. You want that?" He droops his head and she says, "Just wrap me in my blanket and take me there. If you'll do that, I can die in peace."

"Yes, Gram…" he gently lays her hand in her lap then stands.

"Good…" she says. "Now take that hourglass I use for cooking and turn it over. That's right. Once it's empty, I'll be gone, and you should not see me go. You have lots to do, so you best get started. And don't forget to milk ol' Bossy before you come back in, else she'll complain."

"Yes'um…" he nods and pulls on his coat.

"And take your new gloves against the cold…" Though she doubts he'll wear them, he stuffs them in his pocket and heads out the door.

She glances to the waiting letter and waits till she hears him tossing chunks of wood into her father's old wheel barrow then waits till she hears it creaking on towards the hill. Funny how she can hear things — the sand funneling through the hourglass, her heart beat, and her slow-drawn breath like the wind far and near circling the earth.

"Well, I guess…" she sighs and reaches to unfold the last letter.

<hr>

That cold morning in winter of '59 when I pulled the envelope from the mailbox and saw it postmarked "California," for one bright moment I thought Hannah had written to tell me of the new *Ben Hur* movie then being filmed. At second glance I saw the writing was not hers. Fearing the worst, I did not open the letter all that day. Waited until supper was put away and Paul had gone to bed. Stoked the fire and waited awhile yet, dreading what it would say. Finally, I opened the letter and read:

"Dear Mrs. Ross, you don't know me. I was Hannah's common-law husband for nigh 40 years. Asked her to marry but she said why bother, we're married if we say so. She was the best. Sorry to say she died here before Christmas. She talked of you and said you gave her life twice. Once when you birthed her and second time when you set her free, what from she never told me, just said she would have died if not for you. The other day I found her letters and learned she had a son named Paul. I hope he is well.

"She was strong-willed, I know. But that strong will could not save her. It was a cancer in her stomach that got her. The pancreas, they said. She fought hard then just weakened all a sudden. Her pain was awful and hard to watch. I told the doctor to give her all the morphine she wanted. He said it could kill her and I said would you let your horse suffer? So he gave her a good shot and she died peaceful. I had her burned like she asked then tossed her ashes off the cliff there above the ocean where she liked to ride. She said scatter me to the wind and waves. So I set her free one last time. Sure do miss her. Thought you should know of her end. Yours truly, John Benjamin Kale…"

Reading of my dear daughter long lost to me, now truly gone, I wept far into the night. And no, I never told Marion, when he asked of her, let him believe like Paul that she lived forever in the realm of dreams. But I felt my whole life empty out, all those I'd loved fading like characters chaptered in an old fiction. Of my nine lives — mother and father, Liam, Glen, Hagan, Maxie, Danny and Hannah — only Paul remained.

And my remains soon delivered to his hands. Listening now as he again loads the wheel barrow, I place the letter next my breast along with others from Hannah, Danny, and Hagan to hold them close. And sense the old Indian astir on the hill, never quite at peace, nor am I. Wanted to die that night with word of Hannah's death, thought I'd seen enough, yet had a decade to live…

Not all a torment — in 1960 I saw Nixon lose the presidential election to John F. Kennedy, a charming young man of wit and courage who was not afraid to raise a glass with the boys. A war veteran and Catholic to boot, which would've made Maxie smile. And Maxie always made me smile, even in memory. Yet seeing our gallant young President who boldly pointed us to the moon shot dead that terrible day in Dallas, my back bent to the earth and I seldom smiled thereafter.

Truth is Kennedy helped hatch another foolish war in far Asia. Why? As father would say, the old follies of pride, greed, and lust color the doings of every prince and fool. Like Hagan, Kennedy bedded many women other than his wife while striving for noble ideals, both blind to their folly, lost to the turning pages. Soon replaced by others and those gone as well. Many lost in Vietnam, boys I read of playing sports one year, the next pictured in uniform, shipped out and killed in action.

Luckily, the Nietenthall sons are spared, one due to flat feet, the younger serving aboard a submarine deep in the sea — his parent's main concern, his wild sprees ashore. And riots in our cities, Negros long denied liberty, impatient of song and prayer, rising up in anger with perhaps some gain, lately granted equal rights and the vote. Grudgingly given, how long will those rights hold? Now Nixon moves from the shadows, a spiteful man who condemns every protest and promises an honorable end to the war and who I trust no more than God or Devil, both one and the same I suspect.

No, I've seen enough, ready to rest my bones, though I'd love to see those three brave men touch down — all of us a mix of good and bad tumbling through space and few as good as Paul. And I...I wonder of that Word or Will that made us then stands apart to watch us fall...*myself emptying out like the sand through the glass...swirling weightless, mind and thought dissolving in silent awe...*

------------◆------------

Smoke escapes the chimney and the wind howls on for a good half hour before Paul steps in from the cold with a pail of warm milk and his breath steaming the air. He sets the pail to the floor then walks over and kneels by Gram. Doesn't need the mirror, can tell at a glance that she's gone — her head tilted aside, her eyes vague and dim. He briefly touches her limp hands folded on her lap then goes to the tree. Takes the kitten doll and tiny moccasins from their limbs and gently tucks them under her hands then snugs the blanket neatly about her shoulders. He stares a moment puzzled at how still she looks then slowly turns to the tree and yanks it from the bucket, snapping the light cord as he drags it out the door and up the hill, Bing trotting alongside.

Earlier, after rolling four loads of wood to the mound, he'd added a dozen small cedars chopped thereby then stomped them to form a nest where he carefully places the Christmas tree. This not her wish but he wants the best for Gram. The sun nearly set, the hillside darkens. He returns to the house and gently cradles Gram in his arms and carries her to the mound. He lays her body nestled among the cedar boughs, the ornaments and dead lights, their colors fading in the gathering night. He takes a can of fuel oil set by and empties it over the pyre. Waits till he sees the first star blinking overhead then strikes a match and steps back as the dark mound blazes up, lighting the surrounding hillside, warming his hands and face. For an instant he sees Gram engulfed in flames then looks there no more. Gazes to the swirl of sparks rising to the stars and listens to the snap of ornaments, limbs, and bones while smiling in wonder of the grand fire Gram has made. Gazes and smiles till the last smoke ripples to the wind.

Paul and Bing stand silhouetted next to the mound of dying embers blinking blue to red, nothing but scorched limbs and coals, Gram all gone. Then Paul looks to the moon wreathed by a passing cloud like Gram's white hair, and briefly thinks she's replaced the Man in the Moon. But he knows better. He knows she's with the old Indian in the wind, grass, and rocks. Still watching, but he can tell no one. They'll think he's an idiot…

The Mankato Mercantile Weekly
Thursday, January 23rd, 1969

The Voice of the Limestone

"Today marks a month since the passing of Sadie Briar-Corbett-Ross. Born along the White Rock in 1869 on the 9th day of February, by her mother's reckoning, and died Christmas Day, 1968. Sadie was an abiding presence in our region through all that time, in and out of most of our lives from our first memories. Certainly true for my brother Jacob and myself. She had worked the paper with her first husband, Hagan Corbett, then later with my father, Ian Winchell, who always spoke fondly of her. Kind, intelligent, and keenly aware of our world, though I once heard her say she had never left the county. A handsome woman to her ripe old age, Sadie walked straight and proud into her 90s, only bent to the cane her last few years. Such a singular soul, hard to think of her gone, her voice now silent.

"Upon her death, her grandson Paul Ross cremated her remains per her expressed wish on a pasture hill west of their home place. The following morning he walked to the Niethenthalls, their neighbors north, and informed them of her passing. Sheriff Benson and the coroner were called and upon arrival they went to the Briar place to examine the site of her cremation. Inside the house they found a copy of her will and last request, both confirmed and countersigned by her attorney, Jacob Winchell. An unusual circumstance, certainly, but a fitting end for a stubbornly proud, admirable woman.

"Paul now resides at Sunrise Rest Home where he helps with general maintenance and cleaning and also lifts and moves bedridden patients as needed. Claude Arlen says he scooped their sidewalks clear after our recent snow and seems happily content with his new life. Although he misses his 'Gram' as he called her.

"Most days the gentle giant can be seen out walking his little dog, Bing, which would no doubt please Sadie, may she rest in peace." — James Hagan Winchell

Acknowledgement

I wish to express my gratitude to three remarkable Kansas women — Barbara Kerr, Caryn Mirriam-Goldberg, and Sue Shoemaker-Shea — who graciously lent their time and talents to read and comment on *Sadie Briar.* And a fourth, my dear friend and lifelong English teacher, Linda Joler, who gave the story a good stern edit — any faults remaining are strictly my own. Finally, my wife Debra who I met over half a century ago and who still inspires every day.

About the Author

Melvin Litton's latest work *The Kansas Murder Trilogy* presents three novels of shared theme but separate time and character: *King Harvest (1)*; *Banks of the River (2)*; and *Skin for Skin (3)* – all published by Crossroad Press. He has three previous novels (also from Crossroad): *Caspion & the White Buffalo*; *Geminga*; and *I Joaquin*. His stories and poems have appeared in Chiron Review, Pif, Mobius, Foliate Oak, Floyd County Moonshine, Broadkill Review, and The Literary Hatchet among others. He has two books of poetry: *From the Bone* (Spartan Press), and *Idylls of Being* (Stubborn Mule); and a collection of short stories, *Son of Eve* (Spartan).

He is a retired carpenter and lives in Lawrence, KS, with his wife Debra and their border collie Lonae. Formerly captain of the Border Band, he now performs as The Gothic Cowboy with Mando Dan: www.borderband.com